Chris Manby's most recent bestseller was
Lizzie Jordan's Secret Life:

'Very funny, hugely feel-good, and the perfect antidote
for anyone who worries that the only career ladder they've
achieved is a run in their tights' Fiona Walker

'Hilarious city-girl comedy with a message about facing
up to who you are' *Cosmopolitan*

'With a marriage of comic invention and some clear-
sighted emotional honesty, this novel can move as well
as amuse' *Good Book Guide*

'A feelgood romantic comedy for those experiencing,
anticipating or vaguely remembering thirtysomething
angst' *Scotsman*

'Elegantly funny' *Bristol Evening Post*

Also by Chris Manby

Lizzie Jordan's Secret Life
Deep Heat
Second Prize
Flatmates

About the author

Chris Manby grew up in Gloucester and published her
first short story in *Just Seventeen* at the age of fourteen.
Now in her late twenties, she divides her time between
London, Cheltenham and Sheffield, where she is Writer
in Residence at Sheffield Hallam University.

Running Away From Richard

Chris Manby

CORONET BOOKS

Hodder & Stoughton

First published in Great Britain in 2001 by Hodder and Stoughton
First published in paperback in 2001 by Hodder and Stoughton
A division of Hodder Headline

A Coronet Paperback

10 9 8 7 6 5 4 3 2

A CIP catalogue record for this title
is available from the British Library.

ISBN 0 340 76920 3

Typeset by Palimpsest Book Production Limited,
Polmont, Stirlingshire
Printed and bound in Great Britain by
Mackays of Chatham plc, Chatham, Kent

Hodder and Stoughton
A division of Hodder Headline
338 Euston Road
London NW1 3BH

For Clare Elson

Acknowledgements

People sometimes ask if writing is a lonely job, but, fact is, there isn't a book in the shop which is really the sole effort of the person with their name on the spine. From the people whose stories inspire me to the eternally cheerful gang at Hodder who get the finished product from tatty manuscript to swanky paperback, there are plenty of people to thank.

My Auntie Gwenda and cousin Clare Elson have both faced the big 'C' this year and it was their courage, and Clare's story in particular, which led me to create the character of Brandi, whom you'll meet in these pages. I have tried to give a realistic portrayal of breast cancer care in the United States and am very grateful to Barbie Casey and Brandy Jones of the Susan G. Komen Breast Cancer Foundation for their help with my research. Likewise, I am indebted to Nicky Brian and her colleagues at the Imperial Cancer Research Fund and to breast cancer survivor Marcia Hobbs for sharing her inspirational story. Any bloopers within are the author's, but I hope that I have at least been able to accurately convey some of Clare's and Marcia's positivity.

For the facts and more information about breast cancer, you can visit Imperial Cancer Research Fund's website: www.imperialcancer.co.uk

Or write to:

Imperial Cancer Research Fund, PO Box 123, Lincoln's Inn Fields, London, WC2A 3PX

email: cancer.info@icrf.icnet.uk

Onto the usual suspects . . . I need to thank my eternally supportive family, Mum, Dad, Kate and Lee. Thanks to Marty Beal, for letting me turn his LA flat into the British embassy during the spring. To Chris Hobbs and Greg Sachs for letting me infiltrate the Bachelor Pad. To Jenn Matherly, bad influence, for being the first trusting fool to let me drive her car on the wrong side of the road! To Cynthia Harding and Vicki Arkoff for making me an honorary California girl. To Fiona Walker and Jessica Adams for keeping all the GNI balls in the air while I worked on my tan . . . I mean, my novel. To Nikki Jones for all those cups of tea during the final stages. To Tom, Barfy, Baz and Fergs, for putting me up in Sheffield (you will all be in the next one!). To Kate Lyall Grant and the gang at Hodder for their enthusiastic support and a wonderful launch party. To my agent Ant Harwood, for taking the telephone tantrums. And to Rob Yorke, who survived the real ones – Nightmare on Fourth Street and the LAX Incident. Next time, just go fishing!

CHAPTER ONE

There's only one thing worse than being jilted on the day of your wedding and that is being chucked a week before you have to be your best friend's chief bridesmaid.

At least if you're the jilted bride herself, you don't have to go through with the ceremony. As the recently dumped chief bridesmaid, however, you don't have the luxury of locking yourself in your bedroom and sobbing your heart out at that moment when you should have been listening to the organist strike up 'Here Comes the Bride'. Oh no. You still have to walk down the aisle with your head held high, choking back the tears so you don't smudge your mascara, and you can't even choose the bloody horrid outfit you have to do it in.

That's right. Being the just-dumped bridesmaid is infinitely worse than suffering a very late broken engagement, or even being left right at the altar. Trust me, I should know. Because that's what happened to me.

My name is Lizzie Jordan. I'm an actress. And just over a year and a half ago, I thought I was on the fast track to 'happily ever after'. I had recently graduated from drama school and though the casting agents weren't exactly camping on my doorstep with offers from Spielberg or the

RSC, I was optimistic that it was only a matter of time. I had received rave reviews for my dazzling performance as the fairy queen Titania in my graduating class' version of *Midsummer Night's Dream* and had got down to the last two in an audition for the grown-up daughter in the new Bisto ad. Though I had yet to earn a penny from my acting, getting my name in lights still seemed less of an 'if' than a 'when'.

In the meantime I was doing a bit of temping to pay the bills, telling myself that the difficult people I met in London's overheated offices would help inform my performance when I played a secretary turned secret agent in some Hollywood action film. The sun was shining. It was an unusually gorgeous London August. And I was very happy to be living with my boyfriend Richard, a portrait artist, in a cosy little flat in Tufnell Park.

Though life wasn't exactly a whirl of parties and excitement that summer, I found myself feeling strangely content as I sat on the bus in the mornings. I had started smiling at women pushing prams instead of cursing them for trying to fit a double buggy onto a rush-hour bus. I had started to appreciate the things my mother had always said about 'settling down'.

'It isn't "settling down" at all,' she said. 'It's all about "settling up".'

Settling up. That's what I thought I was doing. Life didn't have to be a constant round of fireworks and fiery passion to feel good. Stability was soothing, not stagnating. If Richard and I spent another Friday night in front of the television watching comedy reruns, I didn't worry that I was missing something exciting in Soho's newest bar. I was happy. Happy as a turkey the day after Thanksgiving. Happy as a turkey who hasn't yet heard about Christmas.

But Richard seemed happy too. He spent his days at the little studio space he had rented in an old East End warehouse, working on a set of pictures that had been promised hanging space at one of the hottest galleries in town. His work was in demand, as I had always told him it should be. He had been featured as an artist to watch out for in a couple of the glossier Sunday newspaper supplements. He no longer had to beg people to sit for him. The beautiful people were coming to him and happily joining a waiting list.

Life felt good. We were a golden couple. At least, that's how it seemed to me.

You can't see the cracks until you look back.

When the break-up happened, I remembered the moment nine months earlier when Mary called me at the accountant's office where I was working as a temporary receptionist and said, 'Lizzie, I am going to make your day.'

I waited eagerly for my best friend to tell me that she'd managed to procure a pair of Jimmy Choos in exactly my size. Mary is a talent agent, with a variety of clients from actors who want to be pop stars to pop stars who think they ought to be actresses. In fact, it was Mary who put me in touch with my own agent, Useless Eunice.

Before she became a talent agent, Mary had been a fashion PR. She still got freebies from the designers she once represented, in the hope that she might be able to match an ocelot jacket to an Oscar winner. Except that Mary's clients rarely saw any of the exclusive gifts intended for them. She gave me first refusal on anything she thought might suit me – providing it didn't fit her – which is why I was justifiably excited whenever she called me during working hours. The only thing that could have made my day that day was a pair of designer flip-flops. But that wasn't what Mary was offering.

'What is it?' I asked.

'You'll never guess,' she said.

'A little something from Calvin Klein?' I said hopefully.

'No. Better than that,' she assured me.

'Tickets to Leo DiCaprio's latest premiere?'

'You wish. It's nothing like that. Guess again.'

'Bill's given you the clap.'

'Oh, please, Lizzie. That's disgusting,' she sighed.

'Then give me a clue.'

'Big day. Big dresses.'

'You've got tickets for an outsize fashion show?' I asked.

'Noooo! Oh God, I'll just tell you. I can't wait for you to work it out. I want you to be my bridesmaid,' she said.

'Yeah, right,' I said. 'You are joking, of course.'

'I'm afraid I'm not,' she spluttered.

'Oh, Mary. No!' I shrieked. 'No! No way!'

'Yes! Yes! Yes, way! Yes! Yes! Yes! Can you believe it?' she giggled.

'Frankly? No,' I replied.

'Well, it's true,' she gabbled. 'It's absolutely true. He asked me on Saturday morning. I would have told you sooner, but I had to tell Mum first. I had a feeling something was up on the drive down to Cornwall. He had this really weird expression on his face all the way out of London. Like he was building up to say something important and he was getting really nervous. I thought he was going to chuck me, can you believe? I felt so ill when we got to Padstow. I was ready to throw myself off a cliff when he ended it. I nearly fell over when he pulled out that ring.'

'Must have been wonderful,' I said.

'Oh, Lizzie, it was. It really, really was. Bloody hell,' she sighed. I could imagine her sinking back into her padded leather swivel chair. 'To be honest with you, I'm just so relieved I could cry. What with my twenty-ninth birthday coming up next month and everyone we know lining up to drop babies like it's the new aerobics, I thought I was never going to get there myself. Bill wasn't showing any sign of buckling. You know, I actually cried at Emma's wedding reception last month because I thought I'd never be able to have one of my own. Now I'm really going to. I can't tell you how happy I am.'

'You certainly sound ecstatic,' I said.

'I am. So, you will be my bridesmaid, won't you? Please, Lizzie? Pretty please? I promise I won't make you wear anything vile. In fact, you can even choose the colour of the dress if you want. And the style. Though I'd really like deep pink for my flowers if you can think along the lines of something that would match that.'

'Deep pink?' I suggested resignedly.

'Perfect. That would be nice. We could start looking on Saturday, if you're not too busy. Oh, God, I'm so pleased. You're pleased for me too, aren't you, Lizzie?' She didn't pause for my answer before adding somewhat incongruously, 'You don't feel a little bit weird about it all?'

'Weird? Why should I feel weird?' I asked.

'Well, because,' she hesitated. I heard her tap her pencil against her teeth. It was a nervous affectation she'd had since college. 'You know, you're the same age as me and you and Richard . . . well, you've been together officially for even longer than Bill and I have, if you think about it, and yet you still aren't really showing any signs.'

'Signs? Signs of what?' I asked.

'Of tying the knot yourselves,' she whispered. 'Lizzie, I

don't want you to think I'm abandoning you to singledom.'

'Mary!' I laughed. 'I hope you know you are utterly ridiculous. I'll pin him down one day. *If* I decide that I want to. Unlike you, I'm not desperate to be rescued from the shame of my maiden name before I hit thirty. And in the meantime, I'd be happy to be your bridesmaid.'

'Yippee!!' said Mary. 'I've never been so happy in my life. I've asked Bill's sister if her little Trinny can be a flower girl,' she continued.

'What? Little Trinny with the ringlets?' I asked.

'That's her,' Mary confirmed. 'The sweet one.'

'You mean, the sweet one who filled my shoes with fromage frais at your birthday barbecue? The sweet one with the howl like a randy tom cat and the extraordinarily sharp teeth? The sweet one who has to be kept off orange squash with additives in case she kills other children?'

'Yes. She's really looking forward to it,' said Mary as if she had missed all that. 'You'll be able to keep her under control.'

'Am I allowed to use a cattle prod?' I asked.

'Oh, Lizzie,' said Mary. 'You love kids. You know you do.'

'I couldn't eat a whole one,' I told her.

Mary had to hang up on me to talk to some soap actress client of hers (who was having histrionics because she'd just discovered that her character was about to snog Ian Beale and have a fatal car accident) but not before we had made arrangements to meet that weekend and choose her dress. I spent the rest of the day at work feeling faintly shocked.

Though I had known Mary for ten years and we were

both nearer thirty than twenty, I just couldn't quite get my head around the idea of her and marriage. It struck me that afternoon that no matter how long you know someone, it's almost impossible to see people as anything other than what they were when you first met them. That's why you usually have to change companies in order to shake off the office junior image and get promoted. It's why your mother and father will always think of you pooing your nappies even when you're telling them you're shacking up with your boyfriend or you've just been elected MP. And it's why I would always picture Miserable Mary in the tattered black *Bauhaus* T-shirt she treasured all through college and not in an Elizabeth Emmanuel fairytale wedding special. Shocked? Of course I was. It was as if Eddie Izzard had just announced that he was pregnant.

I told Richard about the impending wedding that evening.

'When is it?' he said.

I told him the date.

'I think I might be doing something that weekend,' he told me, without looking up from the newspaper.

'How can you know that?' I asked him. 'It's still nine months away yet.'

'I'm joking,' he said.

'You'd better bloody be.'

Saturday morning. First stop, Blushing Bride. Mary would be having her wedding dress custom made of course, but she wanted to get a general idea of current trends by hitting the high street first. My dusty Caterpillar boots looked

somewhat incongruous on the red carpet that led from the
front doors to the area where the wedding dresses were
kept. I felt like the Tin Man en route to Oz, not believing
that we would ever get there. Mary, however, was like
bloody Dorothy, racing up the staircase to be the first
blushing bride that day to benefit from the shop girl's
attentions.

'Which one of you is the bride?' the girl asked. As if it
wasn't obvious from the fact that one of us was normal
and the other one needed to be sedated.

'Me, me, me,' Mary shouted.

Apparently, a former air hostess set up Blushing Bride's
chain of wedding emporiums. The shop assistant certainly
looked as though she had learned her make-up application
skills from one and I was slightly amazed that she was
allowed to handle white dresses while sporting so much
sticky brown slap. But Mary cooed as the assistant led her
to a pink upholstered gilt chaise longue and handed her a
brochure from which to pick the dresses she would like
to try on.

'What is it exactly that you're looking for?' the assistant asked.

'Think pavlova without the raspberries,' I suggested
irreverently.

Mary looked at me with pursed lips before she told the
assistant herself. 'I want something classy. Not too fussy.
Not too full.'

Which is why it was a shock that the first dress Mary
chose to try on might have made Marie Antoinette wonder
if it was perhaps a little outré for the next state ball. Its
taffeta skirt was so wide that Mary wouldn't have been
able to fit down the fruit and veg aisle at Safeway, let
alone down the aisle at the tiny chapel where she was

actually getting married. My mind boggled at the thought of the dresses she might have tried on if she had decided to push the boat out and go 'fancy'.

'I like it,' she said, fingering the gold embroidery on the bodice. It was thicker than the piping on a guardsman's jacket. 'But what would I wear on my head with this?' she asked.

'I have just the thing,' said the assistant.

She presented Mary with a headdress that looked uncannily like the *Blue Peter* advent candle-holder of our childhood. You remember. They made one every year. It was fashioned from two coat hangers and a string of golden tinsel.

'That's lovely,' Mary murmured.

I turned to share my *Blue Peter* observation with the shop assistant, but I couldn't catch her eye. She was staring at the headdress as though it were as rare and wondrous a thing as King Tutankhamun's funeral mask.

'What on earth do you think you look like in that?' I asked Mary. After our ten-year friendship, we could generally be honest with each other when trying on something crap. Only that month, Mary had nearly choked with hilarity at the sight of me in a pair of leatherette hipster pants in Top Shop. I wasn't terribly pleased at the time, but I knew it was a best friend's duty to prevent you from looking a twat. I was only returning the favour. But Mary didn't take her eyes off the crown.

'Like it?' asked the assistant.

Mary sighed. 'I think it's wonderful.'

Wonderful? Call Mulder and Scully! My best friend's body had been inhabited by a bridal body-snatcher. Mary

Bagshot, aka Miserable Mary. Arch cynic. Cutting Queen. A woman who knew her Versace from her Armani. A woman who could spot a fake Prada handbag at three hundred feet. A woman who only did 'tacky' when she was sticking post-it notes to artist contracts that could have the head of any television network in tears. Stick a ring on her finger and her sense of style fell away like a wart that had been frozen off by the doctor.

I could only look on in horror as the shop assistant stepped forward to help Mary adjust the tinsel tiara until they thought they had achieved the perfect virginal angle. Then they smiled and cooed at each other like two little pea-brained birds.

'This is so exciting,' said Mary, actually clapping her hands together. I'd never seen her do that before. Never. The creature inhabiting her body clearly had a propensity for twee body language gestures as well as a complete lack of style.

'Do I look OK?'

The shop assistant nodded happily, the big soppy grin never leaving her face for a moment. 'Of course you do,' she told my friend. 'Mary, you look incredible.'

And she did. She looked like a bloody loo-roll holder incredible.

'I feel pretty,' Mary sang as she skipped around the red-carpeted changing room swinging her voluminous skirts. 'I feel witty and pretty and ga-a-ay!'

'Oh no, not gay,' quipped the shop assistant. 'You've bagged your man now, Mary! You've done it.'

'Yes, I have bagged my man, haven't I? I'm getting married,' said Mary again, as though she still couldn't quite believe it. Except I knew that a more accurate description of her tone was that she believed it only too well, but wanted to sound modest while she repeated the fact of her fast-approaching marriage for my benefit and her own amusement. She grinned at me now as though she had taken a draught from some secret happiness river that only the engaged can have access to.

'It'll happen to you too one day,' Mary promised me.

'Who says I want it to?' I snorted.

'We all want it,' said the shop assistant, as though she was preaching salvation. 'It's every little girl's dream made reality.'

I felt like the last remaining human being caught at a WI meeting with the Stepford Wives.

Mary reluctantly changed back into her street clothes. Honestly, it was like trying to persuade a six-year-old to change out of her fairy outfit for bedtime. As we walked towards the tube station to catch the next train home, she linked arms with me and tried to engage me in a discussion on the merits of satin versus silk dupion.

'You've gone all quiet,' she said accusingly when I had nothing more to add to the debate.

'No I haven't.'

'Yes you have. You went all quiet as soon as we stepped in the shop. You're not jealous are you, Lizzie?'

'Why should I be jealous?' I asked her. 'It's not as if I haven't got a man of my own.'

'Yes, but . . .'

'What but?' I sighed. 'We don't want to get married, Richard and I. We're happy as we are. I'm still slightly shocked that you're going for the whole horse-and-carriage bit yourself.'

'Why?' Mary asked.

'Because I didn't think you believed in weddings. All through college you said you couldn't see the point in marriage when your own parents were so miserable in theirs. Didn't you once claim that you'd rather have a new bathroom fitted than spend ten thousand pounds on a meringue dress and a round of prawn vol-au-vents for the distant relatives you've been avoiding for years?'

'Did I say that?' Mary asked me.

'Yes, you did.'

'Ah well. That was before I met the right man. I guess that getting married is like having a baby. You don't know that you want one until you're actually having one, then you forget about the varicose veins and the constant peeing and the stretchmarks and just look forward to the christening. I think I was so scathing about weddings because I didn't think anyone would ask me. I wanted everyone to think that I didn't care so that they wouldn't feel sorry for me when it didn't happen.'

'Ah well. Now you've been suckered you may as well make the most of it.'

'You are jealous, aren't you?' said Mary, poking me playfully in the side.

'No. I'm not. I really don't need a wedding ring and a dress with more ruches than my mum's Viennese kitchen window blinds to know that Richard loves me,' I assured her. 'We're happy as we are.'

And back then I was convinced that that was the truth. Which was no mean feat, even for a woman who'd been born long after the advent of feminism. Hell, my mum burned her bra! (Admittedly, it was under the influence of a vodka-laced cheese fondue back in 1973.) But when you're brought up on a diet of fairytales that always end in a white wedding to a handsome prince, it's hard to believe that there's any kind of perfect love except the one that ends that way.

Richard and I were sophisticated people, however. An actress and an artist. We could do the unconventional thing. In fact, back then I thought that weddings were for the insecure. I had seen it happen so many times. After four or five years together a couple run out of things to say to one another. They should split up, but they're afraid of being alone, of never finding anyone better than the person they're starting to despise. Basically, they're scared of never ever getting another shag. So they do the exact opposite of going their separate ways. They decide to get married. And for the best part of a year – or however long it takes to assemble two hundred people for a chicken dinner – they have something to talk about again.

I'm not saying that I thought that was always the case. I didn't entirely disbelieve in the notion of real enduring love with a fancy certificate to prove it. But Richard and I didn't have to get married just because everyone else was doing the ring thing. Our mere *co-habitee* status didn't mean that we loved each other any less than Bill loved my best friend Mary.

Did it?

CHAPTER TWO

Looking back to the horrible events of last summer, I can see now that sometimes Richard was a little fractious. But I just put that down to the fact that he was working so hard; leaving the house at six in the morning and sometimes not getting back until the early hours of the next day with oil paint smeared across his furrowed brow. I joked more than once that he must think I lived in my pyjamas. It seemed that I only ever saw him in the bedroom, either as he crawled into bed hours after I'd given up waiting up for him or woke me later in the morning as he crawled back out again.

But I really didn't see it coming.

The end.

The morning of the dreadful day seemed just like any other. Richard had set his alarm clock for six. It went off. I tried to persuade him to stay in bed for an extra quarter of an hour. He said he couldn't and staggered blearily in the direction of the bathroom. I praised him for his dedication and pulled the duvet back over my head. On his way out of the house to the studio he brought me a cup of tea made just how I like it, in my own special mug, and planted a kiss on my cheek. He muttered 'I love you' into my fringe and then he was gone.

I got up two hours later and began an ordinary sort of

day. Went into the advertising agency office where I had been temping for a couple of weeks, sneakily called Useless Eunice at ten to see if anyone wanted me to audition for the lead role in a remake of *Casablanca* or, failing that, a cornflakes commercial. They didn't.

I had lunch with one of the girls from the office. She talked about her forthcoming wedding. I talked about Mary's wedding which was just seven days away now. We talked about hen nights. I gave my office pal the number of the stripper I had hired to dress, or rather undress, as a fireman for Mary. I did another afternoon at work, calculating the amount I was being paid per minute as I inspected my spots in the ladies' loo. I read that week's copy of *Hello!* beneath my desk when I should have been making speculative phone calls to new clients. I went home.

Nothing about my day prepared me for that evening. Except, if I were superstitious, I might say that I'd had an omen. Though of course, I didn't know it was an omen at the time.

As I turned into the street where Richard and I lived in his scruffy little flat, I heard the sound of a blackbird in distress. As I reached our flat, I saw a female blackbird plummet from the branches of the ornamental cherry tree that overshadowed our bedroom. She was quickly followed by a jay, swooping straight to the ground after her like a hawk. As I looked on, the bigger bird took the poor female blackbird by the neck and by the time I realised what was happening, the jay had shaken the blackbird's head clean from her tiny body.

The jay flew away when I got too close. And the pathetic sight of the dead blackbird made me catch my breath – Richard had once likened me to a blackbird, all bright-eyed and busy, he said. But the horrible spectacle didn't stop me from going into the flat like always, making myself a sandwich like always and settling down in front of the television to wait for Richard's return as though it were any other Friday. It was something to tell him about, I thought. The blackbird killed by a jay. What an awful thing to happen to such a gentle creature. I had no idea that the next time I saw that poor bird's frail body would be as I stepped over it with my bags the next morning, feeling as though my own head had been wrenched from my neck.

Richard came home relatively early that night. He poured me a glass of wine from the bottle he had picked up at the off licence en route. He muttered 'Fine' when I asked him how his day had been. I reminded him that the next day we had to find him a suit to wear to Bill and Mary's wedding. Simply had to. He'd been putting it off for weeks. I threatened to go into Marks and Sparks without him and have him kitted out in brown tweed if he refused to cooperate now. And that's when he told me, 'Lizzie, we need to talk.'

Those words.

'We need to talk.'

Those little words that men are supposed to be so scared of. It was the first time either of us had said such a phrase in the course of our happy-go-lucky four-year relationship and ironically, it wasn't going to presage a deeply soothing heart-to-heart at all. I soon surmised that it wasn't so much that Richard thought that we needed to talk, more that he needed to tell me something. And he did.

That night Richard simply told me that he didn't think

he could see us growing old together. He'd been thinking about it for a couple of months, he said. And now he'd decided that we were all but over and he wanted out. Or rather, he wanted me out. Of his flat *and* his life. As he delivered the killer blow I merely gulped like a landed fish. I couldn't find the breath to argue with him. I couldn't even cry. By the time I regained the ability to speak, to protest my case, to say that I didn't believe him, he had already announced that he was going to sleep in the spare room that night and locked himself away from me.

So I moved out first thing next morning. What else could I do? Richard made it clear that he didn't want to discuss the other possibilities. A weekend apart might make him feel differently, I suggested? Perhaps we could stay together as a couple but go back to living in separate flats? I understood that he needed space, I said. Everybody needs space sometimes. But when I pleaded for a chance to talk things through properly he merely covered his ears like a child who doesn't want to hear that it's bedtime.

And next night I found myself more than a hundred miles away from him, back in Solihull, sleeping in my parents' house again, in the bedroom that they had last decorated in honour of my twelfth birthday. As I stared at the faded 'Diary of an Edwardian Lady' wallpaper that had been so popular in the early eighties, I felt as though I had forgotten how to breathe. The shock of Richard's sudden announcement had yet to really hit me. Every time the phone rang – and it rang all the time since my mother had become coordinator of the local neighbourhood watch – I was certain that it would be Richard calling to tell me that this was all some big, bad joke. Or if not a joke exactly, then just a minor aberration in our otherwise perfect life. Our relationship over? That couldn't be right. We loved each other, didn't we? We could fix it.

Now that I thought about it, I remembered that he had gone quiet every time I mentioned Bill and Mary's forthcoming wedding. At one point he had even said, 'I don't know why anyone still feels the need to get married in the twenty-first century.' Perhaps that was it. Wedding angst. It would explain why he had been so reluctant to buy a suit for the occasion. He didn't want to have to go to Bill and Mary's wedding because he might feel under pressure to be the next one to propose. Obvious.

I thought I had worked it all out. That thought comforted me through one night. If I told him that he didn't have to come to the wedding and promised that I didn't ever ever expect him to propose to me, perhaps he would come to his senses and let me come back home. I called him as soon as I thought he might be awake next morning. But he wasn't at the flat we had shared. I got him on his mobile instead.

'It's five in the morning,' he said grouchily.

'Where are you?' I asked. 'I called you at the flat.'

'Why does it matter?' he retorted, instantly defensive.

'It doesn't,' I said, ready to grovel. 'I just . . . I just wanted to talk to you, Richard. I mean, for heaven's sake, you can't just throw away four years like this. You couldn't honestly have expected me to leave the flat and not want an explanation.'

'I suppose not,' he admitted, very grudgingly.

'So, I've been thinking,' I began, 'about what might have caused this change in your feelings for me. Is it just that you don't want to get married yourself? Did you want to get out of going to Bill and Mary's wedding? Is that why you had to cause a row yesterday? You don't have to propose to me

just because I'm the chief bridesmaid, you know.' I forced
a laugh.

Richard sighed.

'Am I right?' I asked.

'I don't want to talk about this now,' he said. 'I'll call
you later.'

He hung up.

He had never put the phone down on me before – not
without saying 'goodbye' and blowing a half dozen kisses
first. And suddenly I realised that I wasn't about to wake
up and find myself back in our double bed with him
smoothing my hair across my nightmare-ravaged forehead
and telling me not to worry. This was no nightmare. This
was real.

As soon as I had replaced the receiver I went into the
bathroom and was sick. I retched until my ribs ached. And
then I cried until I felt sure that if I cried any more my
desiccated bones would crumble when I tried to stand up
again. When my mother and father got up at seven-thirty,
they found me collapsed on the floor in the bathroom, my
head still resting on the toilet (I had the imprint of the
pine seat on my cheek for the next eight hours). And
that's pretty much the best I could manage for the next
five days.

Believe me, I would have stayed with my head on the
toilet seat for a lot longer than that. Had I been able to, I
would have locked myself in that bathroom until I starved
to death. I'd just been told that my hopes of a long-term
commitment to the person I loved more than any other in
the world were simply 'my reality', entirely unreasonable
given the harsh facts which had just come to light about
Richard's feelings, or rather lack of them, for me. But that
week, the most awful week in my life ever, was also the

most important and marvellous week in the life of my best friend Mary.

You see, while I was dying from the inside out, Mary was preparing for the happy ending to her own grand romance. At three o'clock on Saturday afternoon she would walk down the aisle of the chapel at the college where we had first met and promise herself to Bill, her sweetheart since our student days. And when she took that momentous step towards eternal happiness, she was expecting me to be standing right behind her. When I could finally bring myself to pick up the phone to tell Mary that Richard wouldn't be coming to the wedding, the first thing she said was, 'For heaven's sake, Lizzie, that completely messes up the seating plan.'

She quickly segued into a diatribe about the evil florists who had just called to tell her that the floral arrangements would cost twice their original quote because of a world-wide outbreak of greenfly. I had heard about the unreliable caterers, the horribly expensive wedding-list gifts that had been sent by mistake to an address in Devizes and the fact that Mary could hardly walk in the shoes she was supposed to be wearing down the aisle before I managed to break in and tell her exactly why Richard wouldn't be attending the wedding.

Mary fell silent.

I sniffed in the soundless void.

'Oh, Lizzie,' she said. 'You're not about to tell me that you can't be my chief bridesmaid, are you?'

Of course I was. It was what I had been gearing up to. Mary would understand, wouldn't she? I mean, even without a dumping, being a bridesmaid when you're over the age of fourteen is a nightmare. It's the twenty-first century. They could send an all-female shuttle crew into

space. Women around the world are discovering cures for
diseases and settling wars and writing thought-provoking
novels that might one day change the face of humankind;
but when a girl walks down the aisle behind her best friend,
in a dress better suited to a six-year-old, no one gives a
toss about her achievements. They won't care that she's
just been promoted to head of her department or signed
a three-book publishing deal. Everyone in that church will
want to know what's so wrong with her that she hasn't
managed to bag her own man.

And I had just been dumped. Dumped! It wasn't just a
common or garden dumping either. I had been dumped by
the *love of my life*. My soul mate. My one true love. There
was no way Mary could expect me to be the second most
stared at woman at her wedding, given the circumstances.
Dumped girl in crimson puffball dress? It would be torture. Amnesty International would be horrified. I knew I
wouldn't wish it on my worst enemy.

'Mary,' I began, feeling faint before I even started. 'I really
don't think I can . . .'

I didn't get a chance to finish the sentence. Mary shrieked
into the phone, 'That selfish, selfish bastard. How could he
do this to me?'

'Er, Mary. He's done it to me,' I tried to point out. 'I'm
the one he's abandoned.'

'I'm getting married on Saturday,' she continued regardless. 'Doesn't he know how stressful that is? I've just been
told I need to re-mortgage my house to afford the flowers
I asked for, the caterers are trying to tell me that I want
salmon instead of prawns because they cocked up the
ordering, my off-white satin Emma Hope shoes are full of
blood where they've given me blisters and now you ring
me up to tell me that you're not going to be my bridesmaid

because that selfish bastard Richard has dumped you. I should have known he would try something like this,' she rumbled on. 'He always hated me, Lizzie. All the time you were going out with him he kept making snide remarks about me behind my back. Don't try to deny it. He wanted to ruin my day. Well, I'm not having it. He's not going to spoil my wedding. You're going to walk down that aisle behind me if I have to drag you to the chapel by your hair.'

She was pretty resolved.

'But I look terrible,' I whined.

'Oh for God's sake, Lizzie,' Mary tutted. 'Bridesmaids are supposed to look terrible. I'll pick you up for the rehearsal at two o'clock tomorrow.'

And then she hung up on me. Presumably to finish haranguing the caterers.

That was it then. I knew I was going to have to wear that puff-sleeved dress or risk losing my best friend as well as my lover. Retiring to my bedroom, I lay on the bed for another staring competition with the ceiling. Mum brought in a bowl of chicken soup at five o'clock. I took a spoonful while she watched and forced it down my aching throat.

'What did Mary say?' she asked me.

'She says that she's picking me up for the wedding rehearsal at two o'clock tomorrow.'

'Oh. You're still going to be her chief bridesmaid then?'

'She said she'd have me killed if I didn't.'

Mum patted my hand cheerfully. 'Well, she did spend a lot of money on having the dress made,' she reminded me. 'In any case, you don't want to miss the reception, darling. Chief bridesmaid gets pick of all the single men at a wedding.' She threw out her arm in an expansive gesture as if to show me a hoard of hotties in morning dress lined up along my bedroom wall.

'Thanks, Mum,' I sighed.

Pick of the single men? It was my mother's answer for everything. *Lost one man? Get another.* But how could I even think about having my pick of the single men at Mary's wedding? Losing Richard wasn't just like putting a ladder in a pair of tights. There wasn't going to be another neatly cellophane wrapped Richard at my local Marks & Sparks, looking, feeling and tasting exactly the same as the last one. A quick snog with a new pair of spot-rimmed lips might have been the answer to a broken heart when I was twelve years old and pining for the under-fourteens' cricket captain, but it was not a solution I could consider now.

'Who knows,' Mum continued blithely. 'You might even end up with the best man!'

'Mum!'

Now that was even less likely. If only because the best man was another of my ex-boyfriends. Brian Coren had been at university with Bill, Mary and me back in the early nineties. These days he lived and worked as a banker in New York – which was where he had grown up. He was flying in to the UK especially for the wedding. With his very own fiancée in tow.

'Well, eat your soup,' Mum finished defeatedly, realising that she wasn't going to be able to cheer me up with the promise of fresh totty that day. 'You're looking thin.'

'I can't eat,' I told her. 'I just want to die.'

'You can't die, Lizzie,' she said in a businesslike tone I recognised from my last suicidal phase (back when I was taking my GCSEs in the summer of 1990). 'You've got a wedding to go to. Try not to think about that awful man.'

That awful man. My Richard.

Mum left me alone again and closed the bedroom door behind her. I resumed my stare-out match with the ceiling.

My Richard. How was it possible that we weren't together any more? How was it possible that I was staring at the ceiling in the bedroom I had slept in as a child while the man I had shared the last four years of my life with was probably lying in some strange bed in London with someone else?

Someone else?

Please, no. My stomach lurched at the thought of that.

Like a CD stuck on repeat, I played over our last conversation in my mind. Richard, the man who had once told me that he loved me on a nightly basis, had closed our last conversation – one which admittedly I forced him to have at three in the morning – by telling me that these days he thought I was 'square and common'. *Infra* his *dig*. He had told me that I had *imagined* the depth of his feelings for me. He had even tried to say that the fact that he had told me that he loved me on the morning of the dreadful day was *irrelevant*. That was then, as the saying goes.

Hadn't I seen the clues that should have told me that his love for me was long dead?

What clues? I asked myself afterwards.

Clues like the huge bunch of roses he sent on the fourth 'anniversary' of our first date? Clues like the beautiful framed sketch he surprised me with on Valentine's Day? Clues like the birthday card he had sent to me less than a month before the break-up into which he had scribbled, '*Here's to another wonderful year together*'? Not even *Sherlock* bloody *Holmes* could have seen the harbingers of doom in that.

All alone in my childhood bedroom, I felt like the little girl in the fairytale who loses her best friend to the snow queen when a shard of the frozen bitch's shattered mirror gets in through his eye and pierces his innocent heart. My lovely Richard, the man who had made me laugh and sigh, who cheered with me when life was good and comforted me when life seemed too tough had been replaced by a doppelganger; a man who looked and spoke and even smelled the same as Richard but whose heart was made of ice.

CHAPTER THREE

'I want to die,' I told my reflection next morning.

I certainly looked as though I was about to. Another night without sleep. Another night spent picking through the smoking rubble of my bombed-out relationship, looking for that single sharp-edged crystalline moment when everything went wrong. I was torturing myself with those 'this time last week' thoughts. This time last week, Richard and I were sharing a bed. This time last week I was happy.

At about four fifteen a.m. I had seized upon the possibility that Richard had gone off me when I spilled a glass of wine over an important art dealer he had been trying to impress at some gallery opening. I phoned him right away to ask for confirmation that this was indeed the case and to promise that it would never happen again. I didn't find out that night. Richard had taken the phone off the hook and thoughtfully set his mobile to divert.

Later that day, Mary picked me up to attend the wedding rehearsals. She made the round trip from London specially – no doubt to make sure I didn't go AWOL – and told me in the car that I had the length of the journey from Solihull to the chapel in Oxford to tell her everything that had happened that weekend. After that, she said, with all due respect to my bottomless grief, she was going to have to suspend usual best-friend duties to go about the business of worrying about her big white wedding. I had about an hour and a half. I made the most of it.

I wanted Mary to agree with my diagnosis that Richard just had wedding fever and that the thought of watching me walk up the aisle, albeit from a seat behind one of Mary's numerous cousins, had made him flip and panic.

'He's not into marriage,' I said as confidently as I could manage. 'That's all this is about. I think that's the reason why he ended things when he did.'

'He's just not into you,' was Mary's far grimmer explanation.

'I bet you he calls me tomorrow night, when the wedding's safely out of the way,' I said hopefully.

'I bet you his mobile phone is buried under a pile of some other girl's underwear until Wednesday at the very earliest.'

'I need you to give me some hope,' I pleaded.

We had reached our old college. Mary had circled the building several times, looking for a big space into which to drive her Mercedes, but now resigned herself to the fact that she would have to do some reverse parking.

'I love you, Liz,' she told me, crunching the gears into reverse. 'And I want to be able to offer you some hope,' she continued as she struggled to align her car to the kerb. 'But anything that I say to you today is not going to sound like hope at all. It's going to sound like all the things you really don't want to hear right now. Richard dumped you a week before my wedding. You say that he's afraid of marriage. I say, that didn't even cross his mind. The timing of the dumping is irrelevant in the big scheme of things. Though it shows how little he thought of both you *and* me that he didn't wait another seven days to do the dirty deed.

'No man is really afraid of marriage,' she continued. 'What is there to be afraid of in the prospect of having sex on tap, a smiling face to come home to and dinner on the table night after night? Nothing. But all men are afraid of doing it with the wrong person. Let's face it, women are too. It would be hell to marry the wrong one. And you're Richard's wrong person. That's all. Right, time's up.'

She had backed the car into a space that was far too small for it, left the nose sticking out into the traffic and sprinted into the college chapel, dragging me behind her.

I hadn't been in the college chapel since we graduated. In fact, I hadn't been in a religious building of any type since we graduated almost a decade before.

Stepping through the chapel doors, however, it was as if I had never been away from St Judith's. The smell of the polish they used on the pews. The dust motes eddying like tiny fairy dancers in the shafts of sunlight from the stained glass windows. The oil stain on the flagstone floor where one daredevil student had ridden his leaking motorbike right down the aisle to the altar in 1957. It was as though no time had passed at all.

But so much had happened.

And the chaplain was eager to know what.

'Lizzie Jordan,' he beamed.

I was surprised that he remembered my name. I hadn't exactly been a regular attendee at his services during my time at Oxford. Sunday mornings had been for hangover maintenance, not singing hymns, when I was a student.

'How lovely to see you! Have the years treated you well?'

'Well enough,' I began. 'Until last week . . .'

'Is Bill here yet?' Mary interrupted me. I had promised her that whatever happened that day, I would not talk about my break-up in the place she had chosen for her marriage. Very bad karma, she thought.

'I think Bill went to buy some cigarettes,' said the chaplain.

'He's giving those up once we're married,' Mary retorted. 'Oh for heaven's sake . . .'

The chaplain blanched.

'Sorry, Reverend. I mean, where the heck is he?'

Is 'heck' blasphemy, I wondered.

'We need to get on with this,' Mary continued irritably. 'I've still got to try to find a spare pair of flesh-coloured stockings once this rehearsal is done.'

Bill arrived just in time to save himself from being jilted.

'OK,' began the chaplain, rubbing his hands together to signify his readiness to start. 'Who do we have here? Bride, groom, bridesmaid. Bride's father?'

'Arriving tomorrow morning,' Mary told him. 'Got some unmissable match at Lord's this afternoon.'

The chaplain nodded.

'Best man?'

'Arrives Heathrow Terminal Four at 6.30 a.m.,' said Bill. 'God willing.'

'Well,' said the chaplain. 'Let's hope that England go out and that air traffic control don't, eh?'

'What do you mean?' said Mary snappishly.

'I was trying to make a joke.'

'I'm sorry,' Mary softened. 'It's just I'm quite incredibly

stressed out. They tried to get me to agree to yellow buttonholes,' she told Bill desperately. 'Yellow buttonholes! Can you believe it? White roses dead all over Holland apparently. It's the greenfly.'

'Uh-hmmm,' the chaplain interrupted. 'Shall we crack on? Groom, you stand here.' He hustled Bill to the right of the altar. 'Bride and chief bridesmaid, up to the back. The verger will be with you in the vestibule tomorrow afternoon to make sure that everything runs smoothly. When the organist strikes up "Here Comes the Bride" I want you to wait three bars before you start your procession down the aisle. Slowly. Don't want you to trip over your skirt on the way down. Assuming that you're going to be wearing a long dress, Mary. Had a bride in trousers last week. Very modern. Not entirely sure I approve but I suppose I should be happy to see some of these people in the chapel at all . . . So, walk slowly. But not so slowly that you run out of music before you get to me.'

'Run out of music?' asked Mary in horror. 'Does that happen often?'

'Not very,' explained the chaplain. 'The aisle is only twelve feet long.'

'But if it does happen, surely the organist can just go into a reprise?' Mary persisted. 'I don't want to be walking along and find I've run out of accompaniment.'

'Yes, but then if the organist starts from the beginning again you might have the problem of finding yourself standing idle at the altar for an extra verse. It could be more awkward.'

'Can't the organist just fade the music when he sees me get here?' Mary asked him frantically.

'Mary, it won't be a problem,' interrupted Bill. 'You'll

get up the aisle in time. The music will finish perfectly.'

'Yes,' said Mary as she flounced up towards the vestibule, pulling me behind her. 'And they said that I would be able to have white roses for the buttonholes as well. You can't guarantee anything these days. Doesn't matter how much money you throw at it. Everything's going wrong. It's going to be a disaster.'

'It'll be all right on the night?' tried the chaplain.

Mary snorted. 'It had better be.'

'OK,' the chaplain shouted. 'Everybody ready. Here comes the bride. Wait three bars. Der-der-der-der . . .' He hummed the appropriate tune.

We processed towards the altar at breakneck speed.

'You can walk a little more slowly than that,' said the chaplain when we arrived at the altar. I was almost panting.

'I know,' said Mary. 'And tomorrow we will do. But today I just need to get through this rehearsal as quickly as possible and find a spare pair of tights. Is there late opening in Oxford on a Friday, do you know?'

Unable to confirm whether Debenhams would still be open at half past six, the chaplain raced through the ceremony. Turn here, kneel there, say this, say that, swap the rings, sign the register . . .

'Got that?' asked Mary, turning to me.

I had no idea what was going on.

'So the vows,' began the chaplain.

'You've taken out "obey"?' Mary barked.

'He's taken out "obey",' Bill assured her.

'Well, he better had . . .'

'Presumably you want him to leave in the bit about love?' Bill interrupted.

'Oh Bill.' Mary turned towards her future husband and

visibly relaxed. 'I'm sorry. I'm being a completely neurotic cow again, aren't I?'

'That's the girl I fell for,' Bill sighed.

'I'm sorry.'

Right then, the love between them was palpable. As Bill took Mary's hand in his to mime the exchange of rings, he smiled as though he had just taken possession of the most precious jewel in the world. The tenderness he felt for her shone out through his unmistakably tear-filled eyes. Their shared gaze was so intense that I expected to see laser rays shoot from Mary's eyes into his at any moment.

This was love.

And it was only the rehearsal.

Seeing two people so deeply into one another might be sick-making when you're in the frozen food aisle at Sainsbury's, but watching Bill and Mary practise exchanging their vows at the top of this aisle suddenly felt like a privilege. For a moment I too was lost in their love.

But then the nagging pain of my own loss was back, like a nail in the bottom of a flip-flop.

Had Richard ever looked at me like that? I asked myself while Bill and Mary cooed their words of love. Had he ever looked at me as though he might die with happiness? As though the world could fall down around us and he just wouldn't care as long as he had me safe inside his arms? As though he loved me?

I couldn't remember.

'And at this point,' said the chaplain, interrupting my reverie, 'I'll say, "You may now kiss the bride."'

Bill fell upon Mary's lips hungrily.

'Uh-hm,' the chaplain cleared his throat again. 'You're not actually married yet, you know.'

Mary pushed Bill off playfully.

'Sorry,' she said.

'Oh, don't be sorry. It's wonderful to see two young people so obviously meant for each other.'

It was. Even the two separate pieces of my broken heart agreed.

'Is that it?' Mary asked.

'That's it,' said the chaplain. 'Any questions?'

We shook our heads.

'Wonderful. Then I'll see you at three o'clock tomorrow afternoon.'

We stepped out into the sunlight. Mary, still flushed from Bill's kiss at the rehearsal, was suddenly stressed again.

'Oh my God. It's nearly five o'clock already. I've got to get those stockings before the shops shut. Bill, what have you done with the rings?' she asked. 'You have put them somewhere safe, haven't you?'

He patted his pocket. Then looked horrified to discover that he was patting nothing but emptiness.

'Bill!!!' Mary shrieked. 'Where are they?!!' She punched him in the stomach.

'Oooof!' Bill staggered backwards onto the grass in the centre of the quadrangle – the grass you weren't supposed to step on unless you were a don. Landing on your arse in the middle of it when you only had a BA Hons was strictly not allowed.

'They're in the safe!' he told her as she rained blows on his head with her black Gucci handbag. 'I put them in the safe at the hotel.'

'Well,' said Mary unrepentantly. 'That punch is for teasing me when you know how stressed out I am today. And this one is for buying cigarettes when you were supposed to be ready for the rehearsal. I can't believe I'm marrying such an insensitive, selfish . . .'

At which point the chaplain emerged from the chapel.

Mary linked arms with her future husband and hauled him back onto his feet. 'Just horsing around,' she muttered for the chaplain's benefit. 'You ready to help me find those tights?' she asked me.

'I'll be a couple of minutes,' I told her. 'I think I left my purse on one of the pews.'

Mary didn't question it. 'OK. I'll wait for you here.'

I left Mary checking that Bill really did know where the rings were (by twisting his ear until he told her the hotel safe's lock combination) and scuttled back inside the empty chapel. There I took a seat on the very front pew, although my purse had been safely in my pocket all along.

As a student at this college Mary had studied psychology, cut up a real human brain, pranced around the neurophysiology lab using a spinal cord for a skipping rope and convinced herself and me – an impressionable English Literature student at the time – that there was nothing more to the miracle of life than the reaction between sodium and potassium that sent electrical impulses running through nerve cells. The human being was a bundle of elements no more magical than a lump of coal, said Mary. Emotions were an accident of chemistry, she said. As was love.

But that hadn't stopped her from falling for it and right then I too needed there to be something more to life than carbon and sodium and a dash of H_2O. I needed some magic. I needed to pray.

'Dear God,' I whispered. 'If you're up there.'

No thunderbolt to suggest that he was.

'I know I haven't spoken to you in a long while and I know I haven't been to church for even longer,' I continued.

'I don't suppose I've got too much credit in my celestial bank account, but right now I really need a miracle.'

Still no sign.

'My best friend is getting married tomorrow and I've got to be her bridesmaid. But my heart's just been broken and I don't think that I can get through the day without dying. Please, God, I know I should probably be asking for something bigger and more important on a global scale like world peace and an end to disease and famine and war, but all I want right now is for Richard Adams to want me back again. I know I can make him happy and he's the only person who can make me happy enough not to ruin my best friend's day. Bring him back to me before tomorrow morning and I'll never ask for anything again. I'll believe in you forever. I'll donate all my money to charity. My spare money,' I added quickly. 'I'll stop making jokes about the fish symbol sticker on the back of a car meaning "I ignore the highway code" . . .'

I would have carried on pleading but I heard the chapel door creak open. The collection funds clearly didn't run to a can of oil.

'Have you found what you were looking for yet?' Mary asked me impatiently.

'I hope so,' I said, scrambling to my feet. 'God, I hope so. Whoops, sorry God,' I added. 'For blaspheming.'

'Were you praying?' Mary asked me, eyes narrowing.

I nodded, unable to shake off the feeling that I should be embarrassed.

'No need to ask what you were praying for,' she sighed dramatically.

I nodded again.

'Oh, Lizzie,' she said. 'You are hopeless. How can pray-ing change things? You might as well write your wish on a piece of paper and send it up the chimney to Father Christmas.'

'How can you say that?' I whispered in horror. 'You're getting married here tomorrow.'

'For the pictures,' she explained wearily. 'We're doing it for the pictures. Who wants a registry office in the background of their wedding photos?'

Indeed.

I spent the rest of the afternoon following Mary from department store to department store with all the goodwill of a seven-year-old looking for school shoes. Of course, Mary found the right pair of stockings in the first shop we went to but that didn't mean that the search could end early. Oh no. Mary needed a compare and contrast session in at least another eight shops before announcing, 'I'm going to go back to Debenhams and get the first pair I saw.'

In the hosiery department of John Lewis, Mary shared her frustrations with another bride-to-be. The right tights were the least of it, apparently.

'Nobody understands,' said the stranger, shaking her badly highlighted hair. 'They think you should be beaming all the time from the minute you get engaged. But there's so much trauma involved in planning a wedding. If you can find the venue that you want you can guarantee it won't be available on the right day. Then there's your dress. And the bridesmaids' dresses. Another ordeal. If you've managed to pick a bridesmaid without falling out with all your friends in the first place! Then there's the catering. Don't talk to me about the catering. And the wedding list.'

'I know,' said Mary, sighing dramatically. 'The wedding list. That is such a nightmare!'

The wedding list? A nightmare? Excuse me, but going around Harvey Nichols with a clipboard, ticking off everything you want and then asking your friends to pay for it, didn't sound much like a nightmare to me.

While the two brides compared tribulations, I felt a thin layer of ice grow around my own heart. While Mary moaned that it was 'a mystery' how anyone ever found the right florist, I began to think that the only real mystery here was how these two ridiculous whining women had persuaded two half-decent men to marry them in the first place! What had happened to my fabulous best friend? What was it about an engagement ring that could turn a previously sane, fun-loving, successful career woman into a spoilt, brain-dead complainer whose only topics of conversation were buttonholes and marquee frills?

'Look at me,' I wanted to scream. 'If Richard had asked me to marry him, I would have grinned from the engagement to cutting the cake. I wouldn't be moaning about getting the wrong sugar bowl from Great Auntie Kate because of a cock-up at the John Lewis Brides' Book. I never moaned at Richard. I never nagged. I never told him that he'd have to miss watching England versus Germany in the final of the World Cup because I wanted to be married on the same Saturday as my parents had back in 1966. Why am I only the bridesmaid again? Why do you two deserve to get married and not me?'

I was horrified by the bile I suddenly found inside me. A week earlier I had been the world's best bridesmaid, endlessly patient with the invitation wording worries and the trivial tiara tantrums. I had organised a hen night to end all hen nights (or at least a hen night wild and debauched enough to have parties of single women banned from half the nightclubs on Oxford Street for the next ten years). But an engagement ring suddenly seemed like a life jacket and I coveted one twice as desperately now that my life had hit an iceberg. What's more, I could feel the nastiness inside me heading for the resulting hole in my brittle all-too-human hull.

'I am never going to put myself through this again,' said Mary's new best friend. 'I've had nobody to support me. Nobody understands me. And I know I won't get any thanks from his relatives at the end of the day. It's terrible. Just terrible.'

And the bile broke through.

'You're getting married, for God's sake,' I told her then. 'You're having a wedding, not a funeral. It's a happy occasion. No one's died. No one's been injured. Keep on moaning and you deserve to get divorced before your first anniversary.'

'Lizzie!' Mary breathed in horror.

The other bride just stared.

'I can't believe you just said that,' Mary mouthed at me.

'I can't believe I did either,' I assured her. I put my hand to my mouth in horror. Those words hadn't really come from me, had they?

I ran from the shop and slumped, crying of course, against the automatic door. The automatic door that wouldn't remain closed while someone leaned against it. I fell back into the shop to the great amusement of a couple of schoolboys.

Mary rescued me.

'You upset that poor girl,' she said, yanking me roughly to my feet. 'How could you be so thoughtless?'

'Why her?' I spluttered. 'Why her and not me? Why

does she deserve to have someone want to marry her?
Why doesn't Richard want me any more?'

I had gathered quite a crowd by then and by the way that
they were looking at me, they clearly thought they had the
answer.

That night we were booked into The Randolph Hotel,
Oxford's biggest and most famous five-star establishment.

I had been so excited at the prospect of our night at
the Randolph. As students, surviving on a diet of dodgy
kebabs and jacket potatoes from the van parked outside
college, Mary and I had often pressed our noses against
the window of the Randolph's glamorous restaurant and
wondered what it would be like to be inside. Not even the
sight of a portly man in a tuxedo vomiting all over his shoes
while the waiters drifted by serenely could disabuse me of
the small town girl's notion that this place was the pinnacle
of taste and sophistication. When I was rich, I would stay
at the Randolph. Ten years later, I still wasn't rich. But my
best friend was.

Mary had, of course, booked a sumptuous double room
for me when she thought I would be sharing with Richard.
When she first announced where we would be staying,
right back when we were choosing bridesmaids' dresses,
I had immediately started planning my very own pre-
wedding night. New knickers. Bubble bath. Champagne.
A night away from the little flat in Tufnell Park could
rejuvenate our romance, I thought. Without wondering
too hard why it needed rejuvenating.

Upon hearing that I would no longer need my double
bed, however, Mary had taken advantage of the opportunity to save a bit of money and my room had been

downgraded to a tiny single with a view of the car park. And so much for the romantic bubble bath. As I ran hot water into the tub, which would have been too small for two in any case, I pictured myself reclining not in bubbles but in a pool of blood as the life seeped from my wrists and into the drain.

What would be the worst thing I could do on my best friend's wedding day? Disappear? Kill myself? Or just ruin the happy atmosphere by going through the whole torturous ceremony on the verge of tears?

'I can't do it,' I told Mary again as she sat with her hands in a bowl of warm olive oil designed to make her skin silky smooth for the inevitable new-wedding-ring-flashing that would be required throughout the reception.

'I can't be your bridesmaid,' I continued. 'I know I'm going to spoil your day.'

'You'll spoil my day if you're not there,' she said flatly.

'I'm going to cry all the way through the ceremony.'

'Everyone will think that you're crying with happiness.'

'No they won't. It's a completely different kind of crying. I can't pretend.'

'You've just spent a year training to be an actress,' Mary pointed out with a huff of exasperation. 'Go act.'

But what actress has ever taken on a part that requires her to smile for a whole day when all she really wants to do is fall down on the stone floor of the chapel and beg for a thunderbolt to finish her off? It wasn't as if there would be moments between takes when the cameras stopped rolling and I could return to my personal Winnebago with onboard jacuzzi to sob in.

Having Richard tell me that he no longer loved me was a bullet in the chest. I wasn't quite dead from the wound but every breath I took required more effort than the last as the cold misery of our split grew inside me like fluid building up in my lungs. The very last thing I needed to hear was that one day all this pain would make me stronger. It would make me a better actress, my mother had even dared to say. Couldn't anyone see that I wouldn't live through it to benefit? My wounds were fatal. Head, lungs, heart.

'He really isn't worth it,' Mary muttered one more time as she wiped the oil from her hands and inspected her newly gleaming fingernails. 'Go to bed, Lizzie. Try to get some sleep.'

'I can't sleep,' I whined. 'Every time I close my eyes I see his sodding face.'

She passed me a couple of her herbal sleeping tablets. 'They don't work quite as well as Valium,' she told me. And she should know, having had quite a few of the real thing in her time. 'But if you have a scotch – a single scotch, mind you – as well, you should be able to drift off quite easily.'

'Can't I have a couple more?' I asked.

'No. No, you can't. And leave your door unlocked. I'll come up and check you haven't done anything silly when I've finished my nail varnish.'

'Sure.'

'If you lock the door I'll only get the night porter to break in,' she added.

'I'll leave it open.'

How great was that? My best friend, who should have been worrying about her wedding vows, was having to worry about me committing suicide.

I went to bed and downed the tablets with another silent prayer. Not for Richard to come back to me. (The last-caller display on my mobile phone bore depressing testimony to the fact that he hadn't phoned. No one had phoned that day but my mother.) Richard and I weren't going to be reunited before the wedding. That much was only too clear. The miracle I had prayed for hadn't happened. So this time I simply prayed that I wouldn't wake up.

CHAPTER FOUR

My prayer wasn't granted, of course. And waking up in the Randolph Hotel, in the bed that I was supposed to be sharing with Richard, I had a brief happy moment of fuzzy, dreamy unknowingness before the stiletto-heeled boot of reality kicked in again and I remembered that I had been dumped. To add to my woes, I had a terrifying brain tumour-style headache as a result of the combined action of the dodgy herbal tablets and the contents of my mini-bar. The pain made me suspect that England had played Argentina in my skull overnight. England lost. Fans had rioted.

The banging on the door didn't help. It was room service. Mary had taken the precaution of ordering a cooked breakfast to be sent to my room, accompanied by a note that said, 'Eat this. I don't want you fainting at the altar.' Scrambled eggs on wholewheat toast. Crispy bacon. Done just how I liked it. But I couldn't touch it. I hadn't been able to touch anything except grapes and sips of water for a week. To which there were some advantages.

The *Bastard Ex Bikini Diet*, they should call it. Want to go down two dress sizes in a week? It's not impossible. Just get dumped by the love of your life. Believe me, you won't want chips or chocolate. Unless someone can assure you that a Milky Way contains enough strychnine to put you out of your misery before you've finished the bar.

Years of hopeless dieting, years of jogging around the block three times in penance for every Mars Bar that passed my guilty lips and all it took was a simple dumping to make those pounds melt away like ice in summer sunshine.

When I tried on the ridiculous bridesmaid's dress that six months earlier had made me look like a buxom waitress and prompted Mary's sarcastic PA to ask, 'Have you been to a Harvester before?' it looked as though the dress was still dangling from the coat hanger. My cheeks were more sunken than the *Blue Peter* garden. My clavicle stuck out like a dangerous weapon. My boobs had not gone south, as I was always fearing they would, they had simply disappeared like the *Marie Celeste*. It was as though they had never been there at all.

Mary's dressmaker had done her best to make it look as though the dress had been made for me, with a bit of artful nipping and tucking, but even with a padded bra and two pairs of those jellified breast enhancers on beneath, I could no longer fill the dress as magnificently as I might have done pre-the end of Lizzie and Richard.

'Christ, you look awful,' was Mary's refrain as she watched first the dressmaker and then her mother try to make up for my cleavage shortfall with padded bras and socks and then, in a moment of serious desperation, a couple of small navel oranges.

'I thought I was supposed to look awful,' I retorted. 'It wasn't as though a crimson crinoline was ever going to make me look fantastic, for heaven's sake.'

'There's awful and there's *awful*, Lizzie. The idea is that you won't distract from the bride. But everyone's going to be staring at you. You look like a bloody alien in a sweet wrapper.'

It was true. My head looked way too big for my newly skinny body. Against my misery-pale skin, the fabric of the dress looked as though it had been plucked from a box of Quality Street. Even with my hair bouffanted to the max I looked like a photocopy of my former self. A photocopy that had been left on a sunny windowsill to fade. The specially hired make-up artist added practically another inch in depth to my face with foundation but she couldn't do anything for the dark circles beneath my eyes.

'I just got dumped,' I explained as she hovered dangerously close with a mascara wand and told me to stop blinking. 'By the love of my life. Last weekend. He just told me he didn't want me any more. After four years. Four years we were together. Couldn't give me any explanation.'

'Awww,' said the make-up girl. 'No wonder you look so miserable. Suppose I'd better give you waterproof in that case.'

Then, half an hour later, as she applied a bit more blush – not so much gilding the lily as sticking it in a pot of bright orange Dulux emulsion – she asked, 'You got a boyfriend, then?'

I could have killed her. But I was still far too busy considering the more enticing option of killing myself.

With just twenty minutes until the wedding, I went to the bathroom on the pretence of having one final nervous wee before the car came to take me and the other bridesmaids (Ginny, aged eight, and the dreaded Trinny, six and a half) to the chapel. Mary was too busy fussing with her ridiculous floor-length veil to keep an eye on me now.

We hadn't even got to the chapel and there was already a six-and-a-half-year-old-sized footprint on the back of Mary's train.

I took my handbag. I had a Swiss army knife in there. Just a little one. Richard had given it to me during our second year together, when I went on a girls' only skiing trip to Colorado with Mary and my old flatmate Seema and let slip that I was frightened of bears.

'I'll always protect you,' he said when he gave it to me. 'Even when I can't be there in person.'

Now I held the knife in my shaking sweaty hand, blade extended and knew that I had never felt less protected in my life. I felt naked, flayed. I felt like a gladiator who has been sent out into the amphitheatre with no sword, no shield and a nice piece of prime steak slung around his scrawny neck for the starving lions.

The blade on that knife was pretty sharp. I had never used it for anything difficult. We never did meet the bears in Colorado and since then, my uses for a Swiss army knife had been pretty much limited to snipping stray threads from a jumper or cleaning my fingernails.

Now I pressed it against the soft skin on the inside of my wrist, made even more transparent than usual by a week of hardly eating. I had heard somewhere that if you're going to go this way, by cutting yourself, you should slash up the vein and not across. Quicker, more effective, more painful.

The tears welled behind my swollen eyelids. And bizarrely, I took the time to dab them dry and make sure that my mascara wasn't running before I carried on with my rather undramatic suicide bid. Then I pressed the knife a little harder, began to drag the blade down across my skin. My skin, as if it were too big for me now that I was shrinking from misery, merely moved with the metal, stretching, refusing to tear. Harder still, I pressed the knife. A spot of red. A tiny spot of brilliant red on my white skin told me that I had broken through.

'Lizzie! Aunty Mary says you can pee your pants in the church if you like but we're not going to wait for you any more.'

The door burst open.

'What?'

I whirled around, knife still at my wrist, to face poor little Trinny.

I saw the smile slide from her rosebud pink mouth. Even at six and a half years old, she knew that something wasn't right with Aunty Lizzie.

'Aunty Mary says we've got to go now,' she said solemnly. 'I need you to hold my hand. I'm not allowed in the hotel lift on my own.'

She held out her tiny hand to me.

'You mustn't be sad,' she said. 'We're being bridesmaids.'

Kids. Like dogs. Sometimes they know exactly what you need.

So, while officially I may have been the chief bridesmaid, it was actually little Trinny who held everything together that day. She'd grown up a lot since the fromage frais incident at Mary's birthday barbecue.

'I was only five then,' she reminded me in the car. 'I'm six now.'

Full of the air of responsibility that an extra year can give when it represents almost a seventh of your life, it was Trinny who made sure that Ginny stopped picking her nose while the photographer took official bridesmaid portraits outside the chapel before the ceremony began. It was Trinny who kept Ginny off the back of Mary's train as we walked, still slightly too quickly, down the aisle behind Mary and her father. It was Trinny who reminded me that I was supposed to take Mary's bouquet so that she would have her hands free to receive Bill's ring when her father gave her away.

When we retired to pews on opposite sides of the altar to hear the lesson, it was Trinny who kept me from crying, with sadness at least, with her impression of Mary's mother. Mrs Bagshot had chosen a reading about love from one of St Paul's letters and put just a little too much stress on the word 'faithfulness' with a withering glance at her ex-husband, Mary's father.

When the ceremony was over, Trinny kept the attention firmly off me with her charming antics as she skipped back up the aisle.

'One day,' I told Trinny as we posed for photographs outside. 'You're going to make someone a wonderful bride.'

'Uurgh,' said Trinny. 'I don't ever want to get married. I hate boys.'

'I'll remind you that you said that when you hit puberty.'

'My mum says if I hit anybody else I'll have to go to another school,' she said.

It quickly became clear that I had imagined Trinny's sensitivity. Just like a dog.

'Chief bridesmaid and best man!' called the photographer.

'That's you,' Trinny reminded me.

And the best man. Brian Coren.

Until Richard's recent bombshell, Brian Coren had been

the most important ex-boyfriend in my life. Brian and I had met at college, not far from the worn chapel steps where we now joined each other for our official portrait as principal supporters to the bride and groom. Brian had been sent to Oxford from New York as part of his university's exchange programme. We dated for most of the year he spent in England, then he went back to America to finish his course and start his glittering career in finance. I had thought at the time that he had taken my heart with him.

But eight years later and with a whole novel's worth of water under the bridge, we were friends again. Good friends.

'You did brilliantly,' he whispered while the photographer loaded another film. 'Under the circumstances.'

'Who told you what happened?' This was the first chance I had had to speak to Brian that day.

'Bill told me over the phone,' Brian murmured. 'He was worried that you might not be able to go through the ceremony because of the shock. I spent the whole flight over thinking of ways to cajole you into coming to the church if the worst came to the worst. I was worried I would have to pick you up and carry you over my shoulder.'

'I wouldn't have let Mary down,' I said, conveniently forgetting just how close I had come to doing exactly that.

'But you must be hurting?' Brian asked me.

'Oh, you know me,' I bluffed. 'It's not the first time I've been dumped. I'll survive it. People dump me all the time. Just call me the dumpster girl.'

'I didn't dump you,' he reminded me. 'If things had been different . . .'

If things had been different? I stared at him closely. What did he mean by that? Did he mean that if he hadn't had to return to America at the end of his year at Oxford, *we* might have been the ones swapping rings and vows that day?

'Smile!' said another photographer. Not the official one this time.

Brian's fiancée snapped us swapping wisecracks on the chapel steps instead of promises. Nope. There was no chance now that Brian and I would ever stand on those chapel steps as anything but friends.

'So, when's your big day?' I asked him, trying to grin in a friendly way at his beautiful bride-to-be. We'd met once before, Angelica Pironi and I. Secure in Richard's love at the time, I had decided that I quite liked her in spite of the fact that she made Julia Roberts look like an ugly old heifer and subsequently made me feel like wearing a paper bag for the rest of my life.

'December the fifth,' said Brian in answer to my question. 'I've got your address for the invitation. Tufnell Park, right?'

'Wrong,' I sighed. 'I got kicked out of the flat as well as dumped. I'm back with my parents.'

'What? In Solihull?' Brian looked horrified. 'Jeez.'

'I thought you liked Solihull,' I reminded him.

'Yeah. I did. I mean, as a place to visit, it's great. There's some cool countryside around there. But Lizzie, not to live. You can't live in Solihull. Especially not with your parents.'

'Well, you know how it is,' I said sarcastically. 'I've put my real estate agent onto it but I think it's going to take her a little longer than seven days to find me a bijou apartment in central London for less than three hundred a month.'

'I'm sorry, Lizzie. I didn't mean to insult you like that. I forgot it's only been a week. I'm sure you've had other things to think about.'

'Yeah. Like what I'm going to do with the whole of the rest of my life.'

'Bride's parents,' the official photographer barked. We were shuffled off the step for the next group mugshot.

'Lizzie,' said Brian, clasping my hand. 'We've got to talk some more. I think we both better circulate and do the dutiful bit for now but I really want to hear what's happening with you and I want to help you any way I can. I really do.'

'Thanks, Brian,' I said flatly.

'I hate to see you unhappy,' he continued. 'I still can't believe Richard did this to you. Especially now. Such bad timing. He's a small man, Lizzie. A small man.'

Richard was actually six feet two, but I think I knew what Brian meant.

Brian melted back into the crowd, closely followed by his own adoring fiancée, Angelica, and I found myself suddenly alone again on the edge of all the happy activity. A passing waiter pressed a glass of champagne garnished with pink-red rose petals into my hand. I took a sip. Then I knocked the rest of the glass back in one and held out my hand for another.

That morning, while contemplating the dreadful day ahead, I had decided that if I didn't manage to discreetly kill myself before the whole thing started, I would have to stay completely sober to be able to avoid losing my composure as soon as I got to the chapel and the romantic nightmare began. Now I decided that the only possible way to get through the reception, which was to be held in the college dining room, would be in a state of inebriation bordering on blindness.

I had forgotten that there isn't just the one happy couple to deal with at a wedding. Everywhere I looked, I saw grinning twosomes. Those yet to be married, such as Brian and his fiancée, beamed soppily at one another as they looked forward to their own special day as the centre of attention. Those who had been married for a few years already smiled indulgently as they remembered taking their vows. Even Mary's parents, who had divorced very acrimoniously just a couple of years earlier because of her father's unrepentant philandering, cosied up to present a united front for the photos in honour of their darling daughter, the bride.

Standing in the shadows, with my glass of champagne clutched in a fist and not even a hint of happiness on my own overmade-up face, I felt like the bad fairy at Sleeping Beauty's christening. Hard as I tried, I couldn't stop myself from wishing that everyone would stop looking so bloody joyful while I still felt so much pain.

I willed a block to fall from the chapel roof onto the grinning chaplain. No – that was too awful. I quite liked the Reverend Jones and didn't actually want to see his guts on the pavement. I willed the fluffy white clouds that had been drifting gaily over the quad to club together and get ominously grey. No point – we were about to move inside anyway. I wished for the reception to be cancelled because all the vol-au-vents had been commandeered for British troops suddenly deployed to quash an uprising in Bongo Bongo Land. That would have been perfect.

As if she read my seething mind, Trinny appeared at my elbow like an obliging evil imp.

'They're trying to make me kiss that boy,' she said, pointing towards a spit-cleaned pre-teen Lothario in a jazzy red waistcoat. 'They said it would be romantic for the pictures.'

'Why don't you want to?' I asked her.

'I've already told you, Lizzie. I hate boys.'

'I think you may be on to something there,' I told her.

'Can I play with you all afternoon?' Trinny asked then, grinning through the gap where her front teeth had been last time she bit me.

'Of course,' I said. 'But you have to do something for me first.'

She cocked her head and looked at me slyly from beneath her ringlets. 'I'll do anything to be in your gang.'

I sent a six-and-a-half-year-old child to steal a bottle of champagne from the kitchen. I was going straight to hell.

Blasted. Wasted. Rat-arsed.

By the time the waiters started bringing round the tarte au citron and the Cornish dairy ice cream flavoured with real vanilla pod, I could barely see. I was sitting at the top table, Bill's father to my left, open space to my right. For the first half of the meal I intermittently leaned on Bill's dad and the table. Bill's dad didn't seem to mind that much. In fact at one point he started leaning back on me and telling me all about his days as the most eligible man in Tunbridge Wells. For the pudding course I tried leaning in the other direction, found nothing but fresh air and fell off my chair.

I thought I recovered myself pretty well considering. I got to my feet without too much assistance and staggered past the other guest tables in the direction of the ladies' room. I was at that stage of drunkenness when you think that you're still functioning pretty highly. The stage where you congratulate yourself when you notice that you're pouring champagne straight onto the table-cloth and not into your glass before it hits your shoes. I wasn't yet at that headlining 'oh-my-God-she's-so-pissed-someone-should-put-her-to-bed' stage. Or so I thought.

I was just soppy drunk. I was getting emotional 'I love everybody' drunk. I was suddenly filled with the urge to tell everybody exactly how much I loved them. Coming out of the bathroom, having been careful to check that my mascara was still in place but not having noticed that my dress had gained another extraneous trimming in the form of a long ribbon of scratchy white loo roll, I headed straight for the maitre d'.

The waiting staff were busily collecting up the remains of the tarte au citron. The wedding cake had been wheeled out from the corner of the room to a more prominent position. It was almost time for the speeches.

''Scuse me,' I said, tapping the maitre d' on his shoulder. He jumped back. Or tried to. I was standing on his foot.

'I want to make a speech,' I told him. 'Can you announce that for me?'

'It isn't really etiquette for the chief bridesmaid to make a speech,' the maitre'd said stiffly.

'I know,' I slurred. 'Is s'not etti-ket. But this is different. Mary is my best, bestest friend, you know. And Bill is my second best friend. I only want to make their day extra speshul.'

'I think that perhaps madam had better have a cup of coffee before she thinks about doing any public speaking,' the maitre d' tried again.

'Are you saying I'm drink? I mean, drunk?' I mumbled belligerently.

'Yes.'

'Well, I may be drunk but I'll still be ugly in the morning,'

I said. 'I mean, you're ugly in the morning . . . I mean. Oh, hell. I mean nothing. Just 'nounce me, will you? They'll be pleased. Honestly, they will.'

'I'll ask the bride,' he said.

'Don't ask her,' I told him. 'She'll say no.'

'Exactly. You'd better take your place again, mizz. I'm about to announce the father of the bride.'

'Fine,' I said. 'You be sexist. Men first. All the time.'

'It's tradition.'

So, the maitre d' announced Mary's father who began his speech by saying that he never expected to have to stand up at his daughter's wedding because she was such an awkward little madam as a child that he didn't ever expect her to hang on to a man. Mary's face darkened. Her dad made a good recovery by explaining that she was a lot easier to get along with now that she'd matured.

'Like a mouldy cheese,' someone from the back of the room suggested.

'Like a fine wine,' corrected Mary's father.

'Great,' said Mary. 'I'm not thirty yet, you know.'

'Just slipped in under the cut-off point,' her father reminded her. 'Almost an old maid.'

'Shut it, Dad.'

'The groom,' announced the maitre d'.

Bill's speech was suitably romantic. Beginning with the very first time he saw the woman who would be his future wife, but tactfully failing to mention the fact that she had actually been baring her buttocks at him from across the bar during a Freshers' Week drinking contest when he first caught sight of her. Their love, he reminded the room, had been a pretty on/off affair to start with. He was always on for it and Mary was usually running off screaming. But finally she had succumbed to his charms. Almost six years after she mooned at him. He'd waxed his back and she'd agreed to marry him. He raised a toast to his beautiful wife who was dabbing at her wet eyes with the tablecloth.

'The best man.'

Now Brian got to his feet. A reprise of the Bill and Mary story. A flashback to the night they first kissed at a party where the only entrance requirement was that you were wearing two items of clothing or less. As he got a laugh from the audience with his description of Bill in a spandex catsuit and cowboy hat, I couldn't help wondering if Brian was thinking about the other relationship that had started that night. Because it had been the very same night that he and I first snogged on the steps outside the student union. But it wasn't my gaze Brian kept catching as he reminisced. And when he said, 'Bill and I once told each other that we would never find the girls who could put up with us,' it wasn't me that he winked at. His snap-happy fiancée took another photo and winked back.

'The bride and groom!' Another toast. (Naturally, I was keeping up with those.) And then there were the presents. Big bright bouquets for the mothers who had worked so hard to make the day special (though Mary had complained bitterly throughout the preparations that her mother was only interested in the wedding as another platform from which to humiliate her father). Dolls for Ginny and Trinny, dressed in outfits to match their bridesmaids' dresses. (To the amusement of the room, Trinny announced that she would have preferred a tractor.) And a pair of dangly silver earrings for me. I took the box from Bill and staggered a little when he released me from his big bear hug.

'You've done brilliantly,' he assured me with a dismissive pat on the shoulder.

'I haven't finished yet,' I assured him back.

Since it was obvious by now that the maitre d' was not going to announce my speech, I decided I would have to introduce myself. So, when I should have been retiring gracefully and thinking about having a gallon or two of black coffee before I really started acting the fool, I positioned myself right between the newly-weds and raised my champagne glass in a toast of my own.

'Ladies and gentlemen. Gride and broom.'

A promising start.

'Pray silence, purleese for the chief of the bridesmaids.'

Mary smiled up at me nervously. Bill's eyebrows were knitted together with worry but he too managed to hang on to his grin. I tapped the side of my champagne glass with the handle of a spoon to make sure I had everybody's attention. Bill tactfully took the glass from my hand before I had a chance to break it but he still let me begin . . .

'Ladies and gentlemen, I just want to shay how very happy I am to be here today,' I started. 'No, really, I'm very very happy.'

'Good,' hissed Brian. 'Now you can sit down.'

'In a minute,' I told him. 'I haven't finished yet. Ladies and gentlemen, there's something I need to tell you all. You know,' I picked up my glass again and knocked back some champers to wet my lips. 'When I started crying during the ceremony this afternoon, that wasn't because I got dumped last week. Oh no, it was just because I was sooooo happy. And why shouldn't I be happy that my two best friends in the whole world are getting married to each other?'

'Hear hear,' said Brian, attempting to cut me off with applause this time.

No one joined in. He failed.

'Why shouldn't I be happy?' I asked the audience. 'Even when I've just been left on my own again. That's right everybody. I've just been chucked. Chucked, dumped and abandoned. Dumped like a day-old newspaper. Dumped more carelessly than French nuclear waste.'

A good simile, I congratulated myself. I heard a titter from the back at that one.

'No,' I continued. 'I just want to say that I'm deliriously, gob-smackingly happy to be here today with you all, ladies and gentlemen, watching our dear friends Mary and Bill make their declarations of true love. And I just want to say that even though I've just been dumped by my own stupid b-word of a boyfriend, I hope that Bill and Mary never get divorced because though I've never been divorced myself, I think that after this week I can safely say that I can imagine what that would be like.'

'Lizzie,' attempted Brian.

But I wasn't about to be stopped.

'And it would be horrible, wouldn't it?' I asked my audience. 'To be divorced. Mrs Bagshot knows, doesn't she?' I added with a nod towards Mary's mother. 'It's simply terrible. Being on your own again like you're the last coffee cream left in the chocolate box. Like you're the last lobster in the restaurant fish tank. Like you're the dogshit on the bottom of life's sandal.'

The room was deathly quiet.

'Because there's nothing worse than being on your own again when you've spent the past four years of your precious life giving someone your all, believe me. When you gave everything you had to them. When you loved them and supported them and did their bloody washing. When you ironed their shirts and cooked their breakfasts and cleaned their bathroom and even went to pick up their haemorrhoid cream from the chemist and risked having everyone think it was for you because they were too embarrassed to go themselves. And then they go and dump you so suddenly that you don't even have time to cry before you're out on the pavement with your washbag . . . How fair is that?'

I banged my fist on the table.

'Is that gratitude?' I asked my audience. 'Is that what love's about? All give, give, give and nothing left to take? Do you think I should have seen it coming? Do you think I should have slept with other people while we were together so that when the end came I wouldn't have felt like such a fool? Am I the most gullible woman in England? Should I have stabbed him to death while I had a chance? Could I have got off on a manslaughter charge because of the provocation? What do you think, Mrs Bagshot? What did we do wrong?'

'Take her away, someone,' Mary's mother shouted. 'I think she's been taken ill.'

'She's not ill,' shouted Trinny. 'Lizzie Jordan's drunk.'

Indeed, I was so drunk that when they finally got me back to the hotel I was almost peeing in the bottom of the wardrobe before I realised that I hadn't found the bathroom.

Unfortunately I was not so drunk that I managed to black out before committing the ultimate drunken boo-boo. An even bigger boo-boo than making a ridiculous, bitter speech at my best friend's wedding. I did the one thing that every drunken dumpee remembers forever with crushing humiliation no matter how hard they try to attain a bout of drunken memory loss.

I phoned him. I picked up the phone and called Richard. Not even the fact that I would be paying hotel telephone rates (that is, think of the real cost of the call and treble it) could put me off.

Three rings and the answermachine kicked in. I had expected that. Of course I hadn't expected him to actually pick up the phone because I knew that he had been screening his calls precisely in case it was me.

I had not, however, expected the changed message.

No more 'Richard and Lizzie can't get to the phone right now,' complete with the happy sound of me giggling in the background while he tried to record the message without cracking up. Now the answerphone at Richard's telephone number picked up with a wholly different spiel. 'Hi, this is Richard,' it said. 'I can't answer the phone right now. But you can call me on my mobile. Zero seven seven . . .'

I put the phone down.

He'd changed the message. He'd taken my name off it. Now everybody knew I was gone.

I dialled Richard's number again. Three rings.

'Hi, this is Richard.'

I put the phone down.

He sounded happy, didn't he? He sounded happy *and* sexy. He sounded like a happy, sexy single bloke who had recorded an extra specially happy and sexy message in case a happy, sexy woman he wanted to get a date with called while he was out and got his answerphone.

'Oh God,' I breathed.

I dialled him again.

'Hi, this is Richard. I can't . . .'

Was that a giggle in the background? I could have sworn I heard a new giggle in the background. Who was giggling? Who had been there with him while he wiped my name off his answerphone and recorded that bloody new message in his 'Hi, I'm single. Shag me' tone?

I rang him one more time. I had to know who was

laughing because whether she knew it or not, she was laughing at me!

Three rings.

'Hi, this is . . . click . . . Lizzie, is that you?'

The real Richard had answered the phone this time.

'Yes,' I squeaked.

'Bloody hell,' he sighed. 'Did you just call me three times in a row and put the phone down every time you got the answerphone?'

'Yes.'

'It's one o'clock in the morning, for crying out loud. Are you drunk?'

'I might be. A little bit,' I admitted.

'A little bit? I've never heard you sound so pissed in my life. For God's sake, Lizzie, go to sleep.'

'I can't, Richard. I just can't sleep any more. I keep waking up thinking of you. I'm sad and I'm lonely.'

'I know,' he said. 'I got your letter.'

'What did you think of it?' I asked hopefully. 'Did it help you understand?'

'I think you shouldn't have sent it. It only confirmed what I thought.'

'What did you think?' I asked desperately.

'That I just don't want to be with you any more. Don't try to make me feel guilty, Lizzie. It's over between us. Over.'

'But I can't get over you,' I protested.

'Well,' he said matter of factly. 'I don't think you should expect to be able to get over me completely in a week.'

'I don't think I'll ever get over you!' I whined.

'Lizzie, you really must go to sleep,' he said. 'I've got to get some sleep. I want to get up early tomorrow and finish a painting. I'm putting the phone down now.'

'I'll just keep ringing,' I warned him.

'I'll take it off the hook.'

'I'll get a taxi round to your house and hammer on your door and sit on the doorstep.'

'What? From Oxford?' he sneered.

'From Oxford,' I threatened. 'Mary will lend me the money.'

'Don't do that,' said Richard quietly.

'I will,' I told him. 'That's exactly what I'll do if you don't tell me that you'll see me tonight.'

'OK. OK. I'll see you,' he said resignedly. 'But not tonight.'

'When?'

'I don't know. Soon.'

Exasperation.

'When?'

'OK! Next Sunday. Can you come to London?'

'I'll be there. Oh, thank you, Richard. Thank you. You won't regret it. I'll see you next weekend.'

He had already put the phone down.

And I was just about to call him back to pin him down to a time when somebody rang me.

Mary.

'Well at least you haven't passed out,' she began.

'Oh Mary, I'm sorry, sorry, sorreeeeee!' I cried.

'It's OK.'

'But I got drunk at your wedding reception. I said such awful things. Your poor mother . . . I made a total idiot of myself.'

'Lizzie, I don't care that you got drunk at my wedding reception. Who wasn't? I just want to know that you won't do anything more stupid than make a soppy speech full of expletives while I'm away on honeymoon.'

'I'm not going to kill myself,' I assured her.

'I was thinking of something even more stupid than that. Promise you weren't on the phone to that no-good ex-boyfriend of yours when I called you a minute ago.'

'I was talking to my mother,' I lied.

'Good. Look, just forget about what happened today. OK? I want you to know that I had a wonderful time despite everything and I'm sure that when we watch the video of your speech on our silver wedding anniversary in 2025, it'll all seem terribly funny.'

'For you,' I said flatly.

'For both of us. Listen, you should try to have breakfast with Brian and Angelica tomorrow morning. Brian thinks you ignored him all day.'

'I wasn't ignoring him. I just didn't want to intrude on his *lurve*.'

'You can't spend the rest of your life avoiding happy couples, Lizzie. Have breakfast with them. Angelica's really nice.'

'I know,' I said grudgingly. 'I'll see them if I wake up in time.'

'Good.'

'Mary?'

'Yes, Lizzie?'

'Who caught the bouquet?' I asked.

'I would have thrown it to you,' she said. 'If I thought you were capable of catching it without falling over backwards and cracking your head open on the tiles.'

'I know. But who got it instead of me?'

'Angelica caught it,' Mary confirmed.

'But she's already getting married,' I groaned. A pathetic tear ran down my nose. 'Why did she have to catch it? I *needed* that bouquet.'

'Lizzie, you just *need* to get some sleep,' said Mary flatly. 'It wouldn't have made a difference, catching a stupid bunch of flowers. You know that. Now, I've got to go. Our plane leaves for the Seychelles at eight tomorrow morning. So much for a passionate wedding night. Bill's passed out through too much alcohol and we've got to be up at five to get to the airport. Look, whatever you do, promise that you won't go back to Richard while I'm away, Lizzie. Promise me you won't even see him. After what he's put you through today you mustn't even think about wanting to be with him again. I know I'm never going to speak to him if you do. I won't come to any wedding. Promise me, Lizzie.'

'I promise.'

But I had my fingers crossed behind my back.

I was surprised that I woke up at all the next morning. I was even more surprised that I didn't actually feel that bad. What I didn't know was that I was actually still drunk. My hangover would kick in with a vengeance around lunchtime.

But while I waited for Armageddon, I managed to eat quite a respectable breakfast in the hotel dining room – the glimmer of hope that Richard had restored in me by saying that he would see me to talk the following Sunday had also restored a small part of my appetite. Meanwhile, Brian winced through his hangover with a cup of coffee and his ultra slimline fiancée Angelica sent her English muffin with fat-free butter back to the kitchen three times.

'I asked for it to be toasted, not cremated,' she complained. 'With no butter. *No* butter. Did you get that this time? And do you think we could get some more coffee?

I've had an empty cup in front of me for the past twenty minutes.'

'They'll charge you for extra coffee,' Brian warned her.

'I forgot. I can't believe you don't get free refills here.'

'Neither can I,' I said inanely, not really having a clue what she was on about.

'So, Lizzie,' said Angelica, forgetting her breakfast for a moment and leaning towards me conspiratorially. 'Brian tells me you've just been dumped.'

She patted my hand and gazed at me thoughtfully. Very Oprah Winfrey.

'That's right,' I said. 'After four years.'

'Oh, sweetheart!' Angelica exclaimed. 'That's even longer than I've known my Brian. You must be devastated. I know I'd be devastated if I lost my little hun.'

'Blitzed,' I confirmed.

'Was he very special?'

'He was a jackass,' said Brian.

'Brian!' tutted Angelica. 'Let the girl speak. Tell me all about it, Lizzie.'

'How long have you got?'

'You know,' said Angelica before I even had a chance to start. 'There's no point moping about this. What you need is to get away from London for a while. It's almost impossible to recover from such a blow in an atmosphere that constantly reminds you of what you lost.'

She was right. But it wasn't just London. Right then everything everywhere reminded me of Richard. Even looking at the sugar bowl in an attempt to stop myself from crying all over the tablecloth reminded me of Richard. He took sugar. Waaaaahhh!

'You should come to America,' Angelica continued. 'Brian tells me you're an actress. Why don't you get

your US agent to set up some meetings for you in Los
Angeles and head out there for a couple of months? Get
some sun. Hang out on the beach. You'll feel great in
no time.'

'My US agent?' I laughed. Hollowly. 'I don't have one.'

'You're kidding,' said Angelica. 'Can you believe that,
Brian?'

Brian shook his head and winced again. I knew how
painful head movements could be the morning after a big
night before, and I sympathised.

'What are you thinking of?' Angelica admonished me.
'You've got to have a US agent.'

'I haven't even had so much as a cornflakes commercial
here. Why would a US agent want to take me on?'

'Don't be so defeatist,' she said.

'I'm simply being a realist.'

'If I had been a realist, I wouldn't have ended up with
Brian,' Angelica told me then. 'I was his secretary. Everyone
told me that I couldn't date the boss. But I did it and now
we're getting married.'

'Finding love is a bit different from finding a speaking
part in the new Spielberg,' I told her. Though right then,
getting a major speaking role in a Spielberg movie actually
seemed more likely than my chances of ever finding romantic happiness again.

'Nevertheless, a little bit of optimism goes a long way,'
Angelica persisted.

'I don't think it will get me all the way to Los Angeles,'
I said hopelessly. 'I don't know anybody there.'

'But we do, don't we, Brian?' Angelica announced. 'I
went to secretarial college in San Diego. Lots of my girlfriends moved up to LA. There's Candy, for a start.'

Candy and Angelica? I wondered whether their mothers

had just looked in the kitchen cupboards for inspiration with their names.

'Not Candy,' Brian groaned.

'What's wrong with Candy?' Angelica asked him defensively.

'Nothing, darling. Nothing at all.'

'Now, Candy has just moved into Hugh Hefner's Playboy mansion,' Angelica continued. 'But I give that two weeks so by the time you're ready to move, she'll be looking for a new room-mate.'

Angelica scribbled down a number.

'And then there's Minty.'

More foodstuffs?

'She's a swimsuit model. Gets a bit moody if she's on one of her seaweed diets but she'd show you a good time.'

'Didn't she burn out and go to a Buddhist retreat?' asked Brian.

'She did,' said Angelica. 'But she came back when they told her she couldn't use her hairspray to kill the bugs in her cell. She would love you, Lizzie. And I think she has space in her apartment.'

'I thought she moved the trapeze artist in,' said Brian.

'He was a fire-eater,' Angelica corrected. 'And he moved out a month ago. I knew that wouldn't last long when he singed one of her hairpieces.'

Angelica scribbled down another phone number. 'I'll give her a call to tell her what I've suggested. Isn't this exciting? You could end up as my best friend's room-mate.'

I just about resisted saying 'and you're going to be my ex-lover's wife' as a rejoinder. I took the numbers and slipped them into my purse.

'Thanks.'

'Now, you will call my ladies, won't you?' said Angelica.

'I will,' I promised.

'And you won't call that no-good ex-boyfriend of yours ever again?'

'I promise.'

Fingers crossed. Again.

'Sweetheart, going to Los Angeles will sort you out. I promise you that in less than a year you will call me to say that this was a lucky break.'

A lucky break? It wasn't the first time I'd heard that phrase during the past week and it still wasn't ringing true. I smiled and nodded when Angelica said it but all I really wanted to do was grab her by the throat and say, 'You're lying.'

A lucky break? I was sure I'd even used the phrase myself on some other unfortunate sucker. And I knew that in most cases it was true. Most people moved on to better things after a break-up. A boyfriend who appreciated them was just the start. Think Cher without Sonny, storming up the charts. Tina Turner without Ike. Their break-ups set them free. But then think Ike without Tina. Who remembers him for anything but wife-beating? And look at what happened to Sonny. One goes up. One goes down. What if I was the one on the downward trajectory?

Angelica and Brian left Oxford for Heathrow that afternoon. They were heading on to Italy. The lakes. Having a practice honeymoon, Angelica informed me gleefully. Though I had been *totally* over Brian since 1997, it wasn't exactly what I wanted or needed to hear that day.

For me, it was back on the train to Solihull as soon as I checked out of the Randolph. No practice honeymoon. No heart-warming Italian sun. Just the British summer rain streaking down the dirty grey windows of the 13.51 to Birmingham New Street. Rain on a train and a belated hangover headache and a piece of paper with a couple of telephone numbers I didn't think I'd ever ring.

Los Angeles for the autumn? Nice idea. But Angelica's friends had never even met me. Why should either of them want me to be their room-mate? I decided that Angelica was just being polite in that American way by making an offer that I was supposed to know I should never actually try to take up. I consigned the numbers to the dusty recesses of my wallet and went back to dreaming about Richard.

California dreaming was simply not on the agenda that night.

CHAPTER FIVE

Luckily, or should I say unluckily in retrospect, not all my friends were taking such a hard line on the prospect of my getting back together with Richard 'the Demon King' as Mary had. My old flatmate Seema was a sucker for a happy ending and thought that everybody should at least have a shot at one. So when I told her that I was planning to meet my ex to 'talk' the following weekend, she was more than happy to let me stay at her London flat the night before and even helped choose the outfit that would, in her opinion, impress him right back into loving me.

'You look great,' said Seema, regarding my newly gamine figure in a pair of her ultra-chic Earl jeans and a cropped pink T-shirt that I would never have considered before misery robbed me of my beer belly and helped me rediscover my waist. 'He'll fall at your feet. But make sure that you really want him to. You don't have to have him back just because he asks, you know.'

'I know,' I assured her. As if I would have hesitated for a moment.

Seema squeezed my arm. 'You were made for each other though. That's what I think.'

Seema had been with me on the night I first met Richard. It was her twenty-second birthday. We were celebrating in style – drinking like a rugby team – and had reached that stage where we could only stay upright by leaning against each other for support. So, when Seema tripped in her platform-heeled sandals and fell down the stairs of that backpackers' pub in Leicester Square, I could do nothing but share the fall. Richard softened my landing. Looking back, it wasn't such a fortuitous start.

At the time, Seema and I were sharing a disgusting house in Balham with a guy we called *Fat Joe*. We rarely saw him. He was, to put it bluntly, a lard-arsed computer-obsessed agoraphobic. But though he didn't often show his face outside the confines of his bedroom/bunker, his odour pervaded the place like mustard gas and he left his filthy towelling socks about the house like droppings marking his territory.

Despite that, we were a pretty happy household for the best part of three years. Then Seema went off to Harvard to do an MBA. And Richard asked me to move in with him. Fat Joe wasn't left alone for too long though. He had an internet chat room romance with a girl who called herself 'Venus'. I have to admit that we were all relieved when she did actually turn out to be a girl.

Seema and I flanked Fat Joe's shoulders as the picture of herself she had scanned into an email started to come through. There was a collective sigh of relief when we saw very clear evidence of female secondary sexual characteristics (i.e. boobs). There was a sigh of slight disappointment, however, when Seema and I also noted that while Venus didn't resemble the Botticelli painting, if you'd told us that she came from outer space, we wouldn't have been in the least bit surprised.

Anyway, six months after meeting Venus in a chat room for *Blake's Seven* fans (of which there are plenty in America by all accounts), Fat Joe overcame his agoraphobia for long enough to fly out to Cleveland, Ohio to meet her. They got married two weeks after that. Talk about whirlwind. Seema and I sent them a wooden salad bowl from Habitat. And Fat Joe had been in Ohio ever since.

Seema liked to use Fat Joe's story as proof that there really is someone for everyone.

'And Richard is your someone,' she assured me. 'I really don't know what's going on with him right now.'

Nothing that a good long talk couldn't sort out, I hoped. Anyway, Seema had promised to go out for the afternoon, leaving Richard and me alone to argue in her flat. Neutral ground, she had suggested. But when Richard finally turned up, twenty minutes late, he refused even to step across the threshold.

'Have you eaten?' he asked me brusquely.

'I haven't eaten for two weeks,' I replied.

'Yeah? Well, look, I'm really hungry. Do you mind if we go and get something now?'

'I thought we were going to talk,' I said. 'Here. Seema's gone out specially.'

'We can talk in a restaurant,' he said. 'Come on.'

But of course we couldn't talk in a restaurant. And pretty soon I realised that was exactly how he wanted it. Café Rouge in Richmond on a summer Sunday afternoon. For heaven's sake! Richard couldn't have chosen a more public place to discuss our break-up if he had suggested that we meet on the Oprah Winfrey show.

I sat silently as he ordered a three-course meal from the prix fixe menu and asked for the waiter to make it snappy. He asked me if I wanted anything. I had the waiter bring me a cup of tea but I didn't even really want that. I watched Richard eat a peppered steak with the gusto of someone who has just returned from conquering Kilimanjaro. Separation certainly hadn't affected his appetite. And between courses, with his mouth full of bread roll, he just about managed to ask:

'How was the wedding?'

'Shit thanks,' I told him. What a stupid question. 'I ruined my best friend's day.'

'How are your parents?' he tried.

'They hate you.'

'Oh. Did you manage to call the council about that planning permission before you left my flat?'

'What?' I asked.

'The planning permission? Did you manage to talk to anyone about that?'

I wanted to reach across the table for his steak knife and stab him right through the heart. I wanted to hold him by the throat and stick a fork into his eyes. I wanted to lacerate his stupid face with a broken plate. I wanted to smash his wineglass on the table and grind the broken shards into his groin.

'I don't want to talk about your neighbour's planning permission,' I told him. 'I came here to talk about us.'

'OK. But did you call them?'

'No!'

I started to cry. Richard shifted in his chair as though he had worms.

'Look, there's no need to cry,' he said. 'People break up all the time, you know.'

People break up all the time? What was with the platitudes? Was he really telling me that after four years people break up and that's it? Two weeks later they go out for lunch and she agrees to help him fight his neighbour's planning permission for an ugly kitchen extension so that he doesn't lose any value on his bloody crummy flat?

'How can you say that?' I asked him.

'It's true,' he said, shovelling in a mouthful of lemon tart. 'Could have happened to anyone.'

'What? We're not just anyone, Richard! We're talking about you and me. Honey and Shugs.' I used our pet names but he didn't even register a flicker of my pain. 'We were living together. We were supposed to be in love.'

'Look,' said Richard firmly. 'You told me that if I didn't want to see you again I should just say. You said that you wouldn't try to stop me. You wouldn't give me any hassle, you said. Well, I don't want to see you again and I've said it. Are you going back on your word by trying to make this hard?'

'What word?'

'You said it,' Richard reminded me again, getting pink about the ears with frustration. 'Those were your exact words. If you don't want to see me again . . .'

'Oh stop it,' I said. I had thought it was only supposed to be women who remembered conversations verbatim. Though I remembered only too well the conversation he was referring to now. And exactly when we had had it.

'Richard,' I told him. 'I said those words to you on our third date. *Our third date!* Back then it would have been perfectly acceptable for you to decide that you didn't want a relationship, or you didn't get my sense of humour, or you just didn't like my hair. After three dates it is perfectly acceptable to say, "Hey, we had fun but this just isn't going anywhere. See you around" and not offer a reason why. That does not hold true for a relationship that has lasted three months. Let alone four sodding years including a period during which you've been sharing gas bills and a bloody bedroom. There's got to be a proper reason.'

'Look, it's just the way I feel,' said Richard helplessly. 'I can't help the way I feel, can I?'

'What about the way I feel?' I asked him. 'I don't want this relationship to end.'

'It has already ended,' he said flatly. 'You can't have a relationship if one of you doesn't want to be in it. And I don't.'

'Excuse me,' I snapped.

I jumped up and left the table to lock myself in a loo where I retched into the sparkling porcelain bowl. Nothing came up. There was nothing to come up. But my body wanted to be sick. My body wanted to turn itself inside out so that he could really see how bloody miserable he had made me. My body wanted to stand in front of him, glistening viscera on the outside and say, 'Look. Here's my heart. It's broken already but perhaps you would like to put some salt on it before you go for good.'

This wasn't working out as I had anticipated at all. When planning this meeting, I had known that it wouldn't be a bundle of laughs but I had expected to be able to at least plant some doubt about the sense of our break-up in Richard's teeming mind. I had expected a toehold of residual love to help me climb back up into his affections. I had expected him to look remorseful at the very least. Open to the suggestion that he might have been too hasty after all, perhaps?

But it was clear that Richard was a great deal further removed from the pain of our break-up than I was. He was acting as though my unhappiness surprised him, as though he didn't know why I felt hurt. He acted as though I was being *irrational*. As though the whole of our four years together had been a figment of my imagination. Like I was a stalker he had never given any encouragement. There was no foothold to help me breach the walls around his affection. Far from it. Richard was as impenetrable as Hitler's bunker and right then, he was obviously just as full of love.

I walked back across the restaurant towards him. On my way I told the waiter, loud enough for plenty of people to hear, 'The arsehole in the corner wants his bill so that he can leave this restaurant right away and doesn't have to spend a moment longer not telling me why we broke up.'

The waiter nodded and brought the bill forthwith.

'Give him a tip,' I hissed as Richard signed the credit card slip.

'Service is included,' Richard said.

'Like it was when I lived with you,' I snarled. 'You know,' I stopped the waiter to be witness to my bile. 'I lived with this shit for a year and a half. He earned more than twice the amount of money I did but he had me pay rent at the market rate and on top of that I did all his cooking and cleaning and his tax and VAT returns. In return, during the whole of our relationship, he only once bought me flowers. He forgot my birthday four times in a row. And he never gave me an orgasm.'

'What? Never?' asked the waiter.

'Never,' I confirmed.

Richard was moved to protest.

'He forgets I went to drama school,' I said to cut him off.

'Unbelievable,' said the waiter. 'You're better off without him. And as a matter of fact, service isn't included here. Sir.'

Richard was already halfway out the door.

'Come on,' he said, yanking me out into the sunshine by my collar. 'I think you've humiliated me quite enough for one day.'

'And you haven't humiliated me? We were lovers for four years, Richard,' I shouted. 'Four fucking years. You can't just expect me to walk away from our relationship and our home, spend two weeks sobbing at my parents' house in Solihull and then come back to London all happy to be your friend and talk about your next-door neighbour's bloody planning permission. Is this all I'm worth? Three quarters of an hour in a Café Rouge? Watching you stuff your face with steak and garlic mashed potatoes? I want you to talk to me, Richard. Properly. You promised that you would talk to me.'

'There's nothing left to talk about,' he said.

'What on earth do you mean?'

'Look. I didn't want to have to say this but you've left me no option. We're over, Lizzie. We're over forever. Not just because I don't love you any more but because I've met someone else.'

He might as well have hit me in the stomach with a hammer. I crumbled to the pavement. Literally. Physically. My knees quite simply gave way. I was lucky I didn't black out.

'No!' I cried.

'I'm sorry.'

A passing dog gave me a quick sniff but its accompanying humans just walked on by.

'Lizzie, get up,' said Richard, pulling roughly on my arm. 'You're making an exhibition of yourself.'

'I don't care,' I told him from my position on the ground. 'Tell me that you're lying. Tell me you're just saying that to make me give up and go home.'

'I'm not lying, Lizzie. I've met someone else and I want to be with her.'

'Who is she?' I demanded.

'Get up,' persisted Richard.

'I'm not getting up until you tell me.'

I grabbed hold of his trouser legs and stayed resolutely in my heap on the paving stones while I waited for an answer.

'It's Jennifer,' he said. 'Look. Just get up and go home.'

Jennifer. No! Not Jennifer the model? Jennifer the model whose dot.com-rich boyfriend had commissioned a portrait of her by Richard to hang in his new Notting Hill mansion? Jennifer who was allegedly so sickeningly devoted to her other half that Richard complained she kept interrupting the initial sittings to send text messages via her mobile phone to her true love at his offices. So sickeningly devoted that she'd obviously invited Richard round to make an in-depth study of her anatomy outside the studio, just to make sure the portrait was absolutely right.

'But Jennifer has already got a boyfriend,' I said pathetically.

'He treated her badly,' said Richard with no trace of irony whatsoever. 'He didn't deserve her.'

'Oh, Richard. No!' I moaned again.

'I'm sorry, Lizzie. I didn't mean to get involved with her. We just sort of clicked.'

'Clicked? Clicked?!!!' I raged. 'You mean you couldn't keep your hands off her after getting her to pose topless? Richard, how could you? It's so . . . so tacky!'

'We didn't sleep together until the day after you and I split up,' he said almost proudly.

'Great. That's just great. Richard, thank you for that. You didn't shag her while you were sleeping with me. You're such a gentleman. You're so fucking honourable.'

The dog that had sniffed me when I first fell on the floor had come back for a second go.

'Do you need a hand getting up?' asked the dog's owner.

'She's fine,' said Richard.

'No, I am not fine,' I told the dog-walker. 'The love of my life has just told me that he dumped me for a sodding topless model.'

'She is not a topless model,' Richard protested.

'She's a model. And she was topless. A topless model by any other name, if you ask me. Don't you agree?' I asked the dog-walker.

'Er, I don't know,' he said as he shuffled out of range.

'I can't believe I fell for all that crap you used to spout about not being attracted to the women who posed for you,' I continued to shout at Richard.

'It's never happened before.'

'And it's no sodding consolation that it's happened now.'

The dog owner had moved on, but his pooch was still regarding me with interest. 'Oh, sod off,' I said.

Richard started to walk away.

'No. Not you,' I called after him, reaching out for his ankles. 'Don't go. I was talking to the dog. Richard, come back. I haven't finished talking to you.'

'I've finished listening,' was his retort.

'You'll regret it, you know,' I warned him. 'Shacking up with some airhead glamour model. What we had together went deeper than animal passion. We were soul mates, Richard. Meant for each other. Our love was about more than looks. We had real passion. We had a connection up here.' I pointed to my head.

'And that's exactly where you've lost it,' said Richard. Then he began to run.

Seema returned from her afternoon of tactful shopping with

an expectant look on her face. She turned the key in the
front door as quietly as possible and made a pretence of
creeping past the kitchen.

'I'm on my own,' I called out shakily. On my own in a
puddle of my own making. Forehead on the kitchen table. A
layer of soggy Kleenex six inches deep on the floor around
my feet.

'Oh. Shit.' Seema stopped creeping to survey the car-
nage. 'It was so quiet in here I thought I might have
caught you in the middle of making up. I hoped that was
the case.'

'Fat chance,' I sniffed. 'He's got someone else.'

'Oh, Lizzie. No. Tell me it's not true.'

'It is true. It's a disaster. She's a model. She's five feet
eight, blonde hair to here.' I indicated my bottom. 'And a
pair of tits that men would go to war for.'

Seema, who was as flat-chested as most of the boys in
the prep school three doors down from her house, pulled
a face of disapproval and sat down beside me.

'Did you know her?' she asked me carefully.

'He was painting her.'

'The bitch. Wanna talk about it?'

'I want to have her assassinated.'

'We can start with her character,' Seema suggested. And
we did.

But I could find little to console me in the things Seema
pointed out that afternoon. Sure, Jennifer's stunning model
looks would fade with time. But mine were fading equally
quickly and I wasn't starting from such a good position.
And maybe she didn't have as many qualifications as I
did, but who ever met a red-blooded man who valued a
BA Hons from Oxford above perfect perky breasts?

'He'll get bored of looking at her,' Seema assured me.

'And then he'll realise what he had with you. He'll come back to you, I promise.'

'He'll never come back to me,' I said bleakly. 'I had hope when I thought he was just afraid of commitment. I thought that I could get him back eventually if I didn't apply too much pressure. But he's traded me in for a newer model, Seema. There's no vacancy any more. And when he finishes with this one – if he doesn't go ahead and bloody marry her to spite me – he's going to want an even better one. Did you ever meet a man who went back to driving a Ford Escort after owning a sodding Porsche?'

'I'm sure plenty had to do exactly that during the eighties recession,' Seema pointed out. 'Richard won't always be such a good catch himself, you know.'

But I couldn't believe that. To me, Richard combined the looks of Russell Crowe with the sparkling wit of Alain de Botton and the eligibility of Prince William. And while I had been busy getting comfortable with our lovely couply life in Tufnell Park, he had quietly been moving out of my league.

That was the problem. When Richard was just a trainee accountant who sketched in his spare time and I was an office temp with ambitions of studying drama, we were equally matched, an ideal couple. Now that he was a proper, over-commissioned, successful, in-demand portrait artist and I was just a poverty-stricken ex-drama student who had gone back to being a temp, we were no longer neck and neck. Richard was in a different universe to me now. He deserved a girlfriend like Jennifer. Gorgeous cover-star Jennifer. She was on his level. She had dumped a millionaire for him!

'Console me,' I begged Seema.

'At least your parents aren't trying to marry you off

to the owner of a cotton bud factory in Madras,' she tried.

'Is that the latest offering?' I asked. Seema's parents had been trying to arrange a marriage for her since she hit sixteen.

'Meeting his family for tea next Sunday. I can ask if he's got a brother, if you like.'

'Thanks but no thanks,' I told her. 'I'm never going to fall in love again. I'm through with this, Seema. Finished. I'm nearly thirty. I've got no lover, no job and I'm back at home living with my parents. I might as well end it right now in this kitchen. Your cotton bud mogul wouldn't have me.'

'You'll be all right, Lizzie,' Seema insisted. 'There *is* someone for everyone. Remember Venus and Joe.'

Right then, the phone rang.

'Do you mind if I get this?' she asked.

'No, no,' I assured her. 'Please do.'

I was hoping desperately that it might be him. Richard. Fat chance.

'Fat Joe!' Seema exclaimed. 'We were just talking about you! Sounds like you're in the next room! Lizzie, Fat Joe's calling from America,' she said unnecessarily. 'How's Cleveland?' she asked. 'What? You're in Los Angeles now. Wow! How come you're there? What? Say that again, Joe? You're joking. No. You're getting a divorce? No, Joe, no. Tell me it isn't true.'

There was no point in my trying to sleep that night. Every time I closed my eyes, Jennifer's face loomed large in my mind. Unfortunately I knew only too well what she looked like. I had met her on a couple of occasions. The first time was when she came to Richard's studio to discuss the portrait, with her spotty dot.com boyfriend in tow. I had wondered even then what such an incredibly beautiful girl was doing with a man who looked like a horned toad. Hell, the dot-commer wasn't even a real man. He must have been all of nineteen and a half. His voice was three octaves above mine. He had bum fluff between his spots. Then he mentioned the brand new Jaguar . . .

Well, Richard and I watched Beauty and the Beast drive away from the studio in his new XK8 and had a good bitch about geeks with cash and gold-diggers that day.

'You're lucky that I value looks over money,' I told him.

'You're lucky I value brains over looks,' was his reply.

Next time I saw Jennifer was a couple of months later. I had had a shitty day at work – temping in an advertising agency for some old cow who bawled at me for serving her decaff in a mug instead of an espresso cup. I wanted to know if Richard would meet me at the pub when he had finished, but he wasn't answering his phone. His studio was on the way home from my office so I decided to pop in. Perhaps he had forgotten to charge the battery in his mobile. Perhaps he was playing music really loudly – as he sometimes did when looking for inspiration – and hadn't heard the phone ring.

At the time, I wasn't too taken aback when I walked into the studio to find Richard kneeling in front of Jennifer as she reclined, naked but for a skimpy silver g-string, on his tatty velvet couch. Richard often got up close to his models to match his oil paints more exactly to a skin tone. I had modelled for him several times myself and was used to his avant-garde techniques. But now, looking back from my place on the emotional floor, I knew that I hadn't interrupted a paint-mixing session at all. I had interrupted the prelude to a kiss.

'Hi, Lizzie,' smiled Jennifer coolly.

Richard scrambled to his feet. 'Just, er . . . just er, you know,' he muttered.

'I've had a terrible day,' I said, throwing my handbag onto Richard's reserve posing couch and throwing myself down after it. 'Just thought I'd drop in and see if you fancy going to the pub for a swift one?'

'Er, not tonight,' said Richard. 'I wanted to get some more work done before finishing up today. That's OK with you, isn't it, Jennifer? You're not getting too stiff up there are you?'

'No,' she replied. 'Though I thought you might have been. Getting stiff, that is. From standing at the same position behind your canvas all day.'

It all went straight over my head. I had grown so accustomed to watching Richard paint women in the nude. It bothered me about as much as he would have been bothered by the thought that I might meet a man to fall in love with at the photocopier. Not completely impossible but highly unlikely. Richard often said how grateful he was that I wasn't the jealous type. He painted women for a living and he often painted them nude. It wasn't about sex, he assured me. It was only work.

So, unable to persuade him to come for a drink with me, I heaved myself up from the sofa and bid them both goodbye. Jennifer blew me an air kiss. Richard let me kiss him rather chastely on the cheek. That night I called Seema and had her meet me for a drink instead.

'What's Richard doing tonight?' she had asked me.

'Painting a nude,' I said. 'Some dizzy model.'

'Oh my God. A real model? Nude? And you trust him? I wouldn't trust him.'

'Of course I trust him,' I assured her. 'It's just a job.'

*   *   *

I felt a total idiot looking back on that night now. How naive had I been?

But in all seriousness what could I have done? Insisted on sitting in the studio every time Jennifer was in there with her clothes off? Called her dot.com boyfriend and demanded that he tear himself away from his computer screen to keep an eye on his feckless girlfriend while she lounged naked in the presence of my real, red-blooded man?

Should I have asked Richard why it was taking him so long to paint his latest model? Most commissioned portraits were knocked out in a matter of weeks. Jennifer's sittings had been going on for three months by the time Richard finished with me.

But if I had realised what was happening, could I have prevented him from falling in love with her anyway? Perhaps, if I had cottoned on sooner that Richard's affections were heading elsewhere I might have made changes to myself to tempt him back to me. Lost some weight? Changed my hairstyle? Read a couple of manuals on the art of red-hot sex?

'It wouldn't have made any difference,' Seema assured me when I asked her whether the size of my arse had swung the vote in Jennifer's favour. 'When a man sets his heart on taking a spin in a Ferrari, he's not going to be satisfied by his old Datsun with a new paint job. Don't kid yourself that there's anything you should have done differently, Lizzie. If it hadn't been Jennifer it would have been the next girl who posed for him. Or the next girl. It was never about you. Or them. It was always about his state of mind.'

But what had made him change from the Richard who

loved me to the Richard who didn't? He was too young
to be going through a mid-life crisis. And he had always
been so proud of the fact that his self-esteem came through
what he did, not *who* he was doing. Had that been just
another line?

I wasn't entirely idiotic about love. I wasn't the kind of
girl who expected to hit twenty-one, meet the man of her
dreams, get married and absolve herself of all responsibility thereof. The love I felt for Richard had grown over quite
some period of time. It wasn't instant. It wasn't based on a
floppy fringe, or a sexy smile, or a pair of exceptionally cute
buttocks. It was based on the growing realisation that here
was someone who shared my sense of humour. Here was
someone who listened to my lofty dreams of becoming an
actress and didn't scoff but instead offered helpful advice
and encouragement. Here was someone who looked at me
as though I didn't have cellulite when I took my clothes off.
Here was someone who respected me.

I thought that we had a 'two-way thing'.

It was a long time before I told Richard I loved him and
when I did tell him that, in the middle of Clapham Common
in the summer of 1998, I felt sure that I said those words
in safety. I had known too many men, and women, who
thought that telling someone you loved them was a sign
of failure; that you lost the game of love by being the first
one to capitulate or even, having had the other person say
those words to you, by admitting that you felt the same.

I remembered my old work mate Rupert – who, admittedly, was an estate agent and shouldn't be given too much
credence on matters of emotion or morality in any case –
telling me that as soon as a girl told him that she loved
him – and they seemed to do so on a weekly basis where
he was concerned – it was 'game over'.

'I lose interest instantly,' he said. 'It's the human condition, to always want what you think you can't have.
You've always got to be chasing. Where's the fun with
nothing to chase?'

For Rupert the romantic philosopher, love was all about
the sick, hollow feeling you get when you dial someone's
number and you're not sure if they'll pick up the phone.
It's the feeling you have when you know that if they're
not answering the phone they could be anywhere with
anyone. Richard knew that if I didn't answer the phone
it was because I was cleaning the oven or scrubbing the
bath. No chance that I would be wrestling on the sofa with
the milkman. He had nothing to fear.

And a lack of fear leads to complacency. And complacency leads to boredom. And boredom leads to someone
else.

When I told Richard that I loved him, I thought I had
found the only man in London who saw love as a gift
without strings rather than as the cheese on commitment's
mousetrap. But in reality, Richard was the same as the rest
of them. Just the same.

So it was back to Solihull. Only now it was worse than
before because now I had no hope left whatsoever. Though
I had tormented myself daily since the split with thoughts
of Richard getting it together with someone else, I could put
myself through ten times as much agony now that I could
actually picture the someone he was getting it on with.

I tried to distract myself. I watched daytime soaps until
my brain bled. But I couldn't clear my mind of the image of
Richard's lovely body on top of Jennifer's. Every time someone with long straight blonde hair like hers appeared on the

TV screen I had to change channel; which was OK while I was in the house alone during the daytime but would not be tolerated during Mum's favourite, *Coronation Street*.

I still didn't feel like eating much. I barely felt like getting up any more. In fact, I soon stopped getting up during the daytime at all, preferring to lie in my bed in a darkened room until I heard the sound of Mum's car on the gravel as she pulled into the driveway on her return from work. Then I would spring out of bed and put my clothes on, pretending that I had been up and about all day. I don't know if I ever convinced her.

My only contact with the wider world outside Mum and Dad's house was through the long analytical telephone conversations I had with anyone I could get hold of. Once, when Seema was in a meeting and Mary was still on her honeymoon, I subjected a hapless telephone survey call-operative to a blow-by-blow account of the Richard affair from first snog to last bitter goodbye. Even the Samaritans started to sound as though they couldn't wait to get onto another more interesting suicide call.

I started going to bed straight after *Neighbours*.

My life was over.

CHAPTER SIX

My friends and family would have been perfectly justified in giving up on me but about a month after the split, I was woken at seven in the evening by an animated conversation going on in the room beneath my bedroom. I could tell that my parents were trying to keep the noise down but the 1960s house we lived in was as good at transmitting sound as the whispering gallery at St Paul's cathedral and I could hear every single poorly stifled word.

'I don't know what to do with her,' said my mother desperately. 'She's starting to fade away.'

'I'd have thought she would have snapped out of it, by now,' said someone else.

'Me too. But she's convinced she's still in love with him. Even now he's gone off with that model.'

'I always knew he wasn't good enough for my little girl,' said my father.

'Well, she will insist on picking the flighty ones,' the mystery someone pronounced. 'Thinks the lads here in Solihull are beneath her and gets mixed up with those drug-dealing London types instead.'

'You don't think that Richard was on drugs do you?' asked my mother in a panicked whisper.

'They're all on drugs in London, Mum.'

I knew exactly whom the unfamiliar voice belonged to then. It was my twin brother, Colin, who had last been to London in 1995, encountered the Gay Pride march in Hyde Park while he was looking for the Natural History Museum, got felt up by a six-foot builder in a wedding dress and had been convinced that London was nothing but a hotbed of depravity ever since.

'Don't tell me that, Colin. You'll worry me,' said Mum.

'You've got good reason to worry, Mum,' said Colin wisely. 'London isn't like Solihull, you know.'

Exactly. London is more different from Solihull than champagne is from tap water, which was why I had chosen to flee the outskirts of Birmingham for the Metropolis and why Colin had stayed put in the pit of despair that was our home town. He preferred tap water over Evian.

Colin had inherited all the sensible genes in our family, or so he used to tell me. He had been to college in Solihull, got a job in Solihull, married a girl from Solihull and was on course to fill a plot in the Solihull cemetery in, oooh, approximately sixty years time if everything went according to his minute-by-minute schedule.

My relationship with Colin defied every twin study a psychologist had dared to carry out in the last two hundred years. We didn't look alike, we didn't talk alike, we didn't think alike. We certainly didn't share the same outlook. I voted for the Green Party. He voted true blue. He read the *Telegraph*. I read *OK* and *Hello!* He thought I was irresponsible. I thought he was old before his time. And now he obviously thought that having sorted his own life out, he had the right to make a start on mine.

'They've got no sense of responsibility, those artists,' Colin continued knowledgeably. 'It's all intense passion for one girl one minute, then the next thing you know

they're in search of a new muse. Looking for a new muse,'
he scoffed. 'That's just another name for philandering, if
you ask me.'

'I thought that one day he might marry her,' said my
mother.

'After she moved in with him?' snorted Colin. 'Not likely,
Mother. Why buy the cow when you're getting the milk
for free?'

'Exactly. I think it's always a mistake to live with somebody before you're married to them,' added Sally. Soppy
Sally, my brother's lovely wife, who had recently refused
a promotion at work so that she would have more time
to concentrate on her folic acid intake prior to trying for
a baby. Bear in mind that they weren't actually going to
start the exciting part of family planning for at least another
three years.

'What incentive is there to make a commitment?' she
continued. 'If you don't get married first, it's all too easy
to walk away the moment you get bored.'

'Oh, what can we do for her, Colin?' asked my mother.
'If only she could have been a little bit more like you. I
never had to worry about you coming back to live at home
aged nearly thirty. You had everything sorted out as soon
as you left school. Mortgage, marriage, pension. But not
our Lizzie. Sometimes it feels like Lizzie's been a teenager
for the best part of twenty years.'

'Don't worry, Mum. I'll sort her out,' said Colin. 'I'll give
her my brotherly talk.'

His brotherly talk? I couldn't take any more of this. I
pushed open the sitting room door and stood in the door
frame in my nightie. The inhabitants of the sitting room
turned towards me as though I were Banquo's ghost at
Abigail's mother's dinner party.

'I couldn't sleep,' I said.

'Oh, hello Lizzie,' said Sally, still looking jumpy. 'We were just talking about how nice the garden looks at this time of year.'

'Were you really?' I asked her flatly.

'The roses are doing really well, don't you think so?' She looked to Colin in the hope that he would agree and diffuse the rising tension.

'Enough about the garden, Sally,' Colin interrupted. 'Lizzie knows why we've come round here tonight and it's not to have a chat about greenfly.'

'Come to have me taken away in a straitjacket?' I said facetiously.

'Might do you some good,' said my brother. 'I'm certainly all for it. But Mum and Dad don't want that. All they want to know is when you plan to start getting on with your life again.'

'Never,' I told him. 'I'm already emotionally dead.'

'Very funny to your London crowd, I'm sure,' said Colin. 'But I'm not interested in your pathetic self-indulgence. I want to know exactly when you were thinking of going back to work. You can't stay here sponging off the family forever.'

'I could put in a good word for you with the personnel department at my office,' said Sally quickly. 'You've got lots of office experience, haven't you, Lizzie? And you can type, can't you? What's your wpm?'

'I don't want to work in your office,' I said, cutting her short. 'In fact I'd rather die than work in any office in Solihull.'

'Don't be so ungrateful,' barked Colin. 'Sally's trying to help. Just like we all are.'

'I know she's trying to help. But I can't work in an office.

I can't live with Mum and Dad for another month and I can't get a job in Solihull.'

'Then what can you do?' asked Colin.

'I went to drama school. I had a dream.'

'So did Martin Luther King and look what happened to him,' Colin sneered.

'He got shot,' Sally reminded me, in case I didn't know.

'But not before he'd changed something, he didn't. Not before he had inspired millions of people to do something to make the world a better place.'

'Hark at Linda McCartney,' said Colin. 'Vegetarianism. World peace. Whatever next?'

'Acting,' I said sarcastically. 'Which is what I am trained to do, in case you've all forgotten.'

'Acting the fool?' asked Colin. 'When are you ever going to make a living doing that?'

'Soon.' Then I added recklessly, 'I'll have an acting job before the end of this year. Just watch me.'

'Yes,' laughed my brother. 'And I'll be manning the next mission to the moon. Who's going to give you an acting job, Lizzie Jordan? You've been arsing about in London for the best part of a year since you graduated from that poncey drama school and you haven't even had an audition.'

'I did actually. For the grown-up daughter in the Bisto ad. I got to the final two.'

'But that didn't exactly get you on the gravy train,' quipped Colin.

'I know that,' I said, screwing my hands into fists to stop myself from slapping him. 'So perhaps I've realised that London isn't the best place for my talents.'

'Well, at least you're seeing some sense,' Colin started but I interrupted him before he could mention Solihull again.

'That's why I'm going to Los Angeles.'

Cue four very slack, astonished jaws.

To be honest, even I wasn't quite sure where that revelation had come from. Mum, Dad, Colin and Sally all stared at me. The room was so quiet, I could hear my heart thump against my ribs.

'Los Angeles,' breathed Sally finally, as if I had just said that I was about to set out on my white charger to discover Avalon. 'You don't mean you're going to America, Lizzie? Do you?'

'Yes, America. Of course I mean America. I'm going to Hollywood.'

'Whatever for?' asked my brother brusquely.

Good point. But I found an answer from somewhere.

'I'm going to do what I should have done the day I graduated,' I said quickly. 'I'm going to go out there and get myself a part in a film.'

Colin had managed to regain control of his jaw. 'And when did you come up with this bright idea?' he guffawed, in a tone that clearly intimated he thought my idea was as bright as a dead sparkler on November the 6th.

'I've been thinking about it for quite some time,' I said boldly. Though in reality I hadn't thought about it much at all. In fact, the idea had just popped into my head, when Colin made that crack about coming to my senses. Prior to that I had never had the inclination to go to California. Or rather, I'd never had the guts to consider it as a serious option, vaguely hoping instead that I'd end up there naturally after doing a couple of big British films. But I would have gone to a war zone if it would piss off my brother. I would certainly go to Los Angeles to prove him wrong about my ambitions.

'And just how do you plan to manage once you're out there?' asked Dad sensibly. 'Where will you stay, Lizzie? You don't know anybody in America except Brian Coren and he's in New York.'

'Actually, he's not the only person I know out there any more. I'll be staying with Fat Joe in Venice Beach,' I announced proudly. 'He's got a house just three blocks from the sea and he needs a new room-mate.'

I knew that much was true. Seema had been keeping me up to date with the developments in Fat Joe's post-divorce life which were only marginally less disastrous than mine. 'He already shares with an actress who'll be able to introduce me to some very influential people,' I added for effect. I didn't know whether that bit was true or not.

'But you didn't like Fat Joe,' said Sally. 'Wasn't he the one who made the funny smells in the bathroom?'

'He made funny smells all over the house,' said my brother.

'He's changed,' I said.

'I hope he has,' said Sally.

'You seem to have it all worked out,' said Mum. She at least was still too shocked to start protesting.

'Well, I think it's a stupid idea,' said Colin. He was never too *anything* to protest. 'Flying halfway round the world to stay with that half-mad loser? It'll all end in tears, you know. Don't expect us to bail you out when you discover that the streets of Tinseltown aren't paved with gold.'

'No fear of that,' I assured him. 'Just don't expect me to ask you to escort me to the Oscars.'

'The Oscars? What will you be doing there?' Colin laughed. 'Hoovering the red carpet?'

I suddenly stiffened. And though I was still wearing my
nightie – the nightie with Mickey Mouse on it that I had
been wearing for most of the week – I hoped that I looked
suitably intimidating when I drew myself up to my full
five feet two inches, set my jaw and intoned, 'I don't care
whether you think I'm going to make it or not, Colin. It's
what I'm going to do with or without your support. I'm
going to go to Hollywood as soon as I can and I'm going to
make it as a movie star. Whatever happens, whatever you
think of me, I am not going to sit in Solihull and rot!'

Solihull and rotting. The combination of words most
guaranteed to make my brother fly off the handle. Colin's
jaw hardened to match mine as he prepared the perfect
comeback. Sally beat him to it.

'Well, isn't that lovely,' she said, clapping her hands
together to signify an end to the row. 'Let's hope it works
out for you, Lizzie. Does anybody else want another cup
of tea?'

CHAPTER SEVEN

That was it then. I had announced my intention to go to Los Angeles in front of my brother Colin. If I didn't go to Tinseltown now I would never hear the last of it. Not until one of us died.

But was my rashly composed escape plan really feasible? When Sally and Colin had finally gone home – Colin still tutting loudly at my foolishness as he reversed his sensible car out of our parents' drive and crunched the gears with agitation – I chewed my fingernails for half an hour before I could pluck up the balls to dial Fat Joe's new number. Well, actually I rang Seema first.

I mean, why should Fat Joe want to give house room to me? I hadn't exactly kept in touch with him since he left the UK to marry Venus almost two years before. I only knew what was going on in his life because Seema was an inveterate gossip who kept in touch with everybody, from her American college friends to the mad Iraqi poet who sat next to her on the National Express and picked his nose between sonnets all the way from London to Leeds.

'You never know who's going to provide you with your next hot tip,' she reasoned, when I pointed out that she had an address book full of numbers of people she regularly had to hide from. I knew that Fat Joe, who had been working as a computer programmer in Ohio, had given her some inside advice on software firms to watch but I didn't think the mad poet was likely to spot the craze to replace Pokemon. Seema also blamed her incessant networking on being a Gemini. 'Our *raison d'être* is to communicate.' She was a strange mixture of hardheaded MBA and crackpot, that girl.

'Call Joe,' she said in true Gemini style. 'I know he would love to hear from you.'

'Do you think he'll let me stay?' I asked.

'Of course. He needs another room-mate.'

'But do you think he's got over the time I set fire to all his socks in the back garden?'

'Just don't bring it up,' Seema laughed.

'Do you think he still wears the same pair of socks for three weeks at a time?'

'Look,' said Seema. 'You and I both know that it's unlikely Fat Joe has become Laurence Llewelyn-Bowen since we last saw him. He probably still thinks that hoovering and washing up deplete your "chi". But if you're looking for a free place to stay, I think you have to face up to the fact that beggars can't be choosers. He's in the right city at least.'

'You're right.'

'And perhaps Venus house-trained him,' she added hopefully.

'Why do you think she's divorcing him?' I asked meaningfully.

'Perhaps he left the cap off the toothpaste?'

'Perhaps she discovered that he doesn't use toothpaste in case it's been poisoned by the FBI?'

'It's a bad option but it's your only one,' Seema pointed out.

She was right. But when she put it in those blunt terms,

I couldn't help but think back to a moment when I did have options. When Richard asked me to give up sharing with Seema and Joe to get a flat with him instead, I had been elated. When I carried my worldly goods out of the Balham Hilton (that's like the Bangkok Hilton, not the London one), I thought I had reached the next stage of life's game.

Let's face it, flat-sharing is actually the antithesis of the communist ideal you might suppose it to be. The only thing you're sharing is an address. Inside the house, we had our own kitchen cupboards and three separate bottles of semi-skimmed in the fridge. Unclaimed calls on the itemised phone bill could herald the start of a war. But I was no longer a flat-sharer. I was a co-habitee.

'Never again,' I said, as Richard drove us towards the flat he had bought in Tufnell Park.

'Never again,' he agreed.

But you can never say 'never', can you? So, I phoned Joe. And he didn't sound at all surprised to hear from me. He didn't say, grumpily, as I might have expected, 'You haven't phoned me for years. I suppose you want a favour.' He just said how nice it was to hear from me.

'Your accent's changed,' I told him. It had. From *Crossroad*'s Benny to a low-rent Loyd Grossman.

'That's not the only thing about me that's changed,' Fat Joe assured me in his new mid-Atlantic drawl.

'Of course,' I said. 'You're an American citizen now.'

'I'm a Yankee Doodle Dandy, all right,' he said somewhat disturbingly.

'That's nice. Er, Joe, has Seema told you about my predicament?'

'I know that Richard dumped you,' he said. 'That's too bad, Lizzie. I really feel for you over that.'

I laughed nervously. He 'felt' for me? The Fat Joe I

remembered had no truck for feelings. For him, emotions had been all but replaced by email style *emoticons*. Towards the end of our time in Balham together, when he wanted to express disappointment, Joe would actually trace out a colon and a left-hand bracket instead of bothering to frown.

'Lizzie, you gotta know that we're all with you on this one,' he said now. 'You're a good, kind person. You can do better than end up with a man who has so many issues.'

Issues?

'Thanks, Joe,' was all I could think to say.

'So, are you coming to stay?' he asked me kindly.

'I think I'd like to. Can I call you when I've sorted out a flight?' I asked.

'Call me any time. Any time at all. It's good to talk, you know.'

'Yeah. Right.'

Good to talk? I guess Fat Joe wasn't an emotionally retarded agoraphobic any more. Which was a relief. And I had a place to stay. I should have been ecstatic. But when I put down the phone to Joe, the fluffy bundle of excitement I'd felt in my stomach prior to calling him had suddenly grown into a scaly monster of fear. Prior to the phone call, Los Angeles had simply been a swanky idea with which to irritate my brother. Now the idea had taken on a coating of possibility with the promise of a roof over my head, I wasn't quite sure what to do.

I called Mary. I was due to go round and look at her honeymoon photos in any case.

'I need your advice about Los Angeles,' I told her.

'Go,' she said simply.

'I need a bit more detailed advice than that.'

I travelled down from Solihull to London next day to spend the weekend with the newly-weds. Bill was putting up shelves when I arrived. Putting up shelves! It seemed like a very long time since the only outlet for Bill's hands-on creativity had been making bongs from empty Evian bottles.

'They'll have to come down again,' Mary muttered as she surveyed his handiwork. 'I'm having that wall knocked through to make the kitchen bigger.'

'I can't believe this is your life,' I told her. 'Husband. Semi-detached house. Having your kitchen knocked through. It's so glamorous.'

'Glamorous?' Mary laughed. 'You must be joking. Glamorous is jetting off to Los Angeles on a whim. I'll trade you my husband for that.'

'To stay with Fat Joe?' I said.

'Hmmm.'

We left Bill knocking the house down and headed for Knightsbridge. Mary wanted to buy the Harvey Nichols' sugar bowl that no one had bought from her wedding list. Sugar bowl found, we headed for the cafe and I told Mary all about my hastily assembled plans.

'Sounds great,' she said. 'Spending the summer in a beach hut.'

'Fat Joe's beach hut,' I corrected. 'You don't think it's a stupid idea?'

'Staying in Solihull would be a really stupid idea,' said Mary.

'But I don't want to go,' I admitted. 'I just want my old life. Here in London.'

'What? Spending hours on the Tube each day and temping?'

'No. I still want Richard back.'

'Lizzie, he's got someone else,' said Mary sensibly and more than a little wearily. 'You've got to move on.'

'I wish I could. But I can't. Every time I think about the future, I'm just filled with this dread that I'll never be happy again. I'll never meet anybody like him again. I'm doomed to be single for the rest of my life.'

'Rubbish,' Mary told me. 'You'll be beating them off when you get to the States. And at least you've had a relationship that's lasted for more than a month. Some girls our age haven't even had that. At least you know you can do it again. Sustain a relationship, I mean. Isn't it better to have loved and lost than never to have . . .'

'Stop right there,' I said. 'If one more person says that to me, I swear I will take a knife to their throat.'

I picked up a teaspoon to demonstrate. Better to have loved and lost? That missed the point entirely. I wasn't able to look back on my relationship with Richard and comfort myself with the thought that once upon a time we had both been happy. Remembering the good times? That was the worst part. That was what hurt the most.

'You know what,' I said to Mary then. 'There's another saying I think is much more apt under the circumstances. I can't remember if it was Auden or Waugh who said it, but it goes like this, "Love is remembered as something different when it's gone." And that is how I feel right now. I'm not sure whether I ever really loved or not. I'm certainly not sure whether I was ever loved in return. People keep telling me that I have to look upon this as some kind of bereavement, but sometimes I'm left thinking that this is far worse. It would actually be easier to take if Richard had died because then I could look back on the time we spent together without the knowledge that he made the decision to end things.

'Richard made the decision to break my heart because he doesn't want me any more. When someone dies they don't usually leave you with the abiding sense that you must be an utterly worthless human being as well as a single one. I wish that he were dead, Mary. I really do. Perhaps I should have taken a knife to his throat while I had the chance.'

'Right. Retail therapy,' said Mary, suddenly getting up. 'You need to buy some new knickers to take your mind off this miserable rubbish.'

'Why? When will I ever need new knickers again?'

'For crying out loud, Liz,' Mary snapped. 'You're not Miss Havisham. Lizzie, I promise you – and I'm willing to bet the cost of your flight to Los Angeles on this – that within a year you will be able to look back on splitting up with that bloody stupid man and be glad that it happened. Honestly, one day you will wake up and look back and be able to see him for the arrogant, bigoted, humourless pig that the rest of us knew he was all along. You had a lucky break.'

Those words again.

'Did you really think he was humourless?'

'Totally without a funny bone. Funny as an enema in fact,' said Mary.

'I thought he had a great sense of humour.'

'You thought he was being faithful to you too,' she reminded me. A blow straight to my heart. 'Now you've got the chance to leave all this shit behind and go to Los Angeles. Los Angeles, California, Lizzie! A place where the sun always shines! For heaven's sake, what's stopping you?'

We had reached the doorway to Sloane Street by now.
It was raining outside. Mary turned me around and led
me back to the lipsticks while we waited for the rain to
pass. She picked up a tube of pearlised pink gloss called
'Los Angeles'.

'An omen?' she suggested.

The one I picked up was called 'London'.

'Look, one of your friends is offering you a place to stay,'
she continued. 'I'm willing to lend you the air fare and a list
of everyone I know there and all you can do is worry about
what will happen if Richard changes his mind and wants
to be with you. For a start, the chances of him changing his
mind and dumping the supermodel for the old model are
slightly less favourable than the odds of your being struck
by lightning. And secondly, if he does decide that he wants
to be with you, he can bloody well get on a plane and come
and find you, can't he? It's up to him to make the effort
this time.'

I blinked back tears.

'Oh, Lizzie. Go, go, go,' she implored me, taking my
hands and squeezing them hard. 'Go to Los Angeles. I'll
miss you like mad when you're not here but I know it will
make you happy. There's no reason on earth for you to stay
here in London now. No reason at all.'

She was right. What did I really have to leave behind?
No lover, no job, no place of my own. The alternative was to
carry on living with my parents, rotting away in Solihull or
to start commuting backwards and forwards from there to
central London, putting myself through the misery of more
job interviews and temporary assignments in offices with
no air-conditioning or windows. Add to that the absolute
torture of trying to find myself a new flat through *Loot*
with the high probability that whoever agreed to let me

stay with them would be madder than Fat Joe knew how
to be. What kind of option was that compared with the
possibility of spending at least three months in the sun,
staying in a house just three blocks from the beach? Three
blocks from the beach! Not three hours from the nearest
mudflats, which was the distance between Solihull and
Weston-super-Mare.

Even if I did have to share with Fat Joe again, it was still,
as Brian would say, a 'no-brainer'. Like the first question
in a round of *Who Wants to Be A Millionaire*. If I couldn't
get this one right then I didn't deserve to crawl out of a
petri dish.

'I should do it, shouldn't I?' I finally admitted.

'Hooray,' said Mary, throwing up her hands. 'You've
seen the light. Let's go to the travel agent now before you
change your mind.'

Within half an hour Mary had waved her credit card like
a magic wand and booked my return ticket. I had a place to
fly to and a plane to fly there in. As an All-American Girl
would say, *I was outta there*.

And when I told anyone who cared about my plans they
responded with unequivocal approval. But I have to admit
that even with the ticket in my pocket, I didn't think I
would actually go.

I still believed that Richard would stop me. I convinced
myself that he would hear on the grapevine that I was about
to leave the country and that news would spark the fear that
he might be about to lose me forever. While he thought I
was going to end my days pining at my parents' house in
Solihull there was no chance of him suddenly wanting me
back, but the idea of me leaving on a jet plane, heading for

the sun, heading for a place where, Brian's fiancée Angelica had assured me, an English accent would have me beating off new suitors like a toddler defending a lollipop from a freshly disturbed nest of wasps . . . Surely that would change his mind.

I'm afraid I was hoping that Richard would have that classic male reaction – there's no view the average man likes better than a view of a woman's backside. Run away and a man will chase you. Stop and shout 'catch me' and he'll run straight into the brick wall of commitment fear that miraculously materialises by your side.

But, as I had known while we were together, Richard wasn't like any other man I had ever met and he wasn't about to live up to a stereotype now, even though it was the first time in my life that I actually wished he would.

Seema, my old flatmate, bumped into him in some trendy Soho bar about a week before I was due to leave town and made the mistake of calling to let me know. He wasn't with Jennifer. My heart soared until I heard that was only because she was on some super prestigious modelling assignment in Japan. My heart lost all aerodynamic ability altogether when Seema added that upon hearing that I was leaving for Los Angeles, Richard's reaction was to say, 'At least she's getting out of Solihull.'

'At least she's getting out of Solihull!?'

Was that all?!

He didn't ask when I was going away, or for how long, or why. Though surely even the newly insensitive Richard must have guessed that he had something to do with my decision to run away from England. He didn't ask who I was going to be staying with, or who had put the crazy idea of emigration into my head. He didn't ask if I had met an American multi-millionaire playboy who was demanding that I fly out first class to be by his side. He just said, 'At least she's getting out of Solihull,' and then asked Seema how her Internet start-up business was getting on.

Having managed to limit my crying to once or twice a day, I suddenly hit another wall of despair. 'Was that really all he said?' I asked Seema again and again. I made her describe their chance meeting in minute detail to me, in face and over the phone, at least ten times over the next two days. 'What did his face look like? Was there no twinge, no tiny downward flicker of his perfect, kissable lips that suggested he might not be overjoyed at the news of my going away?'

'He looked exactly the same as he did when I told him about my business plan,' Seema told me. 'Not really all that interested. Just being polite.'

I went into some kind of crisis then. I suppose that a bigger part of me than I imagined had been hoping that Richard would try to stop me going away. With that hope finally, incontrovertibly extinguished by Seema's news, that part of me had to deal with a new grief. Whereas before I had been able to recount my Los Angeles plans with a strange carefree bravado borne of the belief that I would never actually have to carry them out, now the thought of the days to departure ticking away made my stomach turn. It was as though I had gambled on a hand of seventeen and gone bust to the croupier's blackjack. So much for my exciting foreign adventure. I may as well have been on death row.

I suppose I could have cancelled my plane ticket. Lord knows, I wanted to. I woke up in the middle of the night having dreamt that I had. But Mary and Bill were already arranging a departure dinner party in my honour. A fabulous themed party in their newly-marrieds' home. 'Go West, Young Girl!' said the bright pink invitations sent out to all my friends. The dress code was cowboys and Indians. Drinks were tequila or Bud.

I stuck with the tequila. I spent the first half of my 'going away' party challenging all-comers to slammers and the second half with my head down the toilet bowl, homemade Pocahontas headdress drooping like my heart. I was as miserable as someone who has been granted permission by St Peter to go back to earth to attend their own wake, only to discover that the person they loved most in the world hasn't bothered to turn up.

I prayed for a calamity. I prayed for an all out air traffic control strike at Heathrow. I prayed for an irresistible offer from the RSC that would allow me to stay in England with dignity and commute to Stratford from Solihull until I felt strong enough to try a bigger adventure again. As Mary led the gang in a rendition of 'Leaving On a Jet Plane' in my honour I just wanted to shout, 'Not yet! Not yet! I'm not ready!'

I was being forced out onto the stage half-dressed. Out into the spotlight without my wig or my make-up. I wanted to run back into the wings and through the stage door and into the dark, lonely night. But then Mary was presenting me with my going-away present – a lovely Louis Vuitton vanity case. So expensive. Everyone at the party had chipped in to buy it. The party had been thrown. The song had been sung. The present had been presented. I was going to the United States whether I wanted to or not.

Heathrow, three days later. Sitting in the departure lounge with my new Louis Vuitton vanity case on my knees like a security blanket. My parents had driven me to the airport but I refused to let them come into the terminal and wave me off. I didn't want them to see me crying and there was no doubt that I would be sobbing like an abandoned baby before the plane even got off the ground.

As the other passengers for British Airways flight 269 to Los Angeles gathered at the gate while we waited to board, they looked excited and happy. All of them smiling. They were going on holiday, going home, going to meet the person they had been missing for so long. I, on the other hand, felt like a sheep-rustler waiting for the prison ship to take me to Australia. I felt as though I would never see the people I loved again. I wasn't even convinced that I would make it to my unfriendly destination without succumbing to scurvy on the way (which is, of course, a very real danger when it comes to aeroplane food).

I waited until the last possible moment to board the plane that morning. Everyone of my acquaintance, from my parents and my friends to the lovely man behind the counter at the corner shop, knew which flight I would be on and exactly when it left for America. And for that reason I stared hopelessly at the doorway to the main terminal, waiting, wishing, begging, until the tannoy announced the final call for flight 269 – in fact, until the tannoy announced my name specifically, followed by a warning that my luggage was about to be unloaded – and I had to board the plane.

No last-minute dash to the airport by the love of my life to stop me. Perhaps Richard, wherever he was, looked up at the sky at the moment when my plane finally left the tarmac. More likely, he hadn't even looked up from Jennifer's super-flat tummy. As flight 269 climbed into the clouds my heart was falling through the centre of the earth.

At least someone familiar would be there to meet me at the other end.

CHAPTER EIGHT

O r so I thought.

I was tired and faintly deranged by the time my plane landed at Los Angeles International, better known as LAX. It had been a bumpy journey. Turbulence over the Atlantic. Followed by even more turbulence in the seat right next to me after the chap by the window bolted his airline dinner. I couldn't escape because the chap on the other side of me, in the aisle seat, had taken three knockout tablets and fallen asleep before take-off. Not that it would have made much difference. One hour into the flight, the air-con was only recycling the air from the toilets in any case.

So, after eleven hours in a tube full of flatulence, you can imagine how keen I was to find my host among the crowd of grinning and grimacing faces in the arrivals hall and get back to his place for a nice long bath. If you had told me just one short year before that there would come a moment when I would actually look forward to seeing Fat Joe, I would have laughed. But right then, the sight of Jude Law strolling through customs surrounded by hangers-on and paparazzi was only the second thing I most wanted to see.

In fact, when Jude Law did walk past I was only annoyed that the gang of people tailing him was keeping me from searching the crowd properly.

'Where are you, Joe?' I hissed through gritted teeth.

Where was he? My plane had landed slightly late. It had taken me the best part of an hour to convince immigration that I wasn't coming into the country to seek work illegally or commit acts of moral turpitude. I knew that Fat Joe had always been a bit on the tardy (as well as lardy) side but surely he wasn't an hour late to pick me up after my first transatlantic flight?

I scanned the crowd again. But how could I have missed him? No one could have missed Fat Joe. He was six feet two. And that was just his width. Though I'd never seen him in anything but Desert Storm style camouflage gear (Arctic Fox colours for winter) during the year we lived together, that wouldn't have been helping him to blend into the background now. And yet I couldn't see him anywhere. Perhaps he had sent his other room-mate, the actress who went by the thoroughly made-up name of 'Brandi Renata', to fetch me instead.

Or a car? Perhaps he'd just sent a car. I knew that he was very busy at work these days. I scanned the names scrawled onto bits of card by taxi drivers who could barely speak English, let alone write it. Did that say Lizzie Jordan? I wondered. No, I think it was supposed to say Mister Jones. I was about to give up and head for the information desk when I heard my name announced over the tannoy.

'Mizz Elizabeth Jordan. Mizz Elizabeth Jordan. Please go to the Encounter Restaurant where your friend Joe Green is waiting for you with a special welcome cocktail.'

I was so relieved I burst out laughing. A cocktail with Joe? The only cocktails I'd seen him make were Molotov ones, from a website recipe. They didn't work, thank God, on account of him using acetone-free nail varnish remover instead of petrol. But now apparently he was waiting for me in a *cocktail* bar called Encounter, which I was soon to discover is one of the craziest cocktail bars in the world.

A nun collecting alms at the bottom of an escalator directed me to the white spider-like building at the centre of LAX with such enthusiasm that I almost felt guilty for palming her off with three five-pence pieces instead of the dimes she was hoping for. She even gave me a rundown of the building's history. Encounter, which straddled the centre of LAX like a creature straight out of H. G. Wells's *War of the Worlds* was built in the 1960s when space travel was all the rage and everyone was certain that by the end of the century Los Angeles International would be LA Intergalactic. But the package tours to the moon had never happened. And the bar, revamped by Disney's *imagineers*, seemed strangely old-fashioned now. Like a building based on a lava lamp.

This is right up Joe's street, I thought as ten minutes later (it took me that long to cross the ring-road around the terminals) I rode up to the top-floor restaurant in a purple elevator complete with groovy sci-fi music. Fat Joe is probably at the bar right now, making furious notes in one of his ubiquitous notepads on how he should write to the President and beg him to reconsider appointing Joe as captain of the next manned mission to Mars.

Good old Joe; social retard, uber-geek, married to the Net, married *via* the Net even. Probably setting up a website for divorced fans of *Blake's Seven* in his spare time these days. I wondered if he was still emailing world leaders to warn them of impending alien invasion? Hacking his way into websites of the rich and infamous? Checking his eyeshadow in the mirror behind the bar . . .

'Joe?'

I just dropped my case and stared.

'Lizzie! You look so . . .'

'Different?'

'Your hair. You've changed it.'

'And you. You . . .'

'It's just a rinse,' he said.

'Just a rinse?'

'OK. And a few highlights.'

'Joe?'

'People are calling me Joanna these days.'

And that is how I came to discover that Fat Joe was no longer half the man I remembered.

'I didn't think it was appropriate to try to tell you over the phone,' Joe said as we walked to his car. He was striding ahead of me as I dragged my cases. Wearing women's clothing obviously excused him from offering to help with the bags.

'There it is,' he said, pointing to a soft-top Cadillac.

It was bright pink. A bright pink car to match his leather jacket!

'Skirt doesn't quite match the seats,' he tutted, as he smoothed the short cerise mini over his much reduced thighs and slid into the driver's seat with finishing-school finesse.

Even if he hadn't been wearing women's clothing, I don't think I would have recognised Joe that day. He had lost more weight in a year and a half than Oprah Winfrey and Roseanne Barr combined had managed over their entire yo-yo dieting careers. Now he had cheekbones! (Very nicely highlighted ones at that.) Fat Joe had gone from an uncooked doughnut to a chic finger biscuit in the space of eighteen months.

'You've lost a bit of weight,' I said inanely.

'One hundred and eighty pounds,' said Joe. 'I've practically lost a whole person.'

'And found a new one,' I commented.

'Have you ever tried finding tights that will fit a ninety-inch-wide ass?'

I could only shake my head at that.

'Just need to adjust the mirror,' he said, tilting the rearview mirror to get a better view of his lipstick. 'Shocking,' he muttered. 'This stuff is meant to stay on all day. One cafe latte and it's all over the place.'

'You drink cafe latte?'

He'd always been a strictly Horlicks boy.

'My new drink. Skim milk. No sugar. Shouldn't really drink coffee because of the cellulite, of course. Better if you rub it on your thighs rather than drink it. Seema told me that.'

I remembered only too well the coffee crisis when Seema used all the Nescafé as a body scrub. This was so surreal. As Joe straightened his skirt before starting his car up, I wondered whether I had actually landed yet. Perhaps I was still dreaming halfway across Hudson Bay. Perhaps this wasn't really Joe? The Joe I remembered had eyebrows that met in the middle. This Joanna had false eyelashes.

'You're shocked, aren't you?' said Joe with incredible understatement as he exited the multi-storey car park and joined the queue of cars nudging their way onto the highway.

'Well, the last time I saw you, you were . . .'

'Agoraphobic?' he suggested. 'Unable to communicate except via email? Hygienically challenged?'

'A man?'

* * *

What a difference two short years can make. Apparently, Fat Joe's transformation to Joanna started pretty quickly after his arrival in America. On his honeymoon night, in fact. An hour after their quicky marriage in some Cleveland state office, Fat Joe and Venus retired to her room at her parents' house – they were going to live there until they had enough cash for a place of their own – to consummate their marriage.

Fat Joe told me the story as we drove to the beach house. I was too tired to do anything but listen, though the story he told was far from small talk. It deserved to be made into a mini-series.

'It was Venus who made me realise the truth about myself,' he explained. 'I mean, strange as this might seem, I'd never actually seen a real woman naked until I saw Venus on our honeymoon night and when I did, I knew instantly that I wasn't attracted to her.'

Now that didn't seem strange to me. Given that Fat Joe, at best, had looked like one of the contestants on *Robot Wars*, I would happily have placed bets on him never seeing a naked woman in his life. And remembering the photo Venus had emailed him at the start of their courtship, I thought plenty of men might prefer to go gay. But that wasn't what Fat Joe realised about himself when Venus stood before him in her honeymoon trousseau.

'I wasn't attracted to her,' he said. 'But I was attracted to her nightie. And her knickers. And her suspender belt.'

'Too much information?' I started to suggest.

But Joe wasn't about to stop. 'I tried to distract myself by focusing on Venus's underwear while she made me do the job, but it wasn't long before I realised that I wanted to be wearing it myself.'

'Her nightdress?'

'And her fluffy clogs.'

'And how did Venus feel about that?'

'She's been very understanding. It came as a huge relief to both of us. She didn't fancy me either. She let me try on her nightie and that was it. I knew at once. I still fancy girls but I also want to be one. I'm a gay woman trapped in a man's body.'

It was a lot to take in with the jet lag.

'Isn't it great?' he said.

'You certainly look well on it.'

'Bronzing powder,' Fat Joe suggested.

'So, I suppose that's why you're getting a divorce.'

'Yes. Though not until my green card comes through. Venus is already quite keen to remarry. She's met a guy called Merlin in a chat room for people who know people with gender reassignment issues.'

'Is she sure he won't turn out to be Mer-linda?' I cracked.

Fat Joe rose above my cheap shot and continued. 'All this explains why I was always so much more comfortable around women. I loved living with you and Seema, Lizzie. You were like a couple of rare birds with those gaudy rags from Top Shop. But I know you both thought I was odd.'

'No,' I protested. Conveniently forgetting the time he created a tracking device attached to an Alice band so that MI5 could find him if he was kidnapped by the forces of darkness while surfing the net. (He'd watched *The Matrix* far too many times.) Or the strange immortality elixir he brewed in the bathroom cabinet (a mixture of wholemeal flour and vinegar, Seema had decided after daring to take a sniff). Or the big black diary filled with tightly packed scribblings on the alien nations that were massing in a giant underground bunker near Milton Keynes.

'Joe,' I protested too much. 'We did not think you were odd. I loved living with you too.'

'Well, now we're going to do it all again. I'm so glad we've got this chance to become better friends. Girl friends!' he added excitedly. 'We can have girly chats and go shopping. We can borrow each other's clothes.'

It was a lot to take in from a man whose socks were put to the torch for being terminally unhygienic.

'Just one thing,' I had to ask. 'Was it you who burned the hole in my fake Armani jacket?'

'I swear I never touched it. You're going to love it here in America,' Joe continued. 'This is the place for new beginnings, Lizzie. Look what it's done for me!'

'I would happily change my orientation if it could stop me from thinking about Richard.'

'Yes, Richard,' Joe nodded. 'You know, I never really liked him that much.'

'Didn't you?'

This wasn't what I wanted to hear.

'I just had this feeling,' Joe carried on. 'But it doesn't matter now. You're here to start your new life and the "R" word must be struck from your vocabulary. Your past doesn't matter here, Lizzie. Only your potential. Everyone in Los Angeles is equal. You can do anything you want.'

It was a comforting thought. And if Fat Joe could make a living as a computer programmer in a miniskirt then it must be true . . . Of course, I would later discover that he still wore a suit to go to work.

'Joe,' I began. 'I really can't believe . . .'

'You're here? I know. Isn't it wonderful?'

I suppose it was. We were driving along by the ocean now. Warm sea breezes purged the stagnant plane air from my lungs. Joe's car was open-top and his newly long blond hair flew out behind him like a flag of tri-umph.

'Welcome to the land of opportunity!' Joe shouted and punched the air while we paused at some traffic lights.

I cringed slightly. I wasn't entirely ready to be seen driving in an open-top car with an overdressed transvestite. You can take the girl out of England but . . .

'We're in California now!'

Bloody hell. I was.

Venice Beach, California to be precise.

Well, it has canals. But that's where this Greater Los Angeles suburb's resemblance to its Italian namesake ends. No Doge's palace here. No beautiful painted chapels where the tourists 'ooh' and 'aah' at the work of Renaissance craftsmen. But plenty of dogs. And plenty of crackhouses. In fact, I was living just two doors down from one of those.

I'm not sure what I had been expecting to find when I arrived in Los Angeles, tired and faintly delirious after eleven long transatlantic hours spent sobbing over the Bas-tard Ex and worrying about my unhappy future without him. OK, let's face it. I had been hoping and praying to find Fat Joe in a beautiful 1920's villa on a cliff overlooking the sea, a bit like the kind of place I thought Tom and Nicole (Cruise and Kidman) would live in. Whatever, I had not been expecting to find my newly glamorous Eddie Izzard-style flatmate living in a hut that wouldn't have looked out of place on the sea front at Weston-super-Mare, complete with dirty broken windows and a picket fence that only had two pickets.

'Oh, yeah,' said Brandi, my other new room-mate when I

asked her about the dilapidated fence. 'Those got pulled up after the LA Lakers won last summer. People were using them to hit people and stuff.'

Charming.

As the newest inmate, my room was the smallest in the glorified shed. Instead of a proper bed I had an ancient futon that was so uncomfortable I soon ditched the wooden frame and started sleeping straight on the floor. Which was fine until the night I awoke to find a cockroach investigating my nasal hair.

Yes. Cockroaches! I'd never seen a real one in my life before and now suddenly I was living with hundreds. They acted like they owned the place. They were in the bathroom. In the kitchen. Sometimes they didn't even have the manners to scatter to a dark corner when you turned on a light. One night, I found two of them stuck up to their knees in the butter dish. And as if sharing my space with those critters wasn't bad enough, the whole paint-peeling place stank of cat's piss. We had a colony of feral cats living in the basement and the stench of their territorial sprayings drifted up through the broken air conditioning vents to fill the house far more effectively than the plug-in air fresheners we used to combat the smell.

Stepping outside wasn't much better. We often awoke to find that random winos had set up camp in the front yard, parking their shopping trolleys full of filthy blankets and hare-brained religious pamphlets on the tiny square of dirt that masqueraded as a lawn. To get to the corner store in the morning was like walking down the worst street in Cairo wearing nothing but a fur coat and a platinum Rolex. Everyone you passed asked for money. Some quite nicely. Most of them not. On my first couple of mornings in America I found that by the time I got to the store I had given all my change away and not left myself with enough for the milk I came out for. A month later I would be doing as the Venetians do and only coughing up to the ones who looked as though they might have been able to afford a gun.

'At least you've got the beach,' wrote Mary in an email shortly after I arrived.

Yeah. But it wasn't the kind of tropical bay where you'd expect to find Leo DiCaprio. Venice Beach is otherwise known as Muscle Beach. More like Tussle Beach, I thought. Imagine shoving your way through a crowded cattle market to a strip of sand about as wide and restful as Oxford Street on a Saturday afternoon. Just about as clean as well. And with double the number of menacing hagglers trying to sell you knock-off designer gear or your name on a grain of rice.

The Baywatch Babes didn't hang out here, that's for sure. It was more like the badly painted backdrop for a circus freak show than a set for a multi-million-dollar mini-series. Everywhere you turned there was something new to shock (and probably disgust) you. Think you've seen the most tattooed man alive? Look over there and see a man getting the last chapter of the *Kama Sutra* written on his foreskin. Only don't look too closely in case he takes offence and pulls a gun.

Far from being sexy, most of the body builders who worked out in the infamous caged gym on the boardwalk, which gave Muscle Beach its name, looked as though they should be led around by a ring through the end of their nose if they were allowed out of the zoo at all. And that was just the girls.

Venice Beach was like the Los Angeles of the popular imagination seen through the bottom of a beer bottle. It was

darker and hideously distorted. Like London's Camden
Town, Venice Beach was a Mecca for tourists who came
because they'd heard of it, only to discover that the beautiful people had already been and gone – just like the groovy
young things who made Camden Town the place to be in
the 1960s and 70s. In their wake the in-crowd left a far more
cynical crowd selling crappy mugs and oversized T-shirts
printed with the legendary place name, to be passed on via
the tourists to their ungrateful friends back home. Venice
Beach, Camden Town, Times Square, wherever. All the
T-shirts were made in Taiwan.

'It's Times Square Sur La Mer,' said Fat Joe hopefully.

Yep, Venice Beach was as far from being declared an
area of outstanding natural beauty as I was from becoming
the new Calvin Klein spokesmodel. I was sure that Los
Angeles' infamous smog was thicker there than anywhere
else in the city. Back at the beach house, it wasn't long
before it struck me that the only birds we ever heard
were the helicopters (or 'ghetto birds' as Brandi called
them) that circled the area at night with their bright lights
beaming straight in through our cracked windows as they
searched for the crack kings. One night I thought I heard
gun shots.

'You probably did,' said Brandi at breakfast.

By the end of my first week in Los Angeles I was
wondering how long I would have to stay out there before
I could go back to Solihull without looking like a quitter
and having to face Colin's 'told-you-so' glee. I didn't relish
such an untimely conclusion to my big adventure but was
it really worth getting caught in a drive-by shooting just
to save face in front of my bro?

*   *   *

But as awful as my new home seemed, the sun really did shine every morning. And on weekdays when the beach wasn't crawling with tourists or muscle men out to impress them, it was nice to be able to paddle in the Pacific. The Pacific. Paddle in *the Pacific*. Just saying those words gave me a frisson of childlike pleasure. So much more glamorous than the Med.

As I walked out one morning with the intention of finding a reputable travel agent who could get me back home early, I saw porpoises from the end of Venice Pier. The sleek black creatures bobbed and weaved through the shimmering waves like horses on an aquatic carousel. Bright pink and purple bougainvillea flowers bloomed like fireworks between the empty oil cans in the back garden. Someone tied a yellow ribbon round the palm tree at the end of our street. I met a wino who told me a new and funny joke every morning and didn't ask for change. And Fat Joe and Brandi, my room-mates – well, they were something else.

There was nothing left of the Fat Joe I remembered from Balham but his way with a website. I soon realised that, other than the suit he had to wear to the office, he had no items that could be described as men's clothing left in his wardrobe. He had trousers, sure, but I couldn't imagine any other man I knew wearing the skintight white jeans embroidered with roses that he wore on my second day in Los Angeles.

Fat Joe was still working with computers, making fairly obscene money in fact, as a troubleshooter for a big international bank with an office near the airport. But he squandered all his wages on Gucci and Versace instead of moving to a better area. There were legal fees to save for too. Venus was only too happy to let Fat Joe have his divorce, but she wasn't going to pay for it. Neither was she willing to pay the legal fees that would transform Fat Joe and his green card into a fully fledged American passport holder.

But in any case, Joe's job wasn't his life any more.

'Do you remember how much I liked music?' he asked me on my first evening.

I only remembered that Fat Joe played Queen's *Greatest Hits* five times a day, day in, day out for the whole of the time I spent with him in Balham. Hearing 'Bohemian Rhapsody' could still send me into convulsions. 'I always had a passion for singing,' he now claimed. And so he had decided to spend all his spare time working towards a new dream. To be the greatest diva since Maria Callas.

'Or Danny La Rue!' said Seema when I emailed her with the revelation.

Whatever. To that effect, Fat Joe spent three nights a week moonlighting as Joanna Boisvert, chanteuse francais (sic), belting out classic show tunes with a regular guest spot at a transvestite nightclub called Ladyboys. They got someone good in for the weekends.

Brandi too was trying to break into Tinseltown. She was having a little more luck than her room-mate. Though not much. Brandi Renata was an actress. More accurately, she was a model/actress/whatever. A *MAW*. She whiled away her 'resting time' between non-speaking parts in teen soaps and commercials by modelling but at five feet two, with a bust you could have served a buffet on, Brandi didn't get offered many jobs apart from lingerie work. Or work without even lingerie to model. The money was good but that didn't stop the idea from sending her into a moral tailspin every time she agreed to take her top off.

'I'm supposed to be an ACTRESS,' she'd wail.

'You've certainly got the tantrums down to an art,' Fat Joe commented.

The week I arrived in Los Angeles Brandi thought her agent might have got her a walk-on part in the *Drew Carey Show*. A week later than that, when it transpired that her agent hadn't delivered – again – we weren't allowed to watch anything with Drew Carey on it while Brandi was in the house. A week later than that, the television was stolen. Brandi was especially upset, since between auditions and modelling jobs she spent all her spare time working out to tedious calisthenics tapes with eighties soundtracks or watching motivational videos with subtle titles such as *How to Marry Rich*.

'You've got to have a back-up plan,' she said.

Brandi's was to marry well. Fat Joe's was to marry better. What was mine? Fact was, as I was soon to discover, everyone in Los Angeles is there to follow a dream and with so many people chasing the same single glittering prize – fickle fame – the chances of real success get slimmer and slimmer the older and uglier and more jaded you get.

Back in London, taxi drivers regaled their passengers with stories of the famous people who had ridden in the back of their cabs. In Los Angeles, the taxi drivers wanted to tell you which celebrities they once starred opposite on the silver screen. During my first week, I met a cabbie who claimed to have starred in *Rawhide* with Clint Eastwood. I'm pretty sure that he drove me the extra scenic route from downtown Los Angeles back to Venice just to give himself time to talk about it.

'I'm just driving this taxi to keep myself busy between jobs,' he told me optimistically. He had last worked as a stunt man in 1973 when he leapt in the wrong direction

from a mock-up of a burning skyscraper and landed on the
film set's catering van instead of the carelessly positioned
crash mat. 'Broke my back,' he said. 'But these days I'm
right up to speed again.' He invited me to feel his biceps.

'They said I was gorgeous,' he assured me.

'Really?'

The cabbie's tan was so dark he looked as though he had
covered himself in Cuprinol. The fact that his badly-fitting
wig was the same colour as his skin only added to the
impression that he had been hewn out of mahogany and
varnished. And he must have been nudging eighty now. I
couldn't imagine anyone would be calling on him to double
for Tom Cruise anytime soon.

Likewise, every diner was staffed by women who looked
as though they might once have given Farrah Fawcett
Majors a run for her money, still slapping on the war
paint and tonging their hair into flicks though the casting
calls were long gone. The posher hotel bars, which Brandi
insisted on frequenting for the purposes of making useful
'contacts' though we couldn't actually afford the drinks,
were staffed by young men and women who wouldn't have
looked out of place in the fashion pages of anything published by Conde Nast. Everyone always smiling. Everyone
always friendly.

But I quickly learned that the incredible friendliness of
the Los Angelenos was simply surface gloss. The grins
weren't actually warm, they were manic. Question number
two in any LA conversation was always 'And what do you
do?' Hell, sometimes they didn't even wait that long. And
if you weren't a director, a producer or a big hotshot
agent, it wasn't long before your new 'friend' was off
in search of someone new. Someone more *useful*. I hadn't
found myself in a situation where people dismissed new

acquaintances so instantly since my primary school days and friendships which hinged on whether you preferred *Adam Ant* or *Buck's Fizz*.

But despite that I soon felt as though Fat Joe and Brandi had become real friends. Good friends. (I counted Fat Joe as he was now as a completely different person from the Fat Joe who had lived, and often smelled as though he might have died, in a camouflage-print sleeping bag.) And though the beach house I shared with them was anything but smart, they had gone to the effort of cleaning my murky room out before I moved in and even left a single yellow rose in a vase on my windowsill to welcome me. On my first Sunday in town, when Fat Joe didn't have to work at Ladyboys and Brandi had a brief break from her busy schedule of Pilates, aerobics, yoga and yet more Pilates, they took me on a grand tour of Hollywood itself.

We piled into Fat Joe's beaten-up pink Cadillac just after lunch (he'd done the paint job himself – it looked as though the car had been caught in a hit-and-run accident with an ice-cream van) and drove up the San Diego freeway.

Well, I thought I had seen a lot of cars on the M4 heading into London but I had seen nothing like the San Diego Freeway, aka the 405. At some points there were seven lanes in each direction and even on a Sunday afternoon every one of those lanes was full. This was a road so wide that not even a chicken crossed with champion sprinter Iwan Thomas could have got across it. I was terrified and I wasn't even driving.

'Would you like to drive?' asked Joe.

'I haven't got my licence,' I lied.

I leaned back against the soft leather of the passenger

seat and tried not to wince every time a car came sailing
in my direction and managed not to hit us.

'This reminds me of a film,' I said.

'*Easy Rider*?' suggested Brandi.

'*Mad Max*.'

As if on cue, a juggernaut in shiny chrome missed us by
an inch and sounded its horn.

'Will you drive a little more carefully?' Brandi snapped
at Joe.

'I didn't see him coming,' Joe protested.

How could he not have seen a lorry the size of a cruise
ship?

I looked up and concentrated on the palm trees and the road
signs to stop myself from whimpering. Washington Boulevard. The Santa Monica Freeway. Pico. Olympic. Wilshire.
Sunset Boulevard. *The* Sunset Boulevard. A street only
marginally less famous than Broadway or Fifth Avenue.
Its name a byword for glitz and glamour and broken
dreams.

'Broken dreams, sure. But a lot of dreams that made it to
reality,' Fat Joe pointed out as he pulled his Cadillac wildly
across five lanes of traffic to find the right exit. This was
where we were getting off.

As soon as we were off the freeway it was as though we
were in the set of another film. From *Mad Max* to something
altogether more genteel this time. The road was suddenly
bordered on both sides by beautifully manicured trees.
We sailed on past Bel Air, the gated enclave of the rich
and famous, with its extravagant rococo sentry posts and
uniformed security men.

'Everybody lives there,' Brandi told me. 'My friend
delivered a pizza to Tom Jones. He asked for extra
anchovies.'

There was a small boy at a set of traffic lights selling maps to the homes of the glitterati.

'That must be annoying,' I said. 'To have people selling maps showing where your home is.'

'Oh, I would just love it,' said Brandi. 'I'll know I've made it when there are people lining up outside my house for me to set the dogs on.'

So this was it, I thought as I sat up straight to watch the view unfold. This was the city I had dreamed of. And this was the street that represented it best.

Sunset Boulevard *is* Los Angeles. From west to east. From heaven to hell. At the west end, Malibu and Pacific Palisades, where the stars have their barbecues on the golden beaches and David 'Baywatch' Hasselhoff cavorted with girls too thin to last a second in the icy Pacific, let alone save a drowning sailor. Inland to the leafy exclusivity of the canyons of Bel Air where the only 'people of colour' are watering the gardens and every home boasts 'armed response'.

Past the elegant campus of UCLA from whence a plethora of beautiful people, far removed from the scruffy students I had been used to back home, set out on roller blades, skateboards or jogging – no one walks in Los Angeles, even when they're not in a car. Past the edges of glamorous Beverly Hills; crossing the top of Rodeo Drive, where Julia Roberts struck a blow for any girl who's ever been ignored by a shop assistant. Past the surprisingly well-kept park where George Michael met the LAPD. Past the corner where Hugh met Divine.

Onto Sunset Strip – Hollywood's own version of Piccadilly Circus where young guys cruise in their soft-top cars past

lines of uniformly beautiful girls queuing to get into that
week's nightspot sensation. Past Larry Flynn's Hustler
store, a sex shop about as erotic as Marks and Spencer.
Past Book Soup. Past Tower Records, dwarfed by its own
giant billboards. Here the chi-chi mansions make way for
corporate skyscrapers plastered with Calvin's girls, sixty
feet high.

Past the conspicuously anonymous white gates of the
ultra-exclusive Mondrian, the famous House of Blues, the
wittily inverted sign of The Standard. 'Why is that upside
down?' I asked Fat Joe. 'So you can read it when you've
passed out?' On to spooky Chateau Marmont – where
John Belushi took his overdose. To the Viper Room, where
River Phoenix allegedly took his. 'I cried for a week,' said
Brandi.

Past the Marlboro man, still standing after all these years
but with his cigarette drooping now, finally admitting that
you won't improve your sex appeal with a fag. Then
the skyscrapers give way to low-rise nail parlours. Signs
claiming that this is the 'best place to get your bail bonds'.
Korean liquor stores.

'I got held up by a guy with a gun there once,' said
Brandi.

'Don't tell her that,' said Fat Joe.

'Too late,' I confirmed.

On past car parks that didn't seem to be connected to
any buildings in particular. More liquor stores. Drive-in
burger bars. French manicures, a dollar. As much sushi as
you could eat for $5.99. And suddenly Sunset was gone.

All on one street. Winding through the hills above Downtown Los Angeles. Twenty miles from beginning to end.
From American dream to nightmare.

* * *

We cruised back down Hollywood Boulevard, stopping outside the red and gold pagoda of Mann's famous Chinese Theater to look at the marble stars set in the pavement and the handprints of Tinseltown's favourite alumni. I put my hands in Arnold Schwarzenegger's prints and was surprised to find that his fingers weren't much longer than mine.

'He's a midget,' said Brandi.

'Makes me wonder if I'll ever be asked to come up here and do this for real,' I said.

'Just believe it enough,' said Fat Joe. 'And you will.'

'Wish upon a star, that's what we say in California,' Brandi added.

I stood up from Arnie's handprints and smiled at Fat Joe and Brandi's optimism. Everything and anything was possible according to Brandi. While the British actors I knew back in London grew increasingly despondent with every audition that didn't lead to a part, Brandi in particular viewed every failure as a step towards the day she finally cracked it. Everything could be achieved with self-belief. So California. So Hollywood.

That night, back in Venice, the cockroaches and the crackhouses seemed like a small price to pay for the possibility of living forever in celluloid. For the first time since arriving in Los Angeles I felt something approaching sure that I'd made the right decision by heading out there. After all, this was a city built on the premise that it could turn ugly ducklings into swans. How many stars had flipped burgers or waited tables until they got their chance? I thought of Hilary Swank living in her car while she waited for auditions. Five years later she held an Oscar in her hand. I could make it too, couldn't I?

Brandi told me that she'd heard that British actresses

were in big demand since Minnie Driver and Catherine Zeta Jones made their mark. Fat Joe agreed that I had the hot look of that season, even if he did term it 'slightly wishy-washy'. I decided that he was just struggling to remember the phrase 'English rose'.

As I lay in the bath that night I pondered what colour nail varnish to wear when Mr Mann asked me to stick my hands in the concrete outside his Chinese Theater. Would I wear Versace or Armani? They'd both send free outfits to my apartment, of course.

CHAPTER NINE

I quickly grew closer to Brandi. My first impression of her, looking as she did like a brunette Pammy Lee, had not been especially favourable. Her entire life seemed to revolve around getting thinner and fitter with better hair and breasts. I wanted to play a Tolstoy heroine. She wanted to play Jim Carrey's girlfriend.

But we had far more in common than I expected. She may have looked a bimbo but she was far from being one. While she played the sex appeal card to the max when she was looking for an assignment, at home she was a girls' girl, more than happy to share her clothes, her make-up and her heart.

It wasn't long before I told her about Richard, of course. And she sympathised in a way that Fat Joe, even in his new incarnation, never would. She made hopeful noises when I told her that I thought he was my soul mate and one day, when Fat Joe was safely at work and Brandi had finished that afternoon's dose of Pilates, she got out her tarot cards.

'My grandmother was a gypsy,' she said, tossing her black hair back over her shoulder as she handed me the well-worn pack. 'She predicted that one day I would have a

life-changing experience in Los Angeles right back when I
was still a kid and had never even heard of Hollywood.'

'Life-changing?' I said.

'Yeah. Life-changing. Those were her exact words. And
she said that I'd have the chance to change the world
because of it. That's got to be getting famous, right?'

I nodded. It was a pretty loose interpretation but a
good one.

'She might have meant that you'll become a UN hostage
negotiator and divert a world war,' I suggested.

'Pur-leese! Looking like I do? Anyway, I inherited my
grandmother's gift,' Brandi continued. 'It skipped my
mother's generation and reappeared with me when my
grandmother died. So, let's find out what's going to happen
to you. You've got to blow on the cards before you shuffle
them,' she told me. 'Gets rid of any other person's energy
that might still be lingering in the pack. If you don't do
that, they'll give you a reading for Joe. He was the last
one I did.'

'What did Joe's reading say?' I asked.

'It said that he wouldn't get the Farrah Fawcett Majors
part in the remake of *Charlie's Angels*.'

I could have told him that just by looking at his birth
certificate but I tried to look impressed by Brandi's psychic
abilities all the same.

'Shuffle them now,' Brandi instructed. 'Then cut the pack
into three piles.'

'Equal piles?'

'However you like. However the spirit moves you,' she
added.

'I don't think it does,' I joked, thinking back to the last
time I had my tarot cards read. I had hired a reader as
a special treat for Mary, as part of her hen weekend.

The 'Genuine Romany' – all the way from Witney in Oxfordshire – had been doing well until she told me that I would find myself pregnant by the end of the year. That was frightening enough. But then she told me that I was about to enter a three-year period of celibacy, starting the very next day.

'So how can I possibly get pregnant before the end of the year?' I asked her.

'Make sure you don't hang out with any archangels in December,' quipped Mary.

That gypsy woman definitely wasn't worth the silver we crossed her palm with.

'Since we don't have silver these days, I can take Gold cards,' she'd told me.

At least I wasn't paying for Brandi's bad advice.

I split the pack into three. Brandi had me reassemble them into one pack and shuffle them one more time before she finally started to deal them out face down.

'Concentrate on what you want to know,' she said.

What did I want to know? I took a sip of my coffee. My brain was instantly crowded by a thousand questions. Was I doing the right thing? Would I ever be famous? Would I ever have my own star on Hollywood Boulevard? Would Richard ever come back to me?

Richard. Richard, Richard, Richard.

As I looked at the backs of Brandi's cards with their intricate Celtic design, the question of what would become of me and Richard floated to the front of my mind like a piece of rotten wood floating to the surface of a dirty river. Hardly surprising. Richard was all that I had been concentrating on for almost two months. Even when I thought I wasn't thinking about him, I knew that all my actions, whatever they were, were in some part motivated by what my ex-boyfriend might think of them. From trying to get auditions – he'll want me back if I'm famous, I thought – to accidentally stepping out in front of a lorry – will Richard feel guilty if I die?

Brandi had her eyes shut tight.

'Is anything coming through yet?' I asked.

'Wow. Yeah,' she nodded. 'You know, something's coming through really strongly.'

'Tell me,' I said impatiently. 'Only don't tell me if something really bad shows up,' I amended quickly as she turned over the first card, which was The Death card. Reversed.

'That looks bad,' I said.

'Not necessarily. Wow. I'm getting some really big vibes here. You must be really in tune with your psychic side.'

'What does it mean?' I persisted.

'Well, this card,' said Brandi, pointing at a card which was covered in nasty-looking swords, 'means endings. Endings in your recent past.'

'That certainly makes sense.'

'But this,' Brandi continued, 'represents a new beginning at the place where those endings left off. And this,' she said, pointing excitedly at a card decorated with a beautiful overflowing cup, 'I think that this means marriage.'

Endings. New beginnings where the endings left off. And a marriage? Was this the answer to the Richard question? Were the cards showing our break-up and predicting that not only would we get back together, there would be a marriage at the end of it? I felt my heart begin to rise inside me.

'How psychic did you say you were?' I asked Brandi, hoping that the laugh at the end of that question disguised my desperation for her interpretation to be right. 'Is this really what's going to happen to me?'

'The cards don't work like that,' said Brandi disappointingly. 'They don't deal in absolutes. They present possibilities. They're saying that this is what could happen in your life. But only if you really want it.'

Of course I wanted it!

'They're not saying that it will happen without your making an effort,' Brandi continued.

Oh God, I thought. To get Richard back I would make enough effort to save the universe.

'Or that, if it does eventually happen, it would necessarily be a good thing.'

How could it not be the best thing in the world?

'But it is likely to be a good thing, isn't it?' I asked.

Brandi shrugged.

'And how long until it happens?'

'Not long,' she said, tapping a card decorated with three pentacles. 'At least, I don't think so because it seems to say that these things will take place out here.'

I frowned. How could that be right? How could I get back together with Richard if I was still in Los Angeles?

'Does it definitely say that I'm going to be getting back together with Richard?'

'I think so. If the ending it's referring to is your break-up.'

'And a marriage?'

'That's this card.'

'Well, that's not what I expected to hear. But God, I hope you're right.'

'Careful what you wish for,' said Brandi, rearranging the cards into one pile.

'Can you wish something into existence?' I asked her

then. 'Do you really believe that one day you will be famous just because you want to be?'

'Stupid as it sounds,' said Brandi. 'I really do. I've always thought it. Even when I was a little kid in New Jersey. When my mom got on at me about my bad school grades I used to tell her that it wouldn't matter because I didn't need to get good grades to be an actress. I just knew I was going to be an actress. I never wanted to be anything else. My first heroine was Carrie Fisher.'

'Princess Leia?'

'I liked her hair.'

'I wanted to be Drew Barrymore in *ET*,' I admitted.

'Oh yeah,' Brandi nodded. 'I thought she was great too. I told Mom that I was going to have Drew's part if they ever made a sequel to that film.'

'I used to say the same sort of thing to my parents,' I told Brandi then. 'When they were going on at me about having to work harder to get a place at the grammar school. Getting to the right school was so important, they said, if I wanted to go to university and get a decent job. By that they meant becoming a doctor or a lawyer. But I promised my mum that one day I would send her on a round-the-world cruise with my fabulous riches from stardom.'

'I think you will,' said Brandi. 'I'm getting a psychic feeling about it. Maybe not this year but . . .'

I laughed. 'I think Mum's given up on the cruise. Right now she thinks that the best Christmas present I could give her is to get a sensible job again. Or marry a sensible man. And stop buying shoes that give me blisters and get a mortgage and start my pension. Just before I came out here, I heard her tell my brother that I've been a teenager for the best part of fifteen years and it's making her hair go grey.'

'I got that from my mom,' said Brandi.

'Is she still trying to persuade you to give it all up and get a real life?'

Brandi smiled down at the cards. 'No. No, she's not. In fact, she's not with us any more,' she sighed.

'What do you mean?' I asked.

'Mom passed away three Christmasses ago. I waited until she died before I came out here. I worked in a used car dealership until then.'

'Oh, Brandi, I'm sorry. I take it that it wasn't . . .'

'Sudden? No. I knew she was leaving us for months. She had cancer. In the end she was on so many painkillers that she said it would be a relief to die.'

'That's terrible.'

'Well, everybody has to go sometime,' Brandi shrugged.

'Yeah, but not . . . she must have been pretty young.'

'Forty-eight,' said Brandi.

'That's young.'

'Die young, stay beautiful,' said Brandi, quoting with a smile the phrase that had been applied to her own favourite star, Marilyn Monroe, again and again since her untimely death. 'That's the way to live forever. Captured in your prime on celluloid. Beats living till you're ninety and ending your days having some spotty kid wiping your ass in the seniors' home.'

'When you put it like that,' I sighed. I raised my empty coffee cup and chinked it against Brandi's bottle of mineral water. 'Here's to living forever, Hollywood style.'

'To living forever,' said Brandi.

But big screen immortality still wasn't exactly around the corner for either of us – psychic predictions or no. Upon arriving in Los Angeles, I called every single one of the contact numbers that Mary had given me (and the two numbers that Useless Eunice, my agent in London, had grudgingly handed over when I told her that I was leaving town – both of which turned out to be disconnected). I was terrified of cold-calling these strangers but I forced myself to do it and, over the telephone, I was met with much friendliness and gushing promises of lunch. However, getting an actual date with these Hollywood people was more difficult than closing a deal on double glazing for a static caravan.

Brandi and Fat Joe did their best to introduce me to the few useful people that they knew (Fat Joe knew only one and that was Brandi). Brandi forced me to pile on the slap and attend a few Hollywood parties with her. Once there, we would split up and work one side of the room each. With her incredible chest and bubbly, big-toothed smile, Brandi would inevitably come home with a fistful of producers' phone numbers and requests to send her showreel at the earliest possible opportunity. I would inevitably meet the guy who had been hired to tend the bar.

Meanwhile, the rot under the brittle veneer of glamour was becoming increasingly obvious to me. One day Brandi burst into my bedroom full of excitement because she had been called back to audition a second time for a part she thought had already been decided a week before.

'The girl they cast originally was in a car wreck this morning,' Brandi explained to me breathlessly. 'It's going to take months to rebuild her face.'

'Fantastic!'

I was horrified to find myself agreeing with Brandi that this was indeed a stroke of incredible luck. For her. It was only a matter of time before I picked up Fat Joe's appalling new catchphrase and said, 'One step nearer for us,' every time we passed an ambulance that might be carrying another hopeful actor/singer/whatever to the morgue. Oh dear. Someone should have told me that by the time you can see the rot in your attitude, it's already too late. It's already making Swiss cheese of your brain tissue.

But Brandi and I really hit rock bottom when we attended a 'producer's' party, only to discover that he didn't produce movies at all but pornographic websites. We left that party early. Brandi was convinced that the dodgy-looking photographer who had been taking snapshots of the party guests would somehow cut and paste images of our heads onto a couple of porn actresses' bodies. Personally, I wasn't too bothered but for Brandi, who already had the porn star's body and was desperately trying to break away from the shady roles that her pneumatic assets had her firmly typecast in, such things were a serious issue.

On the drive home, I tried to put her straight about the likelihood of her fears coming true. She had to be over-reacting.

'Nobody does that any more,' I told her. 'Not with unknowns like us. Maybe if you were Cameron Diaz or Jennifer Lopez someone would take the trouble to splice your head to a porn star's body but why bother otherwise? Besides, these days, the rage is for realistic stuff. Who wants a picture of two fully clothed girls drinking champagne from plastic cups at a crappy party when you can log on and see live web camera pictures of college girls in the shower? Or even on the toilet.'

We had reached a set of lights. Brandi turned and looked at me in pure horror. 'Ohmigod. They put web cameras in the toilet,' she breathed.

'Yes, they do,' I laughed. 'It's really gross, isn't it? Can't say I'd want to look but those kind of sites get hundreds of hits every second.'

'Lizzie, I'm not *asking* you whether they do it,' said Brandi. 'I'm *telling* you. They had web cameras in the bathroom at that party. I just know it.'

'Don't be ridiculous,' I said.

'Then why did the host ask me whether I had ever looked up a site called "squatters.com"?'

'Squatters.com? Oh no.'

I tried to tell myself that it was just one of those sites that helps people to find somewhere to live when they arrive in a new town friendless and homeless. At worst it was an on-line store for bidets. But I couldn't even console myself with the fact that I was unlikely to have been caught on camera that night. Attending parties thrown by people I hardly knew always made me nervous and getting nervous always made me want to pee. I had been to the bathroom as soon as we arrived at the house. And now I remembered asking the party host exactly where I would find it.

'There's one downstairs and one upstairs,' he told me. 'I'd use the one upstairs if I were you.'

Now I was convinced that rather than simply directing me to the more salubrious of his guest conveniences, he had in fact been sending me to the pan with the Panavision trained upon it.

Brandi was distraught. She'd been suffering from a touch of diarrhoea that weekend, following a couple of days on a ridiculous cabbage juice fast to help her drop ten pounds for a big audition. It would have been less embarrassing and more effective to go for colonic irrigation.

'Can't we sue?' I asked her later as we drank strong black coffee to drown our sorrows in Jerry's famous all-nite diner.

'Are you willing to identify your privates in a court of law?' asked Brandi. She was shredding a napkin in her frustration.

'Man,' she sighed. 'I'm just so pissed about this. I hate having to go to all these crappy parties and talk to crappy men who are full of nothing but . . .' She searched hard to find the right word. 'Crappy crap.'

I had to agree. The highlight of my evening had been having a conversation with a man whose claim to fame was having slept with somebody who slept with someone who once slept with Kirstie Alley. I was supposed to be impressed by that. Still, at least that guy had talked to me for longer than thirty seconds. The first person I had introduced myself to at the party that night had simply said, 'I don't need to meet any new people tonight. Thanks.'

'Isn't there an easier way to get auditions?' I asked. 'Can't we just get better agents?'

'Lizzie,' said Brandi with a patronising half-smile. 'The only way an unknown actress gets to talk to a decent agent in this town is if she's cleaning that agent's swimming pool. Unknowns don't just turn up in Hollywood and get agents to get them parts. These are the rules. First, you get the decent part. By whatever means necessary,' she added. 'Then the good agents call you. Then they send you flowers. Then they take you out to lunch. Then one signs you up. And then that interstellar agent who's done nothing more than buy you some spaghetti in a bistro on the wrong side of La Brea takes ten per cent of the fee for the job you got yourself in the first place. It's a classic Catch-22.'

She leaned her head in her hands and sighed loudly.

'Something big will happen soon,' I reassured her.

'Something tells me I'm more likely to drop dead than drop into a decent role right now. I'm just so tired of all this bullshit.'

'Brandi,' I said, shaking her arm in an attempt to chivvy her. 'You're not supposed to be like this. You're supposed to be filling me with courage, remember? What about the tarot cards?'

'The tarot cards are a load of bullshit too.'

'Don't say that,' I begged her. If only because my dreams rested heavily on them too. 'You're just having a bad day. PMT.'

'You're right. I'll get over it,' said Brandi, whipping out her compact and reapplying a smile with her lip gloss. 'I always get miserable around this time of the month. And while we're on the subject of misery, rent cheque's due tomorrow.'

'Fine. I'll cash some more traveller's cheques,' I told her.

But when I got to my bedroom that night I discovered that I had spent far more than I thought during my month in the sun. I was down to my last two hundred dollars.

CHAPTER TEN

S o, having overcome my initial misgivings about Venice Beach, and feeling that I had settled in with Brandi and Fat Joe, I had my first proper wobble. I sat on my futon and stared at my last two remaining hundred dollar traveller's cheques in disbelief. I couldn't understand how I had managed to run out of money so soon. I hadn't been that stupid with my cash, had I?

My wardrobe confronted me with the evidence to the contrary. It was stuffed full of new clothes and knick-knacks. When I first arrived in America I told myself that I needed new togs for the auditions that Eunice would be setting up from her office in London. A week later, when it became clear that Eunice couldn't organise a bonfire party in hell, let alone kickstart my glittering career long distance, I went on a shopping spree to cheer myself up.

Then, of course, there were the obligatory presents to self that I needed as consolation every time I thought about Richard. Or got an email from someone back home that didn't say, 'Richard's been asking about you.' Or 'Richard's been dumped by Jennifer.' Or, best of all, 'Richard's real-ised what a tosser he was to end things with you and he's just given Jennifer up.'

I had needed a lot of consolation that month. The kind that comes in the shape of three pairs of almost identical

black satin mules. Mules I couldn't even walk in. I blamed
Fat Joe for encouraging me to buy those. I had also bought
three different multi-coloured bikinis. Two pairs of new
sunglasses. A thirty-dollar pot of lip gloss . . . Lip gloss?!!!
Thirty dollars? That was almost twenty pounds!

No wonder the money that was supposed to last me at
least three months had been used up in less than four
weeks. I had been living a champagne lifestyle on beer
wages, as my mother often warned me I did. And now I
needed money to pay for it. And quick.

But I couldn't get a job. At least, I thought I couldn't get
a job. I had officially entered the United States as a tourist.
I had ticked the box that said I was definitely not coming
in to seek work. I didn't have the proper working visa and
no one would employ me without one of those. No one
law-abiding, at least.

'They're looking for more waitresses at Ladyboys,' Fat
Joe told me, when I explained my predicament over breakfast. 'Antonio doesn't worry about visas. He let me start
work before my green card came through.'

'But Ladyboys? Don't you have to, er, be a ladyboy to
work there?' I asked.

'No,' said Joe. 'Some of the waitresses are actually real
women pretending to be men pretending to be women.'

'I see,' I nodded.

'I could get you a job there. You'd be perfect.'

'What? You mean that I look like a woman pretending
to be a man pretending to be a woman?' I asked.

'Sometimes,' said Joe. 'In a good way.'

'How on earth can there be "a good way" to look like a
woman pretending to be a man in drag? Oh my God, no
wonder I'm not getting any parts out here.' I stared at my
knuckles. Were they big and hairy enough to be a man's?

I'd always hated my knees. They were huge. 'My knees aren't manly, are they?'

'I wasn't saying that. The point is . . . Look, what I'm trying to say is this. You shouldn't be insulted that I think you could work at Ladyboys. Everybody there is beautiful. Really beautiful. Like geisha girls.'

'Who's like a geisha?' asked Brandi, coming into the kitchen to look for her moisturiser, which had to be kept in the fridge. (In fact, Brandi's moisturiser was the only thing kept in the fridge since I discovered the cockroaches in the butter dish.)

'The girls at Ladyboys,' said Joe. 'Don't you agree?'

'Er. Whatever,' said Brandi, curling her top lip.

That was all I needed to hear for Fat Joe's damage limitation tactics to fail. Geishas? When he went into work, Fat Joe looked about as much like a geisha girl as Lily Savage. I didn't talk to him for the rest of the day.

But the fact was, as I had to admit to myself on a mind-clearing beach walk later that afternoon, I was in trouble. If I wanted to stay even for the three months my tourist visa allowed me legitimately, I still needed a job.

Fat Joe's offer to put in a good word for me at Ladyboys was the only lead I had found so far. It wasn't as though I could just walk into an employment agency or even any other, more salubrious, bar. I knew that any remotely reputable business would not want to risk hefty fines by hiring an illegal immigrant. Ladyboys, however, was not a remotely reputable business. At least, it didn't look like one from the outside with its forbidding metal shutters, decorated with an array of bright spray-painted obscenities, all of them incorrectly spelled. Maybe they were actually French Connection adverts . . .

I sat down on the sand near to Venice Beach Pier and

went through my options one more time. Option one, don't get a job, run out of money by the end of the week, go back to Solihull. After all, a month in Los Angeles had brought me no nearer to that elusive acting job. I had secured exactly zero auditions despite my hardcore networking. None of Mary's contacts had called me back with real appointments to back up their gushing promises of lunch and my only screen appearance was likely to be on a coprophiliac's website. I wasn't making it in Hollywood yet, by any definition. Autumn was approaching fast. If I went back to the UK soon enough, Eunice might be able to get me a winter season in panto. And was Solihull really so bad?

I watched a surfer scrambling onto his board, ready to catch the next wave. That was what people did during their lunch hours in Los Angeles. They dashed down to the beach and *surfed*. During your lunch hour in Solihull you could dash down a rainswept street to Marks and Spencer only to find, if you hadn't had the sense to buy your lunch before eleven o'clock that morning, that the only sandwiches left were egg mayonnaise or that month's special – the never-to-be-repeated crispy duck and cold kidney bean. I smiled, very briefly and somewhat bitterly, at the thought of getting a job as the inventor of such vile sandwich fillings. Perhaps I could offset my depression at having to go back to Birmingham by inventing ever more unusual sandwich combinations that would spoil other people's days as well.

At least in Solihull I would have my family around me. There had definitely been times that month when I missed my mum and dad; Sundays, for example, when I sat down to a beansprout salad while Colin would be getting Mum's roast.

And if Sunday lunch wasn't enough to keep me in

Solihull, I could go down to London at weekends to spend time with Bill and Mary. I always had a good time when they were around and if they were being boring, then Seema was always up for a girls' night out.

But it didn't take long for me to remember the reality. Mum and Dad would be driving me mad before we got out of the airport car park. Bill and Mary – well, they had Bill *and* Mary. They were newly-weds. They didn't need me hanging around the house. And Seema, while she was sweet enough, would inevitably score on any girls' night out and thought nothing of leaving me to find my own way home from the middle of nowhere while she snogged that evening's catch round the back of some pub.

Fact was, without Richard, I didn't really have anyone to go back for. No one whose absence in my heart couldn't be cured with a three line email that reminded me how much I loved them while at the same time reminding me why I couldn't spend more than three solid days with my parents, with Bill and Mary, or with any of the other friends I'd left behind without wanting to get on a plane and flee the country again.

Sitting on the beach and weighing up the pros and cons, it was as though I had reached the midway point on some mythical journey. It would have been just as easy to turn back as to carry on. I didn't miss Solihull enough for it to be obvious that I wanted to go back. I didn't love Los Angeles enough for it to be a tragedy if I didn't stay. And yet . . . how would Brandi's prediction have a chance to come true if I didn't.

Pah! I tried to put Brandi's ridiculous soothsaying to the back of my mind and approach the decision process logically. I couldn't base a life-changing decision on a pack of cards. Particularly not if that life-changing decision involved Richard. He was no longer a factor in my life's equation. I had to plan for a future without him and, so, bearing that in mind, these were the real facts with which I had to work . . .

Choice One. Solihull, West Midlands. Surbuban hell with a light, but fairly constant, smattering of drizzle. Choice Two. Venice Beach, Los Angeles. Even the name sounded better. Sure, there were winos, guns and druggies. But there was also sunshine, sand and sexy surfers. Roller skating on the promenade. Sun bathing in the garden. Denny's diners. Pancakes for breakfast. Vibrant C smoothies from Jamba Juice.

I know you shouldn't try to make a decision while you're hungry but there really was no contest. The food in itself was a good enough reason to emigrate. Another no-brainer. I had to stay in Los Angeles. The only difficult question was, would I be prepared to work as a waitress in a bar where everybody would assume that I was a man dressed as a woman to maintain my place in sun?

The surfer I had been watching jogged up the beach with his long board.

'Hi,' he said, with a smile like summertime itself. 'How are you today?'

'Better now,' I told him.

Hmm, I even loved how friendly the locals were. The only strangers who spoke to you in Solihull or London were the nutters; exactly the kind of people who would send me fan letters if Eunice got me a season as a chorus girl in *Babes in the Wood*.

'I'm staying in LA,' I told myself. 'I have to.'

I went straight back to the flat and asked Fat Joe to tell his boss that I wanted to audition for a job at Ladyboys that evening. I even promised to help him do a French pleat in his red 'Joanna Boisvert' wig as a peace offering.

'Just swear to me that I don't look like a man,' I said.

'Lizzie,' said Fat Joe. 'You look like a peach.'

What do you wear to an interview for a job as a waitress in a bar where all the girls are pretending to be boys pretending to be girls?

'Hotpants,' said Joe, with authority. 'Antonio loves hotpants.'

I had been hoping that he would say 'come as you are'. But no. As with Brandi's approach to auditions, Fat Joe assured me that the way to ace this interview would be to go along 'as if'.

'As if I'm already a girl pretending to be a boy pretending to be a girl?' I asked somewhat despondently.

'Yeah. Like in *Shakespeare in Love*,' said Joe. 'Didn't do Gwyneth Paltrow any harm.'

'You said the "G" word!' cried Brandi, covering her ears.

Gwyneth Paltrow's name was mud in the beach house. As was the name of anyone who got to snog Ben Affleck, Brad Pitt *and* Joe Fiennes.

'Gwyneth, Gwyneth, Gwyneth,' Fat Joe teased as he handed me the outfit he thought I should wear to impress his boss, Antonio.

'Gwyneth Paltrow's costume did not show her vagina!' I protested when I unfolded a pair of pants so short they could hardly have kept me lukewarm let alone hot.

'You'd need a Brazilian to wear that,' said Brandi, wincing.

'A Brazilian?' I asked.

'Brazilian bikini wax. Everything off,' Brandi confirmed. 'Did I tell you guys about my friend Cynthia? She let a junior aesthetician give her one on a training day. She was trying to save some money. Next thing you know, she's in the emergency room having twenty-six stitches. Lost three pints of blood. Still can't wear tight jeans.'

'Too much information!' I handed the hotpants back to Joe. 'I think I'll pass on these, thanks.'

'Well, what are you going to wear?' he asked in exasperation.

Half an hour later I stood outside Ladyboys in a leopardskin miniskirt, a bubblegum-pink halter top, knee-high boots and a blunt-cut red wig borrowed from Brandi's vast hairpiece collection (honestly, that girl had more wigs than the cast of *Dangerous Liaisons*). I looked a bit, I hoped, like Julia Roberts in *Pretty Woman* before she gets hold of Richard Gere's credit card and goes crazy in Fred Hayman.

I must have looked as though I worked in the same profession as Roberts' character at least. While I waited for Fat Joe's boss to summon me inside for my interview, two Hispanic guys in the most beaten-up car I had seen in Los Angeles slowed down as they passed me and shouted 'Want some business?'

My pithy reply in pure Anglo-Saxon was drowned out by the sound of an aircraft coming in to land. Ladyboys was situated right at the end of Los Angeles International Airport's runway. Believe me, this place failed on all three counts of the estate agent's mantra: location, location, location.

In the following five minutes, I was asked if I wanted business another five times. I had to resort to standing facing the wall so that the passing drivers didn't think I was trying to make eye contact. This clearly wasn't the kind of stretch frequented by the likes of Hugh Grant and when Fat Joe's boss finally opened the door to me, I was almost grateful to be able to step into Ladyboys' seedy, stale interior.

'You must be Lizzie,' said Antonio Sardi, the proud proprietor, ushering me inside the dark club with one hand on my butt. Antonio Sardi dressed like he had stepped straight out of *Starsky and Hutch*. White suit over a shiny black shirt. Pointed shoes with Cuban heels that clipped loudly as he led me across the dancefloor towards his office.

'Joanna told me you were pretty,' he said, with a downturn of his mouth. 'But he lied.'

'Great,' I muttered. Now a man who looked like a dessicated lizard was going to tell me that I was too much of a dog to work in a trannie bar but . . .

'You're absolutely beautiful!' came the punchline.

He laughed at his own joke. Still fraught from my disturbing wait outside the building, I laughed somewhat hysterically back. Antonio waved me towards a chair and sat down opposite me. Then he leaned on the table between us and, fixing me with an approving stare, said, 'I like you, Lizzie. I really like your style.' He nodded as though he recognised a true equal.

I hadn't even said a word.

'And I know you're going to like me,' Antonio continued precociously. 'I take very good care of my girls here at Ladyboys. They're my family. My sons and daughters. I don't have no real family any more, Lizzie. Which don't mean to say I won't avenge them one day,' he added somewhat menacingly. 'But you come and work for Antonio, I'll treat you like my own. Like a princess. You wanna work for me, Lizzie? You wanna work for your Uncle Antonio?'

'I don't know. What's the pay deal?' I ventured.

'Three dollars an hour and free pasta,' he said quickly. 'As much as you can eat when the club closes at three a.m.'

'Er, three dollars?' I said incredulously. 'Isn't that a little less than the minimum wage?'

'Lizzie, my darling,' Antonio smiled. 'For a girl without a work permit, three dollars and the promise of Uncle Antonio's protection is big money in this town.'

'I see,' I nodded.

'You get to keep the gratuities.'

'Great. That really makes a difference,' I sighed.

Tips. I thought back to my stint as a waitress in The Harvester bistro at Solihull where the best tips I'd received were a handful of foreign shrapnel from a bunch of lads just back from Tenerife and a suggestion that I tie my long hair back so that I could see where I was going when I brought plates out of the kitchen. That second much more useful tip was from a customer who had just received a bowl of tomato soup in the lap of his fake Armani. Despite the fact that I had actually tripped over his stupid girlfriend's carelessly stowed Hermes rip-off handbag, the cost of cleaning that suit did, of course, have to come out of my wages. So, with that experience behind me, Antonio's assurance that if I worked for him I could keep the 'grat-oo-i-dies' hardly cheered me up.

'I don't know,' I began.

'OK. Three dollars twenty-five,' said Antonio straight away.

'Four dollars?' I tried.

'You trying to make me bankrupt? Three fifty.'

Three fifty? That was still only just over two pounds. I'd have to work twenty-four hours a day to be able to afford my bus fare, I thought indignantly. But could I afford to be proud?

'OK,' said Antonio, sensing that I was wavering. 'I give you three seventy-five and my children starve.'

'I thought you didn't have any children,' I pointed out.

'You got me,' he grinned. 'I like a clever girl. You going to come and work for your Uncle Antonio? My pasta's worth another ten bucks a night and I'd go down on my knees for you if I didn't have my old wound from 'Nam.' He winked.

'Oh all right,' I grinned back. What choice did I have? Even three seventy-five an hour would keep me from Solihull for a little bit longer and the free meal at the end of the shift would save me having to buy food with what I did earn.

'You made a smart decision,' said Antonio. 'When can you start?'

'When you want me to?' I replied.

'Good answer. Tonight?' he suggested. 'Davina has just called in sick. Again. Is getting to be a regular occurrence on a Monday night. I might have to pay her a visit and find out what's wrong. I don't like it when my girls get sick.'

'Of course not.'

Despite Antonio's assurance that he treated his 'girls' like family, I couldn't help thinking that a sickbed visit from Antonio would not be the avuncular treat one might imagine.

'Can you dance?' he asked me then.

'Dance? Sure. What kind of dancing?' I began but even as I asked, I caught sight of the shiny fireman's pole sticking up from the centre of the dancefloor. 'You don't mean?' I jerked my head in the pole's direction.

'You might want to think about it,' Antonio told me. 'I'll double your wages if you're good enough and you get to choose your own songs. OK, Lizzie. We open in ten minutes. What you're wearing now will do for tonight but you'll need to show more leg in future. Got any hotpants?'

I shook my head.

'Get some. Just one more thing.'

'What?'

'Those,' he said, nodding towards my chest. 'Are they real?'

CHAPTER ELEVEN

A crash course in waitressing at Ladyboys from a six-foot stunner called Atalanta ('After the Roman goddess of sport, don't ya know?') revealed the club to have more rules and etiquette than Hugh Hefner's Playboy mansion, or even Buckingham Palace for that matter.

'We don't really have to do a bunny dip, do we?' I asked in horror.

'No,' said Atalanta. 'That's optional. But Antonio likes us to keep the check in our cleavage and bend over like this so that the client can take it out for himself when he wants it.'

'What?' I said, as Atalanta tucked a scrap of paper into the front of her sequinned bra-top and leaned so far over backwards that her head almost touched the floor.

'It earns bigger tips,' Atalanta assured me, straightening back up effortlessly as though she had been performing such contortions since she was a baby.

'It would have to,' I told her, thinking of how my back cracked when I even tried to touch my toes. 'How much bigger tips?'

'Last night,' Atalanta whispered, 'I went home with enough money to fund the final stage of my operation.'

'What operation?' I asked naively.

'Fifteen hundred dollars. Enough to finish my . . .' She pointed coyly to her crotch.

'Oh.' I was shocked. But actually less shocked than I was by the size of her gratuities. Fifteen hundred dollars! In tips! In a place that was so run down that the dancers had to put money in the juke box to start the music before they stepped up to the pole? It didn't add up.

'And that's all from one table,' Atalanta continued. 'Ladyboys may not look like much but, believe me, this old place is legendary. We've had them all in here.' In a confidential whisper, she reeled off a list of Hollywood's great and good that left me open-mouthed and blinking. 'I swear to you, Lizzie, the *National Enquirer* would pay me a hundred times what I earned in tips last night to hear some of the stories I get told here.'

'Then why don't you just tell them and retire?' I asked.

'You think Antonio puts on that Italian accent for effect?' she retorted meaningfully. 'You know he's a *made man*,' she added. 'Like in *Goodfellas*.'

'I see.'

So, that is what it had come to. I was about to start work as a waitress in a transvestite pole-dancing club with a Mafioso boss. A Mafioso boss who defended the privacy of his rich and infamous clients with the threat of a pair of concrete platform heels and a walk off the pier at Dockweiler Beach (which, for your information, has more dead bodies washed up on it per year than any other beach in the world).

This is how nice girls end up going bad, I told myself as I considered the financial rewards that Atalanta had hinted at and weighed them up against the potential dangers of working for the Mob as though I was considering a Saturday job at Marks and Sparks versus staying in on Saturday mornings to watch Zoe Ball and Jamie Theakston.

Fifteen hundred dollars was a lot of money by anybody's

standards. She hadn't earned that just for waitressing, surely? The only minor comforting point in my conversation with Atalanta had come when she assured me that at least the police would never bother to check up on the legitimacy of my working status while I worked at Ladyboys. Antonio had an arrangement with the boys in black who patrolled this particular beat which meant that a blind eye was turned to work permits and smoking alike.

'It was much harder to get them to agree with me about the smoking,' Antonio would later explain.

'I didn't think anyone smoked in Los Angeles any more anyway,' I told him. 'I can't believe how difficult it is to bum a fag in this town.'

Antonio looked at me as if I had just told him that it had been very hard to persuade any gay men to have anal sex with me in California, which, as far as he was concerned, I had.

'I meant borrow a cigarette,' I corrected quickly.

'You wanna learn to talk proper English,' said my new boss.

With just five minutes to go before the bar opened that night, I was in the loo, putting on Atalanta's spare false eyelashes. 'The subtle ones for you,' she said. They were bright neon pink and glittery and made me look as though I had conjunctivitis.

I might have felt less scared if Fat Joe had been there to talk to, but Joanna Boisvert was giving a guest performance at a bridal shower in Long Beach that night. I was on my own.

'Think of it like any other acting part,' I told my somewhat nervous reflection as I jabbed myself in the eye again and had to retouch my liquid liner. 'Go out there. Switch the part on. Go home. Switch the part off again.'

In any case, how difficult could waitressing in a transvestite bar be for a girl who had spent the best part of a year acting such challenging roles as 'stick' and 'stone' at a top London drama school? I got top marks in the class for my 'stone'. Quartz sandwiched between granite, I called it. I just sat still and grimaced.

No good. Even thinking about how easy it had been to impress my drama school tutor with my improv abilities couldn't prevent the butterflies that overwhelmed me as I stepped out of the restroom in my Ladyboys' regalia that night. Noticing my nerves right away, Atalanta squeezed my arm, gave me a sticky kiss and said, 'You look great. You'll knock 'em dead, girl.'

I didn't believe it. Great? Atalanta looked like the goddess she was named after in her silver minidress. But me? In Fat Joe's clothes, Brandi's wig and the borrowed make-up that suited Atalanta's shiny black skin so well, I just looked like a little girl in her mother's lipstick.

'Were you this scared when you started?' I asked.

'The customers were always more frightened of me,' she growled. I could see that. Who wouldn't have been scared by a cross between Oprah Winfrey and the sixty-foot killer Barbie. 'Lizzie, you'll be all right,' she added.

'I'll be hopeless.'

'You'll have a scream!'

And I did. In the American sense of the word, thank goodness.

Atalanta was right, the first night really wasn't that bad. After all, it was a Monday. Never very busy, according to the other 'girls' who were working that night. And I was given the easiest tables to start with. Table six and table eleven, right by the bar and the kitchen door respectively so that I didn't have to carry anything too far in my borrowed high heels. Antonio handpicked my clients for me that night too.

When three old guys who looked like they might have heart attacks if they saw what some of the waitresses looked like beneath their glitzy uniforms turned up, Antonio sent them straight over to me. The old guys looked somewhat bewildered by the whole Ladyboys' experience. They explained that they were only in town for a high school reunion and that they had last been to the club in the fifties. Back then, however, it was a straightforward pool hall and the men who served behind the bar were real men in real men's clothing.

Despite the shock of Ladyboys' transformation to Los Angeles's hottest new deviant nightspot, my first customers decided to stay for the duration. And they were darlings. Polite and easy to get along with. Chivalrous even, to a girl who certainly didn't look like she deserved much chivalry, I thought, when I caught sight of myself looking like the bastard child of Bananarama in the mirrored tiles behind the bar.

I made excuses in advance for my newness to the job but I was surprised to discover that I quickly remembered how to juggle three plates with just two hands and get through the double doors to the kitchen bottom first. I didn't spill any of my customers' drinks and even managed to open a bottle of champagne without having to hand the job over to someone with bigger arm muscles.

When the old guys finished their meal, however, I bent the Ladyboys' rules and handed them the bill rather than tucking it into my cleavage to be retrieved. Which was a good job, since one of the guys told me that I reminded him of his granddaughter when he handed me my tip.

My next table was also surprisingly well-mannered. Antonio sent me a couple of diminutive Japanese business-men who had stumbled into Ladyboys since it was the nearest bar to their airport hotel. Or so they said. I would soon learn that everybody had an excuse for visiting a transvestite bar. No one would admit they were actually interested by what might be inside.

Anyway, the Japanese guys were too small to give me any trouble. Or to take their liquor. Three single shots of whisky had them lolling in their chairs like a pair of drunken schoolboys on their first trip to the pub with false ID. When one of them tried to pinch Atalanta's bum as she sauntered past like Naomi Campbell on her day off, he fell from his chair and lay giggling on the floor for a good ten minutes before he could collect himself enough to get back up again. I couldn't help giggling too as I watched his companion's laughable attempts to haul him back onto his feet. They kept tipping over like a couple of real-life Weebles and saying 'Velly velly solly' for taking the opportunity to look up Atalanta's short skirt. She didn't mind, as long as they kept tucking those dollar bills in her stocking tops.

'You having fun?' she asked me when we passed each other in the kitchen.

'It's not bad,' I was able to confirm after a couple of hours.

It really wasn't.

'Don't think those Japanese guys have got their heads round the currency,' Atalanta commented as she retrieved their tips from her garters. 'First they gave me a single.

Now the really little one's given me a hundred-dollar bill.'

'Are you going to tell him?' I still had to read every banknote myself though every American assured me that it was actually easy to tell the difference between the notes which were all exactly the same size and colour.

'No way,' said Atalanta. 'I'm sure he meant to give me a hundred. Besides, he might make the same mistake when he's tipping you.'

Sadly, he didn't. But at the end of my first night at Ladyboys I did go home with twenty dollars from Antonio and a very respectable fifty-three dollars in tips. Hard cash, the lot. Obviously, I wasn't quite up to Atalanta's private medicine fees standard yet, but I was still pleasantly surprised. In fact, I felt rather proud of myself as I folded my ill-gotten gains into my wallet and took off Brandi's itchy wig. Proud of myself and surprisingly happy. I had survived my first evening as a waitress at Ladyboys. I hadn't dropped any plates. No one had complained. Or been nasty to me. And if I continued to bring home more than sixty bucks a night I would be able to afford to stay in Los Angeles indefinitely. Goodbye Solihull.

Unfortunately, the feeling of triumph I had as Atalanta gave me a lift back to Venice Beach that night was fleeting. My self-confidence took a dive again when I found a letter from England waiting for me on the kitchen table. It was postmarked Solihull.

'Dear Sis,' began the letter from my darling brother Colin. He was the only member of our family who hadn't succumbed to email, despite working in the telecommunications sector. In fact, he was rather proud of the fact that whenever someone asked for his email address, he gave them the number for his fax. Colin still thought that email would go the way of Betamax. To be replaced by what, I often asked him. 'Nuclear-powered carrier pigeons?'

Anyway, at least the fact that he insisted on writing the old-fashioned way and would never call long distance, meant that I had escaped his brotherly haranguings for the best part of a month. I had no doubt that this letter would make up for that though.

'Given up on seeing your name in lights yet?' he asked. 'If you haven't, I thought you might like to read this. It's from the *St Expedite Oracle*. Makes interesting reading, I'm sure you'll agree.'

And he'd attached a newsclipping. If you can count the *St Expedite Oracle* as news. It was the free paper produced four times a year by my parents' local church. As a general rule, it didn't carry anything more controversial than the results of the Sunday School colouring competition or a new and unusual recipe for cake.

But for this particular issue, someone had clearly decided that the *St Expedite Oracle* needed jazzing up with a Ricki Lake-style confessional. 'Local girl encounters *true evil* in Los Angeles' was the headline. It was all about Sandy Smith, who had seemed destined for stardom when she got a part in the church's production of *Annie*, aged twelve. In fact, I remembered her only too well. She had got the part I coveted. The lead role of the marmalade-haired orphan. Everyone knew that I had a far better voice than Sandy Smith but I just didn't have the right hair.

Anyway, to cut a long story short, Sandy went on to play one of the seven wives in the church's smash-hit production of *Seven Brides for Seven Brothers*. Then she came to Los Angeles on holiday. Came to see Disneyland but spent an

afternoon at Universal Studios. Got the Hollywood bug
and thought she'd stay on to see if she could make it as
an actress in Tinseltown. Ended up having to come home
after three weeks working in a cocktail bar with the aid
of an emergency money order from her reverend father,
minister of St Expedite's – the Methodist church of the *St
Expedite Oracle* fame.

'I was only joking when I said we wouldn't send you the
money to come home,' Colin had scribbled on the bottom
of the cutting. 'Call us as soon as you've had enough. Sally
says there's a job going in her office if you're interested.'

I was not.

I screwed the piece of paper into a tiny ball and fired it
at the wastepaper basket.

Had enough? How dare he? There was no doubt in
my mind that Colin had not sent me that clipping out of
brotherly concern and I wanted to be able to ignore it. But
suddenly my new job at Ladyboys didn't seem so great
after all. Was I heading the same way as Sandy Smith? Was
I kidding myself that someone influential would notice my
talents as an actress in this town where everyone from the
haughty maitre d' at the Sky Bar to the street sweeper who
paused on our step for a cigarette every Thursday morning
had once played the lead in his school's production of
Annie, or *Oliver*, or *Joseph's Technicolour* sodding *Dreamcoat*
and fallen for their grandmother's proud pronouncement
that one day they too would see their name in lights. How
long was I prepared to keep leaning on the double-bolted
door to opportunity that wouldn't open for Sandy Smith?

'Sod you, Colin,' I said aloud. 'You will not burst my
bubble. Not yet.'

I was going to keep on leaning.

Colin's rules did not apply to me, I reminded myself. In

Colin-land, everyone had their place in life just as surely as everyone in India knew their place in the Hindu caste system. No one from Solihull had ever become a great actress, he said. Therefore it stood to reason that no one from Solihull ever would. It never ceased to amaze me that Colin, who could expound for hours on why the Royal family were mere parasites on the proletariat and the House of Lords should have been abolished years ago, was at the same time willing to apply such ridiculous arbitrary boundaries to his life. And the lives of those around him.

Let's scrap the class system, he'd say with a mouthful of mashed potato at lunchtime. By evening, through a mouthful of Mum's legendary chocolate cake he would talk about 'people like us' and explain why we lowly Jordans could never hope to be anything more than office slaves. We were born to be mediocre. Photocopier fodder. Escape and be squashed was Colin's motto. In fact, it was your very own people who would be waiting to squash you. There wasn't much point trying to draw his attention to the obvious contradiction in his beliefs. It wore me out to try to explain the theory to him. I would just have to get on with leading by example.

My paper missile had missed the bin. I picked it up again and smoothed it out on the kitchen table to take one last look before I consigned Colin's letter to the trashcan properly. Sandy Smith stared up at me glumly, warning other good daughters of Solihull not to be taken in by Los Angeles's glittering promise. There are devils on every corner, she was quoted as saying. People may even try to lure you into prostitution via what seems like a simple waitressing job. Now she was happy to be working in the parish office once again.

'But I'm not you, Sandy Smith,' I told her. 'I'm not you.'

* * *

Bloody Colin. Despite my best efforts to ignore everything my brother ever said, his letter had left me feeling so weak. And thinking of everything I had run away from. Everything and everyone. Richard.

Richard. Again. Why couldn't I keep him out of my mind for longer than two minutes at a time? I wondered what he was doing back in Tufnell Park. Where he was, it would be almost one o'clock in the afternoon. Would he be in his studio, putting the finishing touches to some masterpiece? Or still in bed? My heart settled heavily in my chest at the thought of the woman he would be sharing that bed with. No, I told myself. He had always leapt out of bed in the mornings.

When he was avoiding you, my heart reminded me. When Richard and I first starting seeing each other we would spend so long in the sack together at every opportunity that it was a wonder we didn't get bed sores. Whole weekends passed with neither of us seeing the sun, only moving from each other's arms to use the loo or open the door to the curry delivery man.

Had he spent every Saturday since our break-up lounging in bed with Jennifer? I wondered. What were their whispered conversations beneath the duvet? Was he eating yogurt off her tum?

Urggh.

How I wished that my brain worked like a computer disk. I wished I could highlight the sorry section marked 'Richard' and click on a box marked 'delete'. The pain wasn't any less, not any less at all, even after a month in the sunshine. Even two months after D (for dumping) Day. Thinking of Richard could still make me want to push away a plate of food untouched, lie down on my bed fully clothed and stare at the ceiling until day became night became day.

Brandi's stupid tarot cards hadn't helped. Allowing myself that brief moment of stupid fantasy that somehow Richard and I would get back together had been like picking a scab. It felt good at the time but like your mother says, picking scabs only leaves bigger scars in the end. I had to put him out of my mind. I had to let all thoughts of a future that included Richard Adams float away from me like a helium-filled balloon. While I tried to hang on to him like this, the string I clung to so desperately was only burning the palm of my hand.

I went to bed (having first evicted a cockroach who thought he had prior claim to my pillow; a cockroach so big this time that he actually had a face), and lay awake in the darkness, staring up at the ceiling fan that didn't work. Overhead, a police helicopter circled the area lazily, the bright beam of its searchlight occasionally illuminating my room like bright daylight. I felt tired. But it wasn't simply that I was tired from a day on my feet, in stilettos, and my first night as waitress at Ladyboys. I felt tired in spirit.

The thing was, this was the first time in my life that I had really attempted to follow my dream alone. Entirely alone. My family didn't think I was doing the right thing – that much was obvious from Colin's latest missive. They wanted me to go back to Solihull, get a proper job, get married, get myself (in their opinion) a happy, *normal* future. My friends – my closest friends Mary and Bill – were more than five thousand miles away and in any case it was hardly fair of me to interrupt their newly-wed bliss with whinging transatlantic phone calls. The biggest, most obvious hole in my life was still that left by the absence of Richard.

Back when I was a disgruntled temp, trying to get into drama school, it was Richard I had turned to whenever achieving my dream started to seem an impossibility. When I came home from the terrible offices where I worked, complaining that life just wasn't fair, that I'd never get a place at drama school because I didn't come from the right family, because I didn't have enough money or know the right people, it was Richard who made the cups of consoling tea and insisted that I continue to write application letters, or at least persevere with the dreadful amateur dramatics group I had joined so that I would have some great set pieces for my auditions. And when I finally did get my place at drama school it was Richard I telephoned first with the fabulous news before I even called my mother. He had champagne on ice when I got home from work that day.

His support had been so valuable to me. Without him I would never have had the courage or persistence to follow my childhood dream.

'That's not true,' he'd said to me at the time. 'I'm just the cheerleader, Lizzie. You had all the resources within you yourself. They would have shown themselves eventually.'

I didn't believe it then and I didn't believe it now. I told him that perhaps I had a fingerful of natural talent but it took having someone believe in me to make me want to get off my butt. My success was one per cent talent and ninety-nine per cent wanting to impress him. Richard was my motivation. Without him, the dream suddenly seemed hollow. Because he was the dream. Everything I had done for the past four years had been for him. For us.

It felt so strange not to have him in my life. I couldn't believe that I didn't know what he was doing in the early hours of that Tuesday morning (Tuesday afternoon for

him). For almost four years I had known what he had
eaten for breakfast every day, what shirt he had worn
to the studio, what television programmes he wanted to
watch when he came home and what he thought of them
when he did.

Now Richard's mind was as closed to me as the mind
of any stranger I passed on the street. I didn't know
what he thought of the new Russian premier. I didn't
know what he thought of the songs that were being played
on the radio now. I didn't know whether he'd given up
smoking. Been to see the dental hygienist? Telephoned his
mother? All the little things that he had once been so happy
to share. I was finding it very hard to swallow the fact that
though he still filled my thoughts all day every day unless
I actively forced him out by humming the theme tune to
Brookside, I was no longer a part of his life. I didn't know
Richard Adams any more.

And he didn't know that right then I was staring at
paint peeling from a ceiling, ignoring the clicking sound
of cockroaches bumping into furniture, still wishing that
Richard would just take me in his arms and rescue me
again. Take me back. Rescue me from my life.

CHAPTER TWELVE

I was pretty miserable that night. Sod it, I was practically suicidal. But it's hard to stay gloomy when the sun shines and next morning, of course, this being California, the sun did shine.

That afternoon Brandi – in best cheerleader fashion – jumped on my bed until I was forced to get out of it and dragged me up to Hollywood to a designer sample sale. I spent all my hard-earned tips on a pair of ankle boots that made me feel like I should have been auditioning for a Duran Duran video circa 1985. When I got them home and put them on in front of a decent mirror, I had to ask Brandi whether she was actually in a bad mood with me for some reason and had coerced me to buy the boots because she thought they made me look a prat.

'Would I do that to you?!' she exclaimed. 'You look a million dollars.'

Well, I must have looked at least a hundred dollars because that is what I earned in tips when I wore the boots that night.

Yes, I had decided that I would stick with the job at Ladyboys. I had given myself a good talking to first though. Pros and cons. And I came to the conclusion that perhaps

Colin did have a point, sending me that cutting about the terrible Sandy Smith. He had only been trying to give me a fair and justifiable warning. Los Angeles was like a pinball machine. If you hit all the right flippers you could make it to the top very quickly indeed. But it only took one wrong flipper to send you out of the game altogether.

Anyone looking at my new life in Los Angeles from the outside would be perfectly justified in thinking that I had taken a wrong turning when I agreed to work for Antonio. But I had convinced myself that I was right to take the job as long as I didn't let it become my career.

I realised that it was possible I sounded like a future junkie after his first crack cocaine cigarette but I told myself that there was nothing wrong with dressing like a prostitute and waitressing for a mobster as a means to an end as long as I noticed when the end was nigh. I would be a good waitress. I would earn big tips and, most importantly, I would put most of the money I made away. And, if I hadn't got myself a decent, bona fide audition within a month, I told myself, then I would use the money I had saved to fund a road trip across the States before heading back to London. You'll notice that I was absolutely determined that I would not go back to Solihull.

'Good for you,' said Fat Joe when I told him my plan. 'You'll get an audition before the end of the month, no problem.'

Four weeks later.

I knew even before I got to work that evening that I wasn't going to have a great night. That morning I had woken up to find that my period had started, explaining why I had been looking like one of Antonio's famous pizzas for the past couple of days. My PMT was not alleviated by the discovery of a cockroach in my boots.

I felt like a fighter pilot getting into his gravity suit as I dressed in my halter-top and cut-off jeans for my Friday night shift at Ladyboys. Friday nights were always the worst night of the week. The busiest and the worst, because the club inevitably filled with office workers keen to let off steam with a crazy night out. They drank like girl rugby players on a hen night in Dublin (that's even more than boy rugby players on a stag night in Dublin, in case you're wondering), shouted abuse that would have made a hardened sailor blush and left tips far more suited to bars in the UK than America when they'd finished. Even Atalanta, who was arguably the most popular ladyboy in Los Angeles, would moan that she could rarely clear a hundred dollars in tips on a Friday night. Even if she danced. Even if she was wearing her specially crafted miniskirted Cleopatra outfit. Even if she offered a free fiddle with her rubber asp for every tequila shot she sold.

On Friday evenings, we would gather around the bar before Antonio opened the doors to his adoring public like an air squadron preparing for battle. We knew that some of us wouldn't live to see another night on the illuminated *Saturday Night Fever*-style dancefloor. Antonio always lost one of his staff on a Friday. A week earlier it had been Frederick/Frederica, who had walked out when an unruly customer tried to insert his tip into a gap in Fred's costume in a very unorthodox manner. I had come to discover that the only way to get through the evening ahead was to dream of the following morning.

Fat Joe was dreaming of the next morning too. He was going to be Joanna Boisvert that night since Sasha Tristelle, who could hold a note and normally did weekends, had

broken her ankle while negotiating the stage in shoes so
high they required planning permission. Fat Joe hated
singing on Friday nights almost as much as the rest of
us hated waitressing. Unlike the polite weekday gang
who would have clapped a burp, the Friday night crowd
thought nothing of telling Joe what his rendition of 'I Know
Him So Well' from *Chess* really sounded like.

'I swear I'll just walk off the stage if anyone so much as
looks as if they're going to boo tonight,' he said.

'We'll get pancakes at IHOP tomorrow morning,' I promised him.

'I shouldn't really,' Joe sighed. 'But I deserve maple
syrup after a Friday night in this place.'

I agreed. The promise of a trip to the nearest branch of the
International House of Pancakes was usually as good as the
promise of dinner at the Ritz for me after a Friday night on
the battle floor. But that night, not even the prospect of big
thick pancakes dripping with sugary goo could cheer me.
Because that night was my fourth Friday night at Ladyboys.
A month had passed. And I hadn't had my audition.

Nothing had happened. Nothing. Not one stinking, soli-
tary call-up. Not even a disinterested 'thanks but no thanks'
to the showreels I had sent out by the dozen. All of Mary's
contacts seemed to have packed up and gone to Lake Tahoe
for the summer. Useless Eunice never returned my calls
when I might actually be awake to receive them. I was no
nearer to achieving my Hollywood dream than I had been
when I first blurted out my plans to Colin.

Gwyneth Paltrow was not shaking in her Winnebago.

Equally, no one had actually asked me to pack up my
dreams and leave the country. I wasn't being hounded out
of town by the people who were really making it already.
But I knew that I had reached my own private deadline

without achieving what had seemed such a simple goal. I had made a promise to myself. I had failed in my objective and I was supposed to get on that Greyhound outta there.

Should I give it another month?

I had wrestled with the justification for that all afternoon. What if I left town that weekend and a casting agent called for me on Monday? What if I met the hottest new director in town at a party on Saturday night?

What if I didn't?

Only that week I had heard a horror story from one of the other girls at work. Her flatmate, a Spanish guy who had come to Los Angeles to act and ended up flipping burgers, had been caught outstaying his visa and sent straight back to Bilbao. He was only a week over the three month time limit but the immigration officials weren't feeling terribly lenient and now it looked as though he would never be able to come back to the States again.

I had been in America for almost two and a half months by now. Should I cut my losses before I got a nasty stamp in my passport too?

I decided I would tell Antonio that it was time for me to leave after the shift that night.

'Ladies, are you ready to sparkle?' Antonio shouted. We plastered on grins. He opened the doors.

And within two minutes of the doors opening, I found myself with three full tables clamouring for attention. Two of the tables, all boys, were relatively well-behaved for a Friday crowd. So well-mannered that I barely noticed the difference between them. But the third, a mixed group of eleven guys and gals, was not quite so easy.

If I had had time to stop and ponder the anthropological

aspect of it that night, it might have interested me that the boys on the mixed table were so badly behaved precisely because they were in the company of women. So much for toning down their behaviour for the gentler sex. In fact, I thought the girls might have been egging their male friends on, encouraging them to lift the skirts of passing waitresses to see if they lived up to the bar's title. It was as though being in a mixed group gave the men an excuse to touch the transvestites. They obviously weren't harbouring gay tendencies if they were acting on the behest of a lady.

Not that there were any *ladies* on my third table that night.

There was an obvious ringleader though. A carrot-topped twit with an impressively rounded belly. He was dressed in a shirt that was slightly too small for him, though it obviously wasn't because he couldn't afford a better-fitting one. He had been thrusting fifty-dollar bills in my face all night. Only to pay with a twenty and pocket all the change when I actually brought the cocktails he ordered over.

As the night progressed, it was getting increasingly difficult for me to continue to smile at his sweaty, smarmy face. I got Fat Joe, who was working behind the bar between singing spots that evening, to start making the mixed table's cocktails weaker and weaker. One of the girls in the party was sitting on Gingernut's knee by this point. He had one hand up her skirt. In the other he held a fat cigar and used it to make suggestive gestures at the passing waitresses. The girl on his knee giggled as he cast aspersions on the true orientation of Atalanta.

'She could have you for breakfast,' said Carrot-top's girlfriend. And she was probably right. Though I knew Atalanta would actually have preferred something more low-fat.

Customers like the ginger guy were a mystery to me. I didn't understand why they came to a transvestite bar only to spend the evening shrieking with faux horror every time one of the waitresses came near. He was the kind of guy who would have gone to an execution, I decided. Perhaps years of being teased for his own red hair had left him feeling bitter and eager to take out his rage on the rest of society's misfits. He was a bully. That much was obvious. All the other guests at his table were there simply to laugh at his jokes. He held court. He set the tone for the evening. The others merely followed.

I was standing at the bar, sneaking a drag on one of Atalanta's menthol cigarettes and watching Fat Joe murder 'Feelings', when the ginger one summoned me. 'Hey, Limey!' he said. He thought that was hilarious. Limey. 'Come over here.'

I stubbed out my fag and obliged. I hated menthol fags in any case. I walked over to Ginger's table with my 'happy to be of service' smile. One of the biggest ever tests of my acting ability was continuing to be nice to some of the customers at Ladyboys long after they had drained me of the milk of human kindness. 'What can I do for you now?' I asked.

'Me and my friend here have been having a bit of a wager. And only you can tell us who's won.'

'How can I do that?' I said innocently, expecting them to ask me to confirm where I was from. Only the night before, a rather charming grey-haired ship-broker and his banker friend had made a bet on whether I was from England or Australia.

'Just stand still,' said Ginger, pushing his sozzled girl-friend from his lap and beckoning me to stand in front of him. 'Right there. That's right. This'll settle it.' Whereupon he grabbed both my breasts and honked them like they were the bulbs on an old-fashioned car horn.

'What? Shit! She's a real one!' he exclaimed for the benefit of his friends.

For a moment, for a very short moment, I was paralysed with indignation. My sunny smile disappeared immediately. I felt my entire body stiffen with anger. As the blood raced to my cheeks, I quite literally saw red. And then, in complete contravention of Antonio's 'the customer is always right' policy, under which we girls were categorically not allowed to retaliate to such slights in the confines of the club (we were supposed to act like ladies at all times, discreetly report the matter to the duty manager and Antonio would have one of his henchmen follow the arsehole out into the car park later), I leaned over and grabbed Ginger by the balls, squeezing them until I was certain that he would have no one to leave his estate to but the local dogs' home.

'How do you like that?' I asked him as I ground his testicles beneath my fist. 'Where I come from,' I spluttered, 'men do not grab a woman by the tits unless they've already bought her dinner. Even then they need to ask first. You need to learn some manners.'

I carried on ranting and squeezing until Ginger's initial shriek of horror had subsided to a whimper. And until Atalanta wrestled me off.

'Lizzie!' Atalanta was so horrified that she had reverted to her best Southern belle accent. Despite the fact she was from Compton.

The club was silent. The money had run out in the jukebox. Fat Joe stopped singing along to Barbra Streisand. Angelica – a blonde waitress who used to work as a mechanic and be called Tommy – stopped gyrating around the pole. Two hundred pairs of frightened male eyes (and several female ones, for that matter) watched me warily, as though I was about to start on a rampage of castration with my handy 'Waiter's friend' bottle opener. Ginger slid from his chair and lay shaking on the floor, like the spineless creature he was. Even Fat Joe, my friend and flatmate, stepped backwards uneasily when I turned to appeal to him for support as I justified my actions.

'You all saw what he did to me!' I shouted.

Antonio, alerted to the debacle by the closed circuit monitor in his office, was already striding across the club towards me.

'Shit,' I murmured.

I had broken the golden rule. And knowing my luck, I had probably broken it over the balls of the only ginger-haired man in the mafia. My concrete boots awaited, I was certain. I consoled myself with the fact that I had been intending to hand my notice in that night anyway.

But when Antonio finally reached me, I was surprised and relieved to discover that he had nothing but disdain for the redhead in his eyes. He stepped over the prostrate body of my tormentor and glowered down on him like a victorious gladiator.

'Get up,' he said, jabbing Ginger in the side with his pointed Chelsea boot. 'And apologise to my waitress.'

'She grabbed me by the balls, man,' Ginger protested as he hauled himself onto his elbows.

'After you had manhandled her magnificent chest,' said Antonio. 'I saw everything from my office. We don't behave like that here in Ladyboys. My ladies are real ladies. You should learn to behave like a real gentleman.'

'Hear, hear,' said Atalanta, beginning a little ripple of

applause. It was a ripple that soon petered out in the unresolved tension.

'I don't need your kind of customer in my club,' Antonio continued. 'You come in here and flash your money and think that you can buy everything you want. Well, I'm here to tell you that the dignity of my staff is beyond anything you have in your wallet. And you're not going to be paying for their services with dollar bills tonight.'

Antonio took Ginger roughly by the collar and marched him in the direction of the kitchen door. Just before they disappeared, he turned to the rest of his customers. 'I want you all to see how Antonio takes care of people who don't respect his ladies.'

The swing doors opened and closed behind them. There was a crash of pans. A collective gasp. No one moved as we waited for what seemed like the inevitable. All the waitresses knew that Antonio's gigantic henchman Fabrizio was in the kitchen tasting the pasta – he'd tasted so much pasta in his time that he made Arnie look positively weedy. Fabrizio certainly needed some exercise but surely Antonio wasn't going to have a customer beaten up within earshot of the restaurant on Ladyboys' busiest night of the week?

I held my breath and prayed. Much as I had wanted the ginger prat to get his comeuppance, I didn't want to have to defend Antonio's actions in court. It wasn't that serious. I hadn't actually been injured. Perhaps he'd get away with an ear tweak, I hoped. A verbal warning. A nasty threat.

Suddenly, the swing doors to the kitchen burst open again and Ginger flew back out into the main room of the club and onto his knees. His sweaty sports jacket had gone and instead he was wearing an apron. In his right hand he carried a dish-mop. Antonio strode out after him and stood over him, one foot on Ginger's fat shaking buttocks.

'He says he is very sorry to you all,' said Antonio to his ladies. 'And he says he can only make it up to you by doing your share of the clearing up.'

And he did. Ginger spent the rest of that evening in the kitchen. He periodically threatened to leave the club and sue but a look from Fabrizio soon changed his mind. His friends, with the exception of one other guy and Ginger's not-quite-so-cocky-any-more girlfriend, all left at the start of Ginger's humiliation. Running.

Only when the last pot had been scrubbed was Ginger allowed to take the apron off. He stormed from the club with his bald pal and girlfriend trotting beside him like a pair of little terriers. He didn't have a backward glance for me or my fellow waitresses.

'See you again soon!' Antonio shouted after his latest washer-upper. We all knew that there was no need for Antonio to ban the Ginger peril from the premises. He wouldn't be coming back.

'I'm really sorry about him,' the girlfriend muttered to Antonio as she too slipped out the door. 'He was drunk. He's not usually like that.'

'Yeah, yeah,' said Antonio with a dismissive wave. 'You want to get some better friends. You all right now, Lizzie?' he asked me, slipping an arm around my shoulder.

I nodded.

'Didn't I tell you I treat my girls like family?' he reminded us all. 'You stick with your Uncle Antonio, you always be all right.'

If a little knackered, I sighed to myself.

'Double pay next Friday for you,' he added cheerfully with a pinch to my drained white cheeks.

No. I shook my head. Not even double pay could tempt me back into my Madonna boob tube and Duran Duran shoes now. I'd done my last Friday night at Ladyboys. Ginger and his loathsome friends were just the final straw. I hated working in that club. I wasn't getting anywhere in Hollywood. I was going home to England. At least I was unlikely to get touched up by drunken strangers while working as a filing clerk.

'Antonio,' I began. 'There's something I've got to say to you.'

'You're not pregnant, are you?' he asked immediately. 'I can't let you work here if you're pregnant.'

'No,' I sighed. Pregnant? Chance would be a fine thing. Unless you could get pregnant from sharing hotpants with a transvestite. 'I'm not having a baby,' I told Antonio. 'But I do think that the time has come for me . . .'

'Lizzie!' Atalanta interrupted. She was racing across the restaurant towards us with a business card clutched in her hand. 'Lizzie, look!'

'You've got a fan,' said Antonio, taking Atalanta's timely appearance as his cue to slip back into his office before I could tell him that I wanted to quit.

'Lizzie, this is fabulous,' Atalanta threw her arm around my shoulders and gave me a tremendous hug. 'Will you just look at this card?'

'Where did you find it?'

'On Ginger's table.'

I gave a big sigh. 'Does he want me to send flowers to the hospital?'

I was used to men leaving their cards on the table for me when they left the club at the end of the night. All the girls

had at least a couple by the end of any evening. When I
started waitressing, Atalanta suggested adopting the same
approach as an air hostess friend of hers. If someone in
first class gave the stewardess his card she would call.
If he gave her a card in business class, she would call if
she really fancied him. If someone in economy class gave
her his card, she might get one of her friends to ring and
tell the poor sucker's wife that she was calling from the
STD clinic.

Of course, the club wasn't divided into classes. But
Atalanta had invented a class system of her own, based on
the champagne that the table had bought. There were three
types of champagne in the house, ranging from vintage
Bollinger to a supermarket brand that Antonio had tarted
up with his very own Ladyboys' labels.

Sometimes on an evening off, Atalanta would invite
us round to watch *Thelma and Louise* on DVD, give each
other manicures and ruin the lives of the silly sweaty
businessmen who ordered Ladyboys' own, tipped small
and still dared to leave the Amazon goddess of waitresses
their cards at the end of the evening.

That night, I had hardly had what I would call a 'first
class table' and I wasn't impressed by the idea that one of
Ginger's nasty mates thought he could add insult to my
injuries by suggesting we went on a date.

I was all ready to screw the card up when Atalanta
handed it over to me, but she snatched it back before I
was able.

'No you don't!' she shouted.

'I don't want to ring any man who hangs out with that
scumbag,' I warned her.

'Oh, I think you might want to ring this one,' she said.

I took the card back.

'It's certainly a nice one,' I admitted, feeling the thickness of the card. 'And very stylish.' It was pure white and embossed rather than printed so that it looked as though the card was blank in the wrong light. In the right light, I could see that it said 'Eric Nordhoff' above a telephone number. A number with a 310 area code. The Los Angeles equivalent of 0207 and shorthand for respectable if not downright posh.

'Look on the back,' Atalanta said excitedly.

I flipped the card over. On the back of the card, Eric Nordhoff had written, in very beautiful handwriting and using a real ink pen instead of a biro, 'A feisty performance this evening – please call me about your career.'

'Oh jeez,' I groaned. 'Do you think he wants me to play dominatrix at some Beverly Hills party?'

'Lizzie!' Atalanta squealed. 'Don't you recognise that name?'

'I don't think so. Is he an actor?'

'No way. Actors don't want you to call them to talk about your career. They want you to call them and listen about theirs.'

'In that case, I have no idea.'

'You know, I thought it was him when he sat down. But there are so many guys in Hollywood who look like that. And so I danced round the pole like a total clutz and you end up with his card. Life is so unfair.'

'What do you mean? Who is he?' I asked in exasperation.

Angelica and Fat Joe had joined us.

'It's in here,' Angelica said. She delved into her bag and came out with a copy of *Hollywood Report*, the bible of Tinseltown aspirants. She flicked through the pages frantically until she found what she was looking for. Then she opened the mag out on the bar in front of me and pointed triumphantly at a small blurry photograph of someone I did indeed recognise as the man who had waited for Ginger that night.

'Oh,' I said. He wasn't exactly the most gorgeous man who had left his card for me since I started my job. 'Not only does he have bad taste in friends, he looks exactly like a toad. Do you still think I should call him?'

'Honey,' said Atalanta rolling her eyes. 'Read what it says! I think you should go round and camp on his door-step right now. This man is the hottest new director in Hollywood. According to Madonna!'

'And we all know how discerning Madonna is when it comes to choosing challenging film roles,' said Fat Joe.

'Who cares if it's challenging or not,' screamed Atalanta. 'So long as it gets you on celluloid. This is it, Lizzie. This is your break.' She brandished the card at me. 'Eric Nordhoff wants to talk about your career. You're going to be a superstar!'

I just sat there feeling slightly bewildered. Like someone who's won the lottery and discovered that the jackpot was in fact six billion pounds instead of the expected piddling two mil. But who was Eric Nordhoff? I still hadn't heard of him.

Atalanta called the other girls around to stare at the card and congratulate me with a mixture of genuine warmth and not a little envy. When she passed the news on to Antonio, he even let us crack open a bottle of Ladyboys' own champagne.

'He's only asked me to call him,' I protested.

'That is just the start,' said Atalanta. She grabbed my hands and looked at me earnestly. 'I had a feeling when I came to work this evening that something wonderful was about to happen.'

'I got into a fight.'

'Which got you noticed,' Atalanta reminded me. 'You know I'm psychic, don't you?'

'Isn't everybody in this town.'

'You better not forget me when you're famous,' Atalanta ignored me. 'I tell you, Lizzie Jordan, this is the start of something huge.'

'Huge. Right,' I nodded. The only huge thing I had that night was a headache.

Though Eric Nordhoff was Madonna's tip for the top that year, he didn't exactly have a big back catalogue of work for me to watch. That Saturday afternoon, Brandi and I hired and sat through his first and only short film, which was called *The Ladies' Room*, hoping to see the genius. Instead, we got bored and began to wonder whether Madonna and Atalanta were just being fashionably ironic when they feted the balding auteur who had written a play during which one of the characters sits sobbing in a toilet cubicle for half an hour. And that's all that happens.

I was about to write the bloke off altogether (bad friends, bad face *and* a bad film) when Fat Joe, who had been flicking through an industry magazine during the boring bits of *Ladies' Room* (about forty-five minutes of the total fifty) suddenly announced excitedly, 'He's casting for an adaptation of *Northanger Abbey*. He's got funding to the eyeballs. Gwyneth Paltrow and Renee Zelwegger are up for the lead role! But he wants someone really English. That's why he wants you, Lizzie. He heard you talking in the club.'

'*Northanger Abbey*?' At least I'd heard of that. Brandi and I borrowed Fat Joe's car and drove straight to Borders bookshop to grab a copy.

* * *

I sent some very excited emails that evening. First to Mary. If anyone could confirm whether Eric Nordhoff was worth impressing, it would be her.

'Bloody amazing!' came her reply on Sunday morning. 'I've been trying to see him for weeks!'

I had to call her when I got that message. Even got her out of bed. I might have expected her to be grumpy but Mary was only too keen to hear how I had come to meet the man she had been chasing round the film festivals from Cannes to Montreal.

'He saw nobody in London but Sadie and Jude,' she said incredulously.

'But he hasn't made any films apart from that terrible one about the ladies' loos.'

'You mean the terrible one that was nominated for the Palme D'Or?' Mary drawled sarcastically. 'Lizzie, that film was hailed as groundbreaking by Stephen Soderbergh. Madonna wants to reshoot it so she can play "sobbing girl". I can't believe he wants to see you,' she said. With just a little too much stress on the last word.

'Why wouldn't he want to see me?' I snapped.

'Oh, darling, I wasn't casting aspersions on your acting ability,' she backtracked. 'It's just that you're hardly well known, are you? I have to admit I'm a little bemused. Perhaps he's after nobodies so they won't detract from the genius of his direction,' she thought out loud.

'Well, I won't be a nobody for long,' I said angrily. 'Perhaps then you'd consider representing me in London yourself instead of palming me off on Useless Eunice.'

'Lizzie,' Mary sighed. 'You know I would have jumped at the chance to represent you. It's just that I didn't think it was a good idea to dirty our hands with business given that we're such old friends. We might have fallen out.'

'Nice excuse,' I retorted. We were well on our way to falling out anyway.

'I'd be happy to look over any contract you negotiate with Eric though,' she tried.

'Doing anything exciting this week?' I asked to steer the conversation back into less touchy waters.

'Not much. Got a meeting with the casting agent for the new Bond film. Premiere for some piece of subtitled shit on Tuesday. Some sort of art award thing on Thursday.'

'Art award?' my ears pricked up. 'What art award?'

'The Lister Badlands Awards.' Mary's voice tailed off guiltily.

'Oh, those awards. Did he?' was all I had to say.

Richard had been shortlisted for the Lister Badlands prize just a couple of weeks before we split up.

'You know, I haven't even had time to look at the pro-gramme,' said Mary breezily.

'Don't lie,' I told her. 'Just tell me if he's going to be there.'

'He is,' said Mary flatly. 'But I promise I won't talk to him and if he does win I certainly won't clap. You know I wouldn't even go to the bloody thing at all but the fiancée of one of my biggest clients is also nominated and if I don't show willing . . .'

'I understand,' I said quietly. 'Besides, if you do talk to him – and even though you are my best friend, you are excused if you find yourself in a position where it would be rude not to – you can tell him that I'm now in demand by some of the hottest directors in town.'

'Attagirl,' said Mary. I could hear the relief in her voice. 'You know, I'm so pleased to hear you react like that at last. Because we were all so afraid that you'd never get over him. Especially with the way you were carrying on before you decided to go to Los Angeles. I honestly thought you'd lost it, Lizzie. All the weight you dropped before the wedding and the drunkenness and refusing to get out of bed. I shouldn't really tell you this, but Eunice was actually considering letting you go.'

'You mean that pathetic woman who hasn't got me a job in the eighteen months I've been signed to her was going to drop *me*? Damn right you shouldn't have told me,' I said coldly. 'Well, you can tell her that she needn't expect her ten per cent when my contract with Eric Nordhoff is drawn up. Mary, you're supposed to be my best friend. Shouldn't you be more understanding?'

'Best friends are supposed to tell each other the truth, aren't they?'

'Only if the pain it causes is less than the pain it averts.'

'I'm sorry. Look, just ace that audition, will you? I know you've got it in you. Haven't I always said so?'

'Mmmm,' I grumbled.

'And if you could mention to Mr Nordhoff that Mary Bagshot would be happy to take him for lunch any time he's in town,' she wheedled, 'I'll send you the pair of Gucci mules that have just arrived at my office.'

'Only because they're not your size,' I sniffed.

'No, because they'd be perfect for you.'

'Who were they meant for?' I asked.

'Gina Harrison,' said Mary. Gina was an up and coming soap star. She had joined the *EastEnders* cast as a regular extra and now she had been promoted to the part of Ian Beale's latest girlfriend. 'Overheard her in the Groucho loos, telling some other slag that she's thinking of moving to ICM. After everything I've done for her. She'll think differently about deserting me when she hears I'm lunching with Eric Nordhoff.'

'Only if I agree to tell him you want to.'

'I'll FedEx the shoes in the morning.'

'You're on. But only if you also promise to set fire to Jennifer's hair if you see her at those art awards.'

'Consider it done. I'll take my Tiffany lighter. Break a leg, sweetheart.'

We air-kissed goodbye.

'I'll break your bloody legs,' I hissed into the dead receiver.

So, my best friend thought it was time I was over the love of my life. And my agent too! How sodding treacherous! Weren't they supposed to be the people who supported me? Instead, my excitement at getting that eleventh-hour audition had been all but squashed by the reminder that Richard had been nominated for the art awards. If Mary really loved me, she would have lied about going to the party. That's what I would have done.

I was still bristling with an uncomfortable mixture of pain and anger when Brandi walked in and caught me staring at the phone.

'What did your friend Mary say?' she asked me. 'Is it bad news?'

'Very. She says Richard's been nominated for the art awards.'

Brandi cocked her head to one side. 'What?'

'Richard's going to win that sodding award and then he'll be really big and he'll never come back to me.'

'Lizzie,' said Brandi. 'What are you going on about?

What about Eric Nordhoff? What did she say about Eric Nordhoff?'

'Oh, him,' I said dismissively. 'Only that he's the biggest director in the world right now and she's been trying to get a meeting with him for the past six months.'

'Then what are you sitting there looking like your cat just died for? Call him at once.'

'What's the point?' I asked.

'Whaddya mean, what's the point?'

'There's no point in my doing anything. It's not going to make Richard want me back.'

Uh-oh. I had no idea that my sympathy engine was running on red.

When I arrived in Los Angeles, thinking that my eyes would be permanently pink from the crying that I'd done over the month since Richard dumped me, Brandi had quickly taken it upon herself to step into Mary's shoes and console me. We spent long evenings in the beach house, bonding over tales of woe. She agreed with me that I couldn't have seen the break-up coming. Our relationship was almost perfect. He'd made a mistake to let me go.

'I'll always be here to talk,' she said.

But it seemed that *always* suddenly had a sell-by date.

Brandi's patient smile had hardened.

'Richard, Richard, Richard,' she groaned.

If I thought that Mary had just been tough with me, I was about to meet a girl who was made of pure diamond.

'You know what, Lizzie? That's all we fucking hear from you some days.'

'What?'

The force of Brandi's sudden invective shocked me.

'Now you've got a meeting with the hottest director in town and all you can think about is what your stupid ex is doing back in London. Well, fuck him. It's time to get over it and get a life. Joe and I have tried to be patient but you're not the first girl in the world to get dumped and you won't be the last. Frankly, this self-pity is getting pretty tired.'

My jaw hit the floor.

'He was the love of my life,' I said pathetically.

'Right. *Was* being the operative word. He's part of your past. You've got to move forward.'

'Like Fat Joe has?' I spat then. 'By wearing a dress?'

'Don't judge him by the clothes he wears,' said Brandi.

'Well, don't you judge me by my . . . my . . .'

'Whinging?' Brandi suggested. 'By your moaning? By the way you drift around this house like you were Richard Burton and Liz Taylor and there'll never be another love like it in the history of the world?'

'I . . .'

'Like you were soul mates?' Brandi cupped her hand to her heart and mugged a heartbreak face. 'Like no one else understands you? Like nobody else will ever touch you the way only Richard Adams can? Your life is worthless without him! Utterly worthless!'

She fluttered down onto the futon like a Brontë heroine bereft.

'My name is Lizzie Jordan,' she squeaked in her Dick van Dyke accent. 'My life has no meaning any more.'

'I'm not that bad,' I told her sharply.

'Oh, you are,' she reassured me. 'And it's time you gave it up.'

'How dare you? It's not that easy!'

Brandi sighed. 'It is that easy. You can choose when you get a new life. There's no mourning period. No one's going to care if you don't spend half of each day crying – in fact, Joe and I would prefer it if you quit with the waterworks now. You're not doing some kind of penance, Lizzie. You can get over this in ten minutes. Or you can mope for the rest of your life.'

'You never even met Richard,' I said petulantly.

'I feel like I know him as well as his mother.' She made little yapping puppet mouths out of both her hands. 'Richard! Oh Richard! Ya-dah, ya-dah, ya-dah.'

'Oh fuck off,' I told her eloquently.

But she warned me, 'I will not. Before you came here, Joe told me what you were like when he knew you in London. I was looking forward to meeting this legendary girl. He said you were feisty and bright and opinionated. The girl I met is as feisty as a jellyfish with no opinion on anything that doesn't relate to her or her ex-boyfriend. You know what your problem is?' she asked me.

'I'm sure you're going to tell me.'

'Your problem is that you defined yourself by your boyfriend in exactly the same way Joe was defined by his pants. They might have fitted. But were they comfortable?'

'You can't compare my relationship to Fat Joe's pants,' I spat at her.

'Will you stop calling him that? He isn't fat.'

'He was when I met him.'

'But he isn't fat now. And that's your other problem. Don't you see what a dickbrain you're being by continuing to define him that way?'

'It's affectionate,' I protested.

'How affectionate is it to insist on dragging up his past when he's made an effort to get away from it? You're not acknowledging the real person he's become. Just like you're not prepared to acknowledge the real you.'

'I don't need you to tell me who I am,' I insisted.

'You want to know who you say you are? You're Richard Adams' ex-girlfriend. You're the girl who came to Los Angeles to run away from the pain that Richard Adams caused you. You're the girl whose only concern when anything happens is how Richard Adams might react. Do you think Richard Adams introduces himself as the man who broke Lizzie Jordan? Do you think he mentions you at all?

'Your Fat Joe was brave enough to ditch a past that hurt him and in doing so he found a group of people who accepted him for who he really is. So he wears dresses? Is that a problem? He realised that there are no rules except the ones we make for ourselves.'

'And your point?' I asked sarcastically.

'Being Richard's girlfriend was your trousers, Lizzie. Without Richard, you don't feel the same. You feel like everyone is laughing and pointing at you but the fact is no one cares. The only person affected when you grieve over that man is you. You're not a lesser person without him. But what if you weren't being yourself when you were together? What if there were things you didn't do because of him? Would you have come to Los Angeles?' she asked.

I shrugged.

'You wouldn't. You wouldn't have had the guts. You'd have carried on temping till Useless Eunice got you an ad. And judging by her track record, she wouldn't have got you so much as a voiceover for a panty-liner commercial. Richard would have got successful with or without you. He would have left you behind.'

I wanted to refute Brandi's bleak view of my future but . . .

'Richard didn't compromise. London's where the art

world's at. But you need to be in Los Angeles. Don't let him hold you back now. He doesn't know he's still doing it and he certainly doesn't care. But we do. Joe and I are your friends.'

'Then why don't you try to be more understanding?'

'You're making excuses in the face of a fabulous chance.' Brandi picked up the telephone and handed it to me.

'Ten minutes,' she said again. 'Ten seconds, in fact, to dial that number and do something for you instead of Richard. And me,' she added a little sheepishly. 'You could drop my showreel off . . .'

'Like I owe you a favour,' I snapped.

'Whatever you want,' Brandi sighed. 'If you want to be an asshole, it's your loss.'

I went to my bedroom to lick my wounds. My face stung with the humiliation of Brandi's tirade, coming as it did on the back of Mary's revelation that she thought I'd lost it and the fact that the most pointless agent on the planet didn't think I was a good enough client for her poxy little firm.

On the inside, I was a woman thrice wronged. Four times, if you went back to the original wrong and counted Richard dumping me. In my mind, I was still the sensitive, delicate being who had given everything in love and received the emotional equivalent of a Glasgow kiss in return. I deserved to be comforted. Constantly, if I still needed it. I am 'hurt' personified, I thought.

I looked at myself in the dressing table mirror; my eyes downcast and ringed by dark circles, my hair falling over my face like a curtain to cover the pain. If I squinted a little I could almost have been Diana. Brave Princess Diana, just as wronged in love as I had been. As misunderstood. As maligned.

I looked just like her when she did that *Panorama* interview. Heartbroken. Sensitive. Tragic.

And just a little bit annoying, perhaps . . .

I sat up and looked about me, waiting for the thunderbolt to strike. It was then that I realised that I had already been struck. I *was* like Diana in the *Panorama* days. But that wasn't necessarily a good thing.

Diana thought that by sharing her pain with the nation she could persuade them to love her more. What she didn't know was that much of the nation thought it was time to put on a brave face.

My face was far from brave that afternoon. Eye rings. A permanent crease in my cheeks from a frown held far too long. Two deep furrows between my brows where they knitted together in pain. But I didn't look like the Lady of Shalott, abandoned and beautifully pitiful. I looked instead like Lady Macbeth. Mad, obsessed, deranged. The kind of girl who could bore you stiff as cardboard with her tales of woe. That was the reason why Brandi was fed up of me. And it probably also explained why Hollywood hadn't snapped me up.

In a moment, I understood that tragic princess so well. She was a wonderful person. People loved her. But if you break your leg, sooner or later the doctor is going to make you try to walk on it. Brandi was doing the same for my broken heart.

Eric Nordhoff's card suddenly looked like the number for the Samaritans.

First, I had to apologise to Brandi. Then I had to call Eric.

CHAPTER THIRTEEN

Brandi was only too keen to make friends. She stood next to me while I dialled Eric's number. But I didn't get through to Eric Nordhoff himself. Instead, I was connected to a very nice young man called Jan who promised that he would pass on my message.

'He'll never call back,' I decided. 'He's forgotten he even left that card.'

But half an hour later, Jan phoned back to say that Mr Nordhoff wanted to see me as soon as humanly possible. Would I be available for breakfast at six-thirty?

'Six-thirty?' I mouthed. 'In the morning?'

'For breakfast, that's right.'

I hesitated. Since I started at Ladyboys, six-thirty had become my bed time. I didn't do breakfast any more. Afternoon tea was my breakfast. But Brandi was giving me a furious thumbs-up from the other side of the kitchen.

'Breakfast is a good slot,' said Brandi when the meeting had been set. 'Not quite as good as lunch but better than three o'clock in the afternoon when you'll get half an hour and a cup of tea.'

'I see. It's still a bit bloody early.'

'Quit whining,' said Brandi.

I looked suitably contrite.

'This is a great sign,' Brandi assured me. 'Wanting to see

you so quickly and giving you an actual meal slot. That's serious. Only don't try to eat. The last thing you want is a mouth full of bran muffin when he wants you to impress him. Did Joe ever tell you about the time he coughed up a mouthful of Kettle chips over Steven Spielberg at the Sky Bar?'

I shook my head.

'Well, if he hasn't, best not ask him. I know he's still a little sore about that. So, whatever you do tomorrow, don't actually eat anything. If he offers you an alcoholic drink, you definitely shouldn't take one in case he thinks you're a lush. Not even if he's having one himself. Likewise cigarettes. Not even if you're desperate. It's probably a test. But if he asks you why you don't want anything to eat, say you had a big breakfast on your way to meet him. Being an anorexic looks even worse than spitting chewed-up food onto his jacket.'

'I'll remember that.'

There was so much I needed to learn about Hollywood.

'And no coffee,' Brandi added as a final note. 'Makes your breath stink. Not a good thing.'

'No. Not at all. Thanks for warning me.'

'One more thing.' A postscript. 'If he asks you what brought you to Hollywood, don't say you came here to get over your boyfriend. It's cute when you tell your girlfriends. When you tell him it makes you a . . .'

She didn't even need to say the word. Just made the 'L' sign with her fingers.

'Win! Win! Win!' she sang, cheerleader fashion, as she headed off for some beauty sleep. Sunday nights were a big night in Brandi's campaign of essential maintenance. If Joe and I didn't get in the bathroom before eight on a Sunday evening, we wouldn't get in there until Monday morning.

* * *

I retired to bed with Ms Austen. *Northanger Abbey* had been one of the books I studied for my degree but I couldn't for the life of me remember what happened inside its covers. I don't think I ever actually read the whole book while I was at college. I just crammed critics' notes and read ideal answers to questions on past papers. But that night I crammed with even more determination than I had shown a week before my finals. Eric Nordhoff wanted to see me for breakfast the next morning. My big break might depend on this mad bit of last-minute revision.

It wasn't as though I was going to be able to get much sleep in any case. If I wasn't cramming Austen, then something else would be cramming its way into my mind. Richard Adams. I was still sore from Brandi's ticking off and determined that I would try harder to put him behind me and yet . . .

When I got to Chapter Eight, I must have nodded off. And suddenly I was at the Lister Badlands Art Awards. I was walking into the Serpentine Gallery, weaving my way through crowds of elegant art-lovers in black tie and ballgowns made of anything but silk. I didn't recognise their faces but, as I passed, they stared at me with what seemed like recognition. As I neared the stage where the awards were being presented, the crowds were parting to let me go by.

I looked down at my body. It's about this time in a dream when you discover that you're actually buck-naked. But I was dressed. I was wearing a pretty respectable black dress, in fact.

It wasn't me who was naked at all.

'Presenting Richard Adams!'

The crowd erupted into applause. I elbowed my way
through the last line of spectators to see what was eliciting
such devotion. And then I saw him. Richard. He was the
naked one. On stage with Jennifer. Naked too but for the
diamond ring on her engagement finger. Richard pulled
her close and kissed her.

'Is this what they call an installation?' asked a woman
to my left.

I ran from the gallery, blinded by my own tears, only
to wake on my bed in Venice Beach feeling hot and sick
and decidedly hollow. *Northanger Abbey* had fallen from
my hands to the floor.

I picked the book up again mechanically but it was quite
a while before my heart stopped hammering in my chest. I
read five pages before I realised that it wasn't making any
sense because I had accidentally skipped a chapter.

It was just a dream. A stupid dream that was clearly born
of my conversation with Mary and Brandi's telling off and
my anxiety about the audition. Yet I felt as though I had
really seen Richard and Jennifer making love. I felt freshly
betrayed.

I thought I would lie awake the whole night, tormented
by the vision that had come only from my own mind. But
I must have fallen asleep again, because at five-thirty in
the morning, I woke unshakeably convinced that I had
somehow got on a bus from Venice Beach to Muswell Hill
and not to Malibu, which was where Eric Nordhoff had
his house.

What to wear to my first Hollywood audition. Luckily,
Brandi was on hand to provide yet more insider advice.
She had a theory about auditions which she had already

touched upon when I went to ask for a job at Ladyboys. The trick was to go along 'as if'.

'You've got to turn up at the audition as though it's actually the first day of rehearsals,' she told me. 'You've got to go into that audition with the mindset that the part is already yours.'

Costume was a big part of the 'as if' agenda. To get a job at Ladyboys, that meant dressing like Madonna during her 'Like a virgin' phase. That is to say, not very much like a virgin at all. To get the lead role in *Northanger Abbey*, Brandi pronounced, 'You gotta look like you were in that other movie. That *Emma* one.'

'You mean the one with Gwyneth Paltrow?' Fat Joe dared to ask.

But how did I dress in order to subtly remind Eric Nordhoff of Gwyneth Paltrow's performance in *Emma* and suggest that I could knock her and her mono-expression acting into a hat if he gave me the lead in *Northanger Abbey*.

'Wear this,' Brandi instructed.

Which is how I came to be standing outside Eric Nordhoff's house in Malibu at six-thirty in the morning wearing a white cotton Victorian-style nightdress, with my hair set in ringlets (I didn't notice that I had forgotten to take out one of the curlers until long after lunchtime) and a pair of Brandi's yoga slippers on my feet.

'Wow,' said Eric Nordhoff when he saw me. 'I didn't mean to drag you straight out of bed.'

'It's the Austen look,' I said, hopefully.

'Right. I thought it was a nightgown. It's . . . er . . . nice.'

I looked so nice that you'd have trusted me with your sheep.

'My room-mate's very into fashion,' I blundered on. 'This look will be all the rage next season.'

'Well, I don't know much about fashion,' said Eric Nordhoff kindly. 'So I'll have to take your word for it.'

'Nightwear as daywear,' I continued pathetically. 'Pyjama bottoms are the new black.'

Eric just nodded.

'Well, you'd better come in.' He waved me across the front step of his house into the hallway.

I followed meekly. Little Bo Peep-style meekly. Pyjamas are the new black? My internal Homer Simpson was already screaming, 'D'oh, d'oh, d'oh.' But at least he hadn't sent me away.

From the outside, Eric Nordhoff's place had been pretty unprepossessing. A big wall covered in fading bougainvillea hid his house from the tourists who chugged slowly up the Pacific Coast Highway in their hire cars hoping to catch Tom Hanks tending his herbaceous borders or Michelle Pfeiffer putting out her rubbish. Fact was, you couldn't actually see much of any of the exclusive Malibu estates from the road at all. Inconspicuous consumption were the key words around here. A double garage door set in the breeze blocks was the only thing to suggest that this was an expensive property.

But once over the threshold, it was obvious that this was a beach house of a completely different order from the one I had been staying in. No common cockroach would have dared to scuttle across the white marble floor of this hallway in broad daylight. Shipped from Italy especially, as I would later learn.

I was immediately struck by how beautifully light it was

in Eric's house. At the centre of the Mediterranean-style villa was a courtyard open to the California sun. Flowers bloomed around the internal walls like an explosion in God's paintbox. The scent of roses and jasmine mingled to create an intoxicating aroma that was considerably more pleasant than the cat's pee and air freshener I had grown used to back in Venice. There was even a fountain in the middle of the courtyard, lending its tinkling song as accompaniment to the chattering of the tiny sparrows who jumped in and out of the water.

It was beautiful. A beautiful garden. Beautiful flowers. Beautiful sparrows.

Their beautiful song was interrupted by an ear-splitting shriek.

'That's Picasso,' Eric told me. 'The peacock.'

Picasso eyed me beadily from his perch on the back of a wrought iron bench.

'He's not that keen on women,' Eric said.

I'm not that keen on peacocks. I gave Picasso a very wide berth.

But a fountain! A peacock! And enough fresh flowers to make Amsterdam's flower market look pretty understocked and shabby. And this was just in the courtyard. I wanted to act blasé about it all; as if I'd been in houses like this for auditions a thousand times before. But Eric Nordhoff's house was stunning and I gawped like a little girl.

'I thought we would have breakfast in the garden,' Eric told me.

'Here?' I asked. Picasso was occupying the only seat I could see.

'No, the proper garden,' said Eric. 'This is just the atrium.'

There was more? I trotted after him down another marble

corridor that led out through the back of the house. And then we found ourselves standing at the top of a perfect green lawn. The kind of vibrant, juicy green that could only have been achieved in California's arid climate by diverting half the water from the Colorado River. And at the end of the lawn, a hundred metre drop to the beach. And the sea. The Pacific. Stretching blue as the sky to the horizon. Right at the bottom of the garden.

'Dolphins!' I couldn't help but exclaim, seeing a pod of four or five of the sleek black creatures porpoising through the shallows.

'Oh, yeah,' said Eric dismissively. 'Every dawn and dusk. We get humpback whales around Easter and October time too.' He didn't even bother to look at the aquatic ballet. 'Would you care for a cup of coffee?'

A white-painted table had already been set for two. I took the seat that faced the sea. Eric poured the coffee.

'Oh. No thanks,' I remembered Brandi's warning.

'Good girl,' said Eric. 'I'm supposed to be giving up myself. Caffeine makes me jittery. But hey, I like jittery people.'

'In that case, I'll have some,' I said. Brandi was probably right about the smell, but I was going to be whatever Eric Nordhoff liked that day.

'Muffin?' he asked me.

And risk choking all over the table? Brandi's warning echoed in my mind.

'I won't thanks,' I said dutifully. 'I ate on the way up here.'

'You did?' Eric looked unconvinced.

I nodded. I hadn't of course. And to make things worse, the muffins looked absolutely scrumptious. Eric picked up one for himself and broke it open. It was still warm inside and the smell of butter melting onto warm dough studded with blueberries made my stomach give a sudden, very audible growl.

'You sound like you've still got room for some more,' Eric observed.

'I think you're right,' I decided. I grabbed a muffin from the plate and resolved to keep my mouth shut while I was eating.

'So . . .' Eric and I began simultaneously.

'You go first,' he said.

'No, you go. I was only going to say something nice about your garden.'

I put my hand to my mouth just quickly enough to stop a half-chewed blueberry hitting the table cloth. I blushed crimson. Eric pretended not to have noticed.

'I expect you're wondering why I asked to see you here today,' he started tactfully.

'Mm-hmm,' I nodded. Mouth firmly closed.

'I asked one of the other girls at the club about you and she told me that you're an actress. She said that you've come to Hollywood to find work but that things haven't been going so well so far.'

'I've only been here for a couple of months,' I said in my defence.

'Whatever,' Eric said dismissively. 'It doesn't really matter to me. I just love your accent, Lizzie.'

'Thank you.'

My mum would be pleased to know that the money she had spent on elocution lessons to beat the Brummie out of me had not been entirely wasted.

'I can do others too. Would you like me to . . .'

'That won't be necessary.' Eric put down his muffin and leaned across the table. 'You've probably guessed that I

want you to work for me,' he smiled. 'I want you to play
the role of your life and I want you to start tomorrow.'

'Lizzie, did you hear that? Can you start work tomorrow?'

Thirty seconds later I was still staring at him open-
mouthed. Too shocked to talk. Too shocked even to close
my gaping cakehole and hide the muffin crumbs. But somewhere inside me, an orchestra was playing the 'Halleluia'
chorus. A crowd ten thousand strong were waving Union
Jacks and singing along.

'Halleluia! Halleluia!'

Had I just hallucinated a job offer or what?

I didn't think I'd misheard.

The 'Halleluia' chorus became a raucous rendition of 'If
they could see me now' – one of Joanna Boisvert's showtime
favourites. Then I was driving up to my brother's house
in Solihull in a limousine the size of a battleship. I was
calling Giorgio to tell him that Calvin had already sent me
an outfit for the Golden Globes. I was picking fluff off my
Versace ballgown and ignoring Sadie Frost at the Baftas. I
was already planning my Oscar acceptance speech.

'I'd like to thank my mother and my father, my brother
and my agent and my best friend and my hairdresser . . .
When I came to Los Angeles I had nothing . . .' I was
wondering whether it would be too bitter and twisted to
finish the speech by saying, 'And most of all I would like
to thank Richard Adams. If he hadn't broken my heart in
seventeen places I wouldn't be here thanking the Academy
today.'

My life, in glorious Panavision Technicolor was racing
through my mind like a DVD on fast forward. I was living

in the house next door to Eric Nordhoff's gorgeous villa
in Malibu. Joseph Fiennes got over his lifelong hatred of
Tinseltown to fly out to Hollywood and marry me. We
had three golden-haired children who would grow up to
write biographies about how I'd been a great filmstar *and*
a great mother. I had my hands in the concrete outside
Mann's Chinese Theater . . .

'Lizzie?'

Eric Nordhoff looked worried. Perhaps he thought I was
having some strange kind of fit.

'Liz-zie?' He waved his fingers in front of my eyes.

Suddenly, I grabbed both his hands in mine and told
him, 'You'll be proud of me, Mr Nordhoff. I'll prove you
right. I'll show the world that though I'm just an unknown
now, you knew that I had star quality when you plucked
me from obscurity to play the role of . . .'

'My girlfriend,' said Eric. 'I need you to pretend to be
my girlfriend.'

'Great. Can I take a copy of the script away with me
today? I learn lines really quickly. Who will I be playing with? Is it true you've cast George Clooney in the
lead role?'

'Lizzie,' Eric stopped me. 'There isn't a script.'

'You mean we're going to improvise the whole thing?
Like Mike Leigh's *Abigail's Party*? We did that at college.
I'm great at improvising. Give me a name and I'll give you
a character. Any name. Try me right now.'

Eric furrowed his brow and looked at me in confusion.
'You can keep your own name if you want too. And I
guess we'll be improvising, yes. But it's for a wedding,
not a party.'

'Weddings. Parties. Whatever.'

'We'll come to an arrangement about the money of

course. It'll be a generous amount but before we start
going down that road I need to know that I can count
on your discretion.'

'My discretion. Of course. Until you can send my agent
the contract I promise I won't breathe a word.'

'Lizzie, I don't want to involve any agents. There won't
be any contract. I don't need the *Hollywood Enquirer* to find
out about this.'

'Eh?'

'Well, how do you think it would look?' Eric asked
me. 'Eric Nordhoff hires waitress to accompany him to
his cousin's wedding?'

'What?'

The 'Halleluia' chorus stopped with a squeal like a needle
skidding across vinyl. My children ran away from home.
Joe Fiennes went off with an actress who understood
Tolstoy. Sadie Frost turned her back on me and Colin
laughed at my bicycle propped against his garden wall
in Solihull.

The penny dropped. Eric Nordhoff wasn't offering me a
film role at all.

'You want me to be your date for your cousin's wedding?' I asked. 'Is that why you got me here? But I thought
you wanted me for a part in *Northanger Abbey*?'

'*Northanger Abbey*?' Eric repeated as though I had just
said something really funny. '*Northanger Abbey*? Oh my
God. I'm sorry. You didn't think? Shit, you did think.
Oh, Lizzie, you're a nobody. I gave that part to Gwyneth
Paltrow. I couldn't cast you in one of my films. I only asked
you here today for a bet.'

'A bet?'

'That's right,' said Eric. 'You remember that red-haired guy on Friday night?'

I nodded slowly.

'Ed Strausser. One of the top agents at KCC.'

I felt sick when I heard the name of one of Hollywood's biggest talent agencies.

'He's an asshole but he's got a lot of clients. He also has a great car. You like Rollers, Lizzie?'

I put my hand up to my hair instinctively.

But Eric wasn't talking about hairdos. 'Rolls Royce,' he sighed. 'I love them. I've always wanted one. And Ed Strausser just took delivery of a rare Silver Shadow built for a Sultan in 1963.'

'What's that got to do with me?' I asked.

'You're going to help me win it.'

I didn't know whether to laugh or cry when Eric explained to me that it was precisely because I was a nobody that Ed Strausser had decided I would be the ideal candidate for the charade he had in mind.

I took a big bite out of my muffin. Didn't matter if I spat crumbs out all over him now. Perhaps I should have flounced out there and then, saying, 'Mr Nordhoff, I am an actress, not an escort girl. How dare you waste my time!' He had embarrassed me. He had made me feel worse than my brother had ever managed.

And yet I stayed to hear him out.

Fact was, I was unlikely to get the opportunity to spend time with such a serious Hollywood player again any time soon. My agent was more likely to write 'return to sender' on my postcards than bother to return my calls. And in the back of my mind was Brandi's advice for getting ahead in Los Angeles.

After the dreadful party when we thought we might

have been caught on a particularly candid camera, I asked her why she didn't react in front of the party's host; why instead she sought him out and wished him a good evening when she wanted to rip his head off.

'You have to remember this shit isn't personal,' she said. 'When you go for an audition and the director asks you to take your top off, you can bet you're not being singled out. It's a pact you make when you come to this city. You take the shit so that one day you can dish it.'

So, I let Eric outline his plan to me. I could say 'no' at the end if I wanted to, but I was damn well going to finish his muffins.

'The thing is,' he began, when he had finished cracking up at the thought that I had been expecting to be given the part he gave to Gwyneth Paltrow. 'Everybody who ever met me knows within two minutes of meeting me that I'm gay. I've got the earring, I've got the funny voice, I've even got a pink triangle tattooed on one of my buttocks. Rupert Everett looks straight beside me. It's an open secret. Except when it comes to my mother.'

There was the rub. Eric Nordhoff wasn't out to his mom.

'I grew up in a family that came to this country to escape religious intolerance in Europe and they've been practising it here ever since. My mother even wrote to the President of the United States to have *Dynasty* taken off the air when the truth came out about Rock Hudson. There was no way she could admit to herself and her hellish sisters that she had her own gay son.'

'That's such a pity.'

Eric shrugged. 'I didn't care as long as she'd still see me. But then this happened.'

He pushed an open magazine across the table towards me. On a colourful party page, Eric was pictured with his arm around a beautiful young man that I guessed must be Jan, his very personal assistant.

'This was something she couldn't ignore. All her friends read this magazine. She saw a copy of it on every coffee table in every house she visited. Everyone was talking about it. Mom called me to say that as far as she's concerned, she no longer has a son. That was almost six months ago. I haven't seen her since.'

'That's terrible,' I breathed. 'But if that's really the way she feels, why on earth do you want to talk to her now?'

'Because nobody gets to treat me that way. And because, if I can get her to invite me to her house for Thanksgiving, Ed Strausser will give me his car.'

'And how do I come into this?'

'You'll help me convince her I'm straight.'

'You want to lie to your mother for a bet?'

'I like to gamble.'

'That's disgusting.'

'So is homophobia. Look, it'll be fun,' he said. 'Bound to be a good party.'

The wedding of Eric's cousin Bobby was to be the biggest gathering of the Nordhoff family since his grandparents' golden wedding anniversary in 1992. 'It will be a festival to celebrate just how straight and God-fearing and normal the Nordhoff family are.' He snorted bitterly at that. 'I can't think of a better opportunity for me to come out as a hetero.'

'And you think they'll believe it?'

'If you're a good enough actress.'

'That's obviously not why Ed Strausser chose me. I know how this works, Mr Nordhoff. Your *lovely* friend has picked the girl he believes most likely to cock up and make the bet difficult for you.'

'Could have been worse,' Eric shrugged. 'He might have chosen that terrible singing one. Now there's a monster.'

'That's my flatmate.'

'Don't let yourself get mad about this, Lizzie. So Ed thinks you'll turn out to be a lousy actress? Here's your chance to prove him wrong. I have great faith in your ability.'

'Gee thanks,' I sniffed. 'Why don't you bet on horses like anyone else?'

'Because we're both Hollywood Big Dicks,' said Eric.

'I agree with that last part.'

Eric narrowed his eyes. 'You'd be stupid not to indulge me, Lizzie. If we pull this off and I get my Roller, I promise that I will make it worth your while. I'll make sure Ed puts you on his client list and when I get the right part, it's yours.'

'Speaking or non-speaking?' I laughed.

'Don't jump the gun. But be honest, Lizzie, do you really have a choice here? You're a nobody. I'm a somebody who wants to have a little fun.'

'You make me feel like an escort girl.'

'There'll be no sex involved.'

It was the Ladyboys dilemma all over again. How had this happened to me? I had been one of the best actresses in my class at drama school. Always up for the lead role, gaining plaudits for my Beckett and my Ibsen. Now I was the subject of some sordid bet, chosen precisely because I looked as though I couldn't act my way out of a crisp packet.

I flicked a muffin crumb in Picasso the Peacock's direction.

'Thinking about it?' Eric asked me.

'I shouldn't.'

I could have walked away but Eric had touched on
a nerve when he suggested I could prove Ed Strausser
wrong. Ed clearly thought that Eric's mother would be
horrified by me. What mother wouldn't be horrified by a
prospective daughter-in-law in a boob tube, even if she did
prove that her son had gone straight? But Ed had made the
classic mistake of confusing the costume with the person
inside it and it suddenly seemed important for me to prove
that I had class.

'Where's the wedding?' I asked.

'Santa Barbara. The Biltmore. Great hotel.'

'Will it be a good party?'

'The best. Bobby is Auntie Marion's only daughter.
They're so relieved that she's stopped hanging out with
her masseur friend Melissa that they're going to spend
all Bobby's inheritance at once on sending her off to
heterosexuality.'

'She's gay too?'

'Like Dusty Springfield. Hides it well.'

'That is fucked up.'

'Will you help me?' This time Eric sounded a little less
smug, a bit more needy.

'I don't see why not,' I conceded. 'If it will get me
into KCC.'

'Clever girl.'

'At least this way I get to have a free lunch.'

'And a part in my next film,' he promised. 'Might not
have any words but . . .'

'One day you'll be begging me to do a speaking part, I
know. What time do you need me tomorrow?'

Eric exhaled loudly. 'Eight a.m. We'll drive to the wedding from here in my Jaguar. Call my number if there's an
emergency, but if not I'll see you then. Just one more thing.'

'It's OK, I won't wear a nightdress.'

'No fear of that. I'll have an outfit biked over from Armani.'

'Can I keep it?'

'Of course. But I'll need your size. And I've also prepared a little questionnaire that I need you to fill in for me before you go.'

He handed me a neatly typed piece of paper. 'Just answer it honestly, Lizzie. Don't try and pad out the part. We've got to keep it simple to keep it realistic. I want that car.'

I turned the piece of paper over. Question one. How old are you?

'We've got to make it seem as though we've known each other for a few months. These are my answers to the same questions.' He handed me another piece of paper. 'You're going to need to learn these before tomorrow. Can you do that?'

'I learned three Shakespeare plays in a month last year. I think I can remember what your favourite kind of jam is.'

'Jelly,' Eric corrected. And then he was ushering me out through the door. 'I'll send someone to collect you tomorrow morning.'

'I won't let you down.'

'I'm very grateful to you, Lizzie,' said Eric. 'I knew you'd understand.'

We shook hands in a very businesslike fashion.

'Here's to your car,' I said.

'And here's to your glittering career.'

Eric Nordhoff closed the door behind me and left me standing on the porch with his questionnaire in hand.

Fat Joe's car stood where I had left it. But while Eric

and I had been discussing the terms of my employment, someone had been over the dust covered bonnet with a polishing cloth. I could see no one around to thank. So instead I headed back towards the 405, going through the conversation I had just had one more time in my mind and wondering what on earth I was going to tell Fat Joe and Brandi.

CHAPTER FOURTEEN

Brandi was horrified to hear about the bet, but agreed that the payoff might be worth the humiliation. KCC, the Kristiansand Creative Company, was currently one of the hottest talent agencies in Hollywood. Recently formed by an agent who had broken away from ICM, the new agency had poached disgruntled superstars from top agents all over the city. It wasn't long before they were able to turn people away. Getting representation by KCC, even if it meant having to see Ginger again, could get me to the big time without having to pass 'Go'.

Fat Joe was less impressed by the agency potential but agreed he would go anywhere to get a good free lunch and the Santa Barbara Biltmore was a pretty safe bet so far as that was concerned.

So, I was going to take my part in my first big Hollywood adventure, under the direction of Eric Nordhoff for the most exacting audience in the world; his mom.

Even with Fat Joe and Brandi's blessing on the whole ridiculous endeavour, I wrestled with my conscience in the moments before sleep. I imagined Eric's mother; an innocent old lady; God-fearing, conservative, brought up to believe that the only family unit worth endorsing was one headed by two opposite sex parents.

But an innocent old lady who wouldn't accept that her son was gay? Surely there were some things in this life that should mean more than ideas based on traditions that sprang up in another millennium?

My mother had always told me that she didn't care what Colin and I got up to, just so long as we were happy with our lives. That didn't stop her from giving me her disapproving look at least once every fortnight, when I dyed my hair or wore a skirt she thought might be better employed as a dishcloth. But I did believe that she would stand by the principle of tolerance if I started bringing girls home. There was no way she would have disowned either of us; Colin or me. We were her children, bonded to her by love.

And if Elspeth Nordhoff didn't love her son enough to stand by him in the face of her bigoted neighbours' contempt, then perhaps she did deserve to be deceived at Cousin Bobby's wedding. Far more important to me was my potential reward for deceiving her. If Eric got his car, would he keep his word?

There was only one way to find out.

The following day, as promised, Eric's butler/boyfriend Jan arrived to drive me to the house in Malibu from whence Eric and I would set out for the wedding in Santa Barbara.

I had brought a suitcase full of possible outfits with me. But when we got to the villa I was taken upstairs to find that Eric had been true to his word and an outfit was already laid out on the bed for me.

A chocolate silk Armani shift dress with a matching long-line jacket. Perfect. Even the gorgeous slingback shoes were exactly the right size for me. The whole ensemble reminded me of Mary's going away outfit. In fact, it was probably exactly the same outfit.

It was the first time I had worn Armani in my life.

Eric looked equally smart in a cream linen suit.

'We look like we've stepped out of a chocolate box,' I said chirpily.

But Eric surveyed me critically. 'Perhaps an A-line would have been better with your thighs.'

I resisted the urge to say, 'Perhaps a wig would be better with your head.'

Whatever. I was determined to enjoy the day, which had started as perfectly as every Californian day since my arrival. A couple of fluffy white clouds scudded across the horizon, for decorative purposes only, as we got into Eric's Jaguar and he folded down the soft-top roof.

'I like your car,' I told him.

'You can have it if I get that Rolls,' he said.

The words tripped off his tongue as though he was offering me first refusal on a secondhand sofa when he upgraded to a better Dralon suite. As we headed towards the Ventura Freeway, that would take us north to Santa Barbara, I sat back in my seat and took in the admiring glances of the other motorists who passed Eric's rather special little 'runaround.' How must we look? I wondered. Like a glitzy Hollywood couple? Who do they think I must be? A film star? A film executive?

In a patch of slowed down traffic, we drew level with a Nissan Cherry and stayed opposite the modest blue car for almost half a mile. The driver of this car was a man whose midriff almost touched the steering wheel. He balanced a huge paper cup full of Coke on his belly shelf and slurped at it constantly.

In the passenger seat, a woman. Perhaps she was about my age. She looked a little older, but I had quickly worked out that a childhood in the California sunshine took its toll. Never thought I'd be grateful for the rain that had blighted my childhood holidays.

As we inched along the freeway, me in the passenger seat of the Jag, her in the Nissan, neither of us talking to the drivers of our respective cars, the girl in the Nissan caught my eye. I wondered if she was thinking 'lucky bitch'. My Armani, my boyfriend, his fabulous Jaguar.

The traffic started moving again. Eric put his foot to the floor and we were soon one hundred miles per hour away.

About halfway to Santa Barbara we talked tactics.

'So what is the story?' I asked. 'How did we meet?'

'Let's keep it simple, eh?' Eric suggested. 'We met in a bar. Which we did. You caught my eye, which you did. And I left you my card and asked you to call. Which you did. That's all most people will want to know, if they want to know anything at all.'

'Which bar?' I said. 'I don't suppose you want me to say Ladyboys.'

'The Sky Bar,' said Eric distractedly. 'Think you can remember that?'

'Hey, buddy. I'm a professional actress,' I reminded him. 'I can remember whole Shakespeare plays. I think I can remember where we met. The Met Bar, right.'

Eric looked at me aghast.

'I know, I know. J for Joke,' I said. 'The Sky Bar. I won't

forget. I'll be the perfect girlfriend. In fact, by the end of the evening, you'll be thinking about going straight and marrying me for real.'

'Don't expect me to put you on the car insurance,' said Eric.

It took us just over two hours to reach Santa Barbara. Before I got there, before I saw the mountains that crumbled into the sea, the jagged cliffs edging white sand beaches, I thought the place sounded rather comical. Santa Barbara. I had imagined something more along the lines of a Californian Whitby, full of American pensioners watching the view from behind their car windows. But Santa Barbara was far from being the deathbed dormitory its name suggested.

As we cruised into town, we passed polo fields. Every other car was a Jaguar now. By the time we turned into the driveway of the Biltmore, Eric's Jag was looking about as impressive as a Fiat Cinquecento. Santa Barbara was the Ascot of California.

At the Biltmore, which looked like a Mediterranean village with its white-walled, red-tiled cottages, Eric stopped the car and got out to let a valet take over. Then he strode ahead of me into the reception as though he didn't know that I was supposed to be with him.

'Eric,' I called pathetically, as I waited for someone to unload our luggage. 'Hang on.'

I caught up with him in the hotel lobby.

'Eric, you could have waited for me.'

Eric rolled his eyes at the receptionist as though I was

always a nag. Perhaps he was better at acting this old married couple thing than I thought.

While he checked us in to the hotel – the wedding wouldn't be taking place until late afternoon, so we were going to be staying overnight – I took in my new surroundings. The lobby of the Biltmore was like the entrance hall to a Tuscan palace, perfectly recreated from its terracotta tiled floor to the vaulted ceiling that inspired the kind of hush more suited to a cathedral.

The other guests drifted around like extras from an episode of *Falcon Crest*, everything about them screamed 'expensive', from their outfits to their hair and to their carefully manicured nails, and I wondered for the second time that day whether I was going to be able to pull it off. When these seasoned Santa Barbarians looked at me, could they tell I had been living in a hovel in Venice Beach for the past two months?

I seemed to have convinced the bellboy at least.

'Madam,' he said, wrestling my overnight bag from my hands.

We followed the bellboy to our room through labyrinthine corridors that I was sure I'd never be able to negotiate on my own. We were to be accommodated in a 'poolside cottage'. One of the best rooms in the house with its own tiny garden looking out onto the pool.

I admired the view while the bellboy busied himself with setting down our cases and explaining about the keys. I thought he was being especially attentive and then I realised why when he said, 'Excuse me for asking, Mr Nordhoff, but are you *the* Eric Nordhoff?'

Eric smiled his most seductive smile and nodded at the boy.

'Amazing! I enjoyed *The Ladies Room* so much, sir. Such

strong characters. I've been using the monologue from the plumber who comes to unclog the waste disposal unit as an audition piece. I hope you don't mind. Perhaps I could do it for you later on today?'

'You know where my room is,' said Eric, handing him the same card he had left for me at Ladyboys.

The bellboy was grinning like a looney as he shifted his gorgeous ass back out into the corridor.

'Cute,' said Eric.

'You invited him back to our room!' I exclaimed.

'Where's your problem?'

'Do you want that car or not?'

'Shit,' said Eric. 'I guess it could look a bit strange.'

'It's just for a day,' I reminded him.

'Just for a day. Man, my head aches just thinking about this.'

Eric helped himself to a vodka-tonic from the mini-bar. He didn't offer anything to me.

We had lunch in a restaurant further into town. Eric talked on his mobile phone throughout the meal, leaving me to gaze around the restaurant and prompting one of the waiters to ask cheekily whether I wanted him to join me.

Later, as Eric talked loudly on the mobile about how he couldn't attend some Bel Air pool party because he was being 'bored rigid' in Santa Barbara instead, I wanted to slap him. I knew that technically I was in his employ, but there was no need for him to treat me like his personal assistant. During my temping career I had met too many people like Eric, who treated the personal assistant as a piece of office equipment with as much need for attention and feedback as the photocopier.

I wanted to tell him that even if he were straight, I wouldn't have wanted to go out with him. He was so offensive that I started to wonder whether his mother had just used the whole gay thing as an excuse not to have to talk to him again.

Eric was so dismissive of me that I toyed with the idea of walking out on him and letting Ed Strausser keep his sodding Rolls. But how would I get back to Los Angeles? I had less than twenty dollars in my wallet and my credit cards had all but melted. I was stuck.

'You're going to have to talk to me occasionally if you want people to believe you're in love with me,' I warned.

'Who's the director here?' said Eric.

At a quarter to four, we went back to the hotel for the wedding. Bobby and her fiancé Greg were to be married on a terrace that overlooked the sea. While we were eating lunch, the Biltmore staff had transformed the terrace from a chi-chi restaurant into a scene fit for a wedding straight out of *Dallas* or *Dynasty*. Rows of gilt-backed chairs with red velvet cushions flanked either side of a red carpet that led to the little stage where the bride and groom would swap their vows.

On each of the chairs was a little golden box decorated with a red ribbon that contained a tiny gift for each of the guests. They looked like the favours that designers left for magazine editors on their seats at major fashion shows. At least, they looked like the free gifts that Mary had sometimes passed on to me.

'Is this so we give the couple a good review?' I quipped as Eric and I took our places.

Eric was suddenly looking about him too nervously to notice any of my jokes.

'Is she here yet?' I asked.

Eric shook his head. 'But that's her sister, my Aunt Katherine.'

As if on cue, a woman who had spent so much time in the sun that she matched her beautiful beige Tanne Krolle handbag, paused at the end of the row where we were sitting.

'Why, Eric, what a surprise! How lovely to see you.' She managed to say it in such a way that we were left in no doubt that she meant almost the total opposite. If her eyes looked as though they were smiling, it was only because her surgeon had got the lid tuck slightly too tight.

'Aunt Katherine, this is my girlfriend, Elizabeth,' said Eric.

'Really.'

Aunt Katherine drifted on by.

'This is going to be harder than I thought,' said Eric.

'I've had warmer welcomes,' I had to concede. 'But that lady over there was smiling at me,' I told him.

'Cousin Erica smiles at everybody,' Eric sighed. 'Since she found out about Prozac.'

It was clearly a dangerous business, being wealthy. As the wedding guests filed in, I amused myself by counting bad chin tucks and boob jobs. Several of the women had strangely blank expressions that Eric explained could be achieved by severing the nerve that makes you frown. The fashion for lips was clearly to look as though you were allergic to seafood and experiencing anaphylactic shock after eating a prawn cocktail. In front of me sat a woman who looked barely out of high school. With the hands of an Egyptian mummy. Clearly, something wasn't right.

When I observed that Eric didn't look much like the other Nordhoff cousins he explained it was because they had all had nose jobs. Those cousins who did look similar to one another had simply been treated by the same surgeon.

'That's a novel way to acquire a family trait,' I commented.

'If only I could acquire the family bigotry,' said Eric.

His eyes were still fixed on the entrance to the marquee but at last his face registered something other than the mere disdain he had for his distant relatives.

'There she is,' he breathed at last. 'That's my mother.'

Eric's eyes softened as he pointed out a petite grey-haired lady, dressed in Queen Mother-style blue, who was entering the garden on the arm of a much younger, and quite handsome, man.

'Is that—?'

'Her toyboy?' asked Eric. 'She wishes. He's her physician.'

'She brought her doctor to a wedding? Is she ill?'

'I don't think so. He's not her doctor exactly. She's on the board of several hospitals. I expect he's agreed to be her escort in return for a new scanner. Pretty buff, isn't he?'

I had to agree. Mrs Nordhoff's companion had an air of confident sensuality to match his dark curls and generous mouth.

'But I don't suppose I'll be making a play for him tonight,' Eric sighed.

'You better hadn't,' I said. 'Not if you want that car.'

Eric's mother and her escort had almost drawn level with us now. When it was clear she had caught sight of us, Eric quickly scrambled to his feet and offered her the place beside him. Eric's mother greeted him with the kind of warmth she might have reserved for the guy in charge of the valet parking.

'Eric,' she said in a very clipped voice. 'You made it.'

'Yes, Mom. I wouldn't have missed Bobby's wedding. Er, this is my girlfriend, Elizabeth.'

I got to my feet and held out my hand, smiling with double wattage to make up for the frozen grimace she was giving me in return. 'Elizabeth Jordan,' I said. 'How do you do, Mrs Nordhoff?'

'English?' Mrs Nordhoff acknowledged. 'Well, well, well. This is a surprise.'

'Will you sit with us, Mom?' Eric asked her.

Mrs Nordhoff looked at the seat that Eric had been proffering and shook her head.

'I'm going to sit where I can get a proper view of the bride,' she told him.

Then, without so much as a 'see you later', Mrs Nordhoff strode on to the front row of chairs at a pace that had her escort almost jogging to keep up with her. 'She hates me!' Eric wailed at once.

'No, she doesn't,' I said. 'She just wants to get a better look at the dress.'

I didn't believe that of course. It was a very tough mother who would have passed up the opportunity to sit next to her only son when she hadn't seen him for six months. I knew then that our mission was going to be harder than we had thought.

The more surprising thing was the way in which Eric had reacted to her snub. With only yesterday's conversation and the way he had sneered about his family on the ride to Santa Barbara to go on, I had drawn the conclusion that there really was no love lost between Eric and his mother and that this was all about a bet and a car. But in the space of that one short exchange, the hard man who hadn't bothered to speak to me over lunch had crumbled.

They may have been about as cuddly as the Alien and

her semi-human offspring in *Alien III*, but there was no doubt that even Eric and his mother had that inexplicable familial bond that makes separation feel like death. Suddenly, I was sitting next to a little boy who wanted his mommy.

'She hates me!' Eric said again.

I took his hand and squeezed it.

'We'll win you that car,' I said but I knew this was about more than winning an old Rolls Royce now.

The string quartet stopped playing Vivaldi and launched into 'Here Comes the Bride'.

Roberta, or Bobby as Eric's cousin was known, was, to put it kindly, not exactly a slip of a thing. When she came down the aisle, she looked like the *Mary Rose* shortly before she was scuppered. The Nordhoff family believed in conspicuous consumption and everything, from the wedding cake that towered in a corner like a Richard Rogers project, to the bride herself, was larger than life.

Roberta was followed by three of her younger cousins. Seeing them stomp towards the altar in dresses that looked as though they were simply parachutes with holes cut in for their arms and heads, I suddenly realised that the bridesmaid's dress Mary had made me wear really hadn't been that bad at all.

Apparently nobody in the family had expected Bobby to get married. She was thirty-two, Eric told me. She worked as a district attorney in San Luis Obispo and spent a lot of time with a masseuse called Melissa who was given to joss sticks and tofu. It came as a shock to everyone, including Melissa, when Bobby met Greg. Greg was also a lawyer. He had wispy red hair and looked as though he would only come up to Bobby's navel even when she took her wedding stilettos off.

'I don't buy it,' Eric had told me earlier. 'I think there's a certain amount of political partnering going on here.'

Eric suspected that Bobby's living arrangements had prevented her from rising within the legal system as quickly as she might have done. Greg was interested in the tax breaks.

Certainly, it seemed that while everything about the ceremony was designed for maximum romance, from the seaview setting to the reading from Gibran's *The Prophet* ('Trees, etc, blah-de-blah.' It was getting somewhat ubiquitous. I'd heard it at three marriages the previous year), this wedding didn't move me at all. Admittedly, I had been in a slightly altered state when Bill and Mary got married, but somehow their wedding had felt much more real. Bobby and Greg said their vows as if they were swearing an oath in court prior to sending down a serial killer.

Eric remained utterly distracted throughout. He didn't look at the bride and groom at all. His gaze was fixed on the blue hat belonging to that little grey-haired woman who had reduced him to a boy. It was as though he thought that if he stared at the back of her head for long enough, she would eventually have to turn around. But she didn't. And when the wedding was over, Elspeth Nordhoff walked up the aisle after the bridal party making sure that her escort was on the side nearest Eric. She didn't even catch his eye.

Eric was ready to leave.

'This is hopeless.'

I persuaded him otherwise.

'She'll relax at the reception.'

We followed the guests to the area of the terrace where

champagne was being served. No one spoke to us, though we were on the receiving end of several meaningful glances. Bobby smiled desperately in Eric's direction at one point, but it was almost as though her smile said, 'You didn't save me.' She stood as far away from her new husband as possible without raising rumours of a divorce.

During the meal, Eric and I found ourselves on a table with Greg and Bobby's work colleagues. I had a brief conversation with the man on my right about the fact that lawyers are solicitors where I come from. Eric didn't bother to talk to the girl on his left at all. Pretty soon, the lawyers were talking shop and left Eric and me with each other.

After the speeches, a swing band began to play. The bride and groom stepped up and did a couple of turns about the floor to 'Let There be Love'. The groom had two left feet but the bride didn't seem to care too much. Bobby was drunk on champagne and pure stress, I would have guessed, given the family situation.

The groomsmen and the bridesmaids quickly joined them. In their sunflower-yellow dresses, with headdresses that made Mary's *Blue Peter* advent candle-holder look positively restrained, the bridesmaids were like hot air balloons landing badly. The dancefloor soon looked like an incomprehensible game from *It's a Knockout*. Were the groomsmen trying to hold on to the bridesmaids or evade them? How many points did you get for knocking over a table?

'Should we dance?' I asked Eric, when all the lawyers had left us to enliven the floor with their bastard version of the Twist.

'I don't dance,' said Eric. 'You can if you want to.'

'I can't very well get up there on my own, can I?' I said.

But Eric ignored me. He was gloomily regarding his mother, who was still sitting on the other side of the room with witchy Aunt Katherine and the cousins from hell. Eric told me that his family was of Norwegian descent. His cousins were definitely pure troll.

'Did your cousin Helena ask for her nose job to look like Michael Jackson's?' I said in an attempt to lighten the mood.

Eric wasn't listening. 'She hasn't said a word to me all day.' Still talking about his mother.

'She's got lots of people to catch up with,' I suggested.

'She hates me,' reasoned Eric.

'She doesn't hate you.'

'She hates you then.'

'Why should she hate me?' I asked indignantly. 'I haven't done anything wrong.'

'I thought she'd like you. What with you being English. She's mad about the Queen.'

'Perhaps you should have told her I'm related,' I said sarcastically.

Eric sniffed wetly. I prayed he wasn't about to cry.

'What will you have to give Ed if you don't get invited to Thanksgiving?' I asked.

'Just Picasso,' said Eric.

'What? That horrible peacock? Then, what are you so worried about?'

'Not the peacock,' Eric sighed. 'The early sketch for *Guernica* that's hanging in my bathroom.'

'You've got a Picasso in your bathroom?'

'Until I make a decision about the study walls.'

Talk about another world.

'So, you have to give him a Picasso. You can win it back with another bet . . .'

'I don't care about the sketch,' said Eric. 'I don't even really care about the car. But I can't stand that my mother won't talk to me. I thought if she saw me . . . Especially if she saw me here with you . . .'

What could I say? *Eric, your mother won't accept you for who you are. She is not a nice person. Time to forget she gave birth to you and move on?*

That's what I was thinking. But what I said to Eric was, 'Look, there's no point just glaring at her from across the dancefloor. It doesn't make a very convincing case that we're madly in love if the only woman you've had eyes for all day is your mother. Just try to look like you're enjoying yourself with me and eventually she'll come over. She'll be intrigued.'

'Do you think so?'

'That's what women are like,' I assured him.

'OK,' he said, brightening just a little. 'Let's try to look as though we're having more fun.'

He oriented his chair towards me and attempted a grin in my direction.

'Christ, Eric,' I sighed. 'That's terrible.'

'I'm doing my best. You don't look like you're having such a great time yourself.'

'I'm not. We need to talk about something.'

'Like what?'

'OK, let's do what we used to do at college when we were doing crowd scenes. Just keep saying "rhubarb" at me and throw in the occasional "cheese".'

Eric snorted. 'That's not going to look very realistic.'

'Well, at the moment we just look as if we're having a row. How appropriate is that for a couple who are supposed to be so newly fallen in love?'

'OK,' Eric groaned. 'Rhubarb, rhubarb, rhubarb, cheese.'

'Gorgonzola,' I retorted.

'Rhubarb.'

'Crumble.'

'Crumble?'

'Cobblers,' I corrected, remembering that was what they called crumble in the States.

'What are you on about?' Eric asked me.

'It's word association.'

'I don't get it.'

'It's . . . oh, just forget it.'

Eric's attention had already drifted in any case. 'Oh my God,' he hissed. 'I think she's coming over.'

He was right. Mrs Nordhoff clipped across the dance-floor like Napoleon ready to throw his glove down at Wellington's boot and challenge him to a duel.

'Eric,' said Mrs Nordhoff. 'I think we need to talk. Would you accompany me to the hotel lobby?'

'Yes, Mom, of course.' Eric leapt to his feet. 'I'll, er, I'll see you later, Lizzie.'

I gave him a thumbs up as he trotted behind his mother.

'Good luck,' I mouthed.

He'd need it.

CHAPTER FIFTEEN

E ric left me sitting alone at the table. I looked about me hopefully. My experience of Americans thus far had been that as soon as they heard my accent it was difficult to dissuade them from talking to me. They all wanted to know about the 'old country', even if they were actually descended from Swedes or Russians or Chinese. They all wanted to talk about ancestry too. While working at Ladyboys, I had met at least three guys who claimed to be direct descendants of King Arthur. If you think the British are obsessed with who your parents are, let me tell you, it's America's favourite pastime after TV.

It's like the past life thing. Anyone who has a past life claims to have been Elizabeth the First or Cleopatra. Never a handmaiden. Never a slave girl. Likewise, if someone wants to engage you in a conversation about genealogy, you can bet they're not going to tell you they're descended from a peasant who worked the peat bogs.

But right then, no one wanted to talk to me at all. Though I got the feeling that perhaps I was being talked about. I caught two of Eric's evil-looking cousins staring in my direction, obviously wondering what a nice girl like me was doing with someone so clearly gay. I gave them a wave. But it didn't embarrass them into coming over and introducing themselves to me.

I toyed with my champagne glass. Even the waiters seemed to be avoiding me now. Was it that obvious that I was just a pretender? An interloper in this close-knit family event? Close-knit? Hah! That was a laugh. More likely they were worried that Eric was about to introduce another person to the clan who would then have a claim on their inheritance.

I moved around the table so that the extravagant floral centrepiece obscured the cousins' view of me.

'Deserted you, has he?'

It was Mrs Nordhoff's doctor. He had crept up behind me while I watched the sniggering cousins from behind the blowsy yellow roses.

'You shocked me,' I exclaimed. Then, recovering myself, I added, 'Eric's gone to talk to his mum.'

'That's why I thought I better come and talk to you.'

'A mercy mission. Thanks.'

'Believe me, it's my pleasure.'

The doctor smiled the only genuine smile I had seen that day. It hadn't taken me long to notice that Eric's family physiognomy included a rictus that could have frozen mercury.

'My name's Scott,' he said. 'Scott Walker.'

'Lizzie Jordan.'

He took my proffered hand and shook it briskly.

'I think Eric and his mother have a lot to talk about,' Scott said, taking a seat next to me. 'I know it's no fun being at one of these things on your own. Everyone's too busy catching up on their family news to look after you.'

'You seem to be doing OK,' I commented.

'Yeah, right. I just spent half an hour diagnosing some guy's haemorrhoids. When you're a doctor, everyone wants to talk to you. But only about themselves and what's wrong with them.'

'Can I show you my knee?' I joked.

'I'm sure I'd be very impressed,' he said.

'What kind of doctor are you?' I asked. 'If you don't mind talking shop for just a minute longer.'

'I'm an oncologist. Cancer. Breast cancer specifically.'

'I guess that means you're a boob man,' I quipped. Scott looked at me blankly. 'I'm sorry. That was tasteless.'

But then he laughed. 'Sorry. It took me a second to work out what you meant by "boob".'

'So, what brings you here with Mrs Nordhoff?' I asked quickly to change the subject.

'Mrs Nordhoff has just raised half a million dollars for my unit with a charity art auction. For that kind of money I'm obliged to lap dance for her if she wants it.'

'That's a lot of money.'

'She's a formidable woman. She's got a lot of very wealthy friends. And I don't think many people who know her would dare not to support her *cause du jour* if she asked them to.'

'That's a good thing for you though.'

'Definitely. She's one in a million, all right.' From where we were sitting we could just about see Eric and his mother in one of the hotel's sitting rooms. They were having what appeared to be quite a heated conversation with lots of gesticulation from both parties. Scott and I were both drawn to the spectacle. He sighed as though he'd seen it all before, then asked me, 'How do you like Los Angeles?'

'What?' I was still watching Eric and his mother. 'Oh. Los Angeles? I love it. I think California's fantastic. I suppose that means I'm dreadfully shallow,' I added. 'I think it's more fashionable to prefer New York.'

Scott laughed softly.

'No. I think you're right to prefer the West,' he said. 'I left New York to be here.'

'To work in a better hospital?' I asked.

'I wish my reasons had been that noble. It's more accurate to say I was running away.'

'From someone?'

Scott took a gulp from his champagne rather than answer me.

'You don't have to say,' I said. 'I know exactly what it feels like. Lovely hotel this,' I continued blandly.

'Great view.'

A white-sailed yacht conveniently glided across the blue horizon.

'It's important to have a good view, I think,' I burbled on. 'Doesn't matter how nasty a place is on the inside if you can look out and see the sea.'

'It makes you feel as though there might be something more to life,' Scott agreed. 'When I get a patient who's having a bad day, I tell them to look at the sea.'

'Doesn't it sometimes make you feel insignificant, though?'

'Exactly. And that's sometimes how I need to feel. We're no different from the flowers on this table, Lizzie. We're part of a pattern so enormous we can't begin to comprehend it. Our little lives and deaths won't stop the waves from breaking and to realise that is a liberating thing.'

'Sounds depressing to me.'

'Shall we dance?' Scott asked suddenly, popping the serious bubble we found ourselves in with a smile.

The band had started to play 'Let's Call the Whole Thing Off'.

'Do you say "potato"?' Scott mimicked an English accent.

Now it was my turn to laugh cagily. 'Let's Call the Whole

Thing Off' was the song that had been the anthem for my short-lived relationship with Brian Coren; best man to Bill and Mary, second most significant ex-boyfriend and the man who had single-handedly changed my mind about Americans.

'This song could be about you and Eric,' Scott suggested. 'He says to-*may*-to.'

'And I hate to-*ma*-toes,' I sighed. 'Are we going to dance or what?'

I got to my feet and let Scott lead me onto the dancefloor. This was the moment when everything could go wrong but I grinned at him as we launched into an easy kind of quickstep. It was still a little strange. Once upon a time this song would have reduced me to tears. Now I could happily take a turn around the dancefloor with any old bloke to the song that had once made me sob for what I no longer had with Brian Coren. I guess that meant I was well over him. Would I ever feel the same about . . .

'*Brookside*,' I muttered to myself.

'What?' said Scott.

'Er, I was just trying to remember the name of a place I visited with Eric last week,' I bluffed.

'Oh.'

'Just keep dancing.'

I concentrated on my steps. If I'd started humming the *Brookside* tune at that point I would have lost all sense of timing. Instead, I tried to lose myself in the rhythm of the song. Scott was a very good dancer. It was easy to follow his lead. He weaved us gracefully between the other dancers on the floor which, I noticed, had become considerably busier now that Scott and I had started dancing.

'Where did you learn to dance like this?' I asked.

'At high school. It was ballroom dancing or wood shop,' he added.

'I love it,' I told him. 'I danced in the college team.'

'Congratulations.'

'I didn't last all that long. I had to quit when I fell out with my partner.'

'Did he step on your toes?'

'Broke my foot in our first competition.'

'Oh.'

'After college it was hard to find an opportunity to foxtrot.'

'I hear English men don't like to dance.'

'Not like this, they don't.'

At that moment, dancing with Scott to Brian's song, I couldn't help but think of dancing with Richard. More accurately of jumping up and down opposite him while he shuffled awkwardly and prayed to be allowed to leave the disco.

Richard's intense dislike of dancing had been a disappointment. But I hadn't allowed it to become a tragedy. After all, you don't spend all day dancing, do you? That said, there was something wonderful about being held like a piece of precious sculpture, guided around the floor by an elegant man with one hand lightly in the small of your back. I could think of nothing more romantic. Or erotic. So much more erotic than being pressed groin to groin as you jerked to Basement Jaxx.

Meanwhile, the band had segued from 'Let's Call the Whole Thing Off' into 'The Way You Look Tonight'. I loved these old standards. The songs that Richard had dubbed my 'granny music'. Scott naturally slowed to a sway that made me realise with a delightfully giddy feeling, how much champagne I must have drunk.

Without knowing it, I closed my eyes.

'Someday, when I'm awful low . . .'

I let my head drop onto Scott's shoulder. He smelled so wonderful. A warm, head-filling mixture of freshly laundered cotton and peppery aftershave that wafted upwards on the heat generated by our dancing bodies. I breathed in deeply, still singing along. 'Dancing Cheek to Cheek' was playing now.

'Heaven, I'm in heaven . . .'

'Ah-hem,' Scott cleared his throat.

I was quickly upright again.

'Your, er, your earring was poking through my shirt,' he said.

'God, I'm sorry.'

I reached for the offending cubic zirconia stud. It wasn't that big but I suppose I wouldn't have wanted it poking into me either. We awkwardly resumed a more proper ballroom-dancing stance.

'So,' said Scott. 'As I was saying, Mrs Nordhoff is a very generous woman.'

'Very generous,' I agreed.

'It would be nice if she and Eric could be reconciled.'

'Wouldn't it?'

'I think your presence here today might be going some way towards that. Have you known Eric long?'

'Feels like ages,' I bluffed.

'Where did you meet?'

'In a nightclub,' I told him. 'A sort of private members club.'

'Like the University Club?' Scott asked me.

'Something like that.'

'He's a very lucky man,' said Scott.

For a moment, I wanted to tell him that I felt like a very

lucky girl. But not because I was attending a wedding with Eric Nordhoff. Scott blinked his soft brown eyes. I licked my lips. He looked as though he was about to say exactly what I was thinking.

'May I?'

Too late.

One of Eric's cousins, one of the hellish set of twins that he had nicknamed after Marge Simpson's chain-smoking sisters, had decided to cut in. 'I'm sure that Eric would like to dance with his *girlfriend* now,' she added. 'You've been dancing for almost four songs.'

'What? Oh, yes.'

Scott suddenly released his hold on my hand as though it were glowing white hot. 'I've been hogging you. I'm sorry, Lizzie.'

'It was my pleasure,' I said.

'Selma' muscled in between us. 'Mine now,' she said with a feral glint in her eye as she grabbed Scott's hand and pressed her body hard against his.

I couldn't help looking back as I left the dancefloor and headed back to the table where Eric and his mother were now sitting, having returned to the terrace after their intensive tête-à-tête. Scott was already halfway around the floor with Selma. His hand was in the small of her back, but he wasn't holding her all that closely. I wondered if I had imagined how closely he seemed to be holding me.

'Elizabeth!' Elspeth Nordhoff patted a seat beside her. 'Do sit down. I was just telling Eric about Doctor Walker.'

'He seems very nice,' I said.

'Yes. Isn't he? Well,' she segued straight into a description of her own problems. 'Doctor Walker said that I must get as much rest as possible but of course he doesn't understand that I have certain obligations. What would the Ladies' Bible Circle do without me? I've left it to Marilyn to organise the meetings before and the next thing I know she's arranged a debate about admitting women to the priesthood that has half the ladies vowing never to come to the circle again.'

Eric nodded.

'And then there's the Friends of the Gallery. Without me, there would be no one to arrange the history of art lectures or the annual dinner dance. It takes a certain level of tact to persuade some of these artists to donate prizes for the raffle.'

'Sounds like you're working yourself to death,' I said.

Eric dropped his coffee spoon into his coffee cup with a plop that sent brown splatters all over the pure white table cloth. Mrs Nordhoff just stared.

'Lizzie,' Eric said gravely. 'Mother has just been diagnosed with a very rare form of cancer.'

And I had contracted foot-in-mouth disease. I could only stare back at Eric's mother as she nodded to confirm his revelation.

'Sorry,' I said.

'You weren't to know,' she told me quietly.

'What treatment are they giving you, Mother?'

'Oh, they've been doing their best. Doctor Walker has been overseeing my chemotherapy himself but he says that at this stage, they're only giving me treatment to make me comfortable. There's no hope of a cure.'

'But there must be.'

'Eric, my darling, don't let yourself get angry about it. Holding anger inside is what makes people ill. I've had a

long life. I hope I've been a good person. I've worked hard.
I've tried to be a good mother.'

'You've been the best mother,' Eric interrupted.

Mrs Nordhoff beamed. Her eyes twinkled wetly. 'That's
all I need to hear. I've had a good life, Eric. If now is my
time to go, then I just have to accept that. At least I have a
chance to say my goodbyes. Not like poor Mrs Addison.'

'Mrs Addison?' asked Eric.

'Electrocuted by her own toning table. Now that'll be a
very interesting settlement.'

Aunt Katherine had sidled across the room to join us.

'So, you've met Eric's lovely young lady at last,' she said
to Eric's mother. 'I have to say, there were those of us in the
family who had all but given up hope of ever seeing Eric
settle down. But you've snared him, Elizabeth. You must
be a very special young lady indeed.'

'Oh, she is,' said Elspeth Nordhoff defensively. 'Edu-
cated at Oxford University.'

'Really? You don't say.'

'And she comes from a very good family. In the Shires.'

I had to bite my lip at that one. My mother would be
delighted.

'So what are you doing here in America, Elizabeth?' Aunt
Katherine asked.

'Oh, you know. This and that. Auditioning. I'm an
actress.'

Eyebrows were raised in a far from friendly way.

I felt obliged to say that I would only consider Shakespeare
or Tolstoy adaptations but Elspeth stepped to my defence.

'She's a classical actress. Though, of course, she'll be
giving that up just as soon as she and Eric are married.'

Eric started to nod but his gesture of agreement turned
into a weird wild headshake when he realised what his

mother had just said. Married? He looked at me. I looked at him. We both looked aghast.

'Oh, I've spoiled the surprise!' said Eric's mother. 'Elizabeth, dear. He made me swear not to say anything to you, but I know you won't mind. Eric was going to propose to you right after the wedding, my dear. Still, it's not as though you won't say "yes" right away. It's just obvious that you two were made for each other!'

Aunt Katherine had to use her hand to close her jaw. Eric was still staring at me in bewilderment.

'Eric,' I said. 'Is this, er, is this true?'

Eric Nordhoff was suddenly down on one knee in front of me.

'Er, Lizzie, will you, er, do me the honour of becoming my wife?'

The entire terrace was silent. The band had been instructed to stop playing. A circle had formed around the table where a nightmare was unfolding before my disbelieving eyes.

Eric took hold of my left hand in both of his. His palms were as hot as my cheeks felt right then. His eyes met mine imploringly. The smile on his face was frozen, his jaw clenched tight. But what did he want me to say? I tried to guess from his eyes. Was that a desperate 'please say no' look? Or was he saying 'say yes now and we'll sort it out later'?

I decided that I had best go for the latter.

'Er, yes!' I said.

Eric's jaw unclenched just a little. I had got it right.

'Yes, Eric. Yes, please. I'd love to marry you. Yes!'

Eric leapt to his feet and grabbed me in his arms.

'Did I do right?' I whispered as he swung me round.

'Yes,' he said. 'Yes. We'll sort it out later on.'

But for that moment, we had to play the happy, newly

engaged couple. The band struck up again with 'Let There
be Love' and this time we were the dancers that everyone
wanted to watch. We set off around the dancefloor in
a manic double-speed waltz, grins fixed, hissing at one
another through our teeth.

'I can't believe she did that to us,' Eric muttered.

'Did *you* tell her we were going to get married?'

'I might have hinted something along those lines.'

'It's going to kill her when she finds out the truth,' I
whispered under the pretence of kissing Eric's ear.

'Don't worry. She'll be dead before the truth comes
out.'

CHAPTER SIXTEEN

'Congratulations,' said Scott. He held his hand out to me quite stiffly. I shook it.

'Thanks,' I said. 'Took me by surprise.'

'It's a very romantic way to end this wedding,' he said.

I wanted to tell him that it was about as romantic as being proposed to at the end of a Jerry Springer show about people who sleep with their domestic animals and that by doing it in front of the entire congregation, Eric had given me about the same opportunity to say no. I wanted to tell him that the only romantic part of the entire day for me had been drifting in Scott's arms while the band played 'Smoke Gets in Your Eyes'. But I didn't.

'I expect I'll see you at Mrs Nordhoff's next charity gala,' Scott told me. He nodded goodbye. Then he turned to congratulate Eric.

'Very romantic,' I heard him say.

'What? Yeah,' said Eric, looking as guilty and harassed as a dog that's done a poo behind the sofa. 'Yeah,' he said again. 'That's true love for you.'

Eric's plan had worked. He was back in his mother's favour all right. But at what cost? He was shaking as we walked back to our room at the end of the party that night. Thankfully Elspeth Nordhoff's recently revealed 'condition' meant that she didn't insist on staying up with us.

'What have I done, what have I done, what have I done,' Eric kept muttering. 'What have I done?'

'You asked me to marry you,' I reminded him. 'Thanks, Eric. No one's ever asked me before. Even if you didn't really mean it.'

'It's not funny, Lizzie,' he snapped. 'It really isn't funny at all.'

'Relax. You got your car,' I said. 'And I won't hold you to the proposal.'

'My mother will.'

'She can't force us. Look, just tell her that we've set a date for the year 2005. She'll be dead by then.'

Eric looked at me like he was a puppy I'd just dropkicked across the garden.

'I'm sorry.'

'No. You're all right. It's the only thought that's kept me from going crazy tonight.'

'Why did you decide to go so far?' I asked him.

'You heard her. She's dying. I had no idea . . .'

'But why . . .'

'I just wanted her to be happy, OK? She started talking about how she'd be able to die happier if she knew I was settled and I just sort of ran with the idea.'

'So you've forgiven her for disowning you when she thought that you were gay?'

'Of course I've forgiven her. I love her. Love isn't rational. Not even the love we have for our parents. Haven't you ever loved someone precisely because they make you feel bad? Then, when they finally approve of something you do, it's like the sun breaking through the clouds. It's like ice cracking on a frozen pond. Like finally getting a fire out of a pile of damp sticks.'

'Poetic,' I nodded.

'That's what it felt like today when I told Mom that you and I were going to get married. She *beamed* at me, Lizzie. She hasn't beamed at me since I won an award for good conduct at pre-school. Do you know what that meant to me? To see her smile at me again as though she is actually proud that I'm her son? She refused to come to the premiere of my first film because she thought that conversations overheard in a Ladies' Room were an "inappropriate subject" for a proper playwright. When I asked her to come with me to the Palme D'Or awards ceremony, she pretended she had conjunctivitis. She's sneered at everything I've done for the past twenty-five years. I've disappointed her in every way imaginable. All she wanted was for me to grow up to be a decent, heterosexual lawyer. Instead she got a poofy, perverted playwright.'

Eric wiped his nose on the back of his hand. He was crying.

'Shit, Eric,' I said banally. 'Here, use this.'

I handed him one of my gloves.

'I didn't want to disappoint my mother. All I want is for her to love me and for her last thought about me to be that I was a good son overall. If I have to lie to her to make her think that, well . . . am I wrong, Lizzie? Am I wrong?'

I bit my lip. I'd certainly lied to my mother enough times to maintain my image as the perfect little girl. Starting with the time I told her that next door's dog had sneaked into our house and eaten all her favourite chocolates out of the box of All Gold that Dad bought her for her thirty-second birthday. Right up to the email I'd sent her only last night, in which I lied that I would be spending the day performing in a drama installation under the direction of Eric Nordhoff.

The best lies, I had discovered, were those that contained at least seventy per cent truth.

'Haven't you ever lied to your mother?' Eric pressed me.

'Yes. Of course I have. Everybody has.'

'Well, what do you think I should do now?'

In my defence, I had been drinking a lot of champagne that day. My judgement, generally weak, was now also exceptionally muddled. I could have pressed him to try to come clean again. I could have offered to stand beside him while he did it and chant a chorus of his positive attributes while his mother threw her fit. Surely it was better for Elspeth Nordhoff to die knowing that she had faced the truth rather than in a happy fog of ignorance. But I didn't take the moral high ground. I said, 'I think we're going to have to go along with the wedding thing for now.'

It didn't seem like such a big deal.

'All your relatives are going to be at the Biltmore until tomorrow afternoon, right?'

Eric nodded.

'I think we should just stay in our room, drinking champagne and watching TV all morning – everyone will assume that we're celebrating our engagement anyway.' I made little inverted commas in the air around those words. 'Then we'll join your mother for lunch, which shouldn't take longer than an hour. And claim that we have to dash back to Los Angeles as soon as we've had a sandwich so that I can catch a plane back to London and tell my parents the good news.'

Eric's face relaxed. 'Are you willing to do that for me, Lizzie?'

'Hey, I don't want a huge Nordhoff family row to spoil the only chance I'm likely to get to stay at a five-star hotel this century. Plus, you'll work doubly hard to persuade Ed Strausser to take me as his client, right?'

'Right,' said Eric.

Next morning, I was too busy nursing a hangover to want to order room service champagne. Eric spent a couple of hours on the phone, talking in a low whisper to someone I could only assume was the real object of his affections at the time. I ran a bath at least twelve inches deep and poured in all the freebie bath oil so that there was another twelve inches of bubbles on top. Then I lay back and luxuriated in the hot water. I hadn't had a bath since leaving England. I'd had a shower, of course, but you didn't want to spend too long in the beach hut's mildewed bathroom.

Elspeth had called to suggest we met for lunch at twelve. Her treat, she said. 'For the love birds!'

Eric had taken to clutching his head in his hands and groaning at regular intervals.

'Just lunch,' I said. 'That's all we've got to get through. Then you can drop me off in Los Angeles, tell your mother I've gone back to London and go back to doing whatever it is you normally do.'

Eric nodded.

'But for now,' I reminded him, 'you've got to act like you love me. And that means carrying my bags to the car so that we're ready for a quick getaway as soon as coffee is served.'

Unfortunately, Elspeth wasn't going to let us get away with a quick sarnie and a couple of air kisses. And we weren't going to be lunching *à trois* as I'd hoped. Oh no.

When Eric and I presented ourselves at the Biltmore's
terrace restaurant that lunchtime, we were led outside
to an a cappella version of 'Here Comes The Bride' to
find ourselves confronted by the entire Nordhoff family,
including its newest addition. Yesterday's bride and her
brand spanking new husband were delaying the start of
their honeymoon especially in order to be able to join
Elspeth in toasting Eric's engagement.

'You shouldn't have gone to all this trouble,' I said on
Eric's behalf. He was dumbstruck.

'You think I'm not going to celebrate the engagement of
my only son?' was Elspeth's incredulous reply.

Eric and I were seated on either side of his mother. Eric
had his Aunt Katherine on his far side. I was sandwiched
between Elspeth and Aunt Madeleine, her other Sister
Grimm. The whole family had turned out. Including the
evil cousins. I noticed to my disappointment that Doctor
Scott Walker was sandwiched between them.

'I've been itching to get to know you properly,' Elspeth
told me. And she'd certainly prepared for the opportunity.
She fired questions at me as though she was interviewing
me to be her personal assistant rather than her daughter-
in-law. Upbringing, education, political affiliation? Prefer-
ences, allergies, genetic mutations? I'm joking about that
last one. But by the time my smoked salmon arrived at the
table (I hate smoked salmon but Elspeth had ordered for
us all), I felt as though I should be in line for a pretty hefty
prize. She'd asked question after question and I'd answered
every one of them. She hadn't narrowed her eyes at me or
tutted so I guessed I was getting the answers right. Then
she asked the question that was, for her, the million-dollar
one. I knew that much, thanks to Scott.

'Do you like art, Elizabeth?'

Art. Elspeth Nordhoff's passion. She was on the board of half a dozen art museums between Los Angeles and Death Valley. Scott had told me that Elspeth had auctioned one of her own Picasso sketches to help raise funds for his new scanner. I had to answer this question in the positive.

'Well, yes,' I replied.

Mrs Nordhoff looked at me expectantly. 'And . . .'

'Er, I like the Impressionists,' I tried.

'Wallpaper,' said Mrs Nordhoff dismissively. 'What's your favourite painting?'

I noticed that Eric had downed his cutlery and was looking in my direction every bit as eagerly as his mother. Not just eager, but desperate, for me to get this right.

'My favourite painting?' I murmured to give myself time. 'What's my favourite painting?'

I felt the same fear that had flooded me when I tried to remember the word for pianist in my A level French oral exam and somehow said 'penis' instead. All I could think of was Monet's *Waterlilies*, but Mrs Nordhoff had already dismissed impressionism. I couldn't say *Waterlilies* then. So instead I blurted out the name of the only other painting I knew apart from the Mona Lisa or Van Gogh's *Sunflowers*.

'*Mr and Mrs Clark and Percy*,' I said. 'By David Hockney. I like the way that the composition turns tradition on its head. The man's sitting instead of standing. And yet he still dominates the picture with his aggressively languid pose.'

'You look transported at the thought of it,' said Mrs Nordhoff.

'Sorry,' I snapped my eyes back to hers, expecting to find that she was being sarcastic, but for the first time that afternoon, she was actually smiling at me. Genuinely.

She was right; I had been transported but not in the way she might have expected. I had, of course, been transported back to Richard. *Mr and Mrs Clark and Percy* wasn't my favourite painting at all. I liked Monet and his common old *Waterlilies*. But even if Mrs Nordhoff hadn't already declared them tacky, I wouldn't have been able to explain why I loved the *Waterlilies*, except to use the old cliché, 'I know what I like.' Richard, on the other hand, could give a thousand reasons, both deeply personal and extremely academic, why he liked David Hockney's most famous portrait. The painting was Richard's benchmark. He aspired to capture his subjects in the way Hockney had captured his best friend and his wife.

And if I was transported, it was because as well as having the painting in my mind's eye, I had an equally strong image of Richard and me, standing in front of the painting where it hung in the Tate Gallery, his arms around my waist, his head on my shoulder, as he whispered the reasons why he loved it into my ear.

'Of course, Mr Hockney is a Los Angeles artist now,' said Mrs Nordhoff. 'In fact, I have a couple of his smaller works myself. And of course, Eric has the small oil that I gave him for his eighteenth birthday. I expect you were delighted to see that, Elizabeth. Particularly fine, don't you think?'

I nodded. Of course I hadn't seen it.

'It's getting awfully late,' said Eric, coming to my rescue at last.

Finally satisfied that she wouldn't be getting a Philistine for a daughter-in-law, Mrs Nordhoff ('Call me Elspeth') deigned to let us go. We practically ran to the car, waving frantically over our shoulders. We bombed, much too fast, about two miles down the highway. Then we pulled in to the first available bar and each had bourbon on the rocks.

'My God, I'm free.' Eric pulled off his tie. 'I'm gay again!'

'Did I earn my money, or what?' I asked.

'You were worth every single cent.'

'You think she liked me?'

'She loved you,' Eric assured me. 'You know so much about art.'

'Not really,' I admitted. 'I was just quoting out of some art textbook I once read.'

'Well, you pulled it off. I was taken in. And so was she. Thank you so much.'

Eric's relief was visible. His mother's approval had worked more effectively than a face-lift at ridding his face of its worry lines.

'You know the best thing?' he asked me then.

'What?'

'She actually asked me how I was doing. While you were in the bathroom getting ready to leave, she put her hand on my arm and told me that she'd seen *The Ladies' Room* and thought that I had the eye of a great director. Not just a good director, Lizzie. A great one.'

'That's nice.'

'It's better than getting an Oscar. And you should have seen her face when I told her what I was going to do next.'

'What are you going to do next?'

'Tolstoy's *Resurrection*.'

'Whoa! Sounds deep.' In fact, I think I had used a copy to wedge the back door open one summer.

'That's what Mom thought too. That's when she told me that she knew I'd make her proud.'

Eric dabbed at his eyes with a napkin. Any minute now, I thought, we're going to have an Oprah Winfrey moment. But we didn't. He recovered himself very well.

'Do you want to see my Hockney before you go home?' Eric asked me then. 'We could drop by the villa en route.'

'I don't really like Hockney,' I told him. 'I think I'll just go home.'

Sitting in the passenger seat of the car, still wearing my Armani 'costume', I thought about that lunchtime's conversation. *Mr and Mrs Clark and Percy*. Eric had a Hockney. Richard would have been delighted. By saying that I wasn't interested in seeing it, I had, in a small way, been giving Richard the finger.

'Look,' I was saying. 'I don't care about the things you care about any more. I don't have any reason to.'

It was a small gesture. A childish one. And one which served only to make me feel sad.

CHAPTER SEVENTEEN

Eric dropped me off about half a mile from home. He didn't think it was a good idea to drive into my part of Venice Beach in a soft-top car. He was probably right.

When I waved Eric off back to Malibu, I knew how Cinderella must have felt. Back at the beach house, I took off my new shoes, wrapped them up again in their tissue paper and put them in a box at the bottom of my wardrobe. My new Armani was replaced by my brightly coloured rags from America's Top Shop, The Limited. I had to go straight into Ladyboys that night.

Fat Joe was still covering for Sasha Tristelle. On the way home after our shift, I told him about the wedding. He roared with laughter when I described the proposal.

'Hope that wasn't the proposal Brandi predicted with her tarot cards,' I sighed. I couldn't wait to ask her about it. She had been out when I got back from the wedding.

'How did her audition go yesterday?' I asked.

'Dunno,' said Fat Joe. 'Haven't seen her.'

When Fat Joe and I got back to the house at six in the morning, Brandi was sitting on the doorstep. Smoking.

'Smoking?' I said. 'I thought you'd given up.'

Fat Joe pinched a snout from Brandi's packet and hurried inside to get the hot water. There was never enough for two showers in the tank. Well, perhaps there would have been if Fat Joe hadn't become such a girl in the bathroom. Honestly, he had gone from being a guy who showered once a month (and then only because he thought that the FBI's tracker dogs were onto him) to a full-blown woman who cleaned her teeth after every Tic-tac. Bathroom hogging was the one area of Fat Joe's diva development that I didn't really appreciate.

Normally, Brandi would have shouted something after him to the effect that he wasn't the only person living in the house and could he perhaps remember that before he condemned the rest of us to an ice-cold sprinkle. That morning, she didn't bother.

Instead she looked up at me, fag still hanging from the corner of her mouth and let the other corner twitch upwards in a pathetic approximation of a smile. There was something very different about her face that morning. I couldn't quite put my finger on it. It was like the day I finally had my brace removed. People kept coming up to me all the time, saying, 'You look different somehow,' but they just couldn't work out what had changed. I soon worked it out with Brandi though. She wasn't wearing any make-up. Nobody ever saw her without make-up, even at six in the morning (unless she was wearing a mashed avocado mask instead). Not that she looked terrible without her slap. But she did look tired.

'What's up?' I asked, sitting down beside her to enjoy the view. (Which was still the burnt-out shell of a car that had been abandoned outside our house almost a week before. Quite romantic in the dawn, I told myself.)

'Nothing's up,' she said.

Which never actually means 'nothing's up', of course.

I knew that Brandi had been called for an impromptu audition in Studio City the previous afternoon. It was a bit-part casting for a new sitcom pilot. No lines. Just lots of hair-flicking and lip-licking from what I could gather. 'Bad audition?' I asked.

'You could say that,' she said, taking another big drag on the cigarette before grinding it out on the step, right in the pathway of an army of ants that had been diligently removing all the free-standing foodstuffs from our kitchen for the past month.

'What went wrong?' I asked. 'Did he ask you to take your top off?'

Brandi nodded.

'Well,' I began. 'If you will keep going for parts in movies with titles like *Dorm Room Dollies*, Brandi. You've got to have a word with your agent about this. If you don't want to get your kit off any more, you really don't have to . . .'

'I don't mind it,' she interrupted me. 'It's never really been a problem.'

'Honestly?'

'Honestly. It's just some Catholic guilt thing makes me feel like I ought to feel bad about it.'

'Then what is the matter?' I asked breezily. 'If you don't mind getting your kit off after all?'

Brandi was sucking in her top lip as she gazed into middle space. Suddenly, there was no mistaking the fact that she was trying her hardest not to cry.

'Did he criticise your acting?' I tried.

'No.'

'Did he say you were too old for the part or something?'

'No,' she said. 'No.' Despite her efforts to maintain some composure, a big fat tear sneaked past her guard and rolled down her cheek. 'No.' She let her head drop forward into her hands, her shoulders heaved upwards. 'That isn't it at all.' Brandi started to cry.

I put my arm around her shoulders. I stroked her hair. I even kissed the top of her head. But Brandi wouldn't stop crying. I didn't know what to do. I had seen her come home from hopeless auditions before. I had seen her sniff back a couple of tears before they had a chance to wreck her mascara, then practise jujitsu moves all over the garden until she had kicked an imaginary director back up his own ass.

I figured that she must have finally had enough. She'd been in Los Angeles for three years. She wasn't sleeping in her car any more but, if you weren't feeling optimistic, then the beach house was hardly any better than a clapped-out Nissan. And though Brandi said she didn't mind getting her clothes off for the parts that she did get, I wasn't convinced. Of course she was crying because another part had been offered and then whipped away from her. It was obvious.

For an actress who made her living playing teens and dizzy students, the notion of a sell-by date was more pertinent than for any of us. Brandi had realised that her time was up. She was never going to put the fear into Cameron Diaz. Jennifer Lopez wasn't fighting her for parts. And now Brandi and the rest of her late-twenty-something peers were being superseded by a new set of wannabes with the same legs, same tits, same hair, who had never even heard of Duran Duran.

'It's OK,' I said hopefully. 'All of us will have to go through this moment. You've just got to change the parts you go for now. You're not finished yet, Brandi. Tell your agent that you want her to put you up for older roles. Character parts. Rene Russo didn't become a household name until she was in her forties. You even look a little bit like her.'

Brandi sat up straight and stared at me. She didn't look remotely comforted.

'That's not what this is about,' she whispered slowly. 'This is worse than getting older, Lizzie. Much worse.' She took a deep breath. 'Oh God,' she choked.

'What is it?'

Brandi screwed her eyes tight shut as though she was steeling herself to repeat something truly unrepeatable.

'When I took my top off at the audition this afternoon, the director's assistant told me there was something wrong with my tits.'

'Charming,' I said facetiously. 'At least they're not made of silicon.'

'I wish they were,' said Brandi then. 'Because then perhaps I wouldn't have breast cancer.'

'Brandi, you're overreacting,' I told her as she led me inside the house to her bedroom. But when she showed me the place on her right breast near her armpit where her skin had puckered in like someone had put a stitch in it, I found that I too was instinctively scared.

'Touch it,' she said. 'Tell me I'm imagining things.'

I put my hand out gingerly and touched her. Too lightly at first to feel anything but acute embarrassment. Then Brandi put her hand on top of mine and pressed it until I thought that perhaps yes, I could feel something after all. But if there was anything there at all, it was just a tiny lump. No bigger than a bean.

'We shouldn't jump to conclusions,' I said authoritatively, guilty that I felt so relieved when Brandi put her T-shirt on again. 'There are lots of reasons why you might have a lump there. The first thing to do is find out exactly what's happening. It's probably benign,' I promised. 'Most of these things are.'

'With my family history? My mother died of breast cancer.'

'But your mother was much older than you are now,' I reasoned. 'There's no need to panic.' I said that as much for myself as for Brandi. 'We'll make an appointment with your doctor for this afternoon. I'll come with you if you like.'

'I don't have a doctor,' Brandi interrupted.

'You mean you're not registered with anyone here in Venice Beach?'

'I mean, I'm not registered with anyone anywhere. I don't have a healthcare plan.'

It took a second for the significance of this announcement to reach me.

'That doesn't matter,' I told her firmly. 'We'll find a way around it.'

I read that last line directly from a motivational poster that Brandi had tacked to the outside of her wardrobe. 'I am invincible,' said a post-it note stuck to her mirror.

'You're invincible,' I told her.

Brandi snorted.

'Honestly,' I said. 'You are.'

Brandi hadn't been keeping up with the payments on her healthcare plan. It didn't seem important, she said. She was young. She never felt ill. Healthcare seemed like something for old people to worry about, or mothers. People with responsibilities and people with real reason to think that they might get ill. For Brandi it was more important to have money to spend on the right clothes for auditions, getting her hair done, a manicure, pedicure. She spent every spare cent on looking right to get the next job to get the next spare cent.

I wasn't about to lecture her about it. I knew that in the same position, I would probably have let my health plan lapse too. I was lucky that where I came from, private healthcare wasn't an issue. Yet. Later that day, as I sat next to Brandi in the depressing emergency room of the nearest hospital we could find, I was profoundly grateful for the NHS. Equally depressing the service might have been but that wasn't the fault of the overworked doctors and nurses. At least in the UK you never got the impression that because you didn't have the right credit card you might not get the best possible level of care.

The emergency room was full of the kind of dispossessed people who asked me for money in Venice Beach. We could hear an argument going on in one of the cubicles. Drunken voices. A fight. Brandi hugged her arms across her chest and drew her feet up beneath her bottom so that they rested on the edge of her seat. I had never seen her look so scared. So distant. It was as though she had been shrinking all that day; growing smaller and younger and more vulnerable until there was no trace of the Hollywood starlet-in-waiting. Just a small girl from a small town who wished that she could be anywhere else in the world right now.

I knew what was going through her mind. Most women would. Most of us know someone who has found themselves with breast cancer. Friends, neighbours, cousins. They're mostly older women. But by no means all.

At my senior school, a woman called Miss Blaine taught us history. She wasn't a popular teacher. She placed more emphasis on getting us through our exams than being liked by her pupils. It's only now in retrospect that I can see she did her best for us. At the time, of course, we all hated her. She seemed to give us twice as much homework as the rest of the staff. We had a litany of terrible names for her. One of which was Teflon Tits.

Miss Blaine had had a double mastectomy. Back in those days it was obvious. Her prosthetic breasts were like two upended ice-cream cones long before Madonna made the look fashionable with her Jean-Paul Gaultier bra.

Perhaps even then, when we sniggered at Miss Blaine's pointy profile from the back of the history room, we were acting out of fear. A mastectomy. It's got to be the worst thing that can happen to a woman, isn't it? Short of rape, there is no more effective way of robbing a woman of her femininity; reminding her of the vulnerability of her form. A woman's breasts are more than a body part. They're symbols, aren't they? Of maturity, sexuality, motherhood.

I knew what Brandi was thinking then. She was imagining waking up with a bandage where once she would have worn a fancy bra. She was imagining months of being unable to look down at herself in the shower or in the mirror. Longer still before she could let someone else see her without a shirt on again. If ever.

And I knew she was wondering whether she had somehow brought this horror upon herself. As if the pride she had in her body – the body that made her living, for heaven's sake – had somehow decided karma to visit cancer upon her and teach her a lesson.

I squeezed her hand. 'It is going to be all right, you know,' I said lightly. 'They'll be able to tell you exactly what's wrong. I bet it's just to do with hormonal fluctuations,' I added pseudo-knowledgeably. 'Then we'll go home, fetch Fat Joe and hit some bars to celebrate.'

'Thanks, Lizzie,' said Brandi, raising her chin from her knees to force a weak smile for me. 'It will be OK, won't it?'

I nodded again. But there was something about the emergency room that afternoon. I didn't think it was possible that anyone was going to come away from there with good news that day.

And we didn't. The overworked female doctor told Brandi that she would need to take a biopsy but her stiff smile told me she was almost certain, just from looking, that Brandi was suffering from something malign.

I hugged Brandi harder as if that might make the words easier to take.

'You've still got to have tests,' I said. 'She can't know for sure just by looking at you.'

Brandi stared at the array of pamphlets she had been given to tell her where to go next.

'My mom had all these,' she murmured. 'I threw them out when she died.'

'I would have done the same,' I assured her.

A nurse with a slightly less hardened expression had replaced the doctor. She handed Brandi a drink of water in a plastic cup and patted her on the shoulder. But then she had to turn her attention to the next in line.

'I've got cancer,' said Brandi very, very quietly.

'Now, that's not what she said,' I reasoned. 'The biopsy could show that everything's perfectly fine. There are lots of reasons why women get lumps in their breasts. You're still young. Cancer is the least likely explanation.'

Brandi raised her finger to her lips in a gesture that was meant to cut me off. 'I know you're trying to cheer me up,

Lizzie. And I'm very grateful. But I know what this means. My mother died when she was forty-eight. Her sister died two years later.'

'You're only twenty-seven,' I reminded her.

'I'm thirty-four,' she said to me then. 'I told you my Hollywood age.'

CHAPTER EIGHTEEN

A week after our visit to the emergency room, Brandi
went back to the same hospital for her FNAC. When
the nurse first spouted the acronym at her, Brandi said it
sounded like some kind of potato chip. Fer-knack.

Fine Needle Aspiration Cytology sounded far less friendly.

My worries that Brandi would be sent away from the
hospital without help had been unfounded. There were
options for people who didn't have medical insurance,
thank God, and while Brandi reeled at the brusque on-
the-spot diagnosis of the emergency room doctor, Fat Joe
and I set about examining her options. I called Cancer
Care, with its 1-800 number ending in HOPE, with far
more trepidation than I had once called Eric Nordhoff.

And within a week, Brandi was having her first diag-
nostic tests. We drove her to the hospital but she wanted
to stay there alone. She wanted to be alone when the doctor
delivered the results of those tests too.

Back at the beach house on results day, Fat Joe and I
waited in companionable silence for Brandi to return. Fat
Joe hadn't put on his make-up. 'Hands shaking too much,'
he said.

As I stood in the shower, I looked at the reflection of my

naked body in the bathroom mirror and ran a hand over my own breasts, almost guilty at the relief I felt to know there was nothing wrong with me.

Outside, the sky had been overcast all morning. Los Angeles doesn't look right when the sun isn't shining. London does overcast. Let's face it, London is almost always overcast. But Los Angeles doesn't wear it well. She doesn't do bad weather nonchalantly. And her people scuttle around looking faintly worried, as though Los Angeles were some giant concrete-breasted, palm-tree-studded mother who's always smiling, never in a mood, so that when she does finally get PMT, everybody knows it.

It is almost as though the city itself is a film set and when the special lighting is turned off you can see that the Hollywood Hills are in fact painted onto a giant curtain. The skyscrapers are just plywood facades. The beautiful people are exactly the same as the people in Solihull when they're not being lit from the right angles.

But that morning I didn't mind the weather. I wanted to sulk and mull over the events of the last few days and it was a damn sight easier to be in the right frame of mind for deep, soul-searching recollection when the street wasn't full of shiny, happy people enjoying the shiny, happy sun.

'Going for a walk,' I told Joe.

He didn't ask to come with me.

I set out alone and headed for the beach. The sea churned restlessly, grey as the clouds. The sand, usually so light and fine, hadn't yet dried out that day.

I turned onto the Boardwalk and headed north towards Santa Monica. Outside a tacky T-shirt shop, tea towels twisted in the wind like Tibetan prayer flags. The shop-keeper who had a word for everyone who passed was

keeping quiet today. It was as though the whole of Venice
Beach waited with me and Joe for Brandi to come home.
Even the fortune-teller where Fat Joe once learned he would
marry a millionaire industrialist turned off her neon green
palmistry sign as I passed.

I stopped by the basketball courts, usually so busy. No
one was playing today so I sat down on the low wall around
them and looked at my feet instead. As I contemplated
Brandi's dilemma, a dark, wet, perfect circle formed just
in front of my toes. I automatically wiped my cheek. But
I wasn't crying.

After a pause of about ten seconds, another perfect wet
circle appeared on the ground in front of me. And another.
And another. Around me, the world seemed to pick up
tempo. The people who had been mooching along beneath
the clouds all day, complaining of the darkness and the
humidity, were suddenly active again, scurrying like ants
now, out of the rain, back to the nest.

And the noise. All morning it had seemed so quiet.
Voices lowered. Car horns muted by the clouds. But now
the rush of the rain on the dry, parched pavement was
like applause. At first, the sound of just one particularly
brave member of the audience clapping while everyone
else sat and pondered. Then another and another. Until
the whole auditorium was shaken up and fizzing with the
sound of hands on hands. The rain pounded the pavement
around me, heavy and crazy as the sounds of hands and
feet. Everyone on their feet now, stamping out their praise
because their hands couldn't clap loud enough.

The concrete floor beneath me soon glittered like the
bottom of a stream. Already, a torrent of rainwater was
sweeping rubbish ahead of it along the pavement like a
miniature tsunami. I got to my feet and started to run

for the shelter of home. Drivers, unused to using their windscreen wipers for anything other than somewhere to park valet stickers, sent up wings of water as they ploughed along roads not built for rain, not ready to cope with anything like this downpour. A tourist bus thundered past me through the newly created puddles. I was so wet I expected my clothes to fall apart at any second.

And then, just as suddenly as it had started, the rain was gone. The sky was still overcast but now there were tears in the grey blanket above and once again the blue was showing through. I pushed my soaking hair out of my eyes, sending a trickle of icy water down my back. My pale pink skirt was red as blood now. My underwear showed clearly through my T-shirt. Catching sight of myself in the window of a passing car, I reminded myself of an illustration I had seen once in a book of children's fairytales. The princess batters on the castle door after being caught outside in a storm.

I looked a wreck. But strangely, I felt better than I had done in a long time. I felt like I did after having a good cry; as if some knot had untangled inside me; as if someone had taken a stone from my chest. It was as though the city felt like that too. Los Angeles had grown tired of being perpetually smiley. She'd had a quick bawl about her responsibilities, her ridiculous working conditions, and now, having made sure that everybody loved her by throwing a small but effective fit, she was ready for business as usual again.

It was like Scott said at the wedding party. Our little lives are part of a much bigger pattern. It rains. And then it shines again. Everything would be all right.

'I'm going to take that as a sign,' I said aloud and walked back to the beach house. The unhappiness that I had been allowing to press me into the ground, the weight of Richard's rejection, suddenly felt no more important than bird shit on a car bonnet. The rain had washed it away.

Right then, I also knew that whatever news Brandi came home with that day, it wasn't going to be the end. Fat Joe and I would help her get through.

'It's going to be good news anyway,' I told myself.

I was sure of it.

Before the cancer shock, whenever Brandi had an audition, we would wait around until she came home, peering out of the kitchen window to catch sight of her as she walked up the garden path.

'Did she or didn't she?'

Fat Joe and I would guess on the outcome of the audition then, knowing that the second Brandi walked into the beach house she would be her inscrutable upbeat self. The walk up the garden path was, in Joe's words, 'The Walk of Truth'. In the rare moments when Brandi thought she was out of her audience's critical gaze, she would reveal her true feelings. Skipping for good news, slouching for bad. When she walked through the door she would be equally composed whatever. Brandi Renata. Actress. Professional.

'Is she or isn't she?' Fat Joe asked now.

We heard the taxi door slam shut. Brandi handed her fare through the window to the driver. The car drove away. Brandi paused and took a deep breath.

Neither Fat Joe nor I made a bet this time as she walked up the garden path. She walked slowly. Straight-backed. Not smiling but not crying yet either. We couldn't have guessed until the minute she opened the door.

'I've got cancer,' Brandi wailed. 'They're going to cut my breasts off.'

'Brandi, no!' I wailed with her.

'I'm going to lose all my hair!'

'Well,' said Fat Joe, trying too hard to look on the bright side. 'At least you've got plenty of wigs.'

CHAPTER NINETEEN

B randi's mammogram had revealed a lump the size of a nickel in her left breast. The needle test had confirmed that it was cancer. When the hospital doctor told Brandi that the cancer cells were 'undifferentiated', she thought it sounded like good news at first.

'No,' he said. 'The less it looks like normal breast tissue, the worse it is.'

Fat Joe and I sat to either side of her, each holding a hand as she told us what the doctor said next.

'You should have let us come with you,' I said. Hearing the diagnosis secondhand was bad enough. I thought of Brandi, alone in the doctor's room as he spouted medical terms at her, as if he was a mechanic explaining the work she needed on her car.

'He said I should have both breasts removed, just in case.' Brandi's voice cracked. 'He's a butcher!' she sobbed. 'I don't want him touching my body.'

Fat Joe and I shared a worried glance.

'I'm sure he's suggested the best possible option,' I said cautiously.

'What kind of option is that?' Brandi snarled at me. 'Lose both my breasts? I'd rather be dead.'

She snatched her hands free and ran for her bedroom,

leaving Fat Joe and me in silence, embarrassed by the failure of our efforts at support.

'Shit,' said Fat Joe eventually.

'Shit,' I had to agree.

'Doesn't sound good.'

'I think perhaps she's overreacting,' I said. 'I mean, not overreacting exactly, but only hearing the worst parts. I'm sure he wouldn't have been quite so blunt as that.'

'It didn't sound like he had the best bedside manner,' said Joe.

'I don't think Brandi believes she's going to get the best care if she can't pay for it.'

'Everyone gets the same care, don't they?' Fat Joe said.

'It's not like the NHS here,' I explained. 'There's only so much they can do for free. Everyone who works is supposed to have private health insurance.'

'Doesn't Brandi have that?'

'What do you think?'

We didn't want to leave Brandi alone that evening. The hospital doctor wanted her to make a decision about treatment as quickly as possible. She had come home with yet another sheaf of leaflets, which remained on the kitchen table while she stayed alone in her room. But Fat Joe and I had to go to work.

I must have spent the entire evening looking miserable. I cleared just ten dollars in tips. Fat Joe's voice cracked when he tried to sing 'My Heart Will Go On'. When we got back to the house, Brandi was still in her bedroom, though it was clear that she had emerged from her room while Fat Joe and I had been gone.

The jazzy pink leaflets that tried their hardest to present

mastectomy as a positive lifestyle choice – only stopping short of saying 'Hey, you'll save money on bras' – hadn't been touched. But Brandi had been doing some reading. A glossy fashion mag lay on the kitchen table next to a half-finished cup of coffee. I flicked through its pages while Fat Joe prepared us a nightcap.

'Bikini special,' I groaned. The pouting models pictured posing in the Caribbean were enough to make Elle McPherson get depressed about her body. I sucked my teeth at the sight of yet another thong that would be better employed as dental floss. But when I turned the page, something altogether more interesting caught my eye.

Complete Woman magazine was running a Breast Awareness Campaign. Two pages after the flesh-fest of 'This Summer's Best Bikinis', the surreal models were replaced by real women, survivors of breast cancer. Three girls, who could only have been my age, grinned out from the magazine's pages. Halfway down one page, a quote jumped out, 'the most positive thing that ever happened to me'. Sheri Liberty had turned her life around, beaten cancer, left her abusive husband and started a new career in hypnotherapy.

On the next page, *Complete Woman* magazine explained where the money raised by their special breast awareness issue would be spent. St Expedite's Hospital in Santa Monica had one of the best breast cancer units in the country. Pioneering treatments. The finest doctors in the world. It looked as though you could just walk into the ultra-modern marble-clad building (same stone as the Getty Museum) and be cured. It was quite different from the depressing concrete block where Brandi had had her biopsy. 'Abandon hope all ye who enter here', might just as well have been hung above that hospital's door.

Fat Joe put a mug of Horlicks down in front of me. His mother had recently sent a tin through the post.

'What are you reading about?' he asked me.

'Guess.'

I pushed the article about St Expedite's in his direction.

'That's just up the road. Can't Brandi go there?'

'Not on Medicaid,' I told him.

'But if she could pay for it . . . How much money does she need?'

'Not sure. Thousands of dollars. Could be tens of thousands.'

Fat Joe exhaled expressively. 'She asked me to lend her some money to pay the rent last month.'

'I know. She hasn't got anything, Joe. And she's petrified. She thinks that she's just going to get butchered if she can't pay for the best care.'

'Is that the truth?'

'I don't suppose so. But it's what she thinks. And thinking like that isn't going to be helping her get better.'

'What can we do?'

'We need to raise some money.'

'How?'

'I don't know. Work extra shifts at Ladyboys?'

'I've got some money put away,' Joe said quietly. 'It was meant to be . . . well, it was meant to be for my operation.'

'Oh Joe,' I sighed. 'You can't spend that.'

'Well, having a penis for a couple more years isn't exactly a life-threatening condition, is it?'

'How much have you saved?' I hated to ask, but I had to.

'About a thousand dollars.'

'Is that all?'

'I've had other things to pay for,' he said defensively. 'I can't just buy size twelve shoes off the shelf.'

'Sorry. Oh, bloody hell,' I raged. 'I'd give her all the money I got for going to that wedding but we've still only got two thousand bucks between us. This just isn't fair. It doesn't seem civilised. Especially when I think of the kind of money some people in this town can lay their hands on. I bet Eric Nordhoff spends more than a thousand dollars a week on cut flowers for his hallway.'

'If only he would hire you for another thousand-dollar date.'

'I don't know if I could survive the stress,' I said. 'You know, those people live in a different world to us, Joe. And if something like this happened to one of them, the specialists would be found within an hour. The poor just die like sparrows.'

'Oh God,' Joe sniffed. 'Stop. You're making me think of that fairytale. The one about the statue and the little sparrow that plucks off bits of gold and uses it to help the needy.'

'I wish I'd plucked a bit of gold from Eric Nordhoff's house. I could have paid for Brandi's op with one of his ashtrays.'

'We could rob him,' suggested Fat Joe animatedly.

'I don't really think that's an option. Though . . . No.' I shook my head. 'Even if we did get hold of some artwork we wouldn't have a clue where to resell it.'

'We could blackmail him instead.'

'Joe, if you could just keep your mouth shut until you come up with a useful suggestion,' I sighed.

I took a sip of my Horlicks and remembered that I hated the stuff.

'This is like a horror movie,' said Fat Joe. 'I mean, it just doesn't seem right that Brandi should get ill. She's too, too full of life.'

'She's nowhere near dead yet,' I reminded him.

'You know what?'

'What?'

'I've been thinking lately that perhaps we've been living in a dream world here. Perhaps none of us will make it. Hollywood is more likely to make a film about the sorry lives of people like us than actually ask us to star in one. I mean, look at us, Lizzie. I'm a pathetic transvestite who can't sing a note.'

'You can sing,' I assured him.

'I *can't*. I overheard Antonio talking to Sasha on the phone. He said that he needed her to come back before I scared all his customers away with my *wailing*. That's the actual word he used.'

'Antonio wouldn't know a good voice if he heard one,' I said.

'But he recognises one that's really bad. I'm just a carica-ture, Lizzie. A stereotype. A big fat bloke who thought he could put on a dress and become a diva. And now Brandi's got breast cancer. Perfect scripting, isn't it? A girl who lives by her looks is afflicted by the worst possible disease imagi-nable. Her chest is her biggest asset and now it's become her biggest problem. Can't you see the billboard?'

I shook my head but I knew exactly what he was get-ting at.

'It's like some made-for-TV movie. Brandi would be played by that dark-haired one from *90210*, with lots of lip-quivering when she gets the diagnosis followed by the most beautiful death you've ever seen. I'd be played by that fat ginger-haired bloke from *Boogie Nights*. Face down in a swimming pool by the end of Act Two.'

'Don't be so depressing,' I pleaded. But I couldn't resist asking, 'What would you have happen to me?'

'You'd be played by Sarah Jessica Parker. Your voice would narrate the whole thing. You've come over to Los Angeles, bruised by love, and had your brush with the bizarre but ultimately, you're a survivor. You'll find my body in the swimming pool and write a book about my sad short life. It'll be a bestseller in New York and you'll refuse to come to California ever again.'

'Is that how you see me?' I asked. 'As an observer.'

'You can be an observer, Lizzie. You're the lucky one. Me and Brandi, we're both trapped by our bodies.'

'But you could both be freed if we threw enough money at your problems,' I said.

'We don't have enough money,' replied Fat Joe sadly.

They say that problems are relative. To a model a split end is as big a problem as a split in a grain sack for a Third World farmer. But I felt very humble after the conversation I had with Fat Joe that day. My broken heart had been merely psychological. Fat Joe and Brandi's problems were physical. And to a certain extent, Brandi had been right, I could choose when my problem with Richard ended.

The beach house was so miserable. Next day, Brandi was still refusing to come out of her room. Poking my head round the door a couple of times to find her staring up at the ceiling, I tried to engage her in conversation but it was clear that she wanted to be alone. Fat Joe had locked himself away too, playing Celine Dion's 'My Heart Will Go On', from *The Titanic* soundtrack over and over. I wondered whether that was contributing to Brandi's depression. It certainly wasn't helping me feel any happier.

If this was a proper studio movie, I thought, as opposed to one made-for-TV, this scene would last just a couple of minutes before my character found the perfect solution. But it wasn't a movie. And however many variables I worked into my calculations as to how much money we three could raise in a month or so, it didn't look good. Not even if I factored in Atalanta-style tips and not spending any of the money I earned on food. We had nothing to sell. I used a few drops of milk in my tea and immediately felt that I was frittering away resources.

'My heart will go onnnnnnn!!!!' Fat Joe crooned from his bedroom. But he couldn't hold the note for as long as Celine and soon dissolved into sobs.

'I can't stand this any longer,' I muttered to myself as I called Antonio and asked whether I could work an extra shift that evening. He was only too happy to have me at the club that night. Atalanta was taking a rare night off through sickness. Antonio suspected that she might in fact be spending the evening with a Russian movie producer who had been in the club the night before.

Whatever. I was grateful to have something to take my mind off the problems at home. I worked extra hard, taking on four tables simultaneously so that there was scarcely a second to spare between fetching cocktails and Cajun-style chicken wings and collecting up the loose change that was left behind on the tables for me. And smiling, even though my grin was very much put on at first, actually made me feel a little better too. Positive feedback from my facial muscles to my brain. It was something to remind Brandi about when I got back to the beach house. She had always been so keen on the power of maintaining a positive attitude. *Act 'as if'! As if we're going to make it!* When I found myself in a sulk about Richard, Brandi would always find a way to make me laugh.

God, I prayed. Please help me do the same for her. I was a little surprised at how close Brandi and I had managed to become in less than two months. And after those unpromising first impressions when I thought she was a bimbo who relied more on accidentally slipping out of her top at auditions than acting lessons. When she thought that I was an uptight English girl whose natural tone of voice was whiney.

Now I felt closer to Brandi than I had done to Mary in a long time. We were shooting for the same goal but that didn't seem to have made us competitors. She had been genuinely thrilled for me when she thought I had a chance of starring in a Nordhoff film. Now I was genuinely terrified for her.

It was all too easy to mentally put myself in her position, having to wait much too long for consultations and test results that could have been with her in hours had she the money to pay for them. The prospect of getting the cheapest level of care rather than the best one. There were surgeons who would do reconstructions for little or no fee but they had waiting lists longer than the call lists for Brandi's auditions.

For a woman who didn't rely on her looks to get her employment, who had a supportive husband, who perhaps already had children, a nice home, a family, the wait would have been bad enough. But for Brandi, who, despite her protestations, had been seeking love as avidly as employment, every second was like an hour. Every day was a lifetime in hell. I had called the beach house twice during my shift that evening. Brandi wouldn't even come to the phone.

'It's like her batteries have run out,' said Fat Joe.

'How are you?' I asked him.

'I've been playing Celine Dion,' he said.

'I know.'

CHAPTER TWENTY

St Expedite isn't your average saint. I should know. When I was a small child, I had to sit through the story of St Expedite at least once a year as part of a Sunday School lesson on the history of our local church.

I hated Sunday School. The women who were too witchy and bearded even to teach alongside the coven in the primary school that Colin and I attended, taught lessons in religious education that were arguably more boring than having to sit through the sermon that the adults endured in the church itself. Not even the brightly coloured stamps picturing Bible scenes that were handed out at the end of the session could convince me that this was a worthwhile way to spend a Sunday morning. My best friend Sian's mum and dad took her swimming on a Sunday morning.

'One day you'll be grateful for this extra education,' said my mum.

Back in the early 1980s I pooh-poohed that preposterous statement, but twenty years later, I would at least concede that those Sunday School days had left me with some interesting biblical trivia and a good idea of who to pray to when things were looking tough. Right then, reading about that hospital in Santa Monica named after my favourite saint seemed like a message from some higher power to me.

In the nineteenth century, the congregation of St Jude's

in New Orleans raised enough money to send to Rome for some statuary. Among the plaster saints that arrived in the first consignment from Italy was one of a young man dressed in the uniform of a Roman centurion. He stood with one foot upon a bird, which may or may not have been a dove. In one hand he held a banner saying 'Hodie', the Latin word for 'Today'. None of the clergy recognised this handsome saint. None of them knew his story. But the box he came in was printed with the word 'expedite', so Saint Expedite he became.

Saint Expedite was soon the most popular saint in the parish, particularly renowned for his ability to deliver a miracle fast. If you needed help 'hodie' then Saint Expedite was the man to deliver it. Everyone was delighted until Saint Jude's received a letter from the Vatican. 'We under-stand you've been praying to one "Saint Expedite",' they said. There was no saint of that name recognised. Expedite was the Italian equivalent of 'Air Mail'.

Saint Jude's were ordered to remove the impostor at once. But by this time, the speedy saint had delivered so many timely miracles that the parishioners were in uproar. The Vatican allowed Saint Jude's to keep their Roman soldier and Saint Expedite was saved.

Finding a prayer card to Saint Expedite in a junk shop near the beach house, despite the fact that my chapel pleading prior to Mary's wedding had come to nothing, I decided to give it one more go. While Brandi was walking the beach in a rare outing from her room, Fat Joe and I joined hands over the picture of the Roman soldier.

'We need a miracle and quickly,' we said.

Then we sat back to wait for the thunderbolt.

CHAPTER TWENTY-ONE

A ntonio was locking up Ladyboys at the end of another long night. As I was waiting for him – he was going to give me a lift home – I smoked one of Atalanta's disgusting menthol cigarettes while Antonio turned off the tills and prepared to count that evening's takings. As he flicked through wads of dollar bills two inches thick I was thinking hard about how I might ask Antonio for a loan to fund Brandi's treatment at St Expedite. I thought that night might be a good time to ask him. Takings were up. Ladyboys had recently become fashionable with a new younger set of Hollywood glitterati and these people had money to burn. Literally. I'd seen one guy light his cigarette with a hundred-dollar bill.

An appointment had been made for Brandi to go into hospital to have the lump and, in all probability, most of her right breast removed. In the space of less than a fortnight, she had gone from being the chief cheer leader at our beach house to a mournful, living ghost. She had lost weight. The nurse had advised her to eat healthily in the run-up to her operation but Brandi was eating nothing. I sent off for every motivational video on the subject I could lay my hands on but Brandi wouldn't even take them out of the box.

'She's already given up,' whispered Fat Joe.

At first I tried to chivvy her but I soon learned that my efforts weren't appreciated. Just as, in the days after my dumping, I had been unable to accept that there would come a day when I didn't feel so awful about Richard, Brandi couldn't believe that her life story would have a happy ending.

'Have you any idea how patronising you sound?' she asked me when I quoted to her from the magazine article in which Sheri Liberty said that having breast cancer had actually helped her take steps to improve her life.

One night she had a visit from a woman who had been diagnosed with breast cancer almost a whole decade ago. Brandi's nurse at the hospital had sent her along. Georgina, as she was called, sat in our kitchen and drank tea while Brandi examined her split ends and politely refused to be uplifted by Georgina's survival tale. Eventually, Brandi said that she was tired and went to bed, leaving me to listen to Georgina by myself.

'If your doctor tells you that there's a ninety-nine per cent chance the thing will kill you, then you have to decide to be in the one per cent that don't die. The minute I got my diagnosis, I told myself that I wasn't going to be a victim. I had things left to do with my life and they weren't things I was going to get done in the six months I might have left without a mastectomy.'

Georgina spoke with an almost evangelical zeal as she described her progress from death's door to our door. She'd just run five kilometres to raise funds for Komen's Race for the Cure. I didn't think I could run five kilometres with a lion at my heels.

'Your mindset is as important as the drugs you take,' she warned me. 'It's all about PMA.'

'Positive Mental Attitude?'

Once upon a time, Brandi had that mantra written on a post-it note tacked to the bathroom mirror.

'Your friend doesn't seem to want to get through this,' said Georgina.

When Georgina left, I forced Brandi to talk to me.

'What's the point,' she said. 'I go through this. I get better and then what? What can I do with my life if I can't use my body to get work any more?'

The hospital where she was being treated didn't have the funds or the facilities to offer Brandi post-operative reconstruction without insurance. To Brandi, anything that affected her figure would stop her working just as paralysis would finish a sprinter.

'Isn't there anything else you'd like to give a try? What about hairdressing? Beauty therapy?'

'Do you think I'd have put myself through all the shit you have to go through in this town if I didn't need to be an actress more than I need to breathe? I did the other shit for almost thirty years. I had to wait for my mother to die before I could come out here. Waiting to be an actress was like a living death.'

I was thinking about that now as I waited for Antonio, about how Brandi was so much more desperate to make it in Hollywood than I had ever been, when I heard a scuffle at the front door.

'We're closed.'

Fabrizio blocked the entrance to Ladyboys with his perfect door-wide belly.

'But I have to see Lizzie Jordan.'

'You'll have to come back tomorrow.'

'I haven't got until tomorrow. Let me in.'

The desperate customer disabled Fabrizio with a swift kick to the knee and was inside the club in a second.

'Lizzie!'

It was Eric.

'Lizzie,' he began. 'Thank God I've found you. There's been a terrible disaster.'

'Oh, Eric. Your mother hasn't . . .'

My first thought was that Elspeth must have died and that Eric was coming to me to talk about it because I was one of the few people of his acquaintance who had met her. Eric certainly looked as though that was the case. His hair was sticking up. His eyes were wide and wild and bloodshot. He looked as though he had been crying all night, then fallen asleep on the sofa in the early hours of the morning, had terrible nightmares and come in search of me.

'Worse!' he said.

What could be worse than Eric's mother dying?

'What is it?' I said, simultaneously directing Eric to a chair and motioning to Atalanta that we needed a brandy for my visitor. She was only too happy to oblige. I knew that she would be polishing up her audition piece even as she fetched Madonna's most up-and-coming director's glass.

'Eric,' I pleaded, as he gulped down the brandy in one. 'Tell me what's wrong.'

'She . . . she . . .' he stuttered.

Perhaps she was dead but he was kidding himself that she wasn't, I thought. Perhaps he had her cooling body in the back of the car. 'Eric,' I placed both hands on his shoulders to stop them from heaving with sobs. 'Breathe deeply. Talk slowly.'

'She . . . she . . . she says she wants to come and live with me!' Eric finally sobbed.

'What?' I let go of his shoulders abruptly and settled

back into a chair of my own. 'You mean, she's not dead?'

'No,' he said. 'Not yet anyway.'

Elspeth Nordhoff was marching on. But she knew that her days were numbered and she wanted to make the very best use of the time she had left. Specifically, she wanted to spend as much time as possible with her only son and his fiancée.

'I never thought she'd want to come and stay.'

Unfortunately for Eric, Elspeth thought that was a wonderful idea. She had woken up one morning, looked around her Beverly Hills mansion, and asked herself why a single, elderly woman, hurtling towards the end of her life, should want to spend her final days in a vast, spotless house that echoed only to the sound of the clock in the hall.

'I want to be around my family,' she told Eric.

Next thing he knew, she'd put all her possessions but a few of her favourite paintings into storage; the Beverly Hills mansion was on the market, and Elspeth Nordhoff had booked a moving van to take her to Malibu.

'So, what do you want me to do about it?' I asked him, when he finished his hard luck story. Despite the fact that Eric was driving a Roller these days, I had yet to get my call from Ed Strausser. If Eric wanted me to play fiancée at a dinner party, it was going to cost him dearly. Little did I know, Eric needed me even more than I imagined.

'I told her that we live together,' said Eric. 'You've got to help me out.'

Eric's mother had made her announcement that afternoon. At first, Eric wasn't actually too bothered by the news. He was about to jet off to Hawaii for two weeks in any case. Not on holiday, but on location for a commercial he was shooting while he waited to start *Northanger Abbey*. His mother wouldn't expect him to turn down a job to spend time with her. She could move into the house and Jan would have to look after her. As for me, he would tell her that I was in England with my folks.

It was all going to be so simple, but then Jan, who had by virtue of his closeness to the boss, been getting somewhat above himself of late, refused to look after Eric's old mother. At least, not if he wasn't allowed to tell her that he and Eric were an item. When, after a long and very emotional row, Eric refused to make their relationship official in front of his mother, Jan packed his bags and left.

Which meant that Eric now had man trouble, as well as peacock and mother trouble. If I didn't help him, he would have to cancel his trip to Hawaii. His mother wouldn't stay in a hotel while Eric made other arrangements. She wasn't well enough to stay in the Malibu beach house on her own. He had tried to call several house-sitting agencies but none of them could provide a house-sitter prepared to deal with Picasso, who, in the meantime, had somehow found his way into the garage and pecked holes in the side of Eric's car.

'All you have to do is look after my mother and feed the peacock.'

'But I've met your mother, Eric,' I pointed out. 'And the bird.'

Panic took up residence in Eric's eyes as he considered the possibility that I might refuse to bail him out. However, my internal meter was already running. Eric had paid me a thousand dollars to go to Santa Barbara and eat canapés.

He'd won a car worth a hundred times that in his bet with Ed Strausser and had been prepared to lose a Picasso if he lost.

How much would it be worth to him for me to feed the peacock and his mother? Two weeks at a thousand dollars a day? Two thousand dollars a day? Three thousand if I kept the bird from shitting on his car?

Eric jiggled his leg nervously as he pleaded with me to reconsider.

'My mother loved you,' he said. 'Picasso loved you.'

'Picasso tried to peck my leg.'

'You can keep him locked outside all day so long as you remember to feed him. Mother will probably have her food driven across from the Beverly Wilshire Hotel in any case. It's just company she wants. You can drive the Mercedes. I'll have Giorgio bike you over an entire wardrobe. Has Ed Strausser called you yet?' he asked.

'No.'

'I'll have him call you in the morning. Please, Lizzie, please. You know you're my only hope here.'

I had become aware of that.

'OK,' I nodded. 'How much?'

When you're a child, one of the best things about becoming an adult is, in your opinion, the ability to do whatever you like, whenever you like, with no need to explain or justify your actions to any other adult whatsoever. Of course, when you're seven, you're only thinking in terms of the ability to eat sweets until you're sick if you feel like it, having spent all your wages in one of those shops where you help yourself to jelly bears and squishy strawberry shrimps with a shovel.

Life will be so good, you think. When I can do exactly what I want.

And then you get there. And you realise that if you spend all your wages on pink shrimps, someone will kick you out of the house you can't afford to pay rent on. And far from having no responsibility to anyone, you are suddenly responsible to so many more people. Bosses, lovers, family. Hell, the minute you start to give your parents' authority the finger, you have to start thinking about how you're going to afford to put them in a decent care home when they retire.

Life is a mess of strings that exist only to trip you up. Your desires and your principles always have to be negotiable. And right now, I was negotiating with my conscience. Eric Nordhoff was willing to pay me seventy thousand dollars – that's five thousand dollars a day – just to live in his house and entertain his cancer-ridden mother while he was away. Of course, it also involved telling a whole bundle of lies. Not necessarily a good thing to do. But my friend Brandi needed seventy thousand dollars to pay for the treatment that could cure her of cancer and save her life. If I refused Eric's offer, he might get someone else to do the job instead and it was possible that the money would go to someone less scrupulous.

If it went to me, however, it could go straight to Brandi.

That was it then. When I told Eric that I would take the job, he let out a sigh like a hot-air balloon deflating at the end of a particularly hair-raising ride over enemy occupied airspace.

'But I need the money up front,' I told him. 'And I need the first cheque to be made payable to the St Expedite hospital in Santa Monica. If I'm going to do this ridiculous thing to make sure that your mother dies happy, I want to make sure that my friend Brandi gets her cure.'

'Whatever you want,' said Eric. 'I don't have time to argue.'

Five minutes later we were driving in the Rolls Royce I'd helped him win to pick up my belongings from the beach house.

It was a moral quagmire but a win-win situation as long as we didn't get caught out. Eric's bacon was saved. Brandi would get the best treatment available and I would get to live in a house with a swimming pool instead of cockroaches, while I earned the dosh.

Hearing that we had a means of raising the cash for her to go to St Expedite's, Brandi laughed out loud for the first time since her diagnosis. We danced around the kitchen, Fat Joe, Brandi, and me while Eric stood in the doorway and watched.

'Very touching,' he said. 'But do you think you could continue the gaiety later? I have a dying mother to pick up.'

And first I had to be installed as the lady of the Malibu beach house. While Eric threw the clothes he needed for Hawaii into three vast Samsonite trolley-cases, I emptied out my Debenhams' special holdall into the wardrobe he was vacating. The contents of my going-away-present vanity case looked pretty paltry in the bathroom cabinet next to Eric's entire range of Clinique. And if I thought that my three pairs of almost identical black mules were an extravagance, I felt a little better seeing Eric's *seventeen* pairs of identical black patent boots.

We did a whirlwind tour of the facilities. Juicer, blender, popcorn maker. The kitchen had every mod con imaginable but I guessed that hardly any were used.

'Pool guy comes on Mondays, Wednesdays and Fridays,' Eric told me. 'Gardener on Tuesdays and Thursdays. Cleaner every morning around nine o'clock, nine fifteen.'

'What day do I need to put the bins out?' I asked him.

'Bins out?' said Eric. 'How would I know?'

Eric truly was a guy whose only chore in life had been to wipe his own bottom. 'Look, if anything goes wrong, just call someone to fix it.' He handed me a credit card. 'This has a thirty-thousand-dollar limit on it,' he warned.

There was nothing for me to do but ensure that Picasso had birdseed and water and that Elspeth Nordhoff was entertained.

'Upset my mother and you get none of the money.'

'Your mother will have a wonderful time,' I said.

Tour of the premises over, Eric took down the silver-framed portrait of him and Jan in Whistler that had been in pride of place on top of the grand piano. I replaced it with my silver-plated framed photo of Mum, Dad, Sally and Colin in Weston-super-Mare.

Eric winced at the family in the photo.

'She'll want to know what you're marrying into,' I quipped.

'But does it have to go on top of the piano?'

'I think it does. As your fiancée . . .'

We were ready to face Eric's Mom.

Eric went to pick his mother up from Beverly Hills at nine in the morning. While I waited for them to arrive, I walked about the house that was to be my home for the next two weeks. I touched the beautiful antique furniture, peered closely at the priceless pictures. Imagine really marrying into all this money, I thought; buying your knicks at La Perla instead of Marks and Sparks.

I changed into the Armani outfit that I had worn to the Santa Barbara wedding. Catching sight of myself in a French eighteenth-century mirror, I couldn't help smiling at the girl who looked back. This was a far better way to raise the cash for Brandi's op than taking extra shifts at Ladyboys. Wear designer outfits, eat gourmet food, feed peacock, join old lady for a chat. Talk about money for nothing . . .

CHAPTER TWENTY-TWO

It was a good job I made the most of those few tranquil moments in Malibu before Eric arrived back at the house with his mother, because I wasn't to get another moment to myself for quite some time. I plastered on a grin and muttered 'seventy thousand dollars' when Eric abandoned me to carry Elspeth's not inconsiderable luggage into the house on my own to the accompaniment of a litany of complaints from the old woman herself.

'Will you be more careful with that box,' she barked. 'It contains a small bust by Rodin.'

No matter that I almost bust my ankle falling down the stairs beneath the statue's weight.

When I had finished carting all Elspeth's luggage up to her room single-handedly, she collapsed onto the sofa and had the temerity to look exhausted on my behalf. I tried to be understanding. She was, after all, a woman suffering from terminal cancer. But it was difficult to maintain such a sunny disposition when, having had me carry her up the stairs to inspect the results of my removal work, she announced that she didn't like the view from the bedroom Eric had prepared for her ('Too much ocean,' she said); then had me carry her back down the stairs before moving her small but surprisingly heavy art collection to the other end of the house.

After that, it was lunchtime. And contrary to Eric's promise that his mother would have everything made by her favourite chef at the Beverly Wilshire and delivered to the house on a motorcycle, Elspeth decided that she wanted her sandwich home-made.

'Just a little egg mayonnaise sandwich,' she said.

Easy enough. I boiled an egg – stretching my culinary capabilities to their limit – before I noticed that we didn't have any mayo.

'Will lightly boiled egg and salad without mayonnaise suit you instead?' I suggested.

No, it would not.

So, I got in the car and drove to the nearest supermarket. In fact, it probably wasn't the nearest, since I had no idea of the neighbourhood beyond Eric's gates and ended up driving halfway up the Pacific Coast Highway to San Francisco before I came across a store that sold something other than Native American knick-knacks or bikinis. When I got back to the house, Elspeth complained that she might have died while I took *for ever* to find her Miracle Whip low-fat homestyle mayo. The boiled egg had gone cold by this time. Elspeth warned me that she liked it warm. I boiled another egg and mashed it into the mayo as though I was mashing a skull.

'Wrong bread,' she said flatly when I presented her with the neat little triangles, crusts cut off, topped with a sprinkling of cress.

'Eric got this bread in especially for you,' I said. 'I thought you liked wholemeal.'

'For anything except egg mayonnaise sandwiches,' she explained. 'For egg mayonnaise I always prefer white.'

'OK.' I snatched the plate back up and marched out to the kitchen, feeling like Basil Fawlty. 'The old bag in the corner says this bread is too brown,' I told the fridge.

'What's that you're saying?' Elspeth called from the other end of the house. I made a mental note to remember that her hearing was in better shape than I had imagined.

'Nothing,' I called back. 'Just cut myself on the carving knife.'

'Well, don't get any blood on my sandwich!' she replied.

That was just the beginning. For the rest of that first day, Elspeth Nordhoff was like Goldilocks gone awry. Her afternoon tea was too hot, then too cold, then too warm. The bedroom she had asked to be moved to, at great expense to my lower back, was first too dark and then too light once I had gone to the trouble of unpicking the lining from the curtains. The pillows were too soft and the bed was too hard.

'Makes me wonder why I moved out of my own house,' she said, as she had me plump her pillows.

'Why did you?' I almost hissed.

'I just wanted to spend some time with my son. And get to know you properly,' she added with a surprisingly disarming smile. 'I expect I'll feel better in the morning. It's difficult to settle in an unfamiliar house. I do wish that Eric were home.'

So did I. Though I was beginning to realise why he had been so determined not to be. But I nodded with the empathy I was being paid for and fetched Elspeth a glass of water – 'thirty-two degrees' – before I turned in for my own first night in this unfamiliar home. This was only for two weeks after all. Two weeks until Eric came back from Hawaii and I pretended that I had to go back to England to see my family. Plus, I wasn't such a heartless woman that I didn't want to make Elspeth comfortable during what might be her last fortnight on earth.

Meanwhile, across the city, Brandi was also settling into an unfamiliar bed. Brandi's first appointment with the oncologist at St Expedite's in Santa Monica was arranged for the following morning. In the meantime, the first doctor to see her had decided that a night under observation was in order. In the short space of time since her brusque diagnosis from the state-funded doctor, she had hardly eaten or slept and now looked as ill as she was supposed to be.

But when she called me from her room at St Expedite's – a hospital room with a sea view, she told me excitedly – it was clear that she had taken on board Georgina's message at last.

'I'm not going to be a victim,' she said. 'I feel as if I'm getting better already.'

'You probably are. You're out of the beach house for a start and I'm sure the filth in that place was making me ill as well. What's the food like?'

'Wonderful,' she said. 'I had the most amazing roquette salad for dinner. What about you?'

'Egg mayonnaise on brown bread.'

'Oh. That's not so glamorous. I thought Eric had a cook.'

'He does. Me. The real one very sensibly ran away last night.'

'Have you called Joe yet today?' she asked.

'No.'

'He came and stayed with me here until they threw him out so I could get some sleep. I don't think he wanted to go back to the house on his own.'

'I wish I could invite him up here but I don't think Elspeth would be too impressed by his miniskirts.'

'What's she like?'

'Difficult. Considering she's supposed to think I'm her daughter-in-law, she's been treating me with roughly the same respect she showed the staff at the Biltmore. I keep having to remind myself that she's ill. Can you believe she just had me get a thermometer out and measure the temperature of the glass of water for her bedside table?'

'You can specify how warm you'd like your water here,' said Brandi.

'You'll be able to choose how wet you want it next,' I sighed.

'When will you be able to come and see what your hard work is paying for?' Brandi asked me then.

'I don't know. When her Majesty will let me get away. She doesn't like to be left in the house alone.'

'She's got the peacock to keep her company . . .'

'Oh my God! The peacock!'

I had completely forgotten Picasso, who was probably even now putting beak holes into some priceless piece of artwork because I hadn't fed him his seed. 'I'll have to call you tomorrow. Sleep well.'

'And you.'

'While I'm on call to the Tsarina? Little chance of that.'

I had to get out of bed to take care of the peacock. I hunted for Picasso all over the garden. He wasn't meant to be out after dark in case a passing coyote fancied a peacock-flavoured snack. Of all the instructions Eric had given me before he left for Hawaii, 'don't let Picasso get eaten by a coyote' was arguably the most important; right up there above 'don't let my mother die on the big rug in the Versace drawing-room.' Half an hour into my garden search I began to wonder whether I was already too late and Wylie Coyote had already made supper of Eric's prize bird. Or perhaps the malevolent feathered menace had wandered too close to the cliff edge and fallen into the ocean? Just as I thought that, I felt a little too close to the edge myself.

'Picasso! Picasso! Come and have some lovely bird seed.' I shook the box half-heartedly in the hope that the sound of dried-up husks against cardboard would tempt him back into the house. I've never been an animal person. Colin and I weren't allowed to have pets as children, though we begged our parents daily for a dog.

'You won't look after it properly,' said my mother.

'We will! We will!' we chorused to no avail.

One summer we brought the class hamster home for the holidays, but, after watching Evel Knievel on a summer-time special, Colin made poor Fluffy an impromptu wall of death out of an upturned umbrella. Colin spun the brolly on its tip. The hamster, which had been calmly inspecting the spokes, suddenly found himself caught up in a centrifuge and flung out into the garden before he could get a grip on the fabric with his tiny claws. The hamster died when he landed 'smack' in the middle of the rockery. Colin told Mum I made him do it. We would never be allowed to have a dog.

Years later, I got to dog-sit for my lady boss while she holidayed with her lover in Majorca. Hercules, the Cavalier King Charles Spaniel, was a fussy eater and an indiscriminate excreter. I left him in the care of Seema, who entrusted him to Fat Joe, who let Hercules loose on Clapham Common in order to test a tracking device he had fitted to the hapless dog's collar. The tracking device didn't work, of course. And Hercules got lost.

Nope. I didn't have a very good record with other people's beloved pets and Picasso was not going to prove to be the exception.

'Aaaa-roooo!!!'

Either next door's Weimaraner or a coyote howled and had me shaking in my slippers.

'Picasso!' I rattled the bird-seed box one more time. 'Come in! Well, you can stay out here all night for all I care!' I shouted when he still didn't show his beaky face. 'There are things in those hills that will eat you! Sod you then. I couldn't give a monkey's if you end up a coyote's midnight feast. I just don't want to have to explain a pile of bones and feathers to the boss.'

I'd done my best to entice the critter back indoors. Though it had been a beautifully warm day, scorching, in fact (the kind of day you would like to spend by a pool if you didn't have to spend it indoors waiting upon your ersatz future mother-in-law like a nineteenth-century Louisiana slave), an onshore breeze had chilled the coast at night-fall. I shivered in my pyjamas on Eric's lush, long lawn.

'I'm going in now.'

I turned to head back for the house and my warm, mile-wide bed and—

'Oooof!'

Tripped over a sodding peacock.

Face down in flailing feathers and claws akimbo, I tried to protect my eyes.

'Wrr-aaauuukkkk!!!'

Picasso let out an otherworldly shriek.

'Get off me!' I shouted. No doubt echoing the sentiments

he had just expressed in fluent peacock. We struggled upright. Picasso hissing. Me swearing. When he took a gratuitous peck at my kneecap, I was ready to wring his neck.

First I had to catch him. I was absolutely determined that when I went inside, he would be under my arm. And he was. But not before I had sustained a nasty gash to my left cheek that ended millimetres below my eye. Three of my fingernails were broken and my pyjama bottoms were torn from wrestling the oversized chicken into submission on the lawn only to have him deposit a very passive aggressive parcel of birdshit all over my arm.

But at least a coyote wouldn't eat him that night.

'What's going on?' Elspeth was waiting for me at the bottom of the stairs when I struggled in with the dirty bird. 'I thought I heard a murder.'

'I was trying to persuade Picasso to come in from the garden,' I explained.

She looked at me in my state of dishevelment, cheek bleeding, both knees grazed, and said, 'Well, you should be more careful. He's a very valuable bird.' Picasso fixed me with a look of haughty disdain before he strutted across the beautiful tiled floor to stand right next to Elspeth. She reached down to give him an affectionate pat on his appropriately pea-brained head. 'Did she frighten you? Naughty Lizzie.'

Naughty Lizzie considered coming between that bird's head and shoulders with an axe. I could feed him to next-door's guard dog and say that a coyote had done it.

'I'll need help to get back up the stairs,' said Elspeth brusquely.

I went to help her.

'Not until you've washed your hands,' she said. 'For heaven's sake, child.'

In the bathroom, scrubbing off the birdshit before dabbing gingerly at the peacock-shaped hole in my cheek, I wondered whether $5000 a day was actually enough.

Next morning I was awoken by the gentle tinkling of a bell. It took me a short while to remember where I was. Having grown used to sleeping on the floor in a room where we used posters to cover the bullet holes, it was disorientating to find myself in a bedroom decorated like Marie Antoinette's boudoir at the Palace at Versailles. All the rooms in Eric's house were interior-designed by people from Gucci or Versace. The Gucci rooms, all quietly expensive suede and metal, were for when Eric was feeling Zen. Full-blown Versace glamour for when he was feeling like Liberace.

I was in the pink Versace guest bedroom, half-suffocated by pillows on a vast divan that reminded me of the bed in the fairytale of the princess and the pea. In that story, the prince's mother leaves a pea beneath a hundred mattresses to see whether her future daughter-in-law is a real princess with a physiology so refined that she will find it impossible to sleep with even such a tiny bump beneath her.

Eric's mother was testing me too that morning. Eventually I realised that the persistent, barely audible, ringing of a bell was coming from her bedroom.

'Lizzie! Lizzie!'

She was calling out feebly when I got to the door. I scrambled straight from bed without bothering to straighten myself up first. She was ringing a bell. There must be something terrible going on. I knew that Eric's mother was supposed to be moribund but I was rather hoping that she would last long enough for Eric to have to deal with the corpse and not me.

'Please don't let her die,' I thought.

But Elspeth wasn't dying.

She was sitting up against her pillows like a desiccated baby doll in her white lace nightie. Either she had slept sitting up like that all night, or she had been awake for some time and had already combed her hair and done her make-up. She regarded me in my newly woken state of disgrace as though I was an urchin come in from the street to steal her Rodin.

'What's wrong?' I said. 'You were ringing the bell.'

'Yes. I'd like some toast, please. White bread this time but toasted only on one side. Butter on the side that hasn't been browned.'

'What?' I said. It was six o'clock in the morning.

Elspeth looked at me with something approaching pity. 'Didn't you sleep well, Lizzie?'

'I slept perfectly well. Just not for quite as long as I had hoped.'

'Mustn't waste the day,' she said cheerfully.

I was about to make a witty rejoinder that making her breakfast at six would be wasting a good portion of my night, then I remembered that Elspeth didn't have days to waste. If I had been given only weeks to live, then in all probability, I would have tried to waste as few of those days sleeping as possible too.

'I'll fetch you that toast.'

I hoped that she wouldn't be awake at six o'clock the following morning but that was obviously to become her pattern. Three days later I realised that I had managed an average of four hours' sleep at night since Elspeth's arrival in Malibu. Elspeth would want to stay up chatting until the early hours, then I would have to spend the best part of an hour hunting for Picasso in the garden. Since our wrestling match on the first night, he was determined to avoid me and never came when he was called. By the time I got to sleep it would be two o'clock. I began to wake automatically at six, just before Elspeth rang her bell for breakfast.

It wasn't as though she spent all day sitting in her armchair being undemanding. As I had gathered from our first conversation at that wedding in Santa Barbara, Elspeth was very much a lady who lunched with a mission. She was on the committee of at least a dozen charities with agendas as diverse as heart disease and neutering stray puppies in southern India. Straight after breakfast I would take Eric's laptop into Elspeth's bedroom and spend all morning taking dictation of letters to pop stars, prime ministers and presidents. I'd spend all afternoon correcting my spelling mistakes.

'There is no "u" in favor, here.'

Then a gaggle of ladies would arrive for afternoon tea. They might have been the ladies from the *Society for the Prevention of Cruelty to Fish* or *The Orange County Art Project* or the *Bibles for the Heathens of Southern England* brigade. To me, they blended into one endless do-gooding catwalk parade of dames *d'un certain age*. From their patent Ferragamo pumps to their hair, so perfectly set that it looked as though it was extruded each morning like the hair in the Playdoh Barber Shop Colin and I fought over as kids, these women were devoted to doing good stylishly.

Elspeth was their Mother Superior. When the ladies came to pay their respects at her bedside, they came weighed down by exotic flowers. When I wasn't preparing Earl

Grey tea – 'What's the English way to pour tea, Lizzie? Hot tea first or milk?' – I was trimming the stems from vast bunches of white and orange lilies that made me think of *Day of the Triffids*. Then I would be expected to join the ladies and nod sympathetically while they told Elspeth how the Mexican maid had been caught with her hand in the cookie jar. 'We pay her a hundred and fifty dollars a week and she has every Sunday afternoon free to see her children in Long Beach, you know.'

Then inevitably it would be on to the wedding plans.

'Have you and Eric set the day yet?'

'Well, as you know,' I'd say, 'he's terribly busy right now.'

And Elspeth would interrupt, frowning, 'I'm going to tell him to get a shift on when he comes back from Hawaii. It's not right for him to leave this lovely girl here alone.'

'Some of those Hawaiian girls,' one lady tutted knowingly.

'I'm sure that Eric wouldn't be tempted at all,' said Elspeth.

I agreed; I didn't know about the Hawaiian boys though . . .

Then Elspeth would sigh and say, 'I may never get to see this lovely young woman become my daughter-in-law.' The chattering charity girls would grow grave and nod sadly when Elspeth told them, 'We really don't know how much longer I have left. Madeleine,' she'd say (or the name of whoever she was talking to at that moment), 'when I go, can I trust you to keep running the Bible Brunchers/Art Loving Lunchers/Stray Dog Munchers society as I would have wanted it to be run?'

They'd agree of course and then for the finale, Elspeth would tell them, 'I know I can trust Lizzie to look after Eric as I would have done.'

Exit Lunching Ladies left, all sniffing. Not properly crying, in case they ruined their make-up. I had a little sniff myself the first time, but by the fourth time I heard the story, I settled on a sympathetic smile.

Ladies gone, it would be back to business. Late afternoons were for checking that day's performance of the Stock Exchange. For someone who was supposed to have her finger firmly on the bell at Death's front door, Elspeth had an amazing amount of energy. 'My final wind,' she called it.

'My final whine,' I dubbed it when I had a minute of my own.

On Elspeth's fourth night in Malibu, after I had carried her upstairs and helped her into bed, she had me sit down beside her. 'Tell me,' she said, 'about how you met my darling Eric. I want to know all about the first time you saw him and when you knew that it was love.'

Now was the moment for me to call upon everything I learned at drama school. 'Well,' I started. 'This is how I remember it. Though I'm not sure if Eric would tell you exactly the same story,' I added, to give him a get-out clause if she asked for his version of events.

'I know, men are far less emotional about these things,' said Elspeth. 'My husband could never even tell anyone who asked what colour my eyes were. He never noticed I'd bought a new dress until it appeared on his credit card. You just tell me the way you saw it, Lizzie. Did you think he was very handsome when you first saw him at that bar?'

I looked down at my hands, hoping that Elspeth would think I was just being reflective. In reality, I was trying hard not to laugh at the thought of finding Eric Nordhoff attractive. Only a mother could describe a man with no hair on a head the shape of a grapefruit that had been at the bottom of the supermarket crate as 'very handsome'. When I raised my head again, Elspeth was looking at me intently. She wasn't going to be fobbed off with a quick, 'eyes across a crowded room'. I needed to spin a convincing tale.

'It was my friend Seema's birthday,' I began.

I told her the story of me and Richard, of course. I moved the action from a London pub frequented by Antipodean backpackers to a chi-chi Hollywood bar. The first proper date was at a posh Pacific Rim restaurant, Chaya Venice, rather than a plate of spaghetti at a pizza place in Battersea. But some details I kept exactly the same.

'And when did you realise that you loved him?'

'When we stood in front of that Hockney painting, *Mr and Mrs Clark and Percy* in the Tate.' I had invented a trip to London to introduce Eric to my family.

'What happened?'

'He just told me what he liked about it. He had his arms around my waist at the time and he was leaning his chin on my shoulder. It struck me then what a passionate yet sensitive person he is. I realised that I wanted to see the world through his eyes. I felt as though I wanted him to absorb me, for us to be joined together for eternity.'

'And now you will be,' said Elspeth delightedly.

'Yes. I suppose we will.'

Thankfully it was enough for her. Elspeth had heard her bedtime story and I went outside to begin my nightly hunt for Picasso.

'Picasso,' I called. But even more half-heartedly than usual that night.

The garden was silent except for the sound of the ocean waves smoothing the sand. I knew that recounting the story of me and Richard was probably not the best idea I'd had that week but I wasn't as melancholy as I had expected to be. I didn't want to cry. Not so long ago, recalling the good times had brought tears to my eyes instantly. But not that night.

I shook Picasso's bird-seed box and was surprised to find him at my ankles instantly.

'Come on inside, you,' I said to him.

He followed. I'd stopped shouting. He'd stopped hiding.

Was that what was happening to my memories of Richard? If I stopped trying to block them out, would they start to fade away of their own accord? Was the pain really starting to go?

CHAPTER TWENTY-THREE

Elspeth didn't talk much about her illness. A week into her stay at Eric's house and I still didn't know what exactly it was that she had been diagnosed with. Was it breast cancer, like poor Brandi, I wondered? I still hadn't had a chance to visit Brandi at the hospital though I called her nightly (when Elspeth let out her first snore) and was delighted to hear that she was still looking on the bright side.

Further tests had suggested that Brandi's cancer was quite localised, though the hospital couldn't be certain until they saw the results of pathology tests on the tissue removed during Brandi's operation, and that would take place in the next couple of days. Much to Brandi's relief, the doctor in charge of her care at St Expedite's didn't see the point of removing both her breasts, given that he thought they had caught the cancer early. Instead, they would remove tissue from Brandi's right breast only and, all being well, would be able to perform reconstructive surgery straight away.

'I've been looking at pictures of the girls they've already worked on,' she said. 'In some cases you can hardly tell anything's been done. They take your nipple off like the lid of a teapot, scrape out the bad stuff and fill you back up.'

'Sounds great,' I said. I mean, what do you say to that?

'I thought about asking if they could lift the other one at the same time. That guy at Peephole Pictures said I was a little saggy.'

'That guy at Peephole Pictures was a jerk.'

'Yeah. I'll have them saggy. Seems a bit of a waste though. If they're going to fix one anyway.'

'That sounds like the Brandi I remember,' I said. 'I'm glad you're finding it funny.'

'Lizzie,' Brandi whispered. 'I'm absolutely terrified. But you remember what we used to say about auditions; how you have to act "as if"? Right now, I'm acting as if I'm going to wake up looking like Anna Nicole Smith.'

'Let's hope you hook a better-looking husband.'

'There's plenty of potential here,' she said. 'My doctor is a dreamboat. I can't believe it's my luck to meet a man I could fall in love with when he's sticking an IV port in my arm.'

Brandi was impressed with the little port that went straight into a vein in the back of her hand. 'I might keep it in and have you pump vodka straight into me when I get out of this place.'

'Isn't it uncomfortable?'

'Darling, this doctor takes my mind off it. You've got to come and see him.'

But when? It didn't seem as though Elspeth would ever let me out of her sight and for five thousand dollars a day, I didn't think it would be appropriate for me to announce that I needed a couple of hours off. I was desperate to see Brandi before she went under the knife. She had no family left that I knew of and Fat Joe, while he meant well, had a bedside manner that could only be described as 'clumsy'. Brandi told me that only that morning, Fat Joe had asked her whether he could have her bras when she didn't need them any more.

Just as I was thinking that I would perhaps have to sneak out in the night while Elspeth was sleeping, she announced that she needed to make a visit to the hospital herself.

'Shouldn't your doctor come here?' I asked. How could a woman who was unable to get up and down the stairs unaided be expected to trek to the hospital?

'Oh no,' said Elspeth. 'I don't want to be a bother. If you could just run me there and wait while I have my appointment . . .'

'Which hospital?' I asked.

'St Expedite's.'

Of course. The premier hospital for a woman who came from one of Los Angeles's premier families. A fact of which she frequently reminded me. 'When you're a Nordhoff . . .' she'd say at least a dozen times daily. I'd never be overlooked in Saks Fifth Avenue again.

On the drive to the hospital, I wondered whether it would be appropriate to ask Elspeth precisely what it was she had been diagnosed with. She referred obliquely to her 'condition' from time to time but made no reference to where it was she hurt. She had her own hair, so I guessed that she hadn't had much chemotherapy. When I asked her whether she would need me to pass by a pharmacy on our way home to fetch her drugs she told me, 'I'm not taking any drugs. What's the point of wasting all that money on drugs when I'll be dead by the end of the year?'

At the hospital, she refused my offer of company while she waited to see her doctor. Perhaps she didn't want a virtual stranger to be with her at such an intimate moment. Though as far as Elspeth was concerned, I would soon be her daughter-in-law, we had only met upon two occasions prior to her move to Eric's house. We had known of each other's existence for less than a month. Whatever her reasons, I was actually relieved.

Around Elspeth I had slipped into the role of a geisha. Though she was clearly a very strong-willed and opinionated woman herself, I guessed that she didn't want the same for her son. Eric was the centre of her world and she would tolerate the interference of a daughter-in-law only as a satellite, a shadowy support act to her son. What is it about mothers and their sons? I remembered the girls that Colin brought home before Soppy Sally. If they opened their mouths they were soon branded as overbearing or brassy. And yet, much as I knew Mum liked the idea of waving me off down the aisle as soon as possible, I had received plenty of sherry-fuelled lectures about the danger of subjugating myself to some man.

I hadn't been a hit with Richard's mother. Oh, she seemed nice enough, all polite and smiley, making a special effort to cook vegetarian whenever Richard brought me over. But much as Richard insisted that his old lady loved me, I suspected otherwise from the start. One Christmas, I thought I had finally broken through to win a place in her heart when she gave me a gift of a tiny golden daffodil pendant on an antique chain.

'It belonged to my mother,' she said.

'Wow,' I thought. She'd given me a family heirloom.

I was busy racing through the implications – family heirloom, she'd want to keep that in the family, she must think I'm going to be part of her family, Richard must have mentioned that he's thinking he might propose – when Richard's mother told me, 'It always brought her bad luck.'

'Thank you so much,' I said.

But now I knew that little golden daffodil was more

like the satanic pendant Mia Farrow is made to wear in
Rosemary's Baby than a fantastic, covetable gift, I put it in
the bottom of my jewellery box and started to count bad
omens. Just before leaving for Los Angeles, I dropped the
pendant and my keys to Richard's flat down a drain.

So, Eric's mother didn't think we were close enough for
her to want me with her while she waited for her check-up.
That was fine by me. I had the bonus of an hour to kill at
St Expedite's. Brandi would get her visit at last.

So far, everything I knew of St Expedite's Hospital, Santa
Monica came from the profile in *Complete Woman* magazine. I recognised the extravagantly coated white marble
building instantly, but was surprised to discover that the
'architectural triumph' of the Sachs-Meyer Wing formed
only a small part of the hospital as a whole. Elspeth had
me drop her off by an altogether more low-key entrance.
'Out-patients,' she explained. The main reception area was
in the Sachs-Meyer building. I headed straight there to find
out the whereabouts of Brandi's ward.

The lobby was as impressive on the inside as it had been
from its postcard perfect exterior. I could see at once why
Brandi had been so desperate to come here. The beautiful
vaulted ceiling made you feel as though God had a hand
in your recovery in this place. Immaculately uniformed
nurses, who looked as though they could just as easily
have been haughty front-of-house staff at the Mondrian,
glided noiselessly through the lobby like extras in a 1970s
movie about the future of the human race. (Brandi told me
that the nurses wore slippers specially designed to ensure
that they didn't make any noise that might disturb the
patients as they floated about the wards.) The overall

atmosphere of this gleaming white place made me expect
to see amputated legs being regenerated in seconds by
laser, such was the air of futuristic medical excellence.

Brandi had been prescribed a programme of radiotherapy
in an attempt to reduce the size of her lump prior to surgery.
At the time I arrived, she'd just returned from one session
of the powerful treatment. She looked tired, but she was
still smiling.

'My oncologist's coming round in a couple of minutes.'

'Then I'd better get out of your way,' I said.

'No. Stay,' Brandi insisted. 'He's only going to check
my vital signs. Make sure I'm still breathing before he
has me blasted with more radiation. This is the doctor
I've been telling you about,' she added. 'I want you to
see what a dish your hard work is paying for. Honestly, Lizzie, the man makes George Clooney look like
a dog.'

'I always fancied the skinny one in *ER* anyway,' I said.

'Forget him. This real doctor is worth getting sick for.'

'Brandi!' I scolded.

But she wasn't taking any notice of me. She was
straightening herself up against her pillows, pushing her
lank hair back from her eyes and trying to boot up as
much of the old Brandi, the girl who slayed producers at
Hollywood parties, as possible.

'Doctor Walker,' she grinned. 'Or can I call you Scott?'

'You, Brandi, can call me any time you want,' said Doctor
Walker.

I turned round slowly while Brandi flirted shamelessly.
'I'll call you Doctor Scott. How about that? I love a man
with a title.'

'Title came free with the stethoscope,' Doctor Scott joked back.

He was scribbling something on the clipboard attached to the end of Brandi's bed. He had his head down and I couldn't see his face but it was definitely him. How many Doctor Scott Walkers could there be in that town?

'This is my friend Lizzie,' said Brandi.

Doctor Scott stuck his hand out to shake mine without looking up from his notes.

'We've met before,' I told him.

He looked up then, startled. 'What? Oh.' His face formed an expression of recognition. 'Yes, I do believe we have. How are your toes, Miss Jordan?'

'My toes?'

'From the dancing at that wedding reception.'

'You didn't step on my toes at all,' I said, thrilled that he'd remembered our dance.

'I was thinking about your fiancé,' he said.

I looked at him blankly for a second.

'Oh, my fiancé!' I laughed. Brandi widened her eyes in wicked amusement. 'Eric's not the best dancer, is he?'

'Can't say I've seen worse,' Doctor Scott agreed. 'Er, how do you guys know each other?'

'We shared a flat,' I said.

'Before she moved up in the world,' Brandi added. 'Malibu suits you far better than Venice Beach, doesn't it, Lizzie?'

'I've moved into Eric's house,' I explained.

'Oh,' said Scott. 'How nice.'

'He's away in Hawaii at the moment so I've been looking after his mother.'

'Cheap labour,' Brandi cracked.

I shot her a 'be quiet' smile.

'Elspeth's moved from Beverly Hills?' asked Scott curiously.

'Yes. She wanted to be closer to Eric because . . . you know,' I said cagily.

'Right.' Scott nodded as though he didn't quite understand.

'I just dropped her off at the out-patients department.'

'You did?' said Scott.

'Yes. I thought she was on her way to see you, as a matter of fact.'

'No. No. I haven't seen Elspeth since the wedding. You will give her my best regards.'

'Yes,' I said. 'Of course.'

'Well, it's nice to see you again, Lizzie,' said Doctor Scott. 'I'd better keep on doing the rounds. Much as I'd like to stay here with my prettiest patient all afternoon,' he added.

'Will you still love me when my hair's fallen out?' Brandi asked him.

'You're beautiful on the inside,' Scott flirted back. 'Bye, Lizzie. Don't forget to tell Elspeth I asked after her.'

'I won't.'

Scott replaced Brandi's medical notes and swept from the room.

'You knew him already!' Brandi squealed.

'I don't exactly know him. I met him at that wedding. He knows Eric's mother. We danced together a couple of times. He's a good dancer.'

'You know what that means,' said Brandi lasciviously.

'Dancing lessons?' I suggested.

'Don't be so coy. Did you see the way he looked at you, Lizzie?'

'Like what?'

'Like you didn't notice,' Brandi snorted. 'Next time you

come in, could you do me a favour and try to look a little less good. I'm going to be losing my hair in a couple of weeks. I can't compete with your Malibu Barbie image.'

'Will you definitely lose your hair?' I asked her.

'I don't know. There's a chance that I might not have to have chemotherapy at all. If the thing hasn't spread I might just get away with Tamoxifen.'

'What does that do?'

'Blocks oestrogen. That might have caused the growth. I'm sensitive to oestrogen apparently.'

'I hope that works for you,' I said.

'I can always wear a hairpiece if it doesn't. Talking of which!'

Fat Joe had arrived. He was carrying a bunch of rather bedraggled carnations.

'Nice hair!' exclaimed Brandi sarcastically.

Joe was wearing a funky brown afro.

'Do you think it suits me?' he asked.

'It's a step backwards,' I said.

'Nooo,' Brandi insisted. 'Joe, sit down here.' She patted the edge of her bed. 'You just need to adjust it so that it sits better on your head.'

I left them trying to turn Fat Joe from a young Michael Jackson into Cleo Laine. I wasn't sure that either look suited him to be honest.

'I'd better go and pick the mother-in-law up,' I said.

'Call me later,' said Brandi but she didn't take her eyes off Joe.

When I got to the car, Elspeth was already sitting in the passenger seat.

'You forgot to lock the door,' she commented.

'Did I?' I still hadn't got the hang of the door locking button on the keyring and often unlocked the door again by accidentally pressing twice.

'I just dashed inside to use the loo,' I explained.

I had decided not to tell Elspeth about Brandi. I figured that closing the loop by introducing Elspeth and the girl whose treatment she was indirectly paying for, would only increase the chances of Eric's scam and my part in it being found out.

'Is the doctor pleased with your progress?' I asked lightly.

'I'm dying,' said Elspeth gravely. 'The progress is all downhill.'

'Mother, are you sure you wouldn't rather be in your own home?'

Elspeth was talking to Eric. She had switched the telephone in her bedroom to speakerphone, thinking that I would want to hear my sweetheart's voice. I had been sitting with her when the telephone rang, taking down a letter to the curator of an art museum in Iowa who wanted money to mount a Hockney retrospective.

'Go back to my own home now? How can you say that to me?' Elspeth exploded. 'Are you trying to make me die of a broken heart? I've got to go to the hospital tomorrow, Eric. If I don't stay positive about my condition I could be gone within a week.'

'Mother!'

'Perhaps you want me to die before you come back from Hawaii,' she said provocatively. 'Then you won't have to live with me at all. Just put me in a box and throw my body in the ocean.'

'Mother!!!'

'Would you like me to come to the hospital with you tomorrow?' I interrupted. 'I could stay with you all day, if you like.'

'No,' Elspeth sniffed proudly. 'I'm obviously imposing on you young lovers far too much as it is. Thank you for offering, Lizzie, but I think I'll be perfectly fine by myself.'

'Are you sure?' I persisted.

'I'm sure,' Elspeth confirmed. 'Perhaps you could just drive me there in the morning and pick me up when my physician has finished with me in the afternoon.'

'Of course I will,' I told her.

'See,' said Elspeth to her son's disembodied voice on the speakerphone. 'At least your future wife has a good heart.'

'I just want you to be comfortable,' Eric insisted. 'I only suggested that you might want to go back to your house because you said you were finding the sea air too chilly in the evenings. Lizzie could go with you to Beverly Hills.'

I could not! What was I? Granny-sitter?

'Lizzie doesn't want to come to Beverly Hills,' said Elspeth before I had to say anything. 'She's busy trying to make a home here. And while we're on the subject of making a home, when are you going to make her your wife?'

'There's really no need to rush,' I began.

'There is if you want your mother to see you marry,' Elspeth told her son.

'Mother, I . . .'

'It's all right,' Elspeth sniffed dramatically. 'After a life of disappointment, why should I expect to go out on a high note?'

'Mother, I . . .'

'I only raised you on my own for twenty-five years after your father died. I might have had other children but I was devoted to your father's memory and to you. All I want is to be able to die knowing that your father's name will go on.'

Shit. She wasn't about to suggest that Eric raced home to get me pregnant, was she?

'Mother, we'll start organising the wedding just as soon as I get back from Hawaii,' Eric said soothingly. Then the line made a crackling noise. A crackling noise that sounded suspiciously like a crisp packet being held close to the receiver to me.

'I'm losing you,' said Eric. 'The signal's bad on this side of the island. I'm . . .'

Click.

The sod. I knew he'd pretended to lose the signal.

Elspeth flopped back into her pillows and raised her hand to her forehead.

'He's hurrying me to my grave,' she said. 'You want to get married before I die, don't you, Lizzie?'

'Er? Well, yes. Of course. But I don't want to hurry Eric,' I added.

'What about your mother? Doesn't she want to meet me? I know I want to meet her. Family is very important, you know.'

'I agree but . . .'

'Then why don't we start planning this wedding immediately? Just you and me.' She beamed at me. 'It doesn't matter if Eric's busy with his work. He doesn't have to have anything to do with the planning at all. He just has to be there to walk down the aisle on the day that we choose for him. We can have everything arranged in less than a week. He gets back from Hawaii on Saturday. We can have you married on Sunday!'

'Elspeth, I . . .'

'Don't worry about me.'

Of course she assumed I was concerned for her health.

'I know you don't want me to over-exert myself on your behalf but I want you to know that I'd put my last breath into planning my only child's wedding.'

Eric would knock the last breath out of me if he came home to discover he was about to be married.

'Call your parents at once and tell them to get ready to fly out here. I'll call Father David at St Expedite's. You have been baptised, haven't you, Lizzie?'

By fire, I thought. A thousand times.

I didn't call my parents, of course. As far as they were concerned, I was still living with Fat Joe in Venice Beach. In any case, communicating with my parents at such a distance was not best treated as a spontaneous event. I found that email was the best way to communicate with Mum and Dad, carefully editing out anything that might be misinterpreted before pressing 'send'.

Mum in particular would be worried by most things that had happened to me since moving to Los Angeles. I had told her that Venice Beach was a bit like St Ives. The beach house was 'decked out in Laura Ashley'. And Ladyboys was a cafe serving vegetarian wholefoods. It was best that way. My mother panicked if she wasn't within twenty minutes drive of a branch of Marks and Spencer. Forget McDonalds, Coca-Cola and Microsoft. If a country didn't have Marks and Spencer then my mother considered it Third World.

So, the last thing I wanted to do right then was call her and say that I was being forced into marriage by a woman with more dollar bills than healthy brain cells. I called Eric instead. I knew damn well that he could get a signal on Kauai. He'd been calling me every night, after Elspeth went to bed, to get the lowdown on his mother's condition and also to find out if Jan had been in touch.

'She's started to organise the wedding!' I hissed to his answerphone now. Eric soon responded to that message. He called me back on the kitchen phone line.

'You've got to stop her,' he said.

'You stop her. She's already booked Father David at St Expedite's.'

'Shit. Shit. Shit. Shit. Shit.'

'You talk to her,' I told him.

'Why should I talk to her?' he said.

'She's *your* mother,' I reminded him. 'It's your job.'

Thank goodness Eric realised that we were facing an emergency. He called his mother on her phone line. I remained downstairs in the kitchen. At first I could hear nothing at all. But then came the shouting. Five minutes after his mother put down the phone, Eric called me again.

'And?' I asked.

'We're doing it.'

'Doing what?'

'Getting married. Next weekend.'

'What!?'

'Look, Lizzie, she just said that if we don't get married before she dies, she's leaving everything she owns to one of her charities.'

'She doesn't mean that.'

'I don't want to take a chance.'

'Eric, haven't you got enough money?' I admonished

him. 'Isn't it time you stood up to her and told her that you're gay?'

'Lizzie,' sighed Eric. 'Have you ever stood up to someone whose estate is worth a hundred million dollars?'

CHAPTER TWENTY-FOUR

That was it. I was being bought. I thought of everyone I'd ever met on the earth. If they pooled everything they owned, the sum total of their worth would still be nowhere near the fortune behind Elspeth Nordhoff.

There was also the small matter of my visa. It was just days away from running out. My 'tourist visa', as Eric reminded me, permitted me to remain in the United States for three months only and it certainly didn't permit me to work.

'Which is how I met you,' said Eric slyly. 'When you were working. It would only take one phone call.'

'You bastard,' I hissed. 'I'd tell them I was working for you.'

'Do you have a contract?' Eric asked me. 'Who do you think they're going to believe, Lizzie? You, the illegal immigrant? Or me, scion of the wealthy Nordhoff family? I know who I'd bet my family fortune on.'

I knew I was beat. 'You're so . . . so greedy,' I said, for want of a better word.

'How would you feel if your parents left everything they owned to a dogs' home?'

'I would be happy to see their wishes carried out,' I said, taking control of the moral high ground.

'I don't suppose you'd be able to do that much with

fifteen dollars in any case,' sneered Eric. 'But I am talking about one hundred million dollars, Lizzie. It's the budget of a Hollywood blockbuster. Hell, it's the budget of the United Kingdom. If that money gets into the hands of my mother's gaggle of ladies who lunch, they'll have spent the lot on fact-finding missions to art restoration projects in Tuscany before the end of the year. I will turn it into a masterpiece.'

'Oh yeah?' I snorted. I was standing in the Versace kitchen – all tarty gilt-edged ceramics. Eric had Versace tea towels, for heaven's sake. He was a clear case of someone who had more money than sense and I didn't see that I should help him make the ratio even greater.

But then he really shocked me.

'Remember when we talked about Tolstoy's *Resurrection* on the drive back from Santa Barbara?' he said. 'Remember what we said about the amount of money it would take to get the calibre of star you'd need to make that book into a movie that people would actually go to see? Well, one hundred million dollars is that amount of money, Lizzie. I'm not asking you to help me save my inheritance so that I can blow it all on Versace.'

Had he read my mind?

'I'm asking you to help me leave something behind for our generation's children. What greater purpose can our lives have than to turn that book which is fundamentally about the struggle for basic human rights into a movie?'

'Eric – I . . .'

'With you in the female lead.'

It was the *coup de grâce*.

'Oh, bollocks,' I exhaled. 'Can you give me twenty-four hours?'

*   *   *

So, Eric had given me not just one, but several compelling reasons why I should marry him the following Sunday. If I didn't, Brandi's treatment might come to a sudden halt, I would be deported and the greatest masterpiece of twenty-first-century cinema could lose out to a project to restore a much lesser sixteenth-century masterpiece in Tuscany. But what was really in it for me? Eric would have the whole affair so stitched up in pre-nuptial agreements that there was no chance I would walk away with more money than he wanted me to have. He'd promised me the female lead in *Resurrection* but back at the wedding in Santa Barbara he had also promised me representation by Ed Strausser. Had that materialised? Had it, bingo. I would be an American. But did I want to be an American?

I certainly didn't want to be married. At least, not to Eric Nordhoff.

What if . . . what if Richard suddenly changed his mind about Jennifer and came running back to me? What if he said that he wanted to get married? How could I explain that I was already married to someone else?

Eric had given me twenty-four hours to think about it.

Who wants to be married to a millionaire?

I decided to phone a friend.

'Mary and Bill can't take your call right now . . .'

'Brian Coren is not in his office . . .'

'This is the voicemail of Seema Patel . . .'

'Please leave a message for Colin or Sally Jordan after the tone . . .'

God knows what I thought I was going to say to Colin. Thank goodness he wasn't in. That night I couldn't get

through to a single member of my lifelong focus group.
I even considered telephoning my old boss, Mad Harriet,
to ask her what she would do in the circumstances, but
she came from a long line of aristocrats who thought that
there was no other reason to marry than to consolidate and
expand the family estate. I knew she'd be all for it.

My fingers hovered over the keypad. I dialled the first
eight digits of Mum and Dad's number . . .

'Lizzie!'

Elspeth called me from her bedroom just in time.

'I want you to come in here and talk to me about flower
arrangements.'

Next morning, with the clock ticking against me, I dropped Elspeth off outside the out-patients department at St
Expedite's. Though I offered once more to sit with her
while she had her unspecified 'treatment', she insisted once
again that she wanted to be alone. I wasn't going to force
myself upon her. To be honest, I was glad of the reprieve.
I hadn't spent time with a human being who required so
much attention since I did my last babysitting job to earn
pocket money.

Our neighbours' children back in Solihull, Shaun and
Christopher, required twenty-four-hour surveillance. I once
left them playing in the sandpit while I went inside the
house to use the bathroom. When I came back out again,
two-year-old Shaun was somehow on the roof of the garden
shed. Five-year-old Christopher was already face down on
the lawn, having demonstrated how to be a Power Ranger
for his younger brother. I vowed there and then that I would
never have children of my own.

And taking care of Elspeth had only confirmed that view.

I felt guilty for even thinking it, but I was more than a little irritated by the fact that Elspeth was such a martyr. You know the type. Martyrs like to think that they're being terribly righteous by refusing help but in reality they very rarely refuse assistance then stiffen that upper lip and get on with their painful lives in stoical silence. Nope, martyrs like to tell you how much trouble they *aren't* being at least a hundred times a day. They may say they don't require your assistance but they sure as hell require an audience.

And now Elspeth had put me in the awful position of having to marry her son. Why couldn't she just die happy in the knowledge that we would tie the knot at some unspecified time in the future? Why did she have to see it happen? Wasn't it enough for her just to think that Eric wasn't gay?

When Elspeth was safely inside the building, I hurriedly parked Eric's Mercedes – the runaround, he called it; it was worth more than my parents' house – across three spaces and raced to Brandi's ward.

Now Brandi was much more my kind of invalid.

'How's life with the mother-in-law?' was the first thing she asked.

'She's very high maintenance,' I confided. 'I just dropped her off for her treatment. She's going to be here all day. I said I'd sit with her but she says that she doesn't want anyone with her. Then she keeps on about how lonely it is to be sitting waiting at the hospital all day. So I volunteered again. And she turned me down again. And she moaned again. So etcetera, etcetera. I'm trying very hard to be sympathetic. It makes me feel so bad to be bitching about her when I see what you're going through and think that she's been through the same and now all they can do for her is keep her comfortable until she finally goes.'

I buried my head in my hands theatrically.

'It's OK,' said Brandi. 'Having cancer doesn't make you a good person. There's a woman two rooms along the corridor from me who really deserves a fatal injection. She's such a witch to the porters.'

'I just wanted to make her life a bit happier but . . . oh, Brandi!' I broke down. 'She wants me to marry Eric.'

'I know,' said Brandi. 'She thinks that you're engaged, right?'

'I mean, she wants me to marry him next Sunday.'

I spilled the story in all its gory detail. Elspeth's insistence that the marriage take place before she died, the inheritance, the visa problem, the bribery.

'Haven't they already made a film called *Resurrection* with Arnold Schwarzenegger?' Brandi asked.

'This is Tolstoy,' I intoned. 'Oh God, what am I going to do?'

Brandi shrugged. Then she said, 'It's not entirely a bad idea from your point of view. Once you're married to Eric, you'll get a green card and be able to work here.'

'I know. But—'

'And perhaps he will keep his promise and give you a lead in that film. *Restoration*, was it?'

'*Resurrection*,' I corrected.

'There's got to be some kind of cash involved too. I know he'll have you stitched up with pre-nuptial agreements but if he's prepared to pay you five thousand bucks a day just to granny-sit, then being his wife has got to be worth at least double that.'

'I know—'

'You could save up and make your own film. We could

make a film together. When I'm better. We could make a film all about me.'

I smiled, remembering the conversation that Fat Joe and I had had in the kitchen.

'It could be really gritty,' I agreed.

'But it would have a happy ending. You know what, I don't see what you've got to lose.'

It was as though the gravity in that room suddenly doubled. I felt myself sag under the weight of Brandi's statement. What did I have to lose?

'Brandi, I know you'll think this sounds silly – but I can't help thinking that the day after I plight my troth in a complete sham of a marriage to Eric, the love of my life will come charging along on that white horse and propose to me himself. What am I going to say then? Er, I'd love to, but I'm already married.'

'You could get a quickie divorce,' said Brandi matter-of-factly.

'I know. But how would you feel if you discovered that the person you were in love with had already been married? No matter that it had been a marriage of convenience and they'd never seen the person they were married to with their clothes off. It just doesn't fit in with the fairytale, where getting married symbolises the start of something new and special. I want to say "I do" once and one time only.'

'Lizzie, these days, that might as well be a fairytale. Once you're over twenty-one it's almost impossible to meet someone who doesn't have a past that they regret in at least a little way. If you meet the man of your dreams the day after you marry Eric Nordhoff, then your marital status won't matter. You'll take steps to make yourself single and the man you love will wait for you.'

I nodded. But I wasn't sure I agreed. Richard and I had never really talked about our love lives before we met each other. Though neither one of us was a virgin, I sensed that Richard didn't want to know who I'd practised my moves with.

'Hey, it's Joe!' Brandi beamed.

Fat Joe was standing shyly in the doorway with an armful of blush pink roses.

'You shouldn't have,' Brandi told him.

'I didn't. Atalanta's new boyfriend sent her two hundred this morning. She said I could bring you a dozen to wish you luck with your operation.'

Looking at those roses, I felt suddenly sick. Elspeth had suggested that we had blush pink roses for the wedding. 'For the English rose!' she said.

'You look sick,' Fat Joe said to me. 'Eric's mother been working you too hard?'

'Lizzie's getting married,' Brandi announced.

'I haven't made my mind up,' I insisted. 'I know you're going to hate me for this but I don't think I can marry anyone except Richard. Not even if it is make-believe. I can't believe that one day he won't come back to me.'

Brandi and Fat Joe shared a worried glance.

'I know that if I don't marry Eric I might be jeopardising Brandi's treatment. I know I'll have to leave the country before Eric grasses me up to immigration. But I just don't think I can do it. You have to understand. I just know that Richard and I are meant to be together. It might take six months. It might take years. But I don't want to be married when he comes back for me.'

'What if he's already married himself?' said Fat Joe.

I didn't hear him.

'I've just got this feeling,' I continued hopelessly. 'I

dream about him every night. Brandi, what about the tarot cards? They said we'd get back together.'

Fat Joe took my hands in his and tried to get me to concentrate on what he was saying. 'Lizzie, I got an email from Seema this morning. She saw Jennifer in a bar last Friday. Seema said she was flashing a ring.'

I crumbled. I fell to the floor in exactly the same way I had fallen when Richard first told me that he was leaving me for Jennifer.

'Tell me it isn't true,' I begged.

'Seema didn't talk to her but it seems the only explanation. She was wearing the ring on her engagement finger. A solitaire diamond, she said it was.'

'That sounds like an engagement to me,' confirmed Brandi.

'H-how? How? Why?' I stuttered. 'Why?'

Fat Joe hugged me close until I started to beat my fists upon his falsies.

'Why!?' I shouted.

'Lizzie, there's no point getting mad about this,' said Brandi.

'He can't marry her. He can't. He can't. He loves me.'

'You've got to let him go,' said Joe. 'There's nothing you can do about it.'

'I want to kill myself,' I told them. 'There's nothing left to live for.'

Brandi regarded me silently. I imagine she knew even then that I would soon look back on my outburst in her hospital room on the eve of her mastectomy and realise just how ridiculous I sounded.

'Let's go outside,' Joe suggested.

He wrapped his jacket around my shaking shoulders and led me away from Brandi's bedside. In the corridor we passed Scott Walker, on his way to see a patient.

'Lizzie?' he asked, as Joe hurried me past him like a suspect on the way out of court.

'It's OK,' said Joe. 'We're just going to the garden.'

Outside, we sat on a bench near a cactus garden designed by the people who had designed the beautiful gardens at the new Getty. This was supposed to be the most uplifting part of the hospital – a formal garden overlooking the Pacific – but it would have taken all four engines of a 747 to lift my heart that day.

Fat Joe sat with me for half an hour but he could think of nothing to say and I guessed that he would far rather be sitting with Brandi, who would be the first patient to go into surgery next morning. When Joe went back inside, I stayed in the garden. But I wasn't alone for long.

'Good view,' said Doctor Scott.

'Is it?' I had yet to lift my head and really look at it.

'Check it out. I think I see a mermaid on the horizon.'

'A what?' I looked up, sniffing. He was joking of course.

'Would you like me to have you put on a rehydration drip?' he asked.

'I'll be fine,' I said. 'Shouldn't you be looking after your patients?'

'I have a patient in room 67 who will remain in a state of some unnecessary agitation until she hears that her friend is OK. Who died?' he asked. 'Not Elspeth.'

'The love of my life is getting married.'

'To you, I hope.'

'I'm not talking about Eric.'

'Oh.'

'He's marrying the girl he left me for. She's a stupid

topless model bimbo who is only with him because she thinks he might be worth some money and he's fallen for it and now he's going to marry her and I don't know if I'll ever be happy again.'

'That's quite a bummer.'

Doctor Scott handed me a paper handkerchief. 'Blow,' he said. I blew my nose and handed the handkerchief back to him.

'Thanks. This is the guy you were running away from, right? The one who made you come and hide in Los Angeles?'

I nodded. He'd remembered.

'How long has it been?'

'Four months and three days,' I said. Of course, I knew exactly.

'That's not long,' said Doctor Scott. 'Having your heart broken is just like breaking a bone. You think it's mended a long time before it's really as strong as it was before the break.'

'What are you trying to say?' I asked him.

'I'm not sure,' he shrugged. 'I just thought you wanted me to say something helpful. I'm not very good at this emotional stuff,' he added. 'Perhaps we should just dance.'

'There's no music,' I said flatly.

'I'll sing if you promise to smile?'

'Scott, I . . .'

'You say po-tay-to and I say po-ta-to . . .'

Scott pulled me to my feet and tried to waltz me round the cacti.

'It worked last time,' he said, when I refused to get into the rhythm.

'I'm sorry,' I sighed, sitting back down again. 'I just can't.'

Scott plonked himself down beside me. 'I've got this all wrong, haven't I?'

'You did your best.'

'Look, Lizzie. I want you to know that your friends in there care what you're going through. You're a long way from home and of course when you get news like you've had today, you'll feel unhappy. When my ex announced that she was getting married I spent two days up at Big Sur plucking up the courage to throw myself off a cliff. You know why I didn't?'

'You were chicken?'

Scott ignored me. 'It was the view. I realised that if I threw myself off that cliff it would take maybe six months before most people had forgotten me. If I jumped at the right time, I could get myself right in the sea and there wouldn't even be a body to cry over. The sea would close around me and carry on. If I didn't throw myself off that cliff, I could take the memory of the view home with me instead. Killing myself wouldn't rob Laura of her happy life.'

'I'm not going to kill myself,' I said, interrupting his clumsy reverie.

'Oh. Good,' said Scott. 'Brandi will be pleased.'

'Can you tell her that I'm sorry?'

'I will,' said Scott, awkwardly getting to his feet again when he realised that I was telling him I wanted him to go back to Brandi now.

As he stood in front of me, clearly wondering how to sum up our little meeting, I found myself wishing that we might have met under different circumstances. He was as good-looking as I remembered from our drunken smooch in Santa Barbara. In his white coat, he was a little like Cary Grant especially when he rubbed the dimple in his chin when he was nervous. He was rubbing it right then.

'Lizzie, I suppose all I want to tell you is that sometimes it feels as though you'll never be happy, but you will be happy again. You'll see someone smile and you'll realise that though it's not the smile you were once so in love with, it could make you just as happy.'

'Thanks, Scott,' I said. 'I'll remember that.'

'Right. Well. I'll go back inside then.'

'Yes. And I must go and see Elspeth. I dropped her off at the out-patients department again this morning.'

'What for?' asked Scott. Suddenly he was back to his doctor self.

'I don't know. She doesn't like to discuss it. And she said that I should just pick her up when she's finished, but I'm going to go and wait with her,' I decided. 'I'll bet she's just like my mum. She never asks anything of Colin and me in case she's disappointed. She just hints and hints and is overjoyed when we finally get it.'

'I see. Well, tell her that I asked after her again. And you might also tell her that I'd be happy to talk to her if she wants a friendly ear.'

'You're becoming a regular counsellor. Thanks,' I added. 'I feel such a prat for bursting into tears in front of Brandi.'

'I think worrying about you has actually been a useful diversion for her.'

'Will she be OK?' I asked.

'Her operation will be carried out by the best surgeon we have at St Expedite's.'

'Well, I'll see you around,' I said glibly. 'Expect I'll see you at my wedding next weekend, in fact.'

'Next weekend?' said Scott incredulously.

I was already heading for the car park.

* * *

'Hi, I wonder if I might see Mrs Elspeth Nordhoff,' I asked the girl on reception at the out-patients department.

'Elspeth who?'

'Nordhoff?' I was getting used to having to say everything twice before the person I was talking to understood me properly. It was the accent. I'd asked for a bottle of water at McDonalds during my first week in the States. But I'd had to point at a picture of the stuff before the girl behind the counter said, 'Oh, you mean war-durr,' like I was the one who couldn't speak proper English.

The receptionist frowned as she looked down her list of names.

'Nordhoff,' I tried one more time. 'I dropped her off this morning for some treatment. She's supposed to be here all day. I'm her daughter-in-law. To be,' I added.

The receptionist had tapped Elspeth's name into her computer now.

'I don't seem to have her here,' she said.

'Are you sure?'

'Nothing under that name.'

It was odd. But I was relieved. I strolled back out to the car feeling virtuous and happy to have time to wallow in Fat Joe's revelation about Richard. And at least Elspeth would be able to have the delayed satisfaction of knowing that I had come to check that she was OK.

I got into the Mercedes and wound up the windows so that no one would be able to look in through the helpfully tinted glass and see me crying. And there I sat in the car in the car park, not caring as I got hotter and hotter, until Elspeth trotted out of the out-patients department at three o'clock. I saw her tapping numbers into her mobile. My mobile rang on the passenger seat.

'You can come and fetch me now,' she said.

'I'm already in the car,' I told her.

When she opened the car door she immediately noticed I'd been crying.

'Lizzie, it's OK,' she said. 'The doctor says I'll definitely live until after the wedding.'

'I came to see if I could wait with you earlier. The girl couldn't find your name,' I said.

Elspeth coloured a little about the forehead. It was pretty hot in that car.

'Well, I expect she was trying to maintain my privacy,' she said. 'I did tell her that I didn't want any visitors today.'

'Not even your future daughter-in-law?' I asked.

Elspeth squeezed my hand. 'You're a good girl, Lizzie.'

'So, what did the doctor say today?' I asked. 'Do you want to talk about it?'

Elspeth lifted up her glasses and pinched the bridge of her nose wearily. 'Not this afternoon, dear. I'm really extraordinarily tired.'

We drove back to Malibu in silence. Elspeth went immediately to bed.

I joined Picasso in the garden and watched the sun go down. For once, the pesky bird seemed to be tuned in to how I was feeling and desisted from ruining the atmosphere with his terrible ear-splitting shriek.

In the short time since Fat Joe told me that Jennifer had been seen wearing a ring, something had changed inside me. I was like Juliet upon hearing that her Romeo was dead. But desperate as I was, I was at the same time resigned to my fate. I wasn't going to kill myself but I was going to marry Eric. That marriage represented my death. The death of hope.

CHAPTER TWENTY-FIVE

Next day, the day of Brandi's operation, was as grey and dreary as the day she received her cancer diagnosis. Picasso moped about the atrium as though the dampness in the air made his feathers too heavy to lift into their extravagant fan. I sat in the conservatory and watched the slate-coloured sea churning. Fat Joe had promised to call me the moment Brandi came out of the operating theatre.

If Elspeth noticed that I seemed preoccupied, she didn't mention it. She was too busy arranging a wedding. As soon as Father David from St Expedite's had agreed to conduct the marriage here at the Malibu house so that Elspeth wouldn't have to drag her dying self to the church, she had made an immediate action plan to get everything else into place in just under ten days.

Her favourite chef at the Beverly Wilshire would be catering. The flowers had been ordered from the florist who did the arrangements for that year's Oscar ceremony. Blush pink roses. A single bud had been sent out in a silver box as the wedding invitation. Elspeth wrote the guest list. The Ladies who Lunched. The art gallery owners. The doctors from St Expedite's. I ran a finger over the label that said, 'Dr Scott Walker and guest'.

'Would you like me to get Eric's address book from his office?' I suggested.

Elspeth made a little moue mouth. 'The guest list is already very long. Not that I don't want to give you guys the wedding of the century, but I'm not very good around crowds just now.'

I had put just four names on the list. Fat Joe, Brandi, Antonio from Ladyboys and Atalanta. Atalanta would have crawled across Los Angeles, breaking every one of her immaculate nails in the process for the chance to meet the kind of people she thought might be at Eric Nordhoff's wedding. Though without any of Eric's friends on the guest list, it might not be such a starry affair.

It was such a long day. Brandi had gone into surgery at seven that morning. By three in the afternoon, I was sitting over the telephone, waiting for confirmation that everything had gone well. The phone rang constantly, but never with the news I wanted to hear. From three-thirty onwards, people began to RSVP to the beautiful invitations that had been sent out from Fantasie Fleurs.

'That's all of my family accounted for!' said Elspeth delightedly after I took a call from one of the malignant twin cousins. 'Isn't this exciting?'

I nodded dutifully.

But Elspeth noticed that my smile hadn't made it to my eyes.

'I know what you're thinking,' she told me. 'You're thinking that Eric is going to have his whole family around him and you're going to be there alone.'

She stroked my cheek almost lovingly.

'Well, this will bring a smile back to that pretty face.'

Elspeth reached into the top drawer of her bedside table and brought out an envelope. I guessed what was inside it before I opened it. Two return tickets from London to Los Angeles. First-class. Fully flexible.

'Call them at once,' Elspeth told me. 'There's no excuse for them not to be here now.'

That afternoon, I'd received an email from Mum and Dad. It was actually Mum who wrote, of course. Just like she always phoned or, when I phoned, took over the call from Dad.

'Dear Lizzie,' she wrote. 'It's been raining all week.' (A very traditional British email, starting with the weather.) 'Your father hasn't been able to get out in the garden or play golf and he's been driving me mad instead. Luckily, Colin and Sally have finished decorating their conservatory and we've been invited to have tea there on Sunday afternoon.' (A conservatory! How very middle-aged.) 'We do miss you here. We want you to be happy with your life, Lizzie, but your father and I can't help wishing that you could be happy with your life in Solihull. Los Angeles seems so far away. We've started looking at the world weather forecast on teletext to see what the weather is doing where you are.'

'It's sunny, Mum,' I murmured.

'We hope that you are looking after yourself. Don't forget to keep your kidneys covered. I know you'll say it's hot where you are but Mrs Mitchell tells me that the sea breezes in Los Angeles are really rather cold. And don't go thinking that you can get away without sunscreen just because it's cloudy.

'Dad spent some time surfing the net for cheap flights this afternoon. If you're still in Los Angeles by Christmas I suppose we shall have to come out and visit you, though

Mrs Mitchell also said that the long flight in those economy seats with no leg-room played havoc with her veins
and you have to watch out for thrombosis.

'I imagine that by the time you get this email we shall
have gone to bed. There's a repeat of *Pride and Prejudice*
on television this week. Mrs Mitchell says that the series
has been quite a hit with the Americans. So you see,
Hollywood isn't the only place where they can make good
films these days. Colin says that he's even seen a film crew
in Solihull.

'Lots of love from your father and mother.'

I felt a sharp pang of guilt as soon as I read the bit about
Dad surfing the net for cheap flights and Mum worrying
about thrombosis. I held in my hand a pair of first-class
tickets from Heathrow to LAX. Mum and Dad could have
reclined in those sleeper seats and quaffed champagne all
the way.

I clicked on the 'reply' button and began to draft a letter
back home. I wrote 'From your daughter, Lizzie' in the title
line. And then I was stuck. It would have been so easy to
write, 'Stop surfing for bucket seats and pack your bags.'
The tickets that Elspeth had bought were fully flexible.
Mum and Dad could be with me in less than a week.

But there was the small problem of how the tickets had
come to be in my possession. How would I explain that?
Here are some first-class tickets. Oh, by the way, they were
paid for by my future mother-in-law.

It just wasn't possible. Not only because of the deceit.
Mum would be furious on one count – that I hadn't told
her I was getting married. But I knew that she would
simultaneously be over the moon. I had long had the

feeling that Mum wouldn't care if I was about to marry an axe-murderer as long as she could go to the Neighbourhood Watch meetings and tell that smug Mrs 'three daughters married, two grandchildren already' Mitchell, that I was finally off her hands.

I could picture the scene in Solihull. The bottle of champagne that Mum and Dad had been saving since they won it at the church's Millennium raffle would be brought out of the fridge for a toast. Mum would take one sip, screw her nose up and ask to have it diluted with lemonade. Colin and Sally would have been invited round to hear the news. Sally would be delighted for me. No woman was complete without a ball and chain to stop her from floating through the newly opened skylight in the glass ceiling as far as Sally was concerned. Colin would raise a glass but he would be more cynical.

In fact, knowing Colin, he might even guess the truth. Though even he would never dare to suggest that to my mother.

Nope. I couldn't let them use the tickets. Or even know that I had moved out of the beach hut and into a mansion. 'Weather's sunny,' I began. 'But kidneys lagged. Don't worry about your thrombosis, Mum. I'll be home by Christmas.'

I told Elspeth that my mother was frightened of flying.

Six o'clock. The telephone rang. By now I was beginning to give up hope that Fat Joe would ring and tell me that Brandi was fine. I'd called the beach house but he wasn't back there. I told myself that he would definitely have called if something had gone wrong. I hoped he'd just

354

forgotten that he was meant to put me out of my misery as soon as he had any news.

'Lizzie?'

I recognised the voice but it wasn't Fat Joe.

'Who's calling?'

'Scott Walker. Doctor Scott,' he added a little self-consciously.

'Scott! Is she?'

'She's fine,' he confirmed. 'Everything went exactly as we hoped. She's back in her room now. Your friend Joe's with her.'

'He was supposed to call me.'

'I think he's been rather preoccupied.'

'And I haven't been?' I tutted.

'Cut him some slack,' said Scott. 'He's pretty traumatised. He came in wearing trousers this morning.'

It was something I had noticed. Since Brandi's diagnosis, Fat Joe had been getting increasingly conservative in his outfits, almost as though without Brandi to tell him he was looking great, he'd lost confidence in his identity as Joanna.

'You will let me know if he starts wearing Arctic Fox camo gear, won't you?'

'Is he likely to?'

'I hope not. So, she's OK?'

'She'll be fine. She may have a few tricky moments when the dressing comes off but from our point of view here at the hospital, she's been a model patient.'

'Thanks for calling to let me know,' I said.

Scott cleared his throat. 'I wasn't just calling to tell you about Brandi.'

'You weren't?'

'I, er, I got the invitation. Very stylish.' He gave a little, nervous laugh. 'I thought you said you were getting married next Sunday when you ran out of the garden but I decided I must have been hearing things. It's so soon.'

'Not much point to a long engagement.'

'I know, but . . .' He cleared his throat again. 'It really isn't my place to say this but . . .'

'What?' I asked quietly.

'I'm just surprised that's all. Given our conversation.'

'You mean because I'm not over my ex-boyfriend.'

I took Scott's silence as agreement.

'Well, my not getting married isn't going to make a difference to him, is it? He's found a new love of his life. I've found someone who can pay the bills.'

'That doesn't sound like you.'

'You've only met me three times,' I pointed out.

'I like to think I'm a good judge of character. And from the way Brandi talks about you, I wouldn't have had you down for such a *pragmatic* kind of girl.'

'Look, I know what you're thinking. You're thinking that I'm rushing into this marriage because my ex has got himself engaged. You're thinking that because I'm not really over the love of my life, my marriage will last two minutes and end in divorce. Perhaps you're right. In fact, I know you're right. Eric and I could do with a little more time to think this over, but Elspeth has less than two weeks to live and if you can't come to the wedding and be happy for me then at least be happy for her.'

'How long to live?'

I put the phone down.

The last thing I needed right then was bloody pseudo-counsellor Scott telling me that I was making a mistake. I knew I was making a mistake. But I couldn't tell him that I was making it for all the right reasons.

'Who was that?' Elspeth called downstairs.

'Doctor Walker,' I said.

'Is he coming to the wedding?'

'I think so.'

'What do you mean, you think so?'

'I mean, yes. He says he'll be there.'

'Wonderful. Can you come upstairs, please, Lizzie. I suddenly feel almost well enough to go out.'

By the time I got upstairs, Elspeth was already out of bed and standing in front of her dressing table. She was holding a smart black dress against her body. It was Chanel. Made to measure.

'I think I'd like to be buried in this dress,' she said. 'But first I want you to take me to an art gallery.'

'What? Tonight?'

'Yes. Now. I don't have many tonights left,' she reminded me. 'My dear friend Alexander Wolper is opening a new exhibition this evening. Rising stars of the twenty-first century. I'd like to see one more exhibition before I die.'

Half an hour later, I helped Elspeth downstairs to the Mercedes. With every passing day she actually seemed to be getting stronger. She barely needed my support at all as she walked to the car that evening. I wondered if I was witnessing that phenomenon whereby in the last days of life, a dying person finds enormous reserves of energy. You hear it often, don't you? People saying that they didn't expect so-and-so to die. 'I saw her in Marks and Spencers only yesterday.' Or, 'He was in the pub watching the funeral.'

Was this sudden burst of energy like the final glittering flare as a Roman candle explodes in the night? If it was, then I wondered if I ought to be encouraging Elspeth to save her last can-can for when Eric got home.

But Elspeth insisted. And so we joined the other art-lovers milling around Alexander Wolper's Arachne Gallery, named for the boastful spinner who was turned into a spider by the gods.

CHAPTER TWENTY-SIX

In the first few weeks after our break-up, I had seen Richard everywhere. Or rather, I thought I had seen him. It seemed that in every crowd there was someone with his hair, his height, wearing the same kind of jacket, walking with the same kind of skippy, casual walk. And my heart would stop in my chest when I caught sight of the familiar figure in all sorts of places where he would never actually have been seen; standing at a bus stop, the Bull Ring Shopping Centre, the fête at my parents' local Methodist church.

Eventually, the Richard sightings had grown more sporadic as perhaps the template of his being began to fade in my mind. And if I was caught out occasionally by a heart-shaped hairline, a black Schott leather jacket, or even a pair of Richard-style shoes, the moment of disorientation and sheer chest-thumping panic passed a little more quickly each time.

'It's Richard,' said my heart.

'It isn't Richard,' said my brain.

At least I'd stopped following complete strangers through the crowd.

The Arachne Gallery was very crowded that evening. The

guests were spilling out onto the street when Elspeth and I arrived.

'Alex is a very popular gallery owner,' said Elspeth. 'He's just such fun to be around.'

As she said that, the man himself minced through his sycophants to greet us. 'Elspeth, you look divine,' he said, air-kissing her on both cheeks.

'That's appropriate,' she replied. 'Since I'm going to wear this dress to my funeral.'

'Oooh. When you go, will you leave me that Rodin?' Alex asked.

'You cheeky boy,' said Elspeth.

'That's why you love me,' winked Alex.

'It's true. I love those gay boys and their wicked sense of humour,' Elspeth told me when he had gone.

I raised an eyebrow. So gay was OK so long as it was someone else's son?

'Benny!' Elspeth spotted another friend handing out refreshments.

'Elspeth, I thought you were . . .'

'Dead?' she said. 'Not quite yet, dear! You received your invitation to the wedding, of course?'

I left her to it. The gallery was full of people who wanted a word with Elspeth Nordhoff. Last-ditch attempt to get a cast-off from her art collection? I wondered. Alex would be disappointed. I knew the Rodin was going to the Getty.

I picked up a glass of wine and headed into the back room. There were fewer people in here. Too far from the Chardonnay and canapés. It seemed that nobody came to a gallery opening to look at the paintings. They came to air-kiss and gossip. One chap was actually leaning on a painting worth fifty thousand dollars as he ran through his latest movie project for an eager-looking lawyer who hankered for a touch of Tinseltown glitz.

The back room was different. In here, voices were hushed. People stood alone in front of the vast, stirring canvasses or held whispered conversations. On one wall hung a painting of a sad-eyed girl holding a wedding bouquet.

'I know how you feel,' I murmured.

Her eyes glittered with the tears that I had been holding in since my disgraceful outburst in front of Brandi.

In the centre of the room stood a sculpture that appeared to have been made from two breeze blocks and a bicycle pump. 'Three articles', the artist had called it. The price tag said $13,000.00. I thought, not for the first time that week, about the ridiculous nature of wealth.

What would the artist think if someone stumped up $13,000.00 for a sculpture that had cost him cents to make? Would he think 'more money than sense' as I would? Or would he think, 'here's someone who knows what my artistic vision is worth'?

Richard had little time for the modern British artists who emptied out their trashcans and added a hefty price tag. He was frustrated by the media focus on artists such as Hirst and Tracey Emin. If I forgot to put my discarded undies in the washbasket, he would ask me if I was going for the Turner Prize.

Richard had been convinced however, that it was just a matter of time before the public turned back to painters. 'People want to see the sweat going into painting, not a pile of sweaty knickers,' he said.

Perhaps it was because I was remembering Richard's pet peeve, that when I saw a guy with fluffy brown hair that stood up in meringue pie peaks, standing in front of a fifteen foot high portrait of a bull terrier, I had one of those 'It's Richard. It's not Richard,' moments.

But this time, the stranger was so like Richard that I continued to stare at the back of his head for long enough for him to catch me looking when he turned to comment on the painting to his companion.

'My God,' said my heart. 'He looks just like Richard.'

'It . . . isn't . . . It . . . isn't . . .' stuttered my brain.

My heart stopped. The man in front of the painting seemed to frown in recognition.

'It is Richard!'

We stared at each other from opposite ends of the room like two ghosts who had outscared each other. I thought I saw his lips begin to form a word. Probably 'Fuck'. I didn't wait around to hear it.

Elspeth caught up with me in the car park. I was sitting in the driver's seat of the Mercedes. Sweltering. Tinted windows wound right up so that no one could look in, which made my fib to Elspeth that I had gone outside to 'get some air' seem more than slightly ridiculous.

What was Richard doing in Los Angeles? Though I had seem him for a matter of seconds, the image of him turning to look at me was burned into my retina. As Elspeth chattered about the paintings she had liked most, I could only picture Richard. I pictured the close fit of his black trousers, the baggy black sweater with a huge neckhole that made him look boyish with his new, ultra-short haircut. He'd changed his style since I last saw him. Or rather, Jennifer had changed it. And hell, his new style worked for him. He looked like an off-duty Calvin Klein model. An advertising agency's version of 'an artist' for an expensive instant coffee ad. He was more Left Bank or Greenwich Village than Tufnell Park now.

But how must I have looked to him? I craned my neck to get a partial view of my face in the rear-view mirror, but the two-inch depth of the mirror afforded me only a close-up of my forehead and three worried wrinkles. While I was examining the damage, I nearly drove the car into the kerb.

'Stop day-dreaming!' Elspeth exclaimed.

I pulled the car back onto the road.

'You're so agitated,' Elspeth observed. 'What's wrong with you this evening?'

'Nothing,' I said, praying she wouldn't probe. If she probed even a millimetre I knew I would have to tell her. Richard. The pain was suddenly back just beneath the surface. The old wound was open and seeping. I took deep breaths. I told myself that it was just possible that the man in the gallery hadn't been Richard at all. Just another doppelganger. Richard wouldn't have let anyone dress him like an arty-farty poof in DKNY.

It wasn't Richard. It wasn't Richard. It wasn't Richard.

'Alex was telling me about some new British painter he's taken on . . .' said Elspeth.

I drove the Mercedes into the back of someone's Porsche.

No one was killed, thank goodness. But Elspeth insisted that we went to the Emergency Room at St Expedite's to have ourselves checked out. The doctor who attended to me thought that I might have a slight case of whiplash.

'You seem unduly spaced out,' he said.

Elspeth had to have X-rays. She was complaining of pain in her collar bone. As they took her to the radiology lab, I stopped the doctor and told him, 'She's an out-patient here already.'

The doctor raised his eyebrows. 'I don't have any notes for her here.'

'You could try the oncology department. She has terminal cancer.'

'She does?' said the doctor. He said it the way Scott had said it.

'Yes. I don't know what of, though.'

'I'll check it out,' said the doctor before he set off in pursuit of Elspeth on her trolley.

I felt shaken. But I couldn't be sure how much of it was due to the accident and how much of it was due to the fact that I thought I had seen Richard. I decided that the best thing to do would be to take a walk. Elspeth would be occupied with her X-rays for a short while. Long enough for me to get to Brandi's ward?

'It's late,' said the nurse at the front desk. 'You family?'

'Sort of.'

'Sort of isn't good enough at this time of night.'

She wasn't going to let me in.

'It's OK, Gabrielle. I know this one.'

Scott emerged from the office.

'What happened?' he asked. I was shaking quite visibly.

'I had a car crash.'

'Are you hurt anywhere?'

'I think I'm just shocked. Elspeth might have hurt her collar bone.'

Scott suddenly wrapped his arm around me and drew

me into his office. He took a pile of patient files off the best chair and motioned me to sit down.

The tears came quickly. I told him about the apparition in the art gallery.

'It's just because he's been on your mind so much lately,' Scott suggested reasonably. 'Did Elspeth say it was him?'

'She was going to say it. That's when I drove into the back of the car.'

'Lizzie, you don't know what Elspeth was going to say. You're overwrought.'

He studied me closely. The room was dark apart from the banker's light on his desk. I was reminded of one of those old movies. Bogey and Bacall. When the girl turns up in the middle of the night, looking for salvation. The guy is a tangle of emotional knots and can't tell her how he feels.

Scott opened his mouth as though he was about to say something that would show me the way through. But all he said was, 'Shall we go and see Brandi now?'

I followed him down the dark corridor to Brandi's room. Scott gently depressed the handle and eased the door open without a sound.

'She was awake for a while this afternoon,' he said.

Now Brandi dozed silently on a pair of big white pillows. With a drip running from the stand beside her bed to her bandaged wrist, and a funky little monitor keeping track of her vital signs, she looked like a space traveller resting in suspended animation on a trip to the dark side of Mars.

On the far side of the room, Fat Joe snored loudly in the seat beside the window. Yet another bunch of flowers drooped from his hands.

'Will Brandi have to have chemotherapy?' I asked.

'At the moment, I don't think so. Her results just came

back from the pathology lab. Her lymph nodes are clear so I'll start her off on a course of Tamoxifen and hope that she doesn't have to come back. It's the best outcome we could have hoped for. She'll be sore. But there's a real chance that everything will be all right.'

'Fat Joe will be relieved to hear that,' I said.

'They're very close, aren't they? They're looking after each other,' said Scott.

I couldn't help sniffing loudly. They were looking after each other. I was looking after Elspeth. Would anyone ever look after me again?

'I'll drive you back to Malibu,' Scott suggested then. 'I've been meaning to have a chat to Elspeth in any case.'

I let him walk me back to the emergency room with his arm around my shoulders, my head inclined to rest on his chest. His aftershave took me back to 'You say po-tay-to'.

CHAPTER TWENTY-SEVEN

Elspeth was fine. The X-rays had revealed no breakages; not even the tiniest hairline fracture. Even so, I didn't expect the hospital to allow her to go home that night, given her 'condition'. But they did. Scott drove us back in his Volvo. A reassuringly sensible car for a doctor, I thought as he took us smoothly back to Malibu. I went straight to bed. Scott promised me that he would stay with Elspeth until she wanted to sleep. I drifted off to the gentle sound of their murmured conversation.

I don't know how late they stayed up that night but Elspeth was awake at six as usual. Awake and excited. When I heard her ring the little bell to let me know that she was ready to start the day, I had already been awake myself for the best part of an hour.

The previous day's events seemed strangely distant. Brandi's operation, the art gallery, the car crash. I lay on my bed, staring at the rococo cherubs on the ceiling, feeling oddly calm. Brandi would be fine, the car would be fine too when it came back from the body shop. And what had happened at the art gallery . . . Perhaps Scott was right. Perhaps I had hallucinated Richard. The news of his engagement had brought him to the forefront of my mind and an art gallery was the perfect place for my subconscious to manifest a vision of him wearing clothes that he would never have picked for himself. There was probably some Donna Karan-clad Los Angeles artist somewhere in the city wondering why a girl had shrieked when she saw him and run out into the street.

'Lizzie!' Elspeth called again.

I got up automatically and drifted to her bedroom. She was sitting up against her pillows like that wizened little doll again. For someone who'd been through a car crash the previous night, she looked irrepressibly cheery.

'I want to give you your wedding present now,' she said.

'Shouldn't we wait for Eric?'

'We can't wait for Eric. Not if the present is going to be finished in time for your big day.'

'Finished? What is it?'

Elspeth beamed at me proudly. 'I've commissioned a portrait of you,' she told me. 'When Eric's father and I became engaged, his mother, who knew lots of the great artists of the time, had us both painted by Cabriolani. Now that Eric's father is gone, apart from my son, that portrait is my most treasured possession. Whenever I look at it, I don't just see my husband's handsome face as it was when I met him all those years ago, I remember the days that it took to make that portrait. I remember the feeling of his arm around my waist as we sat still for so long, the warmth of his breath upon my neck, the sound of his voice as he whispered in my ear while the painter washed his brushes. I remember the things that we talked about. We talked about how one day we would have children of our own and how we would put their prospective spouses through the agony of sitting stock still for hours on end so that they too could have an engagement painting instead of a photograph.' She laughed.

'Most things that are worth anything hurt,' she continued.

'Portraits, childbirth, getting your ears pierced so that you can wear your first diamonds.'

She squeezed my hand and her eyes twinkled at mine.

'So, today we start the sittings. Aren't you excited? Your wedding dress will be delivered this morning. I thought you should wear that. I didn't wear my wedding dress because I didn't want Eric's father to see it before our wedding day but since Eric isn't here and you're going to be sitting for the portrait alone—'

'My wedding dress?' I interrupted. I wasn't aware that I'd chosen one.

'I sent your measurements to Albert Goldstein,' Elspeth said. 'He's taken my wedding dress and made you an exact replica.'

She was thrilled. I was horrified.

'Isn't that a lovely surprise? I knew you'd think it was a wonderful idea. I'm so excited. This is everything I dreamed of. You know, you even look a little bit like I did when I was married, Lizzie. I can't wait to compare my engagement portrait by Cabriolani with your painting by Richard Adams.'

Richard Adams. The sound of my ex-boyfriend's name had an instant effect. Shock, horror, nausea. I clamped my hand to my mouth, convinced I was about to throw up. Racing to the window on the pretence of opening it, I thrust my head out into the air.

'Is he . . .' I stuttered. 'Is he that English chap?'

'That's him,' said Elspeth, clapping her hands together in delight.

I looked down into the garden. The ground seemed to lurch up to meet me.

'So you've heard of him?' Elspeth continued regardless. 'That's wonderful. I first noticed his work when I went to London last year. He was showing at the October Gallery.'

I remembered the show well. I had spilled a glass of red wine on the gallery owner at the show's opening party.

'And then I saw him again at the Arachne Gallery last night.'

Oh God. My heart convulsed at the confirmation.

'His work is so beautiful. So vibrant and modern yet quite traditional at heart.'

She might have been quoting the catalogue blurb. The catalogue blurb which I wrote for him.

'I was entranced by Richard Adams's painting,' Elspeth enthused while I clutched at the window frame. 'So many of today's young painters go for shock value. But you know, there is something about his work that is timeless. He might have been painting in the sixteenth century or the sixty-first century. He knows how to capture human emotion in a way that reaches out to every human being. He must be incredibly sensitive.'

'Yes,' I said in a tiny voice.

'Do you know what the strangest thing is? As soon as I saw his work I said to myself, when Eric finds himself a wife, I'm going to have her painted by this man. And when I came to that decision, I was actually standing in front of a painting of a woman who looked remarkably like you.'

How could I tell her that in all probability, she had been standing in front of a painting that actually was of me? I had posed for three paintings in that October Gallery exhibition. In two of them my face was hidden. But the third, a painting of me sitting in front of the window of the flat we shared in Tufnell Park, had been hailed as an incredible likeness by anyone who knew me. It was the biggest piece Richard painted that year and it formed the centrepiece of the exhibition. It had been reproduced on the front of the catalogue. The catalogue that Elspeth was pulling out of a file on her bedside table now.

'Look, here's the catalogue,' she said. 'Isn't it amazing. You would think you were twins.'

I hadn't seen the painting, entitled 'Lover. No. 1.', since it was sold to an interior design company who were buying art wholesale for the HQ of some merchant bank. Richard joked that it hung in the executive toilets.

'It is a remarkable likeness,' I agreed.

'Her nose is a bit bigger than yours,' Elspeth said. 'But doesn't it seem like fate to you, that I should be attracted to this painting and then discover that I'm going to have a wonderful daughter-in-law who looks so similar to the girl who sat for it?'

'Amazing.'

I put a hand to my temples. My brain was swelling against my skull. I felt hot. I felt dizzy. I had to get out of there.

'So you like it?' Elspeth asked me.

I had loved it. I had loved that painting because I had thought at the time that I could see Richard's love for me in every brushstroke. He had made me look beautiful, I thought, because that was how he saw me. Even though I felt like a lump at some of the sittings; even when I was pre-menstrual and spotty and feeling bloated and looking like I hadn't slept in a month.

I thought that Richard had been able to see through my corporeal cruddiness to the heart of me and found it to be lovely. Now I wasn't sure what he had seen when he looked at me. Perhaps I was just a convenient body to give the picture a more interesting composition. He made me look beautiful because a painting of a beautiful woman would be easier to sell than a lifelike representation of a pre-menstrual twenty-something, throbbing zits and all.

'He arrives at half-past twelve,' said Elspeth. 'I've told him that you'll be ready. Go and do your hair, my dear. You want to look your best.'

Well, this was hardly how I had expected it would happen. My first proper meeting with Richard since that terrible afternoon at Café Rouge would be when he came to paint my engagement portrait at my fiancé's house in Malibu.

If I ever thought that I would see him again, I had expected it would happen the way these things usually happened. When I'd been chucked before, I'd managed to avoid my ex-boyfriends until that day when I left the house in a pair of tracksuit bottoms that I had been leaving at the bottom of the laundry pile to see whether the rumour that, if left long enough, clothes would actually clean themselves was true. My face would be bereft of make-up, but not colour. Oh no, a couple of juicy red time-of-the-month zits on my chin would make certain of that. My hair would be dirty. Perhaps scraped back in an unflattering ponytail. Perhaps I'd even be wearing an Alice band to keep greasy strands out of my eyes. I would be carrying six extra pounds on my belly, while miraculously my tits would have shrunk.

And then I would see the ex-boyfriend. Perhaps I would bump into him as I was walking out of a chemist's shop, reading the instructions on the back of my verruca cure. Or worse, as I was walking out of a bookshop examining the blurb on the back of my latest purchase, something like

'How to get over your ex-boyfriend and get on with your life in ten easy steps.'

And he'd say, 'Lizzie! You look so . . . so . . .'

So fucking awful that I'm really not surprised I chucked you at all.

In the very worst case scenario he would be accompanied by his new squeeze. Called something like Candida or Bianca, she would be the complete antithesis of poor old me. She could have had a career as a supermodel but had decided to abandon such frivolity and better serve the world by becoming a lawyer. Now she represented orphaned children against big corporations who had caused their parents' deaths with dodgy health and safety practice. Either that or she was finding a cure for AIDS and spending weekends giving masterclasses to the Royal Ballet.

So, I should have been glad that I had at least a little notice of my reunion with Richard. I knew that I looked better now than I had done when he left me on the pavement in Richmond. I was browner, blonder, thinner. My wardrobe was full of designer clothes. I was living in a multi-million-dollar beachfront property in Malibu, driving a Mercedes, preparing for a wedding for which the invitations alone had cost fifty dollars apiece. If there was ever a good position to find oneself in when faced with meeting an ex-boyfriend, then this was it. No one would look at me that morning and think that I hadn't done well for myself.

Except that I knew it was all make-believe. If it hadn't been for Ed Strausser and his stupid bet, I would still be in a cockroach-infested hut in Venice Beach. Perhaps I wouldn't even be there. I'd be back in Solihull, temping in Soppy Sally's office. Richard, on the other hand, had done very well for himself. He had looked fantastic. He was wearing designer clothes. He was in Los Angeles at the invitation of one of the city's hottest gallery owners and he had a fiancée who actually wanted to marry him.

From the outside it may have looked as though I had come a long way since that Sunday afternoon on the pavement but if I was kidding anyone, I wasn't kidding myself.

'Oh God,' I breathed as I sat in front of the mirror, studying my suntanned face and running through a hundred opening lines in my mind.

'We meet again.'

That sounded like Bond and Blofeld.

'Fancy meeting you here!'

That was the kind of line Mary came out with when she found herself sharing the top of a toilet cistern with some soap star for coke-chopping activities.

Something will come naturally, I tried to convince myself. What had I said when we first met? Not much, to be honest.

Drunk as the proverbial skunk, I just fell down the stairs and into Richard's arms. He insisted on snogging me even when his first fumbled attempt to run his fingers through my hair saw my fake blonde locks come away in his hand (I was dressed as Agnetha from Abba). I didn't even know his name until the following morning. I didn't prepare for my first night with Richard. It just sort of happened. I threw myself on top of him and by the next morning he had seen my full repertoire of tricks.

I couldn't help being depressed about that now. While Richard and I had been together I had been faintly proud to admit that he and I had got to fourth base so quickly. It proved, I told myself, that you didn't have to prance about like a nun for months in order to get a man's respect. You could satisfy your urges in a thoroughly adult manner and still go on to have a meaningful relationship. Now I considered the possibility that the rot had set in at the very moment that I stopped Richard halfway through cunnilingus to ask him what his surname was. Too much too soon and too little left for afterwards? The implications for the women's movement were far too depressing.

The doorbell rang. I felt another wave of nausea. But it wasn't him. Albert Goldstein's assistant was delivering my wedding dress.

'Mr Goldstein would like to wish the future Mr and Mrs Nordhoff much happiness in their life together,' the young girl repeated chirpily. She held the dress out towards me in a long golden box filled with layer upon layer of tissue paper.

'Thanks,' I said and was about to close the door when Abby Goldstein (she was the dressmaker's granddaughter) reminded me, 'I have to make sure that it fits.'

Abby helped me into the dress in my bedroom and I stood on a stool while she busied herself with adjusting the hem. The narrow bodice with its shoestring straps fitted me perfectly.

'It was considered very risqué to show your arms when I was a girl,' said Elspeth.

The bodice skimmed across my stomach into a floor-length chiffon skirt dotted with diamanté and pearls. On the bodice itself, Albert Goldstein had used more pearls and glittering stones to enhance a delicately embroidered heart that sat in the centre of my breastbone. When I looked at it properly, I saw that he had stitched two 'E's inside the heart's curvy outline. One for Eric and one for Elizabeth.

'It's fate,' said Elspeth. 'There were two 'E's on the bodice of my dress too. One for Elspeth and one for Ernest.'

Ernest. It was the first time I had heard Elspeth speak her husband's name. Until that point, she had always referred to him as 'Eric's father'. Her eyes glittered with tears as she watched Abby pull the bodice tighter around my ribcage with an elaborate web of ribbons.

When Abby had finished, Elspeth asked her to leave us alone for a couple of minutes while she gave me something she had been keeping especially for this moment. With Abby out of the way, Elspeth handed me a small pink box.

'Something old, something new, something borrowed . . . This will be the old part.'

I opened the box to discover that it held a filigree tiara. The fragile gold wire, dotted with pearls and diamonds, had been carefully bent into a heart shape to echo the pattern of the dress. When Elspeth placed it on my head, I had a flashback to that moment in Blushing Bride when the shop assistant crowned Mary with a ring of gaudy tinsel. But this tiara was the most beautiful thing I had ever seen.

Tiara in place, Elspeth covered my hair with her veil. And finally I stood in front of the mirror like a real bride.

'Beautiful,' Elspeth murmured.

'Sad,' I thought. I couldn't get excited about dressing-up any more. As I regarded my reflection, I thought I could already see Miss Havisham. The wedding would never happen and I would spend the rest of my days cursing a man who had forsaken me for another.

'Brrriiinnnggg!'

A jaunty tune on the doorbell.

'That must be Richard Adams!' said Elspeth. 'Come on, Lizzie. Let's go downstairs.'

I grabbed the back of a chair to steady myself as alternate

waves of sickness and excitement overtook me and all I wanted was to be able to freeze that second of incredible, if somewhat unrealistic, potential when I looked gorgeous and Richard was downstairs and there was every possibility that as soon as he saw me he would fall back in love with me.

CHAPTER TWENTY-EIGHT

I imagined that I swept down the stairs like Scarlett O'Hara but Richard soon put me right.

'You look like the fucking ghost of girlfriends past,' he said as he set up his easel in the sitting room. 'What on earth are you doing here?'

It had been different while Elspeth was still in the room. Then, Richard, the consummate professional, had allowed her to introduce us to each other and his face had shown not a flicker of recognition that might betray our intimate past. While Elspeth was still with us, Richard treated me as he would have treated any subject. We discussed poses, settings, and the number of sittings a portrait of this kind might be expected to take. When Elspeth said, 'She'll make a beautiful painting, don't you think?' Richard had agreed with her and said, 'She has a very striking face.'

'I'm sure you'll find lots to talk about while you're doing the painting, seeing as you both come from England,' Elspeth smiled at us. 'Richard lives in a place called Tufnell Park, Lizzie. Have you heard of that?'

'Oh yes,' I said.

'Is this your first time in Los Angeles?' Elspeth asked my poker-faced ex.

'Yes, it is. But I rather like it here,' he said.

'Lizzie likes it too,' said Elspeth. 'She came out here to

be an actress, you know. But then she met my son Eric and
fell in love. It was a whirlwind romance. It's amazing how
quickly it happened.'

'Amazing,' my ex-boyfriend agreed.

'But when one meets the person one is destined to fall
in love with, why wait any longer to do it?'

'You could do it on the first night,' smarmed Richard.
I knew exactly what he was getting at. 'When's the wedding?' he asked.

'On Sunday.'

'Sunday? But that's in . . .'

'Three days time. It's a very tall order, I know, Richard.
But Alex Wolper tells me that if anyone can knock a
painting out quickly, it's you.'

'Unless you find the subject warrants particular attention,' I sniped in return for the 'first night' crack.

'Well, I should leave you two Limeys to it,' said Elspeth.
When neither of us laughed, she assumed it was because
we didn't get the joke. 'Limeys? That's what people here
call you English guys, right?'

Richard certainly looked as though he was sucking a
lemon when Elspeth finally left us alone.

'We meet again.'

I went for the James Bond line after all.

'So it seems,' said Richard. He continued to unpack his
equipment without looking at me. 'I thought it was you at
that gallery the other night. But then I asked myself what
on earth *you* would be doing at the opening of the most
important new exhibition in Los Angeles.'

'Exactly the same thought went through my mind,' I
retorted.

Richard straightened out the legs of his easel. It was the
same wooden easel that he had bought with the money he

earned from his very first commission. The easel that I had once plastered all over with post-it notes saying 'I love you' for his birthday. I wondered if he remembered that.

'This certainly isn't how I expected to meet you again,' he said as he tightened up the screws that would hold the easel steady and at the right height. 'You've done all right for yourself,' he added. In the same way as my brother said, 'You've done all right for yourself,' to his ex-girlfriend Julie. She had worked as an escort girl and ended up marrying her boss.

'I'm very happy,' I lied.

'And about to be very rich, by all accounts.'

'Eric has some money,' I admitted.

'And he'll have even more when the old lady pops her clogs.'

'I'm not in it for the money,' I said indignantly. 'Unlike some people I know, I don't equate status with love.'

'Was it the way he looked at you?' Richard teased me.

'I fell for Eric because he has inner beauty,' I said.

'He would have to have,' said Richard, picking up a silver-framed picture of Eric and his mother from the top of the grand piano. 'Head like a squashed pink grapefruit.'

'I forgot quite how lookist you are.'

'I can't believe you're getting married,' Richard told me. He stood behind his easel with his hands on his hips and looked me up and down as though I was wearing rags and covered in body lice.

'Why not?' I asked him. 'Didn't think that anybody would want me, did you?'

'You've scrubbed up a bit since I left you by that lamp-post in Richmond.'

'You should have taken a picture,' I snarled. 'It's the last time anybody will see me stoop that low.'

Richard shook his head disdainfully. 'Did you ask that old bat to have me paint you?'

'You must be joking. I had no idea this was going to happen until this morning.'

'But you knew I was in Los Angeles,' he accused. 'You saw me at Arachne.'

'Could have been anyone,' I shrugged. 'I wasn't sure I remembered what you looked like. Anyway, you could have told her you were busy when she asked you to paint me.'

'Oh yeah. Like I'd put two and two together? Come and paint a beautiful English girl living in Malibu, about to marry a multi-millionaire? Lizzie Jordan wasn't exactly the name that sprang to mind.'

He placed a sketchpad on the easel and tore off the cover sheet noisily. 'You moved fast,' he said, as he took out a thick black pencil and began to make furious marks on the page.

'I'm sorry,' I said. 'Was I supposed to spend another six months in mourning?'

'Last time I spoke to Mary she said you were working as a waitress in a transvestite bar . . .'

Bitch! She was definitely off my Christmas list.

'Yeah. I saw her at the Lister Badlands Art Awards with that gormless husband of hers.'

'Bill's my friend,' I pointed out.

'You had some hopeless friends,' said Richard. 'So, how did you manage to meet this fiancé of yours while dressing up like a geezer-bird? Doing a bit of escort work on the side?'

'Fuck you,' I spat. 'He asked me to audition for him.'

That wasn't exactly a lie.

'Keep your head still,' said Richard. 'I want to get

your nose right . . . Be able to get it fixed now, won't you?'

'Fixed!' I exclaimed. 'And why would I need . . .'

'Getting along all right in here?'

Elspeth popped her head around the door.

'Wonderful,' said Richard. 'We've just discovered we have people in common.'

'How exciting,' said Elspeth. 'You will come to the wedding, won't you? None of Lizzie's friends are able to make it out in time.'

'Rush job?' Richard suggested, when Elspeth left us again. 'In a hurry to tie the knot for some particular reason? I must say I always suspected you might end up trying to trap a man when you got a bit too close to thirty.'

My mouth dropped open as his words hit me like a tennis ball in the stomach.

'So much for "Richard, I'll never be able to look at another man",' he squeaked in a petty, mean impression of me at our very last meeting.

'How dare you?' I hissed at him. 'This is not a shotgun marriage. And even if it were, what business is it of yours now, anyway? You gave up all right to comment on my life when you kicked me out of your flat that Saturday morning.'

'I didn't *kick* you out. You could have stayed until you sorted out a new flat.'

'Oh yeah? How could I have stayed? How could I have stayed in that flat and watched you getting on with your life around me while I picked up the pieces of my heart? You broke my heart, Richard. Have you forgotten about that?'

'I can't believe I'm painting you in a bloody wedding dress,' he muttered, choosing to ignore my last accusation.

'Look, can you move that chair a bit to the left? That vase is casting a funny shadow on your face.'

Talk about surreal. Four months since our last meeting and here we were again in the kind of circumstances that even the most ridiculous novelist couldn't have invented. Shouldn't there have been more passion? Shouldn't we have been physically fighting or something? Shouldn't I have been tearing clumps of his hair out for putting me through so much pain?

Instead, we had fallen straight into a bitter little bicker of an argument. It was the kind of argument that we *didn't* have when we were together. Nasty little tit for tat. It hardly fit with my notion that what Richard and I had shared had been a passion worthy of Antony and Cleopatra, Lancelot and Guinevere, Taylor and Burton.

'You took that Morcheeba CD,' Richard announced at one point. 'I think you'll find I bought that.'

'Well, you can swap it for the dance half of my George Michael collection. You had that in the CD player at your studio when we split up.'

That was a particularly unsuccessful parry, since I instantly thought of Jennifer vamping it up to 'Fast Love'.

But that's how it was between us. Pretty soon I forgot that I was sitting there wearing a wedding dress. The seismic potential of that incredible, theatrical, sensational moment when Richard saw me at the top of the stairs, wearing that dress, looking like a filmstar in my sumptuous Malibu home, had come to nothing. My well-rehearsed lines were unspoken. Richard scowled as he scrawled my features onto his sketchpad. Shock had subsided to annoyance.

Where was the passion?

Had it ever been there?

I found myself staring at the hands that had once roamed all over my body, leaving my skin a-tingle, caressing the most secret parts of me until I was so turned on I thought I might cry.

What did Richard see when he looked at me? Didn't he remember how I used to touch him? Didn't he remember the smell of my skin as I remembered the masculine scent of his skin straight from a bath? Did he see anything other than lines and shadows when he looked at my face?

He sketched for almost two hours without saying another word to me except, 'Have two minutes to stretch,' while he sharpened his pencils. Then he would motion for me to sit back down again and carry on scribbling away as though I was a bowl of sodding oranges.

All the time, my mind raced through the things I had wanted to say to him, questions I still had to ask. Specifically, I wanted to ask him about Jennifer. He hadn't yet mentioned her name.

Was she with him in Los Angeles?

'Richard,' I coughed, clutching courage from every part of me. 'Is it true that . . .'

The doorbell rang.

'You'd better get that,' he said.

I wrapped a dressing gown around my wedding dress and headed for the door. Scott Walker stood on the doorstep. When he saw me his eyebrows tipped upwards worriedly. I immediately assumed the worst.

CHAPTER TWENTY-NINE

'**B**randi asked me to give you this,' he said, handing me a plain white envelope.

'Oh God,' I thought. Last will and testament.

I was shaking as I took the letter from him. 'Is she?'

'She's fine.'

'Then what?' I tore the envelope open.

'Please kiss the bearer of this letter,' she'd written in her swirly hand.

I exhaled with a snort.

'Something funny?' Scott smiled.

'What are you here for?' I asked, folding Brandi's note back up. Scott's smile slipped away immediately. 'I mean . . . it's just that I'm in the middle of something.'

'The portrait?'

'Elspeth told you?'

'Is it?'

I closed my eyes and nodded.

'And?'

'Awful,' I murmured.

'Is he?'

'I haven't asked him.'

Scott frowned. Then he looked at the tiara in my hair.

'My wedding outfit,' I explained to him.

'You're still?'

'I have to.'

'Lizzie, there's something I . . .'

'Doctor Walker!'

Too late. Elspeth had suddenly become very mobile. She muscled in between us.

'What have you left Doctor Walker on the doorstep for? Come on in,' she beckoned to him. 'Let's have a cup of coffee.'

'Actually, Elspeth, I thought you and I might go for a ride,' he said.

'In that Volvo?'

'I know it's not quite your usual style but . . .'

'The chauffeur more than makes up for it! Where are you taking me?'

'We'll talk about it in the car,' he said. 'It's kind of a magical mystery tour. Shouldn't take too long. Maybe a couple of hours.'

Scott looked at me intently, as though he was trying to convey something to me with his eyes. Elspeth, a good foot shorter than either of us, was oblivious. Was he deliberately trying to get Elspeth out of my way?

'I'll get my coat,' said Elspeth.

Scott remained on the doorstep. Just then, Richard passed by the front door.

'Lizzie, I need some water for my brushes. Where's the kitchen?'

Scott and Richard regarded each other momentarily like two tigers straying through a piece of unmarked territory.

'Hi,' said Richard before carrying on to the kitchen.

'Is that?' said Scott.

'That's him,' I confirmed.

'Not what I expected.'

'Not what I expected either. He never used to look that good.'

'You look beautiful too,' Scott said then. 'I mean, in that dress. It's a lovely dress. Lizzie, do you think we . . .'

Elspeth reappeared.

'Let's go,' she said. 'All ready?'

Scott nodded curtly and made to escort her to his car.

'I'll see you . . .' he began.

'At the wedding!' Elspeth interrupted. 'You know, Scott, I don't think I've ever been so excited. The wedding preparations are going splendidly. Lizzie was thrilled when I told her that I'd arranged for Richard to paint her portrait. Turns out they have some people in common . . .'

Scott glanced back towards me.

I gave him a wave and shut the door. When I turned back into the house, I discovered that Richard had been standing right behind me.

'Who was that?' he asked.

'Scott Walker. Elspeth's doctor.'

'I thought for a moment that Eric had some competition. You seemed very close. Lots of whispering.'

'He's been treating a friend of mine.'

'Right.' Richard scratched his nose nervously. 'I thought we should have a cup of coffee before we carry on. Couldn't find the cafetière.'

'I'll get it.'

He followed me to the kitchen and sat on a high stool by the breakfast bar while I fixed us both a cup of coffee. I had the dressing gown wrapped tightly around me to protect my nuptial frills. Richard seemed to have declared an entente cordiale. He asked me about the garden. He asked me about Picasso, who was shaking his tail feathers to the sea in an imaginary courting dance.

'Straggly-looking beast,' Richard commented.

'I think he's pretty old.'

'Do you remember the peacocks in Battersea Park?'

I turned towards Richard in surprise.

'What?'

'That Sunday last October,' he continued. 'When we had lunch with Bill and Mary in their house between the Commons and walked back home over Chelsea Bridge? Remember that little dog who poked his muzzle through the wire of the peacock cage and got a peck on the nose for his trouble?'

'Yes,' I half-croaked.

'And then I tried to play football with those kids and ended up on my backside in the mud with a bunch of six-year-olds laughing at me.'

'I remember that too.'

'You found that massive conker and said it looked like my dad's head,' he said.

'I didn't mean to be nasty . . .'

'I thought it was quite funny.'

What was he telling me this for now? Was he about to ask me if I remembered getting back to our flat in Tufnell Park that night, having walked right across the middle of London? The October air was spicy with autumn bonfires. We saw two fireworks as we turned into our road. 'First ones this year,' I'd told him. Autumn was always my favourite season. October was the month that we'd met.

Was Richard about to ask me if I remembered curling up in bed beside him that night and talking about the first Bonfire Night we spent together? That was in Battersea Park as well, watching the fireworks display with thousands of other people but feeling, with his arms around me, as though we were the only people in the world.

Was he going to ask me if I remembered the first time we
made love? Properly made love. Not the drunken fumbling
we indulged in after that night at the backpackers' pub but
two weeks later, when we knew each other well enough
to want to keep the lights on. We'd spent an afternoon on
Clapham Common then too. The tip of his nose was cold
when he pressed it against my forehead and whispered, 'I
think you're really lovely, Lizzie Jordan.'

'You can't beat England at this time of year,' Richard
continued now. 'Los Angeles is all right but there aren't
any real seasons. It may be bloody cold back home but
autumn's so romantic.'

I handed Richard a coffee mug. Milk. Two sugars. Just
how he always had it. Our fingers touched momentarily as
he took the cup from my hand.

'You always had such pretty hands,' he said. 'So soft.'

Was he remembering them caressing his body? I stuttered a thank you. And next thing I knew we had both put
down our coffee cups and reached across the breakfast bar.
My fingers were entwined with Richard's, our eyes were
locked over the cafetière and my heart was beating so fast I
thought it could only be seconds before it exploded through
my chest and splattered blood all over his T-shirt.

'Richard . . .'

'Lizzie . . .'

'I . . .'

We moaned simultaneously.

Richard untangled his fingers from mine and cupped my
face. I leaned forward as far as I could with the breakfast bar
between us. Richard stretched from his side to meet me. As
he drew closer I automatically closed my eyes. I parted my
lips. I waited for the second when his lips touched mine
and . . .

'Crash!!!'

The cafetière hit the floor and shattered into a million tiny pieces, leaking thick black coffee and broken glass onto the pure white marble tiles, *specially sourced from Italy*. Hot liquid splashed against my bare ankles but I didn't feel it. Richard and I were practically wrestling on the breakfast bar. His tongue was down my throat, tangling furiously with my tongue.

Without releasing contact for a moment we shuffled from the kitchen to the bedroom. We were like two starving shipwrecked sailors suddenly finding land. My hands grabbed greedily at Richard's T-shirt and I had soon pulled it over his head. Richard struggled with the ribbons on the back of my wedding dress. I thought I heard a rip as I popped free of the bodice like a lychee from its pod.

'Lizzie!'

'Richard!'

'My . . . oh . . . I!'

It was better than it had ever been. Better than I had dared imagine when I allowed myself to dream that one day we would be back together. Our bodies fitted each other so perfectly that there could be no other lover for either of us. This was destiny, wasn't it? Wasn't it?

We rolled right across the king-size bed and tumbled giggling, wrapped in Versace duvet, to the floor. We tangled on the fake tiger-skin rug and wriggled against the wardrobe doors before we got back to the bed again.

My chin was raw from his stubble. His hair stood on end as if he'd put his fingers in a socket. My wedding dress was thrown to a corner of the room like a dust-rag. My antique tiara was squashed by a careless knee.

'I've missed you so much!' one of us shouted.

Eventually we pulled apart and looked at each other in surprise.

'Should we have done that?' I asked.

'Probably not,' said Richard.

He smiled a little shakily. I reached out to touch his face but short-circuited the gesture at the last moment and instead pushed back my own hair.

'I can't believe . . . it felt right, didn't it?'

'But it's not right,' said Richard. 'I'm engaged.'

'Oh God.'

He had taken me to the top of the world and pushed me off the other side.

'You're getting married too,' he said.

'Yes, but . . .'

I stopped myself.

'What are we going to do?' he asked me.

That implied he thought we needed to do something together, right?

It was the perfect moment for a post-coital fag. But I didn't have any. Instead, we lay side by side like a medieval lord and lady on their cathedral tomb. I imagined a cartoon of us with empty thought bubbles above our heads. Richard sighed. I sighed. Richard sighed again.

'Richard,' I asked him eventually. 'What was it all about? Why did we split up in the first place?'

He shook his head.

'I don't know. I really don't know. I suppose I was going

through some kind of crisis. My work was in demand. People, important people, wanted to hang out with me. I guess my head was turned by all the glamour. A model girl-friend, well, that just seemed like the obvious next step.

'But you were right, Lizzie. She might look great but beyond that there really isn't much to Jennifer. She gets upset if I want to stay in my studio and paint all night instead of going to the latest party. She always wants to be shopping or partying. She's not interested in paintings unless they're printed on a Jean-Paul Gaultier T-shirt. In fact, the only culture she's interested in is the live bacteria in her yogurt.'

I resisted the urge to say I told you so. Instead, I just nodded sagely.

'But we weren't getting along like we used to, you and I. I never saw you in anything except your pyja-mas.'

'You were never home during daylight hours!'

'I know. But when we first met you used to look different. You wore dresses and tight trousers and things that showed your cleavage. Towards the end you started to look like a dyke on laundry day. Everything you owned was grey and fleecy. You never wore make-up any more. I used to like waking up to see you with your mascara all smudged around your eyes like a panda's.'

'Really? I thought it irritated you when I got make-up on the Egyptian cotton.'

'It was sexy. I'd rather wash a few sheets than wake up every morning next to a woman who looked as though she'd given up on men and was about to start growing her armpit hair.'

Ouch.

'Is that really how I looked?' I asked.

'Sometimes I couldn't bare to let you touch me if I didn't have my eyes shut.'

I shrank back to my side of the king-size.

'You didn't say.'

'What could I have said? "Darling, you look like a dog"? You'd have killed me.'

'So you let it kill us instead?'

'Lizzie, I'm sorry.'

I pulled myself up onto my elbow and looked down at him.

'I could have changed. I have changed,' I said, pushing back my California-lightened hair.

'It wasn't just about the way you looked,' Richard told me. 'You seemed to have given up in every other part of your life too. I mean, what were you doing in all those temping jobs? You were supposed to be an actress. Still,' he picked up the crumpled tiara from the bottom of the bed. 'I guess someone's spotted your talent now.'

'Yes,' I took the tiara from him and attempted to manoeuvre it back into shape. 'But you gave up hope in me. You didn't think I was going to make it.'

'You had one audition in a year.'

I pouted at him. I didn't tell him that I hadn't had a genuine audition since. 'What kind of loyalty is that?' I asked instead. 'You make it sound like you did a cost-profit analysis and decided that Jennifer was more likely to keep you in the manner you wanted to become accustomed to.'

'The person I'm with is important for my image too,' he said then, as though it didn't sound like a totally arsehole thing to say.

'Where is she now?'

'She's in London.'

'How long are you here for?'

'I don't know. I bought an open ticket. There's a small chance that I might get to work in David Hockney's old studio for a while. Alex Wolper is investigating the lease.'

'That would be your dream come true.'

Richard nodded.

He stroked my hair and looked anguished for a moment.

'Do you want to marry him?' he asked me.

'Do you want to marry her?'

Richard bit his bottom lip.

A car crunched onto the gravel outside the house. Dashing to the window with my wedding dress held to my chest, I saw Scott's Volvo glide to a halt outside the double garage.

'Fuck!'

Richard was already putting his trousers on.

'Fuck!'

I struggled with the dress, putting my foot through the lining as I yanked the skirt up my legs.

'Fuck!'

Richard sprinted downstairs and left me to it.

Outside, Scott was out of the car and heading round to the passenger door. He held his arm out for Elspeth but she refused his help. I struggled to tie up the ribbons at the back of the dress as I watched from behind the gauze curtains. Elspeth shrugged off Scott's offer of assistance again. She wagged her finger at him. I couldn't hear what she was saying. Scott shrugged and got back into the car.

Seconds later the front door slammed as Elspeth let herself into the house.

'Mrs Nordhoff, can I help you with your jacket?' I heard Richard ask her.

'I can manage perfectly well on my own,' she snapped. 'Please excuse me, I have a migraine.'

I heard her stamp her way up the stairs. Peering from my bedroom door I noticed that she wasn't even using her sticks. She was definitely enraged about something. Where on earth could Scott have taken her to leave her in such a mood? She slammed her bedroom door shut. I heard her crank up the volume on the Shopping Channel.

When I crept downstairs Richard was waiting for me in the sitting room. He had started to pack up his painting gear.

'I'd better go,' he said. 'She's in one hell of a mood.'

'But . . . what about . . .' I could hardly bear to ask him.

'Lizzie, we've both got to think about this very seriously. There are more people than the two of us involved in this thing now.'

'I don't need to think about it,' I started. But Richard put his finger to my lips.

'You've got so much here. I don't know if I can ever give you as much as you deserve.'

'Richard, I don't need this much money . . .'

He planted a kiss on my forehead. 'I treated you so badly, Lizzie. I can't expect you to just walk away from what you've got here.'

'It isn't what you think . . .'

'I'll be back again tomorrow,' he said.

CHAPTER THIRTY

'Lizzie!'

As soon as she heard Richard's hire car leaving the premises, Elspeth summoned me back upstairs.

'I want you to get me the number of the Board of Doctors. The Medical Committee. The – oh, I don't know what they're called. Just find me the number of the most important medical board in this land. I need to have Doctor Scott Walker struck off.'

Elspeth was red with fury. She had been madly scribbling in one of her notepads. 'I need you to take a letter,' she said.

'Dear To Whom It May Concern. I am writing to complain in the strongest possible terms about Scott Walker. He's been guilty of gross medical misconduct. I've never been more humiliated in my life. How this man who clearly doesn't know one end of a stethoscope from another ever came to be head of the oncology department at a hospital as prestigious as St Expedite's . . .'

'Elspeth,' I interrupted. 'What's going on?'

'I can't possibly bear to recount it. Except in a court of law! Needless to say, Scott Walker will not be attending the wedding! Where's Eric? Get me Eric!' She held out a shaking hand for the phone. 'I swear, he's knocked a whole day off my life. I could be dead before the wedding. Get me Eric!'

I dialled his number as quickly as I was able.

'Your mother's having a fit,' I told him.

'Can't you deal with her?'

'No, I can't,' I said.

I couldn't imagine what Scott had done to upset her and to be honest I couldn't really care. Richard was back in my life. Richard wanted me. Elspeth could have dropped dead that very minute and it wouldn't have spoiled my mood.

'Here's your son,' I said to Elspeth. 'I'm going to wash my hair.'

As I let the hot water run over my body, I remembered that wild afternoon. He would be mine again. Richard had come back.

He'd told me that he didn't want to marry Jennifer. I certainly didn't want to marry Eric and now I didn't have to. I'd stuck out two weeks with his mother, he'd have to pay me for that and that was enough to cover Brandi's treatment. Even if it wasn't, what was the hospital going to do? Take her breast implant out again?

But as for marrying Eric so that he could keep his inheritance and make a film of *Resurrection*? I no longer had a need. For a start, I didn't trust that he would make the 'most important cinematic masterpiece of the twenty-first century' anyway. And as for his threat to shop me to immigration? So what? I was going to go back to England with Richard.

I sang in the shower while Elspeth railed at her son over the telephone. They were a despicable family. I hated them. They thought that everyone should bend to their will just because they had a ton of money. Well, they didn't have love and now I did have that again. When Richard came back the next day I would tell him that I was ready to run away. I felt sure that even now he was planning how to break the news to Jennifer.

'Yes!' I punched the air.

When I emerged from the shower, Elspeth was ringing her stupid little bell.

'What is it?' I asked her flatly.

'Eric says he's coming back tonight,' she said. 'He could tell how upset I was so he's going to come back early.'

'That's nice.'

'Aren't you glad he's going to be back tonight?' asked Elspeth.

'Sure.'

One less night with you, you old bag, was what I thought.

I went to my bedroom with Eric's laptop computer and began to send out emails.

'The best possible thing on earth has happened,' I wrote to Seema. 'Richard has come back to me. I'm not going to marry Eric.'

'Thanks for telling Richard I was working in a transvestite bar,' I wrote to Mary. 'You'll be pleased to hear that it didn't put him off me and we're getting back together.'

'Dear oldies,' I wrote to Mum and Dad. 'Get killing that fatted calf. I'll be coming back from Los Angeles sooner than I expected. And guess what? I'll be coming back with Richard.'

'I'm going out,' I announced to Elspeth. 'You can put yourself to bed.'

I left her open-mouthed as I swanned down to Eric's Jaguar (the Mercedes was still in the garage) and drove myself to St Expedite's.

'I'm Doctor Walker's friend,' I reminded the nurse on reception when she opened her mouth to tell me that it was a bit late to be visiting. Then I strode straight up to Brandi's room. She was sitting up against the pillows, eyes closed, listening to Fat Joe read from the showbiz gossip pages of the *National Enquirer*.

'Lizzie!' Fat Joe exclaimed when he saw me.

I sat down on the end of Brandi's bed. She opened her eyes and smiled at me. 'Oh Lizzie. I want to give you a hug but . . .' When she tried to move towards me she winced. 'I feel like I've got a bowling ball under my arm where they took my lymph glands out.'

'How is . . .'

'My new boob? Feels like a sack full of rocks at the moment.'

'What happens next?'

'I just get better. Doctor Scott says I won't have to have chemo this time. He's such a great guy. I'm not going to lose my hair.' She looked askance at Fat Joe. 'Think you should, though.'

He was wearing that vile Afro hairpiece again.

'So,' Brandi turned stiffly back to me. 'How's the blushing bride?'

'That's what I've come to tell you,' I said. 'I'm not getting married.'

'But what about the money,' began Fat Joe.

'It's OK. I've worked it out. The treatment so far has been paid for and Eric wouldn't dare to ask for that cash back. I'd shop him to the papers.'

'Why? What's happened?' Brandi was confused.

'Remember the tarot cards?' I reminded her. 'Well, it happened, Brandi. He's come back to me. Richard came to the house to paint my portrait this morning and by the time he left this afternoon, he'd decided that he doesn't want to marry Jennifer after all. He wants me back.'

'He does?' asked Fat Joe.

'Don't sound so bloody surprised. I knew it would happen. I knew that if I got him on his own for long enough he'd remember what held us together. When he kissed me it was like we both let out this sigh of relief. We were meant to be with each other. Jennifer was just a blip.'

'Has he called the engagement off?' asked Brandi.

'I'm sure that's what he's doing right now.'

'What exactly did he say to you?'

'He said we should both think seriously about what we were going to do but I know what that means. He's going to break up with Jennifer.'

'But he didn't say he was going to tell her tonight.'

'Not in so many words.'

'In any words?' asked Fat Joe.

Then I got angry. 'Don't you want me to be happy?'

Fat Joe and Brandi shared the complicit glance I was growing rather used to.

'Don't do anything hasty,' they said. 'Wait until he proves that he's made a decision.'

'At least wait until Richard confirms that he's called off his engagement before you tell him you're not marrying Eric,' said Brandi. 'And before you tell Eric,' she added.

'I'm not stupid,' I told them.

They looked unconvinced.

'Well, at least you could wish me luck.'

'Good luck.'

'If you don't see me tomorrow, I've eloped.'

As I whistled my way to the car park, I stopped by Scott's office, thinking perhaps that I ought to warn him that Elspeth was trying to have him struck off, but Scott wasn't there. The receptionist told me that he had booked a couple of day's leave but she could contact him in an emergency.

'No need,' I said. 'But you might just tell him that Lizzie Jordan's not going to be at the wedding on Sunday morning either.'

The receptionist wrinkled her nose but duly took the message down.

I floated back to Malibu. I was disappointed that Fat Joe and Brandi hadn't been more immediately enthusiastic about my news but I suppose they had every right to be worried about the implications of my not-marrying Eric for Brandi's treatment. I had that covered though. Eric would be too embarrassed to try and claim back the money he had spent so far.

But they needn't have worried about me. By the time I went to bed that night, I had played over that afternoon's events a thousand times and there was no doubt in my mind that Richard meant to return next afternoon and claim me back. I would wait for him to make the first move but only because I wanted to have the satisfaction of seeing him look just a teensy bit insecure about my feelings for him for just one eensy moment.

Only when we were safely back in the flat in Tufnell Park, would I tell him that there had never been anyone else for me. The revelation would bring us closer together at the right time.

At about three in the morning, I heard a taxi pull up outside the house. Eric spilled out onto the pavement. I could tell from the set of his shoulders that he was not happy to be home again at all. He slammed the door with little regard for the house's sleeping occupants. Not that Elspeth was sleeping. I heard her call out weedily for her son.

'Mommy,' replied Eric. 'I'm home to look after you.'

I just pulled my duvet up to my neck and rolled over. Another twenty-four hours and I would never have to see either of those despicable Yanks again.

CHAPTER THIRTY-ONE

I sang as I prepared Elspeth's breakfast next morning. 'This is the last time,' I told myself as I slapped her fried egg sunny side down onto a piece of wholemeal. It wasn't what she'd asked for and it wasn't what she wanted. But what did I care. Any minute now, Richard would be back to take me away.

'You seem very cheery this morning,' said Elspeth. 'Must be because Eric's home.'

In reality I hadn't even seen Eric since he got back from Hawaii. He had yet to emerge from his bedroom.

'The caterers will be coming to start setting up their equipment this morning,' Elspeth told me. 'Can you make sure they don't damage any flowers when they set up their marquee?'

'Perhaps,' I said cryptically.

'Whatever do you mean?'

'I mean that I might be helping Eric to chase those few stragglers on the guest list,' I said sweetly.

Elspeth frowned at her egg on toast. 'You know I can't eat . . . oh, forget it. You've got plenty to be getting on with.'

My 'plenty to be getting on with' that morning consisted mainly of watching the Pacific Coast Highway for little red hire cars. When would Richard come for me? Was he going to wait until the time when he was supposed to arrive to continue the painting, just in case I'd decided not to leave Eric.

I wished I could have phoned him but I didn't know where he was staying and I didn't want to ask Elspeth for his number. As it got closer to midday I wondered briefly whether he'd abandoned me. Perhaps Brandi was right. Perhaps yesterday had meant nothing to him. Then I saw it . . . The little red Datsun came screeching across the highway into Eric's driveway.

Richard jumped out. He looked dishevelled. As though he had been up all night wrestling with his emotions. He rang the doorbell. I scrambled to get the door but Eric beat me to it.

'Eric Nordhoff?' asked Richard.

'That's right. Who are . . .'

'I need to speak to you. Can we go into your office?'

Ohmigod. My heart thumped like Bambi's best friend's back leg. Ohmigod. Richard was going to tell him. How romantic! Richard had marched in to tell Eric that he couldn't have me. I knew he would do it. I knew he loved me. I knew he would always be mine.

I began to throw my belongings into a suitcase. But when I got the Louis Vuitton wheelie case half full I decided it would really be taking a liberty to abscond with Eric's luggage and decanted my designer dresses into my Debenhams' holdall instead. Meanwhile, I was still in my dressing gown. I laid out my two favourite outfits on the bed I had spent my last night in and wondered which was more suitable for an elopement.

I wanted to create a picture that Richard would remember

for ever. When we recounted the tale to our grandchildren I wanted him to be able to say, 'The moment I saw her in that red Gucci dress, I knew we had done the right thing.'

Or did I want him to say, 'As she stood there in the black Chanel, I knew I would never love another woman more'?

I held them up against my body one after the other. At the same time, I tried to keep one ear on developments downstairs. I couldn't hear any shouting. Did I want there to be shouting? I wasn't sure but it seemed appropriate given that Richard was stealing a bride.

I settled on the red Gucci. I knew that I was risking having Chris de Burgh's 'Lady In Red' as the soundtrack in my mind every time I looked back on this moment, but the dress really was my favourite. Slinky yet understated. The silk jersey accentuated my curves and made me fancy myself as a modern Goldie Hawn.

'I'm ready for you, Richard,' I breathed at my reflection.

A quick slash of red lipstick and I was out at the top of the stairs.

Just in time to hear the front door slam shut.

A squeal of red hire-car tyres.

Eric stood at the bottom of the stairs with a face like my mother when she discovered that her entire collection of Royal Doulton Ladies had been lined up and used for target practice when Colin got an air gun. (He said I made him do it, of course.)

'Going somewhere nice?' he asked me.

'I . . . er . . . Was that Richard?'

'Was that Richard, she asks me? Of course that was your Richard, you double-crossing . . .'

Elspeth, mistress of save-the-day timing, popped her head around her bedroom door.

'Lizzie, have you heard from the leader of the orchestra this morning? I was thinking that you might want something more triumphant than Bach when you walk back up the aisle. How about "The Arrival of the Queen of Sheba"?'

'Mother,' Eric interrupted. 'Lizzie and I need to have a pre-nuptial talk.'

I followed him into his office.

'You can't keep me and Richard apart,' I spluttered. 'It doesn't matter what you threaten. My old boss at Ladyboys is a *made man*.'

'I'm not frightened of your Mafia connections,' sneered Eric. 'But you ain't going to be running away with Richard any more.'

He pushed an envelope across his desk towards me.

'He told me to give you this. I think it's self-explanatory.'

I sat down and started to read.

My Darling Lizzie,

By the time you read this letter I will be gone. As I promised, I went to tell Eric about us and demand that he free you from going through with the wedding. I told him that I thought your engagement was a sham and that I loved you more than he does. But as we talked it through, I realised that I was wrong. Eric is a wonderful man, Lizzie, and he truly loves you more than you could ever imagine. The distress in his eyes when I told him that we planned to elope convinced me that he cares for you more than he cares for his own life. He can make you happy in a way I have realised, in the nick of time, that I can't.

So, don't hate me, Lizzie, for putting you through all this. Have a wonderful wedding day and look forward to

the future without me. You have love. You have passion.
And you have a bloody great mansion! I know that one
day you will realise that I've made the right choice.
　　Yours ever. In spirit,
　　Love Richard

What? Eric cares for me more than he cares for his own
life? I reread the letter six or seven times to see if rereading
Richard's unbelievable words would help them make more
sense. But no. He had abandoned me again. And because
he thought that Eric loved me more.

'What did you tell him? You bastard!'

'Lizzie,' Eric put his hand on my heaving shoulder. 'I
know what you're crying about. And I'm sorry.'

'You made him think that you loved me because you
want your mother's money. You've ruined my only chance
at happiness for your own disgusting, money-grabbing
ends. You've ruined my life.'

Eric sighed and shook his head sadly.

'You poor deluded girl,' he murmured. 'I told your
dear Richard that he could leave this house with only
one beautiful woman and it took him three seconds to
choose.'

'What do you mean?' I spat.

'You. Or the Hockney.'

I whirled around to see the dark red patch on the
sunshine-faded wall of Eric's office. The patch where the
Hockney had last been seen hanging. The painting of the
laughing girl was gone.

'He chose Muriel,' said Eric. 'I'm sorry. As soon as he
had her in his sweaty hands, he seemed more than happy
to believe that you and I are made for each other.'

I was still staring at the one bright patch on the wall

where the painting had once hung. Muriel. The witch. I was ready to blame the woman, of course, even if she was only acrylic paint on paper.

'Don't hate me,' Eric said again. 'Admittedly, I didn't want to have to face my mother if the wedding was cancelled but I did it for you, as well. I suspected that Richard only wanted you because he thought that I had you, Lizzie. And it looks like I was right.'

'How could you make him choose between me and a Hockney?' I asked. 'I didn't stand a chance.'

'But you should have done. Don't you get it? Don't you think that the person you're going to spend the rest of your life with should think that you're the priceless one?'

It was a fair question, but I was hardly in the right mind to give him the correct answer. Instead, I continued to berate Eric for setting Richard an unfair test. I couldn't see that in choosing a painting over me, Richard had shown the same lack of interest in me he had shown when insisting we watch repeats of a football match he had already been to when I wanted to watch the ballet. He could do it because he knew I wouldn't make a fuss. He probably thought that he could safely take the picture and come back for me later when I was going through the divorce that would land me with half of Eric's Malibu palace.

Right then, however, I told myself that this couldn't be the end of it. I told myself that Richard had taken the painting as part of our escape plan. Even as I wiped my tears he was probably at an auction house, having Muriel valued and auctioned and putting down a deposit on our own place in the sun with the proceeds.

'Get some rest,' said Eric. 'We've got a wedding to get through tomorrow.'

CHAPTER THIRTY-TWO

The house was being decked out for a dream wedding. A team of gardeners had been trimming the wayward topiary into hearts for the occasion. Elspeth had suggested dying the water in the fountain pink to match the colour scheme of the flowers and the extravagant ribbons and fabric swags that hung from everything and anything that couldn't move. I had pointed out that rather than being romantic, it might just look as though someone had been stabbed in the water.

Even Picasso the peacock had been smartened up for the occasion. The gardener who had been put in charge of catching the irascible bird and sticking it in a birdbath was going to be suing for damages after Picasso expressed his displeasure with his sharp little beak.

The caterers had taken over the kitchen and set up a van at the bottom of the garden from which they would magically produce a range of canapés as intricate and beautiful as anything that rolled off the production line at Wedgwood.

Thwarted in her quest for a pink fountain, Elspeth had instead struck upon the idea of covering the surface of the water in the fountain and the swimming pool with rose petals. Rose petals were to be strewn all along the path from the house to the altar too.

It was sooo romantic.

But my heart was bleeding in my chest. I carried Richard's last letter to me as if it were the last letter sent home by a soldier at the Somme. Every time I found myself alone – which wasn't often, since Elspeth seemed to have grafted herself to my side for the final wedding preparations – I would read that letter over and try to see if there were some clue among the scribbled words to make me feel less hopeless.

He wouldn't let me go through with this. He wouldn't let me marry another man. Not after the way we'd been together the previous afternoon. That sex was spiritual. It was enough to convince me that we'd been together for several past lives as well as the one we were destined to be sharing now.

Elspeth caught my mood but as usual she misinterpreted it.

'The eve of a girl's wedding is a difficult time. You're probably wondering how you can ever live up to your husband's expectations. You're feeling pretty nervous. But there's nothing to worry about.' She patted my arm and leaned close. 'That side of things isn't as nasty as you might suspect.'

That side of things? Did she think I was a virgin?

'And you're here without your mother,' she continued. 'It makes me sad to think that she's missing all the fun. I'm sure she's thinking of you.'

Perhaps she was. More likely she was down at the Sports and Social Club with Dad and Sally and Colin. If they talked about me at all, it would be to ponder when I was coming home.

'Do you think she's got any auditions yet?' Mum would wonder.

'Don't suppose so,' Colin would tell her. 'It's about time she gave up working in that cafe and came home to get a proper job.'

Never in their wildest imaginings would they suspect that I was less than twenty-four hours away from being married to a millionaire.

Eric wanted to discuss the divorce. He called me into his office and had me sign a couple of pre-nuptial contracts. I had no claim on anything except my wardrobe.

'I haven't got any use for a pile of women's clothes.'

'When will we start divorce proceedings?'

'As soon as my mother is buried.'

Eric attempted a friendly smile. 'I haven't forgotten I promised you a part in *Resurrection*,' he told me.

'The leading female part,' I reminded him.

'Yes. Well, we'll talk about that nearer the time.'

I called Brandi at the hospital.

'She's in consultation with Doctor Walker,' said the bossy nurse.

'I thought he was on vacation.'

'She asked him to come in specially.'

'Is she all right?' I asked.

'I can't discuss such matters over the phone except with next of kin.'

*   *   *

Night fell on the garden laid out for a wedding and soon the whole house was sleeping.

Not me. I sat on the edge of my bed and stared at the wedding dress hanging from the outside of my wardrobe. Abby Goldstein had paid a special visit that day to make sure it looked its best and had been distressed to find a boot mark on the hem.

'Must have happened during the portrait sitting,' I suggested.

'Must have been an energetic sitting,' she said.

I closed my eyes against the memory.

'Oh Richard, please say you're coming back for me,' I murmured. 'I'll do anything. Anything.'

I would have gone back to Solihull and worked in an estate agency for ever and ever. I would have worked in a chicken-plucking factory. I would have signed on and spent my days in a miserable British job club. I didn't want Hollywood any more. I just wanted Richard.

I closed my eyes tightly and took a deep breath. Once upon a time, Richard told me that he thought I had psychic powers. When we were first going out it seemed that whenever I thought about him he would feel compelled to call. More than once we sent each other emails that crossed in cyber-space. It seemed as though we were always thinking about each other at exactly the same time. Either that, or as he claimed, I could compel him to think about me.

'You've put a spell on me,' he said once, when he walked halfway across London to be with me instead of going for a pint with the lads after football practice. Well, if I had any psychic power over him at all I was going to use it now.

I closed my eyes and pictured his face. I pictured him turning around to look straight at me when I caught sight of his back at that exhibition opening. He'd looked straight at me then as though he had felt my eyes burning into his back. Was that psychic?

'Richard,' I said inside my head. 'I know you're still in Los Angeles. I know you're somewhere near by. Come and stop me from going through with this wedding tomorrow. Stop me. Please. Richard. Please stop me.'

CHAPTER THIRTY-THREE

The thirty-piece orchestra struck up 'Here Comes the Bride'.

'That's our cue,' said Antonio, holding out his arm.

I'd asked Antonio to give me away that morning. He was the only man I knew in Los Angeles who didn't wear false eyelashes.

As we processed from the house to the garden, where the congregation waited on dinky gilt-backed chairs, I had a sudden mental flash of my own father holding out his arm to me before we danced at my brother's wedding reception. 'You'll have a reception of your own, one day,' he said. 'And then I'll be the happiest father in the whole wide world.'

As it was, Dad didn't even know I was getting married that day. The memory of his proud, smiling face as we waltzed around the dance floor at Colin's wedding (him in his penguin suit, me in a hideous peach bridesmaid's dress), mocked me as Antonio and I walked down the stairs and through the hallway of Eric's house. How many people was this marriage deceiving? What had started out as a way to take Elspeth's mind off her illness had turned into a fantastical, farcical fraud.

My own parents were probably watching a re-run of *Inspector Morse* in front of the 'living flame' gas fire in their modest house in Solihull while I walked down the rose-petal strewn aisle at a magnificent Malibu villa on the arm of a Mafioso nightclub boss whose own pretend wife for the day, Atalanta, hadn't put on enough foundation to mask his stubble.

Fat Joe dabbed discreetly at his false eyelashes though the only tears he could possibly be crying were tears of laughter. Brandi, who had bullied St Expedite's to let her out for the day, sat beside him and gave me a little clenched fist 'chin up' signal as I passed. The other rows of the congregation were full of slightly bemused faces. But Eric's friends and my colleagues from Ladyboys had all served time as movie extras and no one looked so amused by the notion of my wedding that they would give Elspeth cause for concern.

Elspeth beamed so hard as I passed her and joined Eric at the altar. This was *her* dream come true, the stamp on *her* passport of achievements that she felt she needed to be able to accept whatever happened next. Glancing back at her as Father David began his speech of welcome, I thought that Elspeth looked as impatient as the few children in the audience. Not because she was bored but because she had waited for so long to see her only son settled. That afternoon Eric Nordhoff would be married and all those silly rumours about him preferring boys would be gone and forgotten for ever.

'Dearly beloved, we are gathered here today . . .'

Father David's words floated over me without touching me as I stared at the Pacific Ocean. I wanted to add salt water to the deepest ocean in the world. I wanted to walk to the edge of the cliff and jump off it. My psychic call had gone unanswered. Richard hadn't saved me.

'If anyone here present knows any reason why these two may not be joined together . . .'

How about because the bride is in love with another man, I asked myself. How about because Richard Adams is in love with her? This was Richard's last chance. I looked down at the floor and listened to the silence before the priest carried on.

'Wait!'

'Stop that man!' Elspeth shrieked and the hired security guards jumped on someone at the back of the congregation.

'What's going on?' said Eric.

'It's nothing,' said his mother. 'Carry on with the ceremony.'

'I . . . nnngh!'

A plaintive hand emerged from the scrum of bodies in the back row.

'That man needs to say something,' piped up Brandi.

'Shut up, you,' said Elspeth. 'He doesn't need to be heard.'

'Richard?' I squeaked nervously. 'Richard? Is that you?'

I shoved my bouquet towards Eric and began to run back down the aisle towards the trouble. In a true movie moment, time seemed to expand around me. The aisle that had taken seconds to walk up took a lifetime to run down. In the meantime, my saviour was battling to get out from beneath three bouncers. Again and again his desperate hand broke through only to be submerged again like the hand of a drowning man beneath the ocean.

Elspeth screamed as I passed her. Her red mouth hideously distorted.

'Some . . . one . . . stop . . . her . . .'

But I reached the end of the aisle and punched one of the bouncers in the back.

'Get off him!'

I was like a bridal banshee, kicking and biting to set my white knight free. 'Get off him.'

Time and again the bouncers threw me off them. I had grass stains on my wedding dress but I knew I was almost free.

'This is most irregular,' said Father David. He coughed into his microphone in a pathetic attempt to regain our attention.

Elspeth was on my back now, pulling me off the bouncers as I tried to pull them off my love.

'Get back to the altar, you bitch,' she was saying.

I struck out with my elbow and she tumbled onto her arse.

'Dearly beloved!' yelled Father David. 'There's no place for fighting in God's house.'

'It's not God's house, it's my house,' said Elspeth as she threw herself back into the wrestling. 'Get back to the altar or I'll have you thrown in jail.'

She tried to grab me by the hair but my veil came away in her hands. At the same time I bit one of the bouncers on the ear lobe and sent him running for his mommy. I kicked another in the goolies and had him reeling in a flowerbed. The third one started running when he saw the whites of my eyes.

I had fought like a she-wolf defending her puppies. The adrenaline still coursing through my veins made it easy for me to lift my saviour onto his feet.

'You did it: You came for me.' I kissed him over and over. My eyes were so full of tears it took me a while to recognise Scott Walker.

'Lizzie,' he held me at arm's length.

'Scott.' I shook myself free of him. 'Scott? What are *you* doing here?'

'I came to stop the wedding.'

'What do you care who I marry?'

'This isn't just about you, Lizzie. Elspeth,' he helped the little battleaxe to her feet. 'You're making a terrible mistake.'

Scott strode to the front of the congregation.

'You can't go through with this wedding,' he told Father David. 'He doesn't love her,' he pointed at Eric and me. 'He loves him.' Scott nodded in the direction of the back row where Jan was sitting. He had his suitcase on his lap and was dabbing at wet eyes.

'And she doesn't love him,' Scott continued. 'She's after a visa. And the money, I suppose.'

Elspeth got to her feet again, only to faint dramatically.

I made to go to her rescue but Scott stopped me. 'And she,' he said, nodding in the direction of Eric's mother, 'does not have terminal cancer.'

Imagine the collective gasp.

'She doesn't have cancer of any description. Eric, your mother is suffering from a condition called Munchausens. It's named after the fictional Baron von Munchausen. He told tall tales and so does she.'

'But . . .' I began to protest.

'But nothing, Lizzie. Did she ever show you a medical report? Did you ever meet her doctor?'

'I thought you were her doctor,' said Eric.

'I was only her last-minute date in Santa Barbara.'

'Get him out of here!' Elspeth shouted. She had recovered enough to pull herself back onto a chair. 'He doesn't know what he's talking about.'

'The staff of St Expedite's will back me up, Mrs Nordhoff. There is CCTV footage that shows you entering the out-patients department only to spend a couple of hours in the visitors' canteen.'

'He's lying.'

'I wish I were.'

'You must be,' Eric said angrily. 'Why would she pretend she's got weeks left to live?'

'I don't know. Why do you think she pretended to have a brain tumour last year?'

'That was successfully treated.'

'Eric, it wasn't ever treated because there was no tumour.'

'But the multiple sclerosis . . .' said Eric.

'How many people do you know who develop spina bifida aged fifty-three?' asked Doctor Walker. 'Your mother isn't ill, Eric. Except perhaps in the head.'

Elspeth was sobbing now. Her jaunty hat had slipped down over her eyes. Behind her, the rest of the congregation sat silently. Transfixed. It took a lot to shock a Hollywood audience but right then, they were gobsmacked. And so was I.

'Elspeth,' I said softly, laying my hand on her shaky shoulder. 'Is this true? Is what Scott's saying the real story? Do you have cancer? Or have you been making it all up?'

'Oh, all right!'

Elspeth straightened up and shook me off her so firmly that I almost ended up on my arse. 'I did make it up about the cancer. And I didn't really have multiple sclerosis. But what kind of son is he if the only way I can get his attention is by pretending to have some terminal disease? You,' she jabbed Eric in the chest, 'were always more interested in the Modigliani portraits of this family than the family itself.'

'Mother, that's not true.'

'The only reason you agreed to this wedding was to save your share of the inheritance. I knew I'd raised a greedy son but I didn't think you'd go to the lengths of paying some girl off the street to marry you. You're just like your father.'

'My father's dead.'

'He's not dead. He's in Iowa. All he was interested in was my money. He didn't love me. He was sleeping with the housemaid while I was having you in the hospital. He took a million dollars to get out of our life and never come back.'

'You pretended he was dead?'

'So he wouldn't have an influence on you. How was I to know that he'd reassert his presence through your genes? What did I do to deserve this, Eric? Nobody could have loved you better than I did. And what do I get in return? A call at Christmas? An invite to your premiere with my name spelled incorrectly?'

'Mom,' Eric attempted to interrupt.

'No. Shut up. I haven't finished yet. Lizzie is the first person to show me some love in a very long time. Love with no strings attached. Lizzie was interested in hearing about my life. She didn't write me off as some mad old woman who should just hurry up and die. When I thought I was going to get a daughter-in-law like this girl,' she linked her arm through mine, 'I thought that at last my family would be saved. I thought that I must have done something right for someone as good as Lizzie to want to marry a son of mine. Now I suppose that even Lizzie isn't the lovely girl I thought she was.' She looked me straight in the eye. 'You lied to me too.'

Elspeth let out a deep sigh and held my gaze. I could have shrivelled like the Wicked Witch of the West, leaving nothing behind but my slippers. Elspeth had lied about her cancer because she felt unloved. The assembled wedding guests could only assume that money was my motivation for being in this game.

'Now hang on!' someone piped up from the congregation. It was Brandi. 'Don't go taking it all out on Lizzie. It sounds to me as though she's the one you should all be apologising to. You involved her in your family problems.'

'I should sue her for deception,' spat Elspeth. 'She didn't have to get involved in a charade.'

'She did,' said Brandi solemnly. 'Unlike you and unlike Eric, Lizzie really didn't have much choice. She had to get involved, because of me. Lizzie didn't want to deceive you, Mrs Nordhoff. She only agreed to help Eric out because he agreed in turn to help me.

'Lizzie's part in this was to pay for my medical treatment. Eric promised Lizzie that as long as she helped to keep you happy, he would foot my hospital bills. He was expecting to be able to recoup the money from your life assurance. It isn't the way I wanted things either, but Eric's little game has probably saved my life. Because I've really had cancer, Mrs Nordhoff. And believe me, it isn't a part I would choose to play voluntarily.'

Now that speech really was the showstopper.

The priest, who had been standing silent and open-mouthed throughout, only dared clear his throat after what seemed like a whole hour's silence. 'Well,' he said. 'Obviously, I can't go through with any kind of wedding ceremony now.'

'No,' Eric and I agreed instantly.

'Perhaps we should all just take a moment to pray for understanding?'

EPILOGUE

Two days later I was on a jumbo back to London. The immigration officer didn't even look at the expiry date on my visa as he waved me through passport control.

The wedding party had broken up pretty quickly after Father David called for forgiveness. Eric and Elspeth had a great deal to talk about. But not before Eric hissed something in my direction about illegal immigrants. I made myself scarce and prepared to go home.

In a movie, Scott might have insisted that the priest marry another couple that morning or raced to the airport to stop me leaving town. But it wasn't until quite a while later that I discovered how he felt.

Instead, I found myself travelling back over the Atlantic in much the same way as I had made my journey from London to Los Angeles three months before. That is to say, sobbing. Not even the thought that my brother Colin might meet me at the airport Fat Joe-style dressed as a Birmingham housewife called Colleen could cheer me up. And he didn't of course. When I saw Colin and Soppy Sally waiting for me in the arrivals hall, him with his arms crossed and a look of disapproval already on his face, it was as though less than three days had passed.

Of course, my family knew nothing about the wedding that almost was. They assumed that I'd just made the

sensible decision to come back to the UK in time for the
panto season. Eunice had wangled me an audition for a
production of *Cinderella* conveniently staged in Solihull.
She promised she'd pull strings to get me a chorus role.

'You'll be in a theatre,' Eunice reminded me. But it was
a long way from the lead role in *Resurrection*. I read
in *Entertainment* that casting for the movie was about
to start.

Back in Los Angeles, Brandi was soon out of hospital. A
week after the wedding that never was, Elspeth Nordhoff
sent a cheque to St Expedite's, to fund the remainder of
her treatment. 'Tamoxifen's expensive,' she'd written in the
accompanying letter. 'I should know. I've been pretending
to buy it for years.'

Brandi returned to the beach house in Venice. In her
absence Fat Joe had been decorating. When she walked
into her newly-painted bedroom Brandi burst into tears.
'I realised that here was someone who would do anything
for me,' she told me. They're getting married when Fat
Joe's divorce from Venus comes through. Of course I was
delighted for them, but I dread to think how they're going
to decide who gets to wear the wedding dress.

Fat Joe carried on singing at Ladyboys but Antonio insisted
he take lessons. Atalanta finally saved up enough for her last
operation and hung up her Cleopatra costume for good.

When I got back to England, people knew better than
to ask about Richard. Bill and Mary introduced me to a
couple of the guys from Bill's office – dreadful suits who
expressed their wittiness through pig-patterned ties and
odd socks. Seema invited me out on the pull. She was
delighted to have me back with my bag full of designer
goodies. I let her have the red Gucci dress I'd worn for my
running away.

I don't know what happened to Richard Adams. When I bothered to read any art reviews, the consensus seemed to be that painting was still dead. Then, late one night, when I got in from a day spent dancing variations on the polka to get my stint as a villager in *Cinderella*, I saw an advert on television with her on it. Jennifer the model.

'Dizzy.com,' she lisped. 'It's brought me into line.'

Jennifer the model was still sporting an engagement ring but this time it wasn't from Richard. The toady dot-commer had reclaimed his first proper girlfriend. I guessed that meant Richard wasn't bringing home the Danish with his paintings that looked a bit like Bacons. Or perhaps, I thought in my more reflective moments, that afternoon in Malibu really had meant something to him too.

I guess I'll never find out. In any case, I had come to realise that the Richard Adams who floated back into my life so briefly in Los Angeles was not the one whose life I had crashed into in that pub in Leicester Square.

Autumn limped by. I turned down a part in *Cinderella* – Eunice was apoplectic – and took a couple of temping jobs. Eunice said that she could no longer represent me as an actress and wouldn't listen to my argument that donning a blonde wig with plaits and doing the polka six nights a week was hardly acting. I considered retraining as an accountant. Colin was delighted and offered to pay my exam fees. The London School of Accountancy said they had a vacancy from December.

I was ready to go. I had swapped my subscription to *The Stage* for *Accountancy Today*. Then I got the call.

'Ms Jordan. This is Mr Ed Strausser's assistant at the

Kristiansand Creative Company. He was wondering whether you would be able to come in with your showreel?'

'I'm in Solihull!!!!'

Not for long.

'You've got to go,' insisted Mary.

'I can't afford to fly to Los Angeles.'

'Then tell him you'll meet him in New York.'

Mary was triumphant. She had found a way to make me attend Brian Coren and Angelica's wedding. I wasn't going to go – didn't think I could stand another wedding – and had pleaded poverty as my excuse.

Mary had offered to lend me the fare but I said I couldn't possibly consider it. Now she offered to give me the fare. In fact, she insisted that it would cost her nothing to take me out to New York when she flew there with Bill. She had plenty of air miles, as long as I didn't mind flying cattle class with Bill while she chilled out in First.

'Brian is one of your very best friends,' she reminded me. I knew the subtext was that if Ed Strausser wanted to see me, she wanted an 'in' on the action. Mary was horribly transparent sometimes. But she did know who was hot in the business. I decided I ought to go.

Brian and Angelica were to be married at St Stephen's Cathedral in Manhattan.

The cathedral was an astonishingly beautiful setting. Angelica had insisted that it be decked out with winter white roses, her wedding flowers perfectly complementing the cathedral's own Christmas decorations.

Angelica was the bride that every little girl wants to be, drifting up the aisle towards eternal bliss in a little number by Donatella Versace with matching jewels by

Quality Street . . . Mmm. I mean, Tiffany, of course. From where I was sitting, I couldn't see Brian's face as his bride finally reached him, but I knew that he would be delighted. Angelica lived up to her name.

I closed my eyes as she made her vows to the man who had once been the centre of my fragile little universe. I thought I might need to block my ears to Brian's heartfelt responses to the minister's questions but I didn't. In the pew next to me, Mary rustled through her handbag for a handkerchief. Bill sniffed loudly, though I knew that was only because he had a cold. While some young relative of the bride massacred 'Ave Maria', Mary turned to ask her husband whether he thought it would be inappropriate if she popped into Macy's before they followed the wedding party to the reception venue.

'It's only round the corner,' she said.

One of Angelica's aunts shushed Mary loudly.

I sat back in my pew and looked up at the candles twinkling above the altar. It was a beautiful church and Angelica and Brian had definitely chosen the most magical time of year to get hitched. How much more romantic the candlelight and Christmas decorations seemed than Elspeth's *Dynasty* fantasy on Malibu Beach. This is how I would do it, I thought. If I ever get to do it. Would I ever be the girl in the white dress for real?

Soon Brian and Angelica had signed the register and were processing back up the aisle and out into dusky Manhattan. We stood outside the cathedral and shivered for a few minutes while the photographer took some hasty snaps. One of Angelica's bridesmaids produced a white fur cloak to keep the bride from getting goose-pimply. We threw white confetti that was suddenly lost in the real thing. Snow.

Standing on the steps of the cathedral with her new
husband, Angelica looked like the Snow Queen presiding
over a frozen world and I was taken back to that moment
at the end of August when Richard told me everything
was over. Like the boy who gets a shard of the Snow
Queen's mirror in his eye. Him frozen-hearted and me
broken-hearted.

Brian kissed his new bride on her cheek. Though the
venue was freezing, there was enough love between the
happy couple to keep every one of us warm. We never had
that, Richard and I. We never had the kind of love that is
so big it can't be contained in two bodies. A love so big that
you can't help smiling when you witness it, no matter how
lonely you're feeling inside.

Mary got her trip to Macy's and we were among the last
to arrive at the swanky hotel overlooking Central Park that
Angelica had chosen for the reception. Inside the hotel
ballroom, the Winter Wonderland theme continued. The
champagne cocktails with which we were greeted had
names like Sleigh Bells and Pink Ice. Even the wedding
cake had been made to look like a giant snowball.

I had been seated with Mary and Bill of course. As guests
of honour, all the way from England, we actually had quite
a good table. While Mary and Bill compared Angelica's
glittery snowstorm vision with their own rather more
low-key reception, I played with the name badge at the
top of my place setting and wondered how long it would
take to get horribly drunk on champagne slushies.

There was an empty seat beside me. Someone had been
unavoidably detained. On the one hand, I hoped they
turned up soon. Sitting next to an empty seat at a wedding

reception is worse than being seated next to the groom's mad, lecherous uncle. On the other hand, I didn't really relish the prospect of Noo Yoik small talk that afternoon.

'Where are you from?'

'London.'

'You don't say. Do you . . .'

'Know the Queen? Not personally. No.'

I picked up the stranger's name-card. Scott, it said.

I allowed myself a little smile as I remembered the last time I met a man called Scott at a wedding. Brandi had told me that Scott Walker left St Expedite's shortly after the Nordhoff wedding debacle. It didn't take long for the hospital administration to find out the truth about Elspeth and beg Scott to take back his resignation, but it was too late. Scott had had enough of bending over backwards to accommodate wealthy benefactors who thought that their money gave them the right to tell him how to practise medicine.

Brandi didn't know where he'd gone. No one did.

'Pity,' she told me over the phone. 'I liked him. And he liked you. If only you guys could have met under different circumstances . . .'

'Yeah, yeah,' I sighed.

It might have been nice.

Anyway, the missing guest didn't make it to the reception in time for the appetisers – delicate little blinis heaped with smoked salmon and caviar.

'So nouveau I need my specs to eat them,' commented Mary.

He didn't make it for the entree either – some sort of chicken concoction with a sprig of holly as a garnish.

'Chicken,' Mary pointed out. 'Exactly the same as we had at our wedding, only with added spiky bits.'

The missing guest didn't even make it in time for pudding.

'Let me guess. This must be an avalanche!' sneered Mary when the waiter plonked an ice-cream tower down in front of her so abruptly that it almost slid right off the plate.

I hid in the loos with a packet of cigarettes while the speeches were made, emerging only as Angelica and Brian entwined their hands around a silver knife and made the first cut in the cake.

'Dancing!' the bride clapped her hands and the miniature orchestra started up. There was a singer too. The lights were dimmed as Brian and Angelica took the floor to their song. 'I Will Always Love You'. That great Whitney standard. Mary and I swapped grimaces. Since when had Brian been into Whitney?

The thought of super-cool Brian, the only man I knew who really liked free-form jazz, taking his first dance as a married man to such a cheesy song almost had me laughing. Pretty soon he was desperately beckoning other couples to get up from their tables and join the newly-weds in a whirl.

'I need more bodies to disguise my bad footwork,' he shouted.

'Darling, your footwork is fine,' said Angelica. 'Ow! Mind where you're stepping! These are six-hundred-dollar shoes!'

Mary and Bill went to the rescue and pretty soon I found myself alone again. My specialist subject, I thought, trying to look inconspicuous while left sitting alone at a wedding reception. Brian's mother and father shuffled past. His mum gave me a sympathetic look. I knew what she was thinking.

Sod it, I thought. I'll dance on my own. When the Whitney-a-like had finished warbling, I got up for the next song, heading for the middle of the dancefloor where I began to boogie with abandon. The champagne glass welded to my hand was a good prop. Angelica offered to lend me her husband but I shrugged off the kind thought. 'I'm OK on my own,' I assured her.

I am, I realised. I'm OK on my own. I haven't died of heartache since losing Richard. I haven't died of the embarrassment of my disaster in LA. I haven't even lost my sense of humour after another month in Solihull. I had an audition in New York to go to, and I could look forward to a visit from Joe and Brandi in the spring, now that she had her all clear.

Life was all right, I decided. Life really was all right.

At ten o'clock, Brian and Angelica left on their honeymoon. They were going to be skiing in Austria, of course. Just before they left, the band stopped playing for a moment and the lights were dimmed even further. Brian and Angelica were spotlit in the centre of the dancefloor. As they thanked their guests for coming, Angelica's prankster father gave the signal for a huge bag of paper snowflakes to be released onto their heads. They exited, laughing, into the real snowstorm outside, and the paper flakes continued eddying noiselessly about the glitter-ball while the band started to play again.

And then I saw him, walking across the dancefloor towards me with that same harassed, hurried look he always wore about the hospital. Still wearing his stethoscope around his neck! He was working in New York now. He had lots of family in New York, including his cousin

Angelica. He couldn't believe he'd missed her wedding. It was as though his patients checked his diary for unmissable social events before presenting him with an emergency. He didn't even get to see the happy couple leave. It was hardly worth staying and then . . .

'Scott Walker!'

'You all right, Lizzie?' Mary asked. 'You've gone whiter than the wedding cake.'

I just clutched Mary's arm and gestured towards the vision on the dancefloor.

'Lizzie Jordan?' he murmured.

'What on earth are you doing here?' I asked.

He took both my hands in his as he kissed me 'hello'. And I remembered how much I liked the smell of his aftershave and how happy it had made me to have his hand in the small of my back. When he had kissed me on both cheeks he still didn't let go of my hands. He looked at me as though he was remembering something too. His soft lips curled up in a smile.

'They're playing our song,' he said.

I hadn't been listening. But he was right. The band was playing 'Let's Call The Whole Thing Off'.

'Want to dance?' he asked me.

'Perhaps you should take your stethoscope off.'

He obliged and we moved out onto the dancefloor.

'*You say po-tay-to* . . .' I sang.

'I will. If you say you'll be mine . . .'

CHRIS MANBY

FLATMATES

Have you ever shared a flat with your so-called friends?

Do you remember with a shudder the squabbles over the itemised phone bill, the cleaning rota and whose turn it is to do the washing up? If so, you'll sympathise with the three troubled occupants of No. 67 Artesia Road.

FIONA

– who's been offered a glorious job in New York, but can't bear to leave Tim, her brilliant – but none-too-devoted – fiancé.

KERRY

– who's fed up with spending Saturday night alone in front of the TV, fantasising about her devastatingly handsome – but homosexual – boss.

LINZI

– who won't be tied down by any job or man.

They think they've got problems – but nothing can prepare them for the chaos which ensues when Linzi's latest boyfriend arrives on the scene. Gorgeous but feckless, Gaetano spells Trouble with a capital 'T'. And soon events are spiralling out of everyone's control . . .

'More realistic than FRIENDS, cleaner than THE YOUNG ONES and not as frightening as SHALLOW GRAVE' *Daily Mail*

HODDER AND STOUGHTON PAPERBACKS

CHRIS MANBY

LIZZE JORDAN'S SECRET LIFE

'You're nearly thirty now, Lizzie Jordan. It's about time you started to do something with your life.'

Five years after leaving university, Lizzie Jordan considers herself one of life's failures. Unlike her friends with their highflying careers, Lizzie works as a lowly typist, shares a grotty flat and 'makes do' with her accountant boyfriend.

But Lizzie leads an alternate life – a hectic whirl of extravagant parties and million-pound business deals. The life she describes in her e-mails to Brian.

Brian. The handsome American student she dated at university. The one she's never been able to forget. The love of Lizzie's life.

When Brian announces he's coming to stay, Lizzie is faced with a dilemma. How on earth can she explain that her descriptions of her glamorous lifestyle have been somewhat economical with the truth?

Ever resourceful, Lizzie comes up with a cunning and utterly invincible plan. But the best-laid plans . . .

HODDER AND STOUGHTON PAPERBACKS